The Complete Tales of Lust

(Volumes 1-5)

By Frank Noir

Table of Contents

Volume One

The Secretary

Mr. Bergman had helped Michelle carry her bags up to her room. In the lift down to the lobby, he apologized once more:

"You know, I'm really sorry about this," he said.

Michelle waved her hand.

"Don't be. It's no big deal."

And furthermore, Michelle thought, it wasn't even his fault.

Mr. Bergman had been invited to speak at the conference and had asked Michelle, his secretary, to come along. Whoever had been in charge of the hotel bookings had made a mistake and placed the two of them in separate hotels.

As a result, Mr. Bergman now stayed at the airport Hilton, and had offered to escort Michelle to her hotel - a tourist-class accommodation in a seedy part of town.

"I'm glad you don't think so," Mr. Bergman said as they stepped out into the lobby. "But at least let me buy you a drink."

Michelle looked at him, smiling. She had been working for Mr. Bergman for three years and liked the job. He, too, seemed very satisfied.

He was a handsome man, she thought, tall and dark, in his late thirties. As far as she could make out through the business suits he always wore, he was in great shape. And she was pretty sure he was single - just like her.

Still, he had never responded to her in a sexual way.

Too bad, really. Well - maybe she wasn't his type. Maybe he was being very professional about it. Or maybe - perish the thought - he was gay? Anyway, having a casual chat with Mr. Bergman over a drink would be nice.

If he came on to her, she might actually consider sleeping with him. Otherwise, she could just go back to her hotel. If she had to sleep alone tonight, she had her vivid sexual fantasies to keep her company. Her current favorite - although she was ashamed to admit it - involved being raped by a gang of bikers.

Michelle's mind had drifted, and as the kinky images invaded her mind, she suddenly realized where she was - and that Mr. Bergman was actually waiting for an answer.

"Er, okay," she said, blushing. "Thanks."

"That's the least I can do," Mr. Bergman said. "And I know a nice place just a five minute walk from here."

They left the hotel and walked down the street, Mr. Bergman leading the way. Night was falling and the wet asphalt glistened in the glow of the streetlights.

"It really is a nice city," Mr. Bergman said. "Though it may be hard to tell."

Michelle looked around as they walked. The neighborhood seemed to consist mainly of run-down apartment blocks, the ground floors occupied by darkened bars, sex shops and other businesses to obscure to make out.

"It sure has, ummm... character," she said.

Mr. Bergman laughed.

"You can say that again," he said. "But here we are - I'm sure this will be a pleasant surprise."

As they walked into the bar, Michelle agreed. Like the other bars in the area, this one was pretty dark - but in a very tasteful manner, decorated in dark woodwork and deep reds. The lighting was discrete, and the seating arranged in small booths, enabling guests to have at least a little privacy.

"It's nice," Michelle said.

"What are you having?" Mr. Bergman asked.

Michelle ordered a gin and tonic and sat down at their table as Mr. Bergman got the drinks at the bar. He returned with her drink and an imported beer for himself.

"Cheers," he said.

Michelle took a sip of her drink. God, she needed that. Due to endless delays at the airport, it had nearly taken them all day to get here. Michelle would be turning in early tonight - she was tired.

"So," she asked, "you knew this place? You've been here before?"

"Oh yeah," Mr. Bergman said. "A lot of these conferences take place here. So I've been here several times - but never before with such a lovely companion."

Michelle almost choked on her drink. Had he actually just said that? Mr. Bergman? Mr. discretion himself? She coughed.

"Oh, I'm sorry," Mr. Bergman said. "I didn't mean to..."

"No, not at all," she gasped, coughing again. "Very nice of you to say that. I just never..."

She stopped. She couldn't really complain about his lack of sexual interest. Or could she?

"Michelle," he said quietly. "We have a work relationship. And if we had anything else, I believe it would make both our jobs far too complicated. Which doesn't mean that I can't appreciate female beauty when I see it. Am I making sense at all?"

Yeah, well, Michelle supposed he was. So he was being professional about it. Damn. Looked like she'd spend the night in the company of the hotel mini bar and her biker fantasy.

"You're making perfect sense," she said, forcing a smile. "Sometimes I just wish we didn't have that work relationship - that we were more like normal people."

Mr. Bergman laughed.

"You know," he said, "I shouldn't really say this - but I know what you mean."

Michelle laughed, too - sincerely this time.

They finished their drinks and Mr. Bergman bought another round. They chatted about this and that, but Michelle was tired and found her mind drifting off towards her hotel bed, the mini bar - and the biker fantasy.

"Thank you for the drinks," she said, "but I really must be getting to bed. It's been a long day."

"It sure has," Mr. Bergman said.

They both got up and left the bar.

Back on the street, Mr. Bergman hailed a cab for himself.

"Will you be okay?" he asked.

"Sure," Michelle said. "Like you said, it's only a five minute walk. And the night air will do me good."

"Okay," he said, getting into the cab. "See you tomorrow."

"Bye," she called.

The cab drove away. Michelle looked around and started walking back the way they'd come.

The street was empty, and just a bit too quiet. The combination of streetlights and neon lights was hardly enough to illuminate the neighborhood. Michelle shivered and kept walking.

She had expected to check into the airport Hilton along with Mr. Bergman and was dressed accordingly: In her short black skirt,

loose white blouse and high heels. She had let her long, blonde hair down and looked stunning: A beautiful, young woman of twenty-four walking through the dark, deserted streets at night.

At the next intersection, she stopped for a second. They'd made a turn somewhere. Was it here? Yes, she told herself. It must be. And no - she wasn't lost.

Michelle turned right, down another darkened street, trying to convince herself that this was the right direction. And that's when she heard them.

Footsteps.

She didn't dare stop or turn around. Don't panic, she told herself. It's probably nothing. Just keep on walking.

So she did. And the footsteps - somehow she knew it was a man's footsteps - kept getting closer. And as she stopped at a pedestrian crossing, they stopped, too!

Michelle tried hard not to panic, but this was wrong. Completely wrong. And suddenly she wondered: Had there been one or two set of footsteps? As the light turned to green, she walked briskly to the other side, the footsteps still following her. She increased her pace, and they followed, getting ever closer. And - oh God - there were two men following her.

Michelle ran, but she heard the two men closing in behind her. Oh no, she thought, oh no... She was panting with exhaustion, and as the men got closer, she could hear their breathing, too. Please, she thought...

And then a strong hand grabbed her arm. Michelle screamed.

"Shut up," a rough voice said as another hand grabbed her other arm. "You just come along here."

The men dragged her into an alley, surrounded on three sides by tall brick walls. The asphalt glistened, lit by a single, naked light bulb on one of the walls. A huge motorcycle was parked just below it.

For the first time, Michelle caught a glimpse of her capturers. They were tough-looking biker types. One of them was tall and blond, his hair in a long ponytail. The other was short and squat, completely bald, but with a neatly trimmed black beard. Both of them were dressed in jeans, t-shirts and leather jackets.

"Please," she whimpered.

"Come here," the tall man ordered, making her face the wall and pushing her up against it.

Michelle felt the rough brick wall against her cheek and shivered. The strong hand held her in place. She couldn't move.

"Let me go," she pleaded.

"There, there, honey," the other man said, his voice deep and hoarse. "We're not gonna hurt you."

"No," the tall man said, "we're just going to play with you."

Michelle groaned. Then, she felt his hands between her thighs, strong, rough hands, moving towards her crotch.

"No!" she said, trying to break free.

She felt another pair of hands on her shoulders, forcing her up against the wall: The bald guy had come to his friend's aid. She sighed. This was hopeless.

She felt the fingers pushing against the fabric of her panties, pulling them aside. As a rough finger touched her labia, she gasped.

"No. Please," she whispered.

The finger began moving against her flesh, massaging her. Gently, the biker rubbed his finger rhythmically against her pussy lips, probing at her sex. Michelle closed her eyes as the biker kept massaging her slit, gradually slipping his fingertip into her pussy.

"No. Stop it..." she whimpered.

As the two men pinned her against the wall, Michelle felt the finger entering her again and again, exploring her reluctant crevice. And (oh God, this can't be happening)...

... she was getting wet.

Once again, Michelle struggled to break free. But the two men merely applied even more force and held her still, fixated up against the brick wall.

"P-p-please," she sobbed.

Love juice wet the biker's finger, as it gently poked Michelle's flesh. Slowly, a fraction of an inch at a time, it slipped further and further into her moist flesh. In a slow, sensuous rhythm, the biker masturbated her pussy with his finger.

Then, she felt his thumb reaching around to touch her clit. Michelle jumped as he found it and gently began circling his thumb around the base of her love button. Fucking her with one digit and massaging her clit with his thumb, the biker made Michelle squirm and moan with pleasure.

"Stop it! Stop it!" she sobbed.

"I think she likes it," the bald man said.

"No," she whimpered, ashamed - though in fact she was close to an orgasm.

What was happening? Why would this turn her on? She was a well-paid secretary, working for an important executive. And being raped by two creeps in a dark alley turned her on?

And suddenly she realized: This was her fantasy. Her biker fantasy had unexpectedly come true. Not like a dream, but as a nightmare. But still: Close enough to her fantasy to make her excited against her will.

Something soft and wet touched her labia. Oh God, Michelle thought, it was his tongue. The biker was licking her pussy. She heard him slurping at her wet flesh as his tongue lapped up her juice. Greedily, he licked and sucked at her tender cunt.

Michelle closed her eyes and rested her cheek against the rough brick wall. She gave in to the sensations of pleasure and let the biker lick her pussy. He seemed to sense her surrender. Grunting, he began sucking at her slit with even greater vigor, drinking the wetness from her excited crevice.

"Ahhh," she sighed.

The bald man grabbed her long blonde hair, pulling her head back.

"Look at me," he ordered, and Michelle opened her eyes. His eyes were gleaming, mad with excitement.

"Yeah, I knew you'd like it," he grinned.

"I..." Michelle began.

"You nasty little slut," the bald man said. "Boy, are we gonna have fun with you tonight."

Then, she heard the sound of a zipper opening.

"Spread your legs," the man behind her said. "Spread them wide."

As Michelle hesitated, she felt his hands grabbing the insides of her thighs pushing her legs apart. She steadied herself against the wall. The bald man held her shoulders, keeping her still.

"Okay," he said. "Go ahead."

Michelle's head was spinning. She knew what was next, and sure enough: Soon she felt his fingers pulling the crotch of her panties aside. And then something warm and swollen pushed hard against her pussy - the tall man's erect cock.

"Yeah," he said. "Open wide, baby. Here comes my cock."

"Ahhh," she moaned as he pushed forward, forcing the tip of his tool into her cunt.

It felt big, wide and hard, as it poked her. But she was wet now, very wet, and inch-by-inch the bulging cock entered her slit, slowly opening her tender flesh.

"Oh God," she whispered. "Oh God."

The biker grabbed her ass-cheeks and pulled back. Then he thrust forward again, impaling Michelle on his rigid cock.

"Aaah!" she cried.

Again and again the biker lunged forward, thrusting his excited cock in and out of her slit with fast and powerful strokes.

"Unh! Unh!" he grunted, fucking her hard up against the wall.

Michelle's entire body shook. The biker hammered into her sex with animal savagery - and she was excited, excited as hell. She was being raped, but it felt so good, she never wanted him to stop. She wanted him to keep going, to fuck her like the filthy animal he was.

"Ohhh..." she groaned.

She heard another zipper opening and saw the bald man holding his erect cock. It was about average length, but very fat. The bald man began stroking his cock as he watched his friend fuck Michelle.

"Yeah," he shouted, masturbating. "Fuck her hard. Make her come."

He grabbed her by the hair again.

"Are you coming, slut?" he hissed.

And yes, Michelle realized she was. A powerful orgasm was building up inside her, ready to knock her off her feet. She bit her lip, fighting the urge to scream out loud with pleasure.

The tall man leaned over her, still vigorously hammering his cock into her pussy.

"Come for me, baby," he whispered into her ear. "You know you want to."

Michelle sobbed helplessly, fixing her gaze on the bald man's cock. He obviously enjoyed showed off his erect cock to her, letting her watch as he masturbated - shamelessly.

"Ohmigod," she gasped.

It was happening. No stopping it now.

A few more times the tall man's rigid cock thrust into her juicy cunt, and then - she came.

"Aaah!" she cried. "Aaah!"

It was a powerful orgasm. For a split second she was unaware of anything but the gigantic rush of pleasure pulsing through her helpless body. Her sex kept oozing juice, drenching the fat cock inside her.

"Yeah," the tall man grunted.

He had slowed down his pace a bit, but was still fucking her deep and hard. His cock slid smoothly in and out of her, making little wet noises.

Eventually he pulled out, letting Michelle stand by herself. She leaned against the wall, trembling.

"Oh God," she whispered.

"You can thank us later," the tall man said. "Now get down on your hands and knees."

Michelle turned her head, looking at him. She didn't understand.

"You heard the man," the bald guy said, his stiff cock sticking out of his jeans and jerking slightly up and down. "Get down!"

Michelle looked down at the wet asphalt, rough and shiny, lit by the light bulb on the wall. She couldn't. She was a well-paid secretary, working for a very important executive. No way was she going to lie on her hands and knees on that dirty piece of asphalt.

Finally, the tall man pushed her hard, making her fall to the ground.

"Oooh!" she screamed, as she landed on her hands and knees.

The rough asphalt felt cold and wet on her bruised skin. Michelle looked up at the two men. They were grinning widely. For a second she considered getting up, but that would be futile: They would just push her back down. They had her just the way they wanted her, and there was nothing she could do about it.

The bald man knelt down behind her. His rough hands lifted up her short skirt and began peeling off her panties. Moaning helplessly, Michelle lifted up her knees one by one, as he removed her panties and threw them on the wet asphalt.

She was now lying on her hands and knees in the alley, her naked ass exposed to the bald biker behind her. And soon, she felt the tip of his cock touching her cunt. The other man knelt down in front of her face, pointing his glistening wet cock at her mouth.

"Open wide," he gasped.

Michelle felt the bald biker's cock pushing slowly into her slit from behind. She was very wet, but to yield to the huge girth of his

tool she had to spread her legs as wide as she could, feeling her sex muscle stretch as he entered her.

As she opened her mouth, the tall man slid his cock in between her lips. She noticed the taste of her own juices on his rigid cock. Excited, Michelle sucked on the head of his tool, her mouth rhythmically massaging the bulbous helmet.

"Yeah," the biker groaned. "Suck my cock."

The bald man had now buried the entire length of his hard shaft in her tender insides. Grunting, he began thrusting into her, pumping his fat tool into her pussy. He was relentless. Over and over, he hammered his thick cock all the way into her stretching flesh.

The tall man looked down at his cock, sliding it slowly in and out of Michelle's mouth. He seemed to love watching it glisten, slick and wet from her saliva.

"Make it wet," he whispered. "Make it nice and wet."

Obediently, Michelle slobbered all over the shaft, covering his cock with her spit. She felt his tool growing harder and harder as he slowly moved his cock in and out of her mouth.

The bald man grabbed her ass, stabbing away at her cunt, grunting like an animal.

"You like that, huh?" he said. "Like to feel my fat cock inside your pussy?"

"Mmm!" she cried, her voice stifled by the tall man's cock filling her mouth.

But yes, she realized: She loved it. It was hard for Michelle to admit to herself that being raped gave her such immense pleasure, but her first orgasm had weakened her defenses. And as the bald man kept thrusting his fat tool into her slippery slit, she felt another one approaching.

Michelle's body was trembling. The tall man slowly slid his stiff cock all the way out of her mouth, the shaft glistening with her saliva.

"Oh God," she gasped, as the bald man's savage fucking brought her ever closer to another climax. "Oh God."

The tall man grinned, slowly sliding his cock in between her wet lips again.

"Keep going," he called out to his buddy. "The little slut is gonna come again."

This seemed to excite the bald man even more. Brutally, he drove the entire length of his hardened cock into Michelle's tender flesh. Again and again he thrust into her, uttering inarticulate grunts of pure animal lust.

"Hunh!" he yelled in time with his powerful strokes. "Hunh! Hunh!"

Her head was spinning. Yes - she was about to come. She was about to come right now. It was as if she was no longer the well-paid secretary - she was a horny slut, a biker chick. On her hands and knees in a dark alley, fucked by two bikers, one cock in her cunt and one in her mouth. God, it turned her on...

"Mmm!"

Michelle tried to scream, as the orgasm hit her, her entire body tensing up, overcome with pleasure. Grinning, the tall man removed his cock from her mouth, saliva dripping from the rigid shaft onto the asphalt.

"Aaah!" she screamed, shivering uncontrollably.

She felt the bald man's cock swelling inside her cunt, as he kept thrusting it into her. He was about to come, too.

"Yeah!" he yelled.

To her surprise, he suddenly pulled his cock out of her pussy. She heard him grunting behind her, apparently masturbating, because suddenly the first hot spurt of semen landed on her ass.

"Huhhh!" he roared.

Again and again, his pumping cock shot sperm all over her, landing on her naked ass-cheeks. The biker shouted out loud with pleasure, long creamy jets flying from his cock, spattering her ass.

Is it getting on my clothes, too? Michelle thought. Oh God, please don't let him stain my blouse...

The tall man was masturbating, too, vigorously stroking his erect cock as he watched them. The sight of his buddy ejaculating all over Michelle finally brought him off.

"Yeah," he whispered hoarsely. "Here I go, baby."

He poked his swelling cock against her lips. He wanted to come in her mouth.

Reluctantly, Michelle parted her lips, letting him slide it inside. As his cock made contact with the soft wet insides of her mouth, it immediately exploded.

"Ahhh!" he yelled, as his cock pumped the first spurt of semen into her mouth. "Swallow! Take it all!"

Michelle gulped, drinking down the spicy taste of the tall man's semen. His jerking cock kept squirting its thick liquid into her mouth. She tried her best to swallow it all, but there was too much. Creamy semen trickled down her chin, dripping onto the asphalt.

Finally, his ejaculation subsided, and he slid the warm, slippery cock out of Michelle's mouth.

The two men stood in front of her, zipping up. She thought that maybe now they'd let her go. But then she realized: That was not what she wanted them to do. She wanted more, wanted them to rape her again.

The tall man pulled her to her feet and held her tight.

"Oh yes," she heard herself whisper. "Don't stop."

The bald man walked up to her and ripped open her blouse, pulling it off and throwing it on the ground. She thought she saw specks of semen on it, but she wasn't sure. Next, the bald man tore off her bra and her skirt.

Michelle was now naked, except for her high-heeled shoes, her beautiful body lit by the single light bulb in the alley. The bald man pinched one of her nipples with two fingers. The nipple was already hard. God, she was horny. She just wanted them to fuck her again - fuck her hard and come all over her.

The two men grabbed Michelle's arms and pulled her towards the motorcycle. They placed her on her back on the seat, pulling her hands toward the handlebars. The leather seat felt cold against her naked back.

"Please," she whimpered. "Fuck me again."

The tall man laughed fiendishly.

"Hehe," he said. "Crazy bitch."

"You're gonna get what's coming to you," the bald man sneered. "Don't worry."

Michelle saw that he was holding a roll of duct tape. Seconds later, he was taping her right wrist to the handlebar of the motorcycle. And then, he taped her left wrist, too. Michelle tugged at the tape, but it was no use: She was tied up. Naked and tied to a motorcycle.

"Beautiful," a voice said. "Well done, guys."

Michelle stirred. It wasn't one of the bikers talking. It was someone else, and... she knew that voice. Looking up, she saw a figure appearing from the shadows of the alley.

It was Mr. Bergman.

"Oh God," she whimpered.

She had already been raped by two bikers. And now, as she lay tied to their motorcycle, naked, her boss had to walk in on them. Her boss, whom she had lusted after for years.

Still, all Michelle could think off was: When were they going to fuck her again? She wanted them to rape her once more. Surely, Mr. Bergman would enjoy watching that. Or maybe...

Zzzip!

Mr. Bergman opened the fly of his business suit, and his erect cock popped out. It was quite long and extremely hard. He must have been watching, as the bikers fucked her. Michelle could hardly imagine him doing something like that.

Mr. Bergman walked towards the motorcycle and stood between Michelle's legs, his stiff cock pointing towards her pussy. By now, she was beside herself with lust, wanting to be fucked by anyone. Anyone - but Mr. Bergman would be wonderful.

"Ohhh," she whispered. "Fuck me, please..."

She wanted to touch herself, wanted to masturbate in front of him. But her hands were tied to the handlebars with duct tape. And all she could do was spread her trembling legs, offering him her succulent cunt. She felt her juices trickling down the insides of her thighs onto the leather seat.

Mr. Bergman just stood there, his excited cock jerking slightly. The bikers came closer, curious.

"You want this cock?" Mr. Bergman asked.

"Oh yes," Michelle gasped. "Please..."

"Very well, then," Mr. Bergman said. "Let's go to my hotel room."

Michelle couldn't believe her ears. In her hyper-excited state, she couldn't imagine waiting even a few minutes. She wanted his cock now.

"No!" she cried. "I didn't... no..."

"I'm sorry," Mr. Bergman said, smiling. "I don't understand. What is it you want?"

Naked, tied to the bikers' motorcycle, Michelle was on the verge of tears from lust.

"Fuck me right now," she begged. "Let them watch. I don't care. In fact, I want them to watch as you fuck me. Just give me that big, hard cock right now! I'm so horny, I can't wait any longer..."

Mr. Bergman was grinning. With one hand, he grabbed his erect cock, guiding it towards the entrance to Michelle's pussy.

"That sure sounds like an invitation," he said. "Alright, baby. Here it comes."

And with one enormous thrust, he slid his long, hard cock all the way into Michelle's dripping wet cunt.

"Aaah!" she cried.

Oh God, she thought, this is heaven - this is bliss. At the height of her excitement, she was fucked by the man of her dreams. Her next climax could be imminent, but she wanted to savor every second.

"All right, Michelle," Mr. Bergman said. "This is it. I'm gonna fuck you like you've never been fucked before. Do you hear me?"

He let his cock slide all the way out, and then rammed it in again with one powerful stroke. Over and over, he stabbed her with his bone-hard tool, making her moan with pleasure.

The two bikers stood around the motorcycle, watching the scene with glazed eyes. Slowly, they unzipped their jeans and took out their semi-erect cocks. As Mr. Bergman kept fucking his naked, bound secretary, they began to masturbate.

Michelle bit her lip, realizing that she was about to come again already. Her tender pussy impaled by the rhythmic thrusts of Mr. Bergman's cunt, she felt the pleasure building inside her body, finally reaching an explosive high.

"Aaah!" she screamed, as she climaxed.

Michelle didn't know if she had ever come this hard. Shivering and squirming, she gave in to the sensation of pure physical ecstasy.

Mr. Bergman never stopped fucking her. He slowed down the pace slightly, his rigid tool moving in and out of her slick cunt. One hand kneading her breast, he began gently massaging the base of her clit with his other thumb.

Michelle whimpered helplessly, tears of joy flowing down her cheeks. The bikers stood next to her face, masturbating at the sight. After witnessing Michelle's violent orgasm, their cocks had once more become hard as steel.

The bald man put his cock to her mouth and tried to push her lips apart with his fingers.

"Don't!" Mr. Bergman said. "She's not gonna suck you now. I want to watch her face as I fuck her. Eh, Michelle. Do you like that?"

"I love it," she whispered. "Don't stop."

As Mr. Bergman's stiff tool pounded into her sex, it was as if her last orgasm had never really subsided. But already, she felt the sensations of pleasure building towards a new climax.

"Oh, God," she sobbed. "Oh, please..."

Michelle felt that her next orgasm would be so powerful she'd faint. She wanted him to stop - she couldn't take anymore. And yet, the excitement was too great. If she didn't get her release, it would drive her insane.

She struggled feebly on the seat of the motorcycle, the bikers slowly masturbating, as Mr. Bergman's long hard cock entered her cunt again and again. Pinching her nipple and stroking her clit, he fucked her relentlessly, driving his throbbing shaft in and out her slit in a hard demanding rhythm.

"Yeah," he whispered. "Feel my cock inside you."

Drops of sweat formed on his forehead. He was fucking her with all his strength. Michelle screamed out loud, as she felt what was happening. Mr. Bergman's fat tool thrust a few more times into the wet depths of her pussy.

And she came again.

"Aaah!" she cried, throwing herself about on the leather seat, her tied hands pulling helplessly at the duct tape. "Aaah!"

"Fucking hell!" the bald man cried.

Clenching his bulging cock inside his fist, he ejaculated immediately. The first long jet of sperm shot out of his swollen cock, flying across Michelle's face and landing on her left breast. As semen kept pumping out of his twitching tool, the tall biker climaxed, too.

"Yeah!" he yelled, watching his cock jerking rhythmically, as he came.

For some time, Michelle watched as the two cocks ejaculated across her body. Powerful spurts of hot biker sperm squirted from their hard rods, spattering her flushed skin with creamy white stains.

"Unnnh!" Mr. Bergman yelled.

Michelle felt his cock swelling inside her cunt, as he froze in mid-thrust.

"Oh yes," she whispered, wanting to feel him coming inside her. "Give it to me!"

"Fuck!" he cried as the first jet of semen shot deep into Michelle's pussy.

He grabbed her thighs, pushing his twitching cock all the way inside her. She felt it pumping thick, hot sperm into her tender cunt, filling her insides with his lusty cream.

"Yes," she whispered, shivering with pleasure.

Mr. Bergman's orgasm seemed to go on forever, unloading an unbelievable amount of semen inside Michelle's cunt. But finally, the spurts became weaker, and he slid his glistening, wet cock out of her slit.

"That was wonderful," she whispered. "Really."

The bikers zipped up and untied her without a word. She was still in a daze. She couldn't believe this had happened. Couldn't believe that her boss had been behind it all. And most of all, she couldn't believe how much pleasure it had given her. Hell, tonight had been the best sex of her life.

Mr. Bergman smiled at her, relaxed. As Michelle sat up on the motorcycle seat, the tall biker wrapped a big towel around her.

"Of course," the bald man said, "we'll pay for the clothes we ruined."

Michelle looked at him blankly. Oh yes, she was naked. But she had forgotten all about her clothes. Now she saw them, scattered all over the wet asphalt in the alley.

Mr. Bergman nodded, slowly tucking his soft cock into his suit pants and zipping up.

"Of course," he said.

Michelle looked around.

"But..." she stuttered. "Can you help me get back to my hotel?"

"Your hotel?" Mr. Bergman asked, grinning. "No need for that."

"Sorry?"

"I managed to change my reservation. We now have a double room at my hotel, if that's okay with you."

"Oh, thank you," Michelle gasped, throwing her naked arms around Mr. Bergman.

"Will you call a cab?" he asked. And one of the bikers produced a cell phone.

Minutes later, the cab drove up. As Michelle entered, wearing only high heels and towel, the driver looked puzzled, and then shook his head. Mr. Bergman climbed into the back seat, next to Michelle. As they drove off, she saw the two bikers waving at them.

As Mr. Bergman smiled at her, she smiled back. She briefly wondered whether this was going to have any consequences, job-wise.

Then she realized one thing:

With sex like this, she couldn't care less.

The Bath Attendant

Nicole was hastily packing her bag, just throwing stuff into it:
Bikini, towels, bath slippers, purse...

She looked at her watch. Damn, it was late. The swimming bath
would be closed in less than an hour.

But she had made up her mind that she would go anyway.

Nicole had a perfect body, and she liked to stay fit: Jogging,
cycling, working out, whatever. But swimming was still her favourite
form of exercise. She just loved the sensual feeling of being
immersed in the warm water of the pool.

She zipped up the bag and left her apartment, walking briskly
towards the swimming bath.

Yeah, the sensual feeling of the water - Nicole was a sensual
girl, with a relaxed attitude towards sex.

She wouldn't call herself promiscuous, and she was certainly
not a nymphomaniac: How often she got laid was no big deal for
her. In fact, she frequently went without it for weeks.

Today (like every day this week) she had woken up by herself.
That was okay. She had masturbated, fingering herself to three
satisfying orgasms, before she had got up to go to work.

But on the other hand, if she met a man she liked - why
shouldn't they enjoy each other's company? She had no problems
with one-night stands. Sex could be a purely sensual pleasure - and
why not indulge? It was nobody's business but hers and her
partner's. Was it?

She looked at her watch again. Well, there would only be time
for a brief swim, but that would have to do. She dashed across the
street, narrowly avoiding a car.

People had a strange attitude towards sex, Nicole thought: It
was a very sensual and enjoyable experience, and wasn't that the
most important thing?

Also, a lot of her friends thought that men were kinda scary.
Yeah, well, maybe – but she'd always felt that she was in control.
Once she was naked, showing off her shapely body, any man turned

into a salivating puppy – willing to do anything in the world just for the privilege of fucking her. Men were such slaves to their dicks, it made her laugh.

Nicole rushed through the doors of the swimming bath, heading for the ticket booth.

"Hi," she said to the ticket seller. "I'm late - I know."

"Hey," he said smiling. "I don't mind."

Nicole smiled, too. He was a good-looking guy. Dark, slim and fit - exactly her type.

"No," she stuttered. "No, of course not. I'll be quick."

The guy laughed.

"Yes, very funny," Nicole said, composing herself. "I bet you're thinking about how fast I can get out of my clothes, right?"

"No, no," the ticket guy said. "I wasn't."

He looked at her for a moment. She was dressed in a short skirt that revealed her long, slender legs - and a tight blouse that emphasized her beautiful, shapely breasts. He took a deep breath.

"But now I am," he said.

"You bastard," Nicole laughed. "I really should complain about you."

"Well, that would be the first time, then," he grinned.

Shaking her head, Nicole paid for her ticket and hurried towards the locker rooms.

"See you around," she shouted back at him.

The ticket seller smiled, watching her beautiful ass bouncing along, as she ran along the corridor in her high-heeled shoes. God, she was a sexy thing. It wasn't often his dick got hard at the sight of a fully-dressed girl. But it was getting hard now...

Half an hour later, Nicole was done swimming and just floated lazily in the warm water of the pool. She was all alone in the hall.

Outside the windows of the swimming bath night was falling. The fluorescent lights lighted the hall, but the sky outside was turning a darker and darker shade of blue.

Again, Nicole thought of her flirt with the guy in the ticket sales. She hadn't noticed him before today, but he was really cute. She wished he'd be there again the next time - maybe they could get together. For some reason, she imagined that was really great in bed.

Without noticing it, she let her finger slip inside her panties, and slowly she began caressing herself under water. Carefully she parted her labia and let a finger circle her clit. It felt wonderful.

Shivering with lust, she closed her eyes and visualized the handsome ticket seller. Nicole closed her eyes and let two fingers slide rhythmically back and forth next to her tiny love button. She moaned quietly.

"Everybody out."

Nicole froze at the sound of the deep male voice.

Opening her eyes, she saw the bath attendant walking along the edge of the pool in his white working clothes.

"We're closing."

She looked him over as he stood there in front of her. No, he definitely wasn't her type: A big, thickset man, his crew-cut hair was a remarkably light shade of blonde, and the backs of his hands were covered with blonde hair. Yes, his entire body was probably hairy. Nicole shivered at the thought.

"Are you deaf?" he asked angrily. "Get out!"

She stretched in front of him, letting him see her firm, round breasts swelling inside her small bikini top. Then she brushed her long, dark hair aside and looked at him pleadingly.

"Ah, please?" she purred. "Just a few more minutes?"

Coolly, the bath attendant looked her shapely body over thoroughly. Then he put down his toolbox, turned around and walked by the edge of the pool out of the hall.

Smiling to herself, Nicole laid back in the warm water. Outside the hall she heard the sounds of doors closing and locks slamming shut. And a few minutes later the bath attendant was back.

"Okay. Now get up here," he ordered.

"But, I thought..." Nicole protested, confused.

"Shut up," the attendant snarled. "Get out. Now."

Hesitantly, Nicole got out of the pool. The bath attendant studied her sopping wet body without batting an eyelid.

"Lie down over there," he said, pointing to a wooden bench next to the pool. She looked at him blankly.

"Come on," he said impatiently. "Lie down. On your back."

He's gotta be kidding, Nicole thought, this just isn't happening. She looked at him again: Poor, ugly guy – who would ever want to fuck him? He was probably horny as hell. Typical: Another man – another slave to his dick. And today he was lusting after her.

Fearlessly, smiling quietly to herself, Nicole went over to the bench, water dripping from her body. Then she lay down and made herself comfortable.

The bath attendant came over and knelt down between her legs.

"Show me your pussy," he whispered.

Nicole didn't react, but then she felt his hands softly grabbing her thighs and spreading her legs apart.

"Pull your panties aside and let me see your pussy," he went on. And with one hand she pulled her wet bikini panties aside, while her other hands parted her clean-shaven pussy lips. Ever so slightly, letting the bath attendant glimpse the moist pink insides of her pussy. He panted.

"Masturbate for me," he ordered. "I want to watch."

Shamelessly Nicole spread her legs before his eyes.

And slowly she began caressing herself: Rhythmically, she stroked her labia up and down, slid a finger in and out of her pussy and rubbed her little clit, making it swell and harden.

"Yeah," the bath attendant whispered hoarsely. He had got up and now stood massaging his member though the fabric of his loose pants. "Grab your tits."

Sighing deeply, Nicole slipped her left breast out of the wet bikini top. Still masturbating with one hand, she grabbed her breast with the other, kneading it and pinching her nipple.

She wasn't at all self-conscious — she was not ashamed of her beautiful body or her sexuality.

But still: All the time she knew that the bath attendant was watching her - this big, brutal man who talked so dirty to her. He had lusted after her from the start, but now she was teasing him, turning him on even more. The thought of her situation made Nicole shiver with excitement on the wooden bench.

The bath attendant had pulled down his pants, and his hard cock stood out straight. It was thick and wide, and his swelling balls were covered with a thick layer of blonde hairs. Now he straddled the bench, his member bouncing stiffly in front of her face.

Then he grabbed her chin, fixing her eyes with his firm gaze.

"Suck my cock," he ordered.

As Nicole opened her mouth, the bath attendant guided the bulging head of his cock in between her red lips.

The head alone almost filled her mouth, but the bath attendant wasn't satisfied: Slowly he slid his hips forwards, even further forwards. And inch by inch he filled her mouth with his cock.

"Ohhh yeah, take it all the way," he groaned.

Nicole felt the tip of his cock hitting the roof of her mouth and pressed her hands against his muscular thighs to stop him. And the bath attendant stopped - although only half of his huge member was inside her mouth.

Instead he began making fucking motions. In a slow rhythm he let his hard cock slide back and forth across Nicole's soft tongue, out between her lips and back into her mouth again. With manically precise hip motions he guided his fat tool in and out, in and out between Nicole's softly sucking lips. She felt the hard shaft trembling on her tongue, its wide head swelling like a fleshy dome.

"Play with your pussy," the bath attendant ordered, pumping his cock in and out of Nicole's mouth.

And she immediately pulled off her panties and again began caressing herself. God, she was wet! She spread her legs wide apart. Then she forced two fingers into her pussy, letting them slide in and out, her other hands massaging her little, hard clit. The love juices flowed down Nicole's hot thighs and onto the wooden bench, while the bath attendant vigorously fucked her mouth.

Suddenly he withdrew. With a wet smacking sound the cock slipped out of her mouth, glistening with saliva. It bounced stiffly in front of him, as he stood between her legs and pulled his clothes off. And for the first time Nicole saw the bath attendant in the nude.

His wide body was quite muscular, but she had been right: His chest and stomach, yes, even his shoulders were covered by a thick blanket of blonde hairs. Nicole writhed on the bench, uttering a faint noise of disgust: She didn't want him. She just didn't.

But who was she kidding? She had played her little game, leading him on, teasing him, sucking his cock. He was like an animal in heat. And now, she was afraid, she would just have to pay the price.

The bath attendant just stood there, grinning viciously, his rock-hard cock bouncing eagerly in front of her. Suddenly he bent down and tore off her bikini top, so that she, too, lay completely naked on the bench.

He stood for a while, watching her, his fist clenching his hard cock. She met his gaze. His eyes were lustful, but cold and merciless as well.

"I'm gonna give you the fucking of your life!" he exclaimed - and immediately Nicole felt his rock-hard cock forcing its way into her slit. Its entire length with one single thrust.

Screaming loudly, she twisted beneath him, but the bath attendant had already begun rhythmically driving it into her. With every stroke, he slid the head of his cock all the out between her labia, and then all the way in, in a brutal, relentless pace.

The bath attendant grabbed her shoulders hard, holding her down on the bench, fucking and fucking her. Nicole gave in to her excitement and savoured the sensation of the firm, powerful cock thrusting in and out of her pussy muscle. The sweat poured from the bath attendant's body, dripping down on Nicole's face and breasts, ran down his chest, his stomach, his cock, mixing in her pussy with the juices of her own lust.

"Ooh, that's so good," she purred, the bath attendant gasping with the strain. "Give me your fat cock. Fuck me!"

She clasped her legs around his wide, hairy back and dug her nails into his muscular buttocks.

"Arh," he yelled angrily without slowing down.

He drove his thick, wet cock into Nicole again and again. From the swollen head, the entire length of the hard shaft, until his bristly pubes met her smooth pussy lips. Thrust after thrust into the depths of her quivering flesh, until Nicole finally lost control.

"Ohhh," she cried out loudly, her voice echoing through the swimming-baths.

Her entire body gave in to the pleasure of a violent orgasm. The juices of her lust flowed from her pussy, while the bath attendant mercilessly kept driving his cock into her tender pleasure zone.

"Oh, stop, stop," she sobbed - her climax seemed to go on forever.

Helplessly, Nicole held on to the bath attendant's huge, sweaty body, his cock still pumping into her sex.

Finally he withdrew. Lifting her head, she saw her juices dripping from his shiny, burning red cock.

Then he grabbed her body and quickly turned her over, placing her belly-down on the bench. His strong hands grabbed her hips, and Nicole felt the bath attendant's bone-hard cock slowly entering her hot pussy from behind.

"Ohhh," she whispered huskily, collapsing on the bench, exhausted.

"Yeah, lovely pussy," the bath attendant growled.

He pressed his hips against hers and froze for a few seconds. Nicole felt his blood-filled member throbbing with excitement, swelling inside her tender flesh.

"I'm not done fucking you yet," the bath attendant muttered and slowly slid his fat tool in and out of her.

Yes.

Slowly.

Nicole shivered with pleasure. The motions of his hard cock massaged the insides of her dripping wet flesh. So incredibly good. She closed her eyes and clenched her love muscles around his cock with every thrust. Nicole held on to the bench, as the rhythmic pumping of the batch attendant drove her towards another orgasm.

"Oooh," she whimpered, "oooh, oooh", her entire body shaking on the bench.

Hot love juice drenched his hard cock, trickling down his bulging balls.

The bath attendant's huge hands grabbed her breasts, kneading them violently as his wide member slid into her irresistible pussy. Nicole was gasping for breath, as she felt his tempo increasing. Still more impatiently he buried his cock inside her, and she came again.

A dizzying, unexpected orgasm, leaving Nicole helplessly moaning on the bench. Ready to burst, the bath attendant's cock kept plunging ever faster into her almost numb pussy, until he, too, lost control.

"Ohhh," he yelled into the empty hall as he started to ejaculate.

Nicole's eyes opened wide, as his cock released the first hot spurt.

"Oh," she whispered, impressed, as she felt the bath attendant's wildly jerking cock pumping long jets of semen into her.

"Oh yes," he grunted, satisfied.

He pressed his abdomen against hers, forcing the last thick droplets from his throbbing member. Hard and stiff the cock stood inside Nicole's pussy for a while, until it slowly collapsed, sliding out of her, wet and glistening.

The bath attendant staggered over to the stands and sat down, exhausted. Nicole lay a while on the bench, catching her breath.

Slowly, she sat up, but at the same time she heard footsteps outside the hall.

A figure came out of the darkness and walked along the pool towards them. It was a tall, slim man in a white t-shirt and jeans. Amazed, Nicole stared at the man. It was the ticket seller.

"You?" she gasped.

"Yes, me," the ticket seller grinned. "Hello again, young lady."

Looking at the bath attendant, he asked:

"Been enjoying yourselves, have you?"

"Yeah," the bath attendant said, panting heavily. "I had to teach her a lesson."

"Okay," the ticket seller laughed, "I bet you fucked the living daylights out of her."

The bath attendant sat in the stands, sweating, his cock thick and limp between his legs.

"Well, Jack. You know me."

Jack laughed and turned towards Nicole.

"I don't blame you," he said. "She does look kinda cute. I bet you used the toolbox, too?"

"Nah," the bath attendant said. "I didn't get to that. I got so fucking horny."

"Really?" Jack said. "Okay, baby. We'd better have a look at this then."

Hesitantly, Nicole sat on the bench, looking on in bewilderment as Jack opened the toolbox.

"Oh yes," he said happily, lifting a pair of handcuffs and a shiny steel vibrator from the box.

"It's playtime!"

Before Nicole had time to react, she lay on her back, chained to the bench with the handcuffs. The metal felt icy cold against her wrists. Smiling, Jack knelt down between her legs with the vibrator. She shivered, as the cool metal slid across her labia.

"So, did he fuck you?" Jack asked quietly, and Nicole nodded.

"No, no," he corrected her. "Tell me about it. What was it like?"

He let the cold steel tool slide across her labia, letting it graze her clit, teasing, exciting her.

Nicole squirmed on the bench.

"It was great," she gasped. "His cock was so thick and hard."

"Mmm," Jack said appreciatively. The cold vibrator circled her clit, poking gently at the mouth of her pussy. "Tell me more: Did he fuck you good?"

"Oh yes," Nicole moaned, pulling at the handcuffs.

"He fucked me with his stiff cock. Oh yes, keep going. And he made me come. Mmm. Yeah. And then he squirted all his lovely cum into me."

Jack smiled. Then he turned on the vibrator, letting the cold steel start buzzing against Nicole's clit, eliciting a roar of animal lust.

"Hurhhh," she yelled.

Wild with pent-up lust she raised her hips from the bench and started rotating her abdomen against the vibrator. The bath attendant sat up, staring in fascination at the handcuffed girl on the bench. Jack grabbed her rounded ass, as she impatiently ground her wet pussy against the vibrating tool.

"Is that good, eh? Is that good?" Jack whispered to her, as the vibrator buzzed around her clit, poked in between her smooth pussy-lips, only to touch her clit again.

Nicole's arched her entire body on the bench, as she screamed yet another orgasm out into the hall.

"Yeah," Jack growled.

And with a wild look in his eyes he drove the buzzing steel tool deep into Nicole's wet, pulsating pussy.

"Ohhh," she cried, senseless with lust.

The feeling of the humming dildo buried in her cunt in the midst of her climax was almost too much for her to take. Shamelessly, she stretched her body on the bench, giving in to pure pleasure.

Jack pulled the vibrator out of Nicole's slithering flesh and put it to her mouth. Nastily, she licked the metal tool, savouring the hot taste of her own pussy. Jack's finger massaged her tiny, protruding clit, as he slowly slid the dildo in and out of her mouth.

The bath attendant sat naked in the stands watching them intently, his thick cock still soft between his legs. But the sight of the horny Nicole subjected to

Jack's sexual games excited him, and his fat member jerked involuntarily.

Again, Jack drove the steel vibrator into Nicole's wet pussy, turned it on at the slowest, throbbing speed and let go of it. Chained

to the bench, Nicole squirmed lustfully, her sex muscles rhythmically squeezing the metal tool.

Watching her greedily, Jack unbuttoned his jeans and pulled out his long, rigid member. Nicole gasped at the sight: It was remarkably long - even the exposed, bluish head was somewhat elongated. His cock was hard as rock - the dark, bulging veins clearly visible beneath the skin.

Slowly, Jack caressed his erect cock, as clear liquid quietly ran from its tip, wetting his finger. He let Nicole lick the juice off his fingers, as he turned the buzzing vibrator around inside her pussy, his face an expressionless mask. Then, suddenly, he pulled it out.

The next moment she felt the head of Jack's cock entering her slit. Nicole clenched her teeth, as he slowly forced the entire length of the shaft into her. It felt as hard as the steel dildo, but considerably longer. Slowly he pulled out of her, enjoying the sight of his cock glistening with her abundant juices.

"Yes. Fuck her!"

That was the voice of the bath attendant, hoarse with excitement. With glazed eyes he watched them, as Jack grabbed Nicole's hips, burying every inch of his cock inside her.

"Oooh yeah," she howled.

And eagerly Jack began pumping his rigid cock in and out of her wet pussy. He let the head of his cock slide all the way out between the smooth labia and back all the way in with every thrust. Stab after stab in a hard, relentless beat, while Nicole squirmed on the bench, pulling wildly at the handcuffs, the jingling sound echoing in the empty swimming bath.

"Yeah," the bath attendant grunted. "Fuck her little, wet cunt."

His fat cock was now semi-erect and he masturbated shamelessly. Stroking his cock with his big, hairy fist, he stared at Nicole, helplessly getting pounded by Jack's bone-hard cock.

"Oh yes, fuck me," she gasped. "Give me your long, hard cock. Fuck my wet pussy. Make me come."

"You're gonna come now," Jack hissed - it sounded almost like an order. "My cock will make you come."

And twisting his hips in circling motions between Nicole's widely spread legs, he drove his cock into every corner of her succulent, trembling cunt.

"Ohhh yes," she cried. "I'm coming. Oh yes. Oh yes."

Nicole's juices flowed around Jack's cock, as the orgasm overpowered her. His face was a mad grimace of excitement, as he kept forcing his long, hard cock into her over and over.

"Arhhh," he yelled, desperately trying to hold back his ejaculation.

He felt as if his sperm was about to boil over - the pressure in his bursting balls grew every time he thrust into Nicole's juicy, soft flesh.

The bath attendant stood next to them. Naked and hairy he stood there, masturbating before Nicole's eyes. She saw the round head of his cock bulging, as his hairy fist massaged the fat shaft, until it leaked clear fluid from its tip. Fascinated, the bath attendant stared at Jack's long cock, slipping in fast strokes in and out of the handcuffed girl's pussy.

"Does it feel good?" Jack snarled, fucking her like a madman. "Does the big cock feel good inside your randy cunt?"

"Yes, yes," Nicole whimpered, his powerful thrusts throwing her about on the wooden bench. "Fuck... me... hard."

Immediately she felt something cold and hard entering her anus. Jack had forced the tip of the steel vibrator into her ass, and now he turned it on.

Nicole shouted out, as the dildo began buzzing violently inside her anus. The bath attendant masturbated like mad.

"Yeah, fuck her," he whispered.

Jack had slowed down a bit and now coolly slid his stiff cock in and out of her - sometimes letting it slip all the way out of her pussy, slapping her wet labia - only to let the entire length enter her again. Nicole felt the cock filling every inch of her sex, the steel vibrator teasing her ass, and there was no turning back.

"I'm coming," she cried again. "Oh, help me, I'm coming!"

Her vision went hazy, but she managed to catch sight of Jack pulling his cock from her cunt, yelling wildly as he started to ejaculate. Hot, white jets came pumping out of his cock in long spurts, hitting Nicole's stomach and breasts.

Shivering with excitement the bath attendant thrust his cock against Nicole's lips. Willingly, she opened her mouth, letting his bursting member enter. It still had the spicy taste of her own love juices. She watched Jack masturbating the last drops of semen onto her thighs, and with an animal grunt the bath attendant ejaculated in her mouth.

From the depths of his balls a hot jet of sperm shot deep into to Nicole's throat. The bath attendant's huge body jerked spasmodically, as spurt after spurt of thick, hot semen spouted from his cock and into the sucking mouth of the handcuffed girl. Obediently, she drank the hot liquid in big gulps, until she had emptied him completely.

Nicole gasped, as the bath attendant pulled his fat cock out of her mouth. The two men stood for a while, watching her. The bath attendant stood naked and sweating, as Jack calmly buttoned his jeans. Then she felt Jack unlocking the handcuffs, freeing her hands again.

Jack nodded at the bath attendant and grabbed her feet. She felt the bath attendant grabbing hold of her shoulders, and in the next moment they threw her into the pool. With a loud splash Nicole landed in the warm water. She dived to the bottom and swam back up to the surface, feeling the water wash the two men's semen off her flushed skin.

Surfacing, Nicole shook the water from her hair and looked at the men who had been her lovers. The bath attendant lay exhausted in the stands, as Jack calmly put the handcuffs and the vibrator back into the toolbox. Nicole rested her elbows on the edge of the pool, looking at them cheekily.

"Tell me," she asked. "Exactly when do you really close?"

The two men laughed.

"Just take your time," Jack said.

Smiling, Nicole slowly slid back into the water.

The Subway

It's a hot day. Sandra is on the subway, holding on to the strap as the train roars through the tunnels. The air rushes in through the open windows, cooling her face with a dry and dirty smell. Every time the train stops at a station, the heat becomes unbearable, making Sandra wish it would start moving again. And then, after the loud slamming of the door, it does.

Holding on to the hard plastic strap, Sandra stretches her tall, slim body. She shakes her long reddish-brown hair, letting it fall down her back. The seated passengers glance at her with expressionless faces. Sandra is casually dressed, in a white cotton t-shirt and a short denim skirt. But even today, she's wearing her high heeled shoes and just a bit of makeup.

She's sweating - her skin is damp. Little droplets of sweat are forming, rolling down her face, her arms, her legs. She looks again at the seated passengers. Still no response - she might as well be invisible.

Then she feels a hand touching her behind. It's a man's hand, first stroking the fabric of her skirt, then gently but firmly grabbing her ass. It's a strong hand, grabbing her ass cheek, massaging and kneading it in a slow, sexy rhythm.

Sandra feels the unshaven cheek of the man next to her own. Above the roaring noise of the subway, she hears him whispering into her ear:

"Don't turn around!"

Somehow, she doesn't even want to. This is too exciting. Sandra feels the man's hand sliding under her skirt, pushing her panties aside, touching the soft flesh of her pussy. She moans softly, closing her eyes as she feels his forefinger carefully stroking her labia.

She's standing with her legs close together, the man forcing his hand in between her damp, sweaty thighs. He's masturbating her with deep, slow strokes and Sandra feels herself getting wet.

She opens her eyes. The seated passengers are staring now. The man's hand still moving between her legs, she looks at them: A young black kid is grinning at her. A woman about her own age is looking shocked. A middle-aged man in an expensive suit just sits watching her intently, a faint smile on his face. And between her thighs she feels the man's hand massaging her tender clit.

Then the train stops. The doors open and people get in. And the man doesn't stop, just keeps the motion going. Sandra hangs on the strap helplessly, exposed to the strangers walking by her, her hardening nipples almost piercing the fabric of her t-shirt. The doors are still open, exposing her to everyone on the platform, as an unknown man is slowly masturbating her.

Closing her eyes again, Sandra feels his finger probing her pussy. Wanting to feel it inside her, she spreads her legs slightly. As the rough, dry finger plunges into her wet slit, the doors slam shut and the train starts moving again.

The loud noise of the subway fills her ears once again, as the man's finger slides in and out of her pussy, fucking her with deep, powerful strokes. Sandra is gasping for air. She is so wet.

She holds on to the strap with both her hands as the train turns a corner, jerking them both to the side. Still, the man keeps his finger inside her juicy love muscle, poking it over and over.

Now she hears a different sound - a kind of metallic jangling. And as she feels the cold steel closing around her wrist, she knows: Handcuffs. Someone is chaining both her hands to the same rod the straps are attached to. And as the steel clicks around her other wrist, she's helpless.

Hanging handcuffed in the subway car, Sandra smells the dry, dirty air rushing through the window and feels the man masturbating her. But who did this? There has to be another man behind her. As she yanks at the handcuffs, another man's voice whispers into her ear:

"No. Don't turn around. Please."

Whimpering, Sandra looks at the passengers again. They're still watching, just watching it happen. The woman still looks shocked, but someone has her arm around her - probably her boyfriend. The middle-aged man hasn't changed his expression at all - he's obviously enjoying every second. And the young black kid has unzipped his pants and pulled out his cock, shamelessly masturbating.

"Spread your legs," the first man whispers to her.

And as Sandra stands on the floor, feet wide apart, someone pushes her torso forwards, bending her over, her chained arms stretching to the top of the car.

"Please..." she moans.

But as the man slides his finger all the way out of her pussy, Sandra feels a different sensation. Something cool and hard touches her labia, probing the moist entrance to her pussy. And then she knows: It's a vibrator.

"Yeah," she hears a man's voice saying.

And bent over in middle of the speeding subway car, Sandra feels the vibrator sliding all the way into her burning hot pussy.

"Oh God," she whispers.

She can feel her love juices trickling down the inside of her thighs. This really turns her on. She wriggles her ass invitingly and feels a man's hand slapping her ass cheek hard.

"Ow!" she shrieks.

"Shut up," the man says. "You love it, don't you?"

And he slaps her again, hard, making her skin burn.

"Turn it on," the man says.

Hanging by her cuffed hands, Sandra waits for it. Going through a curve, the car jerks again, screeching, as the man turns on the vibrator.

"Oooh," Sandra moans, as the deep electric throbbing starts.

The vibrator shakes her tender pussy, teasing her, making her wetter still. The man slaps her ass again. And again.

"Yeah," she cries. "Slap me!"

And as one man spanks her burning ass-cheeks, the other starts moving the vibrator back and forth. Purring and throbbing, the electric cock slides in and out of her pussy. Excited, Sandra starts thrusting her hips back and forth. And soon the man just has to hold the vibrator still as Sandra slides her pussy back and forth over the whirring dildo, leaving it wet and glistening from her juices.

The lights go out in the car. In the total darkness, the noise of the subway seems deafening. Sandra feels the man pulling the vibrator out of her slit and hears the sound of a zipper opening. Then she feels the tip of the unknown man's hard cock probing the mouth of her pussy.

"Oh yes," she whispers into the darkness. "Fuck me!"

She feels the man's fingers opening her labia and then his hard cock sliding into her pussy. She hears him groaning with lust as he holds his cock still inside her, letting it swell and harden even more.

Suddenly, the lights come back on: The fluorescent lights, blinking unevenly for a while until the car is lit up like before. The man starts fucking Sandra from behind, while the passengers sit blinking in the light. They can see him, she thinks. And I can't.

She feels the stiffness of the man's long cock, as he slowly plunges into her pussy, then pulls back and slides it into her again. Moaning lustfully, Sandra feels her juices flowing, lubricating the man's powerful tool.

Suddenly, the train speeds into a curve, wheels screeching. The car jerks, throwing them both forward. Sandra's arms are stretched behind her, pulling at the handcuffs, as the man's body slams against her, impaling her soft flesh on his rigid cock. "Aaah," she screams in pain and pleasure.

The train comes out of the curve, and the car stabilizes its movement. Gently grabbing Sandra's hips, the man pulls her back into position, right underneath the straps. Then slowly, he slides his hard, slippery cock out of her pussy. Sandra sighs, as she hears two or more male voices whispering behind her back. She can't make out a single word.

She gasps, as someone pulls a dark, silky strip of fabric in front of her eyes. They're blindfolding her! As a man's hands ties the blindfold behind her head, all is dark. And Sandra, a pretty young woman on her way home from work, hangs handcuffed and blindfolded in the middle of a subway car. There is a quiet murmur from the passengers.

She hears footsteps walking around her. Someone grabs her t-shirt, pulling it out. Then she hears the fabric being torn apart with a ripping sound, and strong hands pull the shredded fabric from her torso. A man's hand grabs her full, naked breasts as soon as they're exposed, other men just grunt in approval.

Rough hands unbutton her skirt and pull if off her. Then something cold and hard grazes her hip, and moments later her panties have been cut apart and discarded. Now Sandra stands naked in the car, except for her high-heeled shoes.

For a while, nothing happens. Hot and wet, she hangs from her handcuffs, listening to the noise of the subway train, waiting for the men to make use of her naked body again.

Then she senses the train slowing down. Pulling into a station, it stops, and Sandra hears the doors open. She hears the noise of passengers entering, passing her naked, chained body. Some of them brush against her, some stroke her breasts, her ass, her pussy. A delicate finger - perhaps a woman's - gently massages her clit, making Sandra whimper with pleasure.

As the doors close and the train begins moving, the slender finger continues stroking her. The woman kisses her breast, gently biting her nipple.

"Oh, yes," Sandra moans.

The finger slides into her dripping wet pussy, slowly fucking her first with one, then with two fingers. She feels the woman kissing her clit, sucking it with loud, slurping noises as her fingers rhythmically probe Sandra's excited slit.

She is gasping for air, pulling hard on her handcuffs, her climax approaching. A man's hand grabs her breasts from behind, squeezing her erect nipples. Sandra throws her head back, crying out with pleasure:

"Oh yes! Ohhh! I'm coming!"

And as the woman sucks her clit into her mouth, finger-fucking her in a furious tempo, Sandra is finally overpowered by her orgasm.

"Ohhh! Ohhh!" she cries out, as her body shakes with convulsions of lust.

The man behind her holds onto her breasts, as the woman licks the love-juice from her tender flesh. Then she gently kisses Sandra's clit and pulls away.

Breathing deeply, recovering from her climax, Sandra feels a man's hands grabbing her thighs and lifting her legs up off the ground. As he stands between her legs, she feels he is naked. Naked and excited. His erect cock brushes against her thighs and her belly, before he gently places it between her labia.

"Oh, God," she whispers.

The man pulls her body against his, slowly forcing her pussy open with the bulging head of his cock. He places her calves on his shoulders and holds onto her ass. Grunting like an animal, the man pulls her pelvis against his, sliding his rock-hard cock ever deeper into her trembling slit.

"Please..." Sandra gasps.

She knows the naked man is not the one who fucked her before. This one's cock is longer and just as hard. She wants to see

through the blindfold, find out who is fucking her. But all is dark, and all she hears is the noise of the moving train.

Laughing fiendishly, the naked man starts pulling her back and forth, sliding her pussy up and down the entire length of his hardened shaft. Sandra is hanging from the handcuffs in the subway car, helpless as the man rocks her body back and forth, penetrating her wet flesh over and over with his long, powerful cock.

"Yeah," a man's voice says behind her back. "That's the way she likes it."

And sure enough: Suspended from the straps, her pussy being slowly fucked by the naked man's huge cock, Sandra savours the waves of pleasure running through her body, making her juices flow hot and wet around the man's cock. As the bone-hard tool probes the insides of her love-muscle, she feels it massaging her tender flesh, making her whimper with excitement.

The man behind her forces his fingers into her mouth. They still have the taste of her own pussy. Withdrawing his fingers, he puts the vibrator to her lips. She kisses it and licks it, tasting her own pussy again. Grunting with excitement, her lover increases the tempo, fucking her in a hard, demanding rhythm. As he thrusts into her again and again, Sandra feels his cock stiffening even more, stretching the soft flesh of her pussy.

"Ooh, ooh," she gasps in time with his strokes.

Holding onto her ass, the man pulls her ass-cheeks apart. And Sandra gasps as something hard pokes at her rectum. It's the vibrator! As the naked man fucks her, the man behind her is forcing the hard plastic vibrator into her ass!

"No. Please, no," Sandra whimpers.

But it's no use. The man behind her slowly buries the vibrator in her ass. And then he turns it on. Sandra almost faints as the electric buzzing shakes the insides of her rectum. Trembling, she gasps for breath as the naked man thrusts his huge, hard cock into her pussy again and again like a madman. He's grunting from the strain, his sweat dripping onto Sandra's body, her breasts, her thighs.

The man behind her starts slowly moving the vibrator in and out of her ass. Turning her head, Sandra bites into her own arm to stop herself from screaming. It's so good! The naked man's cock pumps her pussy, the vibrator slides in and of her ass, and then she can't help herself anymore.

Crying out loud in the subway car, Sandra orgasms again.

"Ahhh! Ahhh!" she yells, throwing her head back in ecstasy.

Immediately, she hears the naked man roaring with animal lust as his rock-hard cock starts ejaculating inside her pussy.

Trembling with the pleasure of her climax, Sandra feels the powerful spurts of the man jerking cock, shooting jet after jet of hot semen into her aching flesh. Yelling and grunting, the man squeezes her ass-cheeks hard, as his bulging love tool pumps her pussy full of thick, manly cream.

Then he gently lets her down, placing her feet on the floor of the subway car, as his cock slips out of her pussy. Breathing deeply, Sandra feels his sperm trickling down the insides of her thigh. Standing blindfolded, arms stretched towards the handcuffs, listening to the noise of the train, she feels the vibrator being turned off and slipping out of her ass.

But only to be replaced by the tip of a hard cock.

Grabbing her hips hard and pulling her ass-cheeks apart, the man slowly forces his cock into her rectum. Sandra tries to relax her muscles, but the man thrusts into her, burying his cock in her ass. It hurts. Sandra moans softly from the pain, as the man holds his cock still in her ass. She feels it stiffening and bulging, an excited fuck tool exploring her forbidden orifice.

"Yeah," he whispers into her ear. "I'm gonna fuck you in the ass."

"No, please..."

"And they're all gonna watch. You like that? They're all gonna watch as I fuck your pretty little ass."

His cock grows ever harder inside her. He pushes forward slightly, filling her ass with the entire length of his cock. Slowly, he slides it out of her and then starts fucking. After a few strokes, the pain subsides, and Sandra gives in to the lustful sensation of the hard cock ploughing into her tight, sensitive ass again and again.

"Oh yesss," she hisses. "Keep going. It's so good."

Sandra arches her back, offering her ass to the man's stiff cock. With a powerful thrust, he penetrates her even deeper, stretching the tender flesh of her rectum. Now his hand reaches around her as he starts gently stroking her clit. Sandra moans softly, as the man skilfully masturbates her, while still pounding his raging cock into her ass.

"Oh yes," she moans, "Fuck my ass. Fuck my ass hard!"

"Yeah," the man grunts, increasing the tempo. "I'm gonna fuck your ass, you nasty little bitch."

His cock flies in and out of her ass over and over, like a piston pumping into a cylinder.

"Yes," she gasps, "I'm a fucking whore. Fuck me. Come in my ass."

Sandra's love juice trickles down the insides of her thighs, as she feels him massaging her clit, driving her toward yet another orgasm. Arms outstretched, she pulls hard on the handcuffs with every thrust of the man's anal assault.

"Ahhh," he grunts. "You dirty little whore. I'm gonna blow. C'mon!"

As the man slides his cock out of her ass, she feels the men feverishly struggling with the handcuffs. They're releasing her. Soon her hands are free, and gently the men place her on her back on the rubbery floor of the subway car. Lying naked on the floor, Sandra hears a chorus of male voices grunting around her.

"Yeah. Let her have it. Ahhh."

Someone pulls her blindfold off, and Sandra looks up.

A dozen men are standing above her, holding their stiff, swelling cocks, jerking off. Their eyes are all fixed on her body, studying her naked breasts, her aching pussy, her sweating, blushing face.

"Yeah," she whispers teasingly. "Look at my sexy body and let me have it."

Sandra starts fingering her pussy, masturbating herself, getting ever closer to an orgasm on the floor of the subway car. She is so wet. The men are out of breath, furiously stroking their explosive cocks.

"Give it to me," Sandra whispers, masturbating, writhing on the rubbery floor. "Wouldn't you like to shoot your delicious sperm all over my lovely tits? Wouldn't you like that? Mmm?"

She is shaking with anticipation, fingering her tender clit while watching the excited men jerking off above her.

"Yeah," one of the men says, "I'm ready. Let's drown her in our fucking come!"

And as the first spurt of thick, hot semen shoots several feet out of his cock, Sandra orgasms again. She moans helplessly, clutching her naked breasts, as she throws herself around on the

floor. All around her, the men are ejaculating, strong white jets pumping out of their jerking cocks.

"Yeah. Unnhh. Ahhh."

They're grunting and shouting, as their semen squirts onto the climaxing Sandra's breasts, her thighs, her face.

They shoot off endlessly, clutching her cocks, pumping boiling hot sperm all over the flushed and exhausted naked girl on the floor. As her orgasm subsides, Sandra closes her eyes, feeling the last jets of love cream spatter across her breasts and cheeks.

Then all is quiet. No-one moves. The train slows down, pulling into the last station on the line.

Everyone gets out, except for Sandra and the men. She lies still on the floor, naked and covered with their semen. They stand around her, quietly looking at her.

The train doesn't move. A couple of black railway workers walk by in their overalls, covered with black soot. They stop and look into the car. Their eyes notice the naked woman on the floor, the handcuffs, the vibrator. They enter the car.

Sandra sits up, naked, covering her breasts with her arms. The men standing around her move aside as the railway workers come forward. Smiling, they start taking their overalls off.

The lights go out in the car.

A Hard Day at the Office

The woman lay on her back on the bed, naked, one hand between her legs, her head thrown back in ecstasy. The man stood at the foot of the bed. He was naked, too, apparently roaring with pleasure. From his erect cock a long, white spurt of semen hung frozen in mid-air, about to spatter the woman's naked body.

I stared at the picture on my computer screen, feeling my cock throb and harden at the sight. I tried to ignore the sensation and focus on my work.

Unfortunately, that picture was my work. Because that's what I do: I'm a photo editor for a glossy men's magazine. Our photographers deliver photos to me in digital format, and I select, crop and touch them up. The magazine takes pride in showing "natural" models in its series – but they still have to look their best. So a little selection and airbrushing is expected.

Yes, I know. When I tell my friends what I do for a living, their first reaction is envy – imagine being paid to look at porn! But then, once they've had time to think about it, the envy turns to horror – how on earth can you focus on doing your job, having to look at sex scenes all day?

But of course, eventually you do get jaded. By now I can look at the pictures in a more abstract way – like they're just highlights, shadows and textures that I can work with and improve on.

Except every once in a while – maybe once every few months – a photo comes along that's just so unbelievably sexy that I can't ignore it. And this was one of them.

I tried to cool off by editing some other photos from the same set. But seeing those two models in whatever poses – clothed, naked, having sex – kept bringing my mind back to the picture of the man spraying his sperm over the orgasming woman.

I was sweating. To make things worse, it was a hot summer day, and neither blinds nor air condition managed to keep the temperature at a moderate level. The office was like a greenhouse. I felt drops of sweat trickling down my skin inside my t-shirt.

And that picture. I didn't care – I just had to look at it again. I clicked it open on my monitor and admired the scene in all its glory.

It was so hot. I could just imagine what it would feel like to be that man. After a long, hard fuck with that beautiful girl, to stand there at the foot of the bed, admiring her sweaty beauty. And feeling the release as the hot sperm shot out of my cock. Feeling the shaft contracting, pumping spurt after spurt of creamy semen over her lovely thighs, her breasts, her pussy...

Breathing hard, I zipped down, freeing my erect cock. I have my own office, and my co-workers hardly ever bother me. I pulled out a drawer in my desk and found some paper tissues. Then I began to masturbating.

Damn, it felt good. I stared at the photograph, almost drooling with lust, slowly stroking my cock at the sight. Ah yes, it would be so good to come now – and an orgasm would clear my head and let me focus on my work afterwards.

Except that's when the door flew open.

I swivelled around in my chair, turning my back to the door as I frantically tried to stuff my hard-on back into my jeans. But the damn thing seemed to have a life of its own – hard as a pole, and either too long or sticking out in the wrong angle to get inside the zipper again.

"Dave?"

Ow. Damn. Fuck. It was the voice of my boss, Jennifer. Bending forwards slightly, I somehow managed to push my throbbing cock back inside and zip up. I took a deep breath before I turned around to face Jennifer.

"Hi," I gasped.

Jennifer is in her mid-thirties – ten years older than me - and still a very attractive woman. Big, red hair and a taste for very tight sweaters that can't help but show off her impressive bust. I bet she's the wet dream of every male staff member – and probably a few of the females as well. She closed the door behind her and looked at me with a curious smile.

"What were you doing just then?" she asked.

"Oh, just looking out the window," I replied casually.

"The blinds are drawn."

"Yeah, I noticed. And I... was planning to..."

"Anyway, I won't keep you long. I wondered: Do you have copies of the 1994 issues?"

Jennifer always keeps a few copies of this year's issues of our magazine in her office. But the main archive is the big filing cabinets in mine. Someone probably figured I might need the old magazines for reference, but so far I haven't used them once.

"Yeah," I said. "Second cabinet from the left. Bottom drawer."

Jennifer stood by the cabinet and bent over. Her short skirt slid up, revealing her thighs and her cute little ass. My cock was still semi-erect and felt big and hot inside my jeans. As I stared at Jennifer's perfect behind, I could swear she wasn't wearing panties – that I could just glimpse the pink folds of her pussy.

My cock grew completely hard again. But no, I couldn't be. She wouldn't. Would she? I swallowed, unable to look away.

Jennifer found the magazines she wanted, stood up and turned around.

"I'll just borrow these for a couple of days, okay?"

"Sure." My voice had a strange, choked sound. Beneath my desktop my erection twitched, stretching against the fabric of my jeans.

"You sure you're okay?" Jennifer asked. "You look a bit…"

"I'm fine," I replied swiftly. "Just a bit tired. Been working on that "sleazy motel room" series all day."

"Oh yeah." Jennifer beamed. "That turned out rather well, didn't it?"

"It's really hot. Really."

"Great."

She opened the door, then turned to me again.

"When you're done with that series," she said. "You can take the rest of the day off. It's too damn hot, anyway."

"Thanks. I appreciate it."

Jennifer left my office, and I returned to work. My cock still felt a bit swollen, but I managed to concentrate on editing the last couple of photos. I just wanted to hurry home to take a shower and jerk off – and not necessarily in that order.

Half an hour later I was done. I took a quick look at the entire series again – ending with what I now considered to be the hottest damn photograph ever taken by anyone. I was just so damn horny.

On my way home, the subway was unbearably hot. And it seemed to be full of young, pretty girls. I kept brushing up against shapely breasts and cute asses. My cock throbbed inside my jeans.

And every single ad poster seemed to show a sexy babe showing her cleavage and flashing me a lascivious look. I tried to look away – tried to hide the erection that felt hot and hard next to my thigh. Damn, I couldn't wait to get home.

I ran into the elevator, which seemed to take forever to get me to my floor. Then I ran to my flat and locked the door behind me.

"Shit!" I gasped, my cock twitching with excitement.

I grabbed last month's copy of the magazine and sat down on my couch. I unbuckled my belt and pulled my jeans halfway down. My cock sprang out, fully erect.

I leafed through the magazine, remembering an especially hot series that I wanted to jerk off to. The one with the huge, black policeman and the brunette hooker with the lovely breasts. The one with the handcuffs and the dildo. What page was it...?

Then my doorbell rang.

"Fucking hell," I hissed, throwing the magazine on the floor.

I stood up, pulling up my jeans.

The doorbell rang again.

"Okay! Okay!" I shouted, zipping up and pulling my belt tight.

Then I went and opened the door.

My neighbour, Brandi, just stood there, smiling awkwardly. I've always liked Brandi. Who wouldn't? She's a sweet young girl in her early twenties, with rather short dark brown hair, which she wore in pigtails today, making her look even younger. She was dressed in blue jeans and a tight white t-shirt. My god, I could hardly handle any more fabric stretched over shapely female breasts today!

I realized my erection was possibly showing through my jeans, but I tried to play it cool.

"Yes?" I said.

"I'm sorry," she said. "But you know something about computers, don't you?"

"A bit."

"It's just... I can't get on the net. Maybe you could help me. I'd be really, really grateful if you came in and took a look."

I sighed. This must be how doctors feel when strangers approach them at a party, asking for free medical advice. But hey – I'm just a guy. And you know we'll do anything for a pretty face.

"Okay," I said.

I walked behind Brandi into her flat. The sight of her shapely ass in those jeans, gently bouncing in front of me... I could have

pulled out my cock and just jerked off at the sight. But of course I didn't.

"Over here," she said, leading me to her computer. "I've tried changing cables and stuff. But it still doesn't work."

She went down on all fours. Shit, what curves she had... ass, waist, breasts. I almost shouted for her to get back on her feet so the sight wouldn't make me come.

"Okay," I said. "I'll have a look."

She stood up.

"You want anything? Coffee? Tea? A Coke?"

"Coke would be nice," I said. "Thanks."

She went into the kitchen, and I crawled underneath her desk. I found the problem easily: Her cable modem wasn't on – the power supply had fallen out. There was a mess of cables around the modem, and I picked up one that wasn't connected to anything.

Then I reconnected the modem, stood up and turned on the computer. It seemed to connect to the net immediately. Just to make sure, I opened a browser, and it brought up Brandi's start page... the website of my magazine.

At that moment, Brandi returned from the kitchen, holding two glass bottles of Coke. She giggled nervously.

"Oh yeah," she said. "I hope you're not embarrassed."

"Not at all."

"It's quite a cool magazine you work for. Really."

She placed the bottles on her coffee table. Dewdrops glistened on the cold glass.

"So what was the problem?" she asked.

"The power wasn't on. Simple. And this – " I dropped the cable on the coffee table. "This, you don't need."

"Oh. Thanks."

We both sat down on her couch and sipped our Cokes.

"No wonder you went for the cold drink," she said. "On a hot day like this."

"Mmm."

Sitting next to her, I could even smell the sweet scent of her skin. There was no way I could hide my erection. I felt her dark brown eyes looking at my crotch. Then she looked my in the eyes.

"Have a... hard day at the office?" she asked cheekily.

"You wouldn't believe it."

"Mind if I…" her voice changed into a husky whisper, "relieve some of the stress?"

"What… what do you mean?"

She swiftly stood up, pushed the coffee table aside, and knelt down between my thighs.

"You know what I mean," she said, pulling down my zipper.

My hard-on sprang out, and she grabbed it with both hands. She parted her lips and took my cock into her mouth.

"Oh shit!" I gasped.

But it felt so good. So goddamn good. Just the wetness of her mouth touching the skin of my cock was pure bliss, but when she began sucking at my meat, I could have climaxed right then and there.

"Wait…" I whispered.

But she didn't. Looking me straight in the eyes, Brandi began moving her head up and down in a steady sensual rhythm, letting my cock slip in and out of her mouth. I couldn't sit still.

"Fucking hell!" I gasped.

I heard the sound of her sucking my cock. The wet, slurping sound of Brandi's mouth slipping up and down over my erect shaft. I closed my eyes, trying to make it last. But at the same time I felt the uncontrollable urge to let go – to ejaculate inside her wet, sucking mouth.

"Aaah!" I cried.

My balls tightened into hard, explosive rocks, and I felt the pressure growing. It was as if my semen slowly forced itself up through my twitching cock, ready to burst forth, as Brandi kept licking and sucking at my sensitive shaft.

"Unnnhhh!" I gasped. "Unnnhhh!"

I didn't think I would come so fast. But I almost fainted with pleasure as my cock began contracting, pumping spurt after spurt of semen into Brandi's mouth. I tried to pull out, but she grabbed my ass and pulled me back in, swallowing load after load of my abundant sperm. As my orgasm receded, she just kept sucking, emptying me of every last drop, drinking it down.

I fell back on the couch, exhausted.

"Oh my god," I gasped.

Brandi sat next to me and wiped her mouth, smiling. Then she reached for her Coke.

"That was quite a load, big boy. Bet you haven't had any for quite a while…"

She took a large sip of the bottle Coke and winked at me.

I looked down at my cock. It looked bright red, but was now slowly growing soft. I felt completely spent.

But I couldn't stop now. It was as if a deep sensation of lust had built up inside me all day. A lust that was not satisfied with just one orgasm.

My cock hung soft between my legs. But as I looked at sweet little Brandi I knew I still wanted more. Didn't want her to get off that easy.

"Take your clothes off," I said calmly.

Brandi's eyes opened wide in surprise.

"You heard me," I said.

She shook her head.

"You naughty, naughty boy," she said.

Slowly, she stood up and pulled off her t-shirt. Her breasts were even more beautiful than I imagined. Then she kicked off her shoes and pulled off her jeans and her black satin panties and stood naked in front of me. Her pussy was neatly trimmed – there was just a small patch of dark hair above the inviting, pink slit.

"Like that?" she said.

I stood up, nodding.

"Lie down on the couch," I said.

Obediently, Brandi lay on her back on the couch.

"No," I said. "Like this. Come here."

I pulled on her legs, dragged her ass towards me, placing it on the armrest. Her shoulders rested on the seat of the couch, but her pussy was up in the air – and directly in front of my face.

I bent down and let my tongue slide over her labia. She moaned. I parted her thighs and began licking her pussy rhythmically. Gradually, I focused my attention on her clit, letting my tongue circle her little pink button until she started grinding her pelvis against my mouth.

She was wet now. Really wet. The intoxicating taste of the young girl's sweet, spicy juices made my head spin. I made my tongue hard and forced the tip into the mouth of her pussy. Then out, then back in. Then out – then in, fucking her with my tongue.

Brandi whimpered with pleasure, her ass gyrating on the armrest.

Her protests just turned me on even more. I saw her juices glistening on the bottle neck as I slipped it in and out of her pussy – increasing the rhythm – going faster, faster…

My cock was getting hard at the sight. I pulled the bottle from Brandi's pussy and put it to her lips.

"Lick it," I said.

And obediently, she stuck out her tongue to lick her own juices from the bottle.

"Yeah," I said, "you just love the taste of pussy, don't you?"

I put the bottle back on the coffee table and pulled off my t-shirt. Then I pulled off my jeans and stood naked in front of Brandi, my cock now fully erect. I made her sit on the couch, her ass resting on the edge of the seat. Her hands were still tied above her head, making her breasts stick out, her nipples hard as glass.

I knelt between her legs, pointing my cock straight at her dripping wet pussy. God, how I wanted to feel her soft flesh wrapped around my cock.

"What a fine piece of ass you are," I said. "You sure deserve a good fucking."

I grabbed my cock in my fist and guided it towards the entrance to her pussy, pushing just the tip of the head inside.

"Mmm," she whimpered.

I froze in position, only half an inch of my cock inside her. She gave me a puzzled look.

"Go ahead," I said calmly. "Fuck me."

Her thighs quivered impatiently.

"But…" she gasped.

"You wanna fuck?" I said. "My cock is right here. But you do the motion. C'mon, wriggle that sweet little ass of yours. I know you can do it."

Brandi bit her lip. Whimpering, with her hands tied above her head, she began moving her pelvis back and forth, making my cock slide in and out of her slippery cunt. Damn, that felt good.

"Yeah," I whispered.

She began moving faster, thrusting against me. I held perfect still, feeling her soft pussy engulfing my rigid cock with every stroke. A torrent of sperm was building up inside me once again, and I wanted Brandi to come with me.

Her gaze was fixed on my cock, as she focused all her energy on thrusting against me. Her lovely breasts bounced gently back and

forth in time with the rhythm. I put my thumb against her hard little clit and began rubbing it.

"Ohmigod!" she gasped.

My cock was slick with juice, as I watched it slipping in and out, in and out of her sweet, juicy crevice. She began sobbing, louder and louder as her climax approached.

"Yeah," I whispered, on the edge of orgasm myself, "come for me, baby! Let me watch!"

Brandi kept thrusting, her sobs building to a loud cry of pleasure, as my thumb kept massaging her clit. And finally, the climax surged through her, making her shiver in ecstasy, her pussy clenched spasmodically around my cock.

"Aaah!" she cried. "Aaah!"

I grunted like an animal, as I pulled my explosive cock from her pussy. As the orgasm shook her body, I grabbed my cock in my fist, not masturbating, just feeling the pressure slowly building up through the shaft. Waiting, waiting. Until finally, the first spurt of semen burst out through my cock, shooting several feet across Brandi's naked body.

"Fuuuck!" I yelled. "Yeah!"

I felt my cock jerking wildly in my fist, pumping load after load of hot sperm onto the skin of the dazed girl. My ejaculation seemed to go on forever, releasing a fountain of creamy juice, making my head spin with pleasure.

And then, the final spurt. And the last, thick drops of sperm flowed lazily from my cock, dripping on to Brandi's floor.

"Yes," I whispered.

I breathed hard, looking at her, naked and tied up, my semen spattered in thick, white drops across her skin. I couldn't believe what I'd just done. And as I came to my senses again, I swiftly untied her.

"I'm sorry," I whispered. "I'm not like that. I don't..."

Brandi rubbed her wrists, smiling.

"It's okay," she finally said. "Really."

She got up, still naked, my sperm running down her belly and her thighs.

"You know," she went on, "it kinda reminded me of some of my favorite series in your magazine."

She walked towards the kitchen, then turned to me, smiling.

"You want anything?" she asked. "Another Coke? Or something... bigger?"

The Prisoner

Tony watched as the officer in charge pulled the piece of paper from his typewriter.

"Okay, Tony," he said. "That's the paperwork over and done with. But you'll be spending the night here."

Tony didn't bother to answer. He just took another draw on his cigarette. At least, by now he was getting used to smoking with his hands cuffed.

"You know, Tony," the officer said, "this is not your first time. And lying about your identity to gain sexual favours is quite a serious crime. I wouldn't be surprised, if they put you away for years this time."

Tony shook his head. So he had sex with a couple of women. What difference did it make if he wasn't the real pool cleaner or the real pizza delivery boy? Big deal. If they wanted sex with complete strangers anyway, why not him?

"Not to mention impersonating an officer," the officer in charge added.

Oh yeah, that was it. He should have known. Dressing up as a policeman had been a bad idea. They were not going to like that. Great sex, though. Some girls really got off on that uniform thing.

"Right," the officer said. "We'll have two police officers escort you to your cell." He hit a button on the intercom. "Steiner. Adams."

Within a minute, the door opened, and two police officers entered the room. Steiner was a big dark-haired guy, looking like something out of the Marine Corps. But Adams was a woman, a pretty young woman with long, red hair in a ponytail and full, rounded breasts bulging beneath her police uniform. And since she wasn't wearing uniform trousers, but a short skirt, Tony had a look at her long, slender legs. She was quite a tall woman, but looked small next to her huge partner.

"Get up," Steiner said. Tony put out his cigarette and stood up, smiling amiably at the policewoman. She stared back at him. Oh,

alright. She had to keep up her facade. But if he could just get her alone...

"This way," she said, pointing at the door leading to the jail cells. And Tony walked towards the door, accompanied by the two officers.

"Bye, Tony," he heard the officer in charge say. "Sweet dreams."

Yeah, yeah. Everyone's a comedian.

When they reached the cell, Steiner opened the door, removed Tony's handcuffs and shoved him into the cell. Tony almost fell over, but regained his balance just as the cell door clanged shut. He had expected the officers to leave, but they just stood there.

"Gonna miss the outside world, eh?" Steiner asked. "What are you gonna miss the most?"

Tony didn't answer. This was annoying. He sat down on the bunk.

"I know what you're gonna miss the most. Pussy, right?"

"Come on," Adams said, "let's go now."

"No wait," Steiner said, grabbing his partner's arm and pulling her towards him. "Let's show him."

"No!" Adams said firmly.

But holding onto her, Steiner lifted up her skirt, exposing her white silk panties.

"Panties off," Steiner whispered into her ear.

"You piece of shit," she hissed.

"All those years on the force, and still a tease," Steiner said. "Alright, I'll do it myself."

Tony watched in amazement, as Steiner twisted the policewoman's arm behind her back, making her squeal. He then quickly pulled off her panties and lifted up her skirt again.

Adams' pussy was almost clean-shaven, leaving only a small patch of red, curly hair above her pink slit.

"There," Steiner said. "Pussy. Don't you think you're gonna miss that?"

He had his arm round Adams, who was struggling to get away, but Steiner was too strong for her. He began stroking her labia with his middle finger, at first gently, but gradually applying more and more pressure. His finger forced itself into her slit, parting her pussy lips, letting Tony glimpse the pink wetness of her sex.

"Yesss," Steiner hissed, masturbating his female partner, as she wriggled in his grip. "Pussy. Lovely, juicy pussy."

"Nooo," Adams sobbed. "Please stop."

But Steiner showed no mercy. He paused, but only to lick his fingers, wetting them with saliva. Then he resumed massaging Adams' pussy, spreading the moisture over her soft flesh. Tony watched, as he caught her clitoris between two fingers, squeezing and kneading it, making Adams gasp for breath.

Then he licked his fingers again.

"Mmm, I can taste it," he growled, as he resumed masturbating her, harder and harder, forcing his middle finger into her moistened slit. Tony felt his cock swelling inside his pants.

"Oh my God," Adams cried out, as Steiner started sliding his finger in and out of her pussy, fucking her with it.

"Yeah?" Steiner whispered into her ear. "Is it good? Does that feel good in your little pussy?"

"You utter creep," she hissed, but Steiner just smiled wickedly, now forcing two fingers into her, making her cry out loud: "Aaaah!"

He made her bend over, still keeping a firm grip on her. From behind he started thrusting his fingers into her soft flesh - over and over, in a hard, relentless rhythm. He only pulled them out to slap her ass hard with the palm of his hand. And then slipped his fingers back into her pussy. And then another slap. And back into her pussy. Tony's cock was getting really hard by now.

Adams was doubled over in front of her partner, subjected to his powerful finger-fucking. She was gasping for breath, still cursing at him. But she seemed to Tony to be just as angry at herself. Because this was actually turning her on. Her cheeks were flushed, and her moans began to sound like moans of pleasure.

Steiner slapped her ass again, then grabbed her ponytail and pulled her up.

"Show him your tits," he said. The policewoman just stared at him.

"Do it!" he shouted.

And staring at Tony, she opened her uniform jacket and unbuttoned the light blue shirt. She wasn't wearing a bra, and Tony's mouth watered as he stared at her big, beautiful breasts. Now Steiner grabbed them, squeezing them hard, showing them off to Tony. Adams' full rounded breasts looked soft as butter, as Steiner's

big, powerful hands were kneading them. Her nipples stood out, stiff and hard.

"You like tits too?" Steiner asked. "Me too. But not as much as... pussy!"

And on cue, he slid his hand back to her clitoris, massaging it vigorously in a fast, manic rhythm. Moaning loudly, Adams threw her head back against his shoulder and flung her arms around his back. Her ponytail had come undone, and her long, red hair flowed freely around her excited face.

"Yes, yes, yes," she hissed, and Tony realized she was about to come.

Steiner was grinning.

"Yeah, that's good, isn't it? You're gonna come. Now spread your legs and let him see your pussy."

Trembling, Adams spread her legs. Only Steiner was holding her up now. Tony went down on his knees to get a good look at her pussy. Steiner took a step forward, pushing Adams up close to the steel bars of the cell. And still his fingers were furiously vibrating her little pink clit.

"Oh yes, oh yes," she gasped, now holding on the steel bars. Tony saw her juices flowing from her pussy down the insides of her thighs. He could even smell the spicy scent of her wetness, as Steiner masturbated the policewoman ever closer to her climax.

"Now!" she cried. "Aaahhh!" Tony saw her juicy love muscles contracting, as the orgasm hit her. Again and again, Adams cried out with pleasure. Then, shivering, she dropped to her hands and knees on the floor of the jail. She breathed deeply, fighting to compose herself. Steiner stood over her, smiling, his cock bulging in his uniform trousers.

"Christ," Tony gasped.

"Yeah," Steiner said, licking Adams' juice off his fingers. "She's really something, isn't she? But I don't know why she has to play hard-to-get. It's like this every time me and the boys wanna have some fun. You know, she's like 'please, no' and 'don't touch me' and all that shit. So we have to hold her down or tie her up. And then we go to work on her."

Steiner had taken off his jacket and shirt and was now unbuttoning his trousers. His cock was long and semi-erect, twitching slightly with anticipation.

"I mean, she should know we're not gonna take no for an answer. So we lick her pussy and stuff. There's a senior officer really knows how to use a vibrator. That's pretty cool. She actually fainted one time. Didn't you, baby?"

Adams was still crouching on the cement floor "Fuck off," she murmured.

"Well, as I said: We go to work on her real good. It might take some time before she lets go. Which might be a good thing. Gives me and the boys a chance to get hard. And I mean real fucking hard. You've never seen hard-ons like on 'Adams night', I tell you. But sooner or later - well, you saw what happened. She comes all over the place."

Steiner was completely naked now, except for some reason he'd kept his policeman's cap on. His long cock stood out, stiff and hard.

"Then, once she's ready, we untie her and fuck her fucking brains out. And she fucking loves it. And now you're gonna watch me fuck her. Get up! I said, get up, what the fuck's the matter with you?"

Steiner pulled Adams to her feet. He placed her, bent over slightly, facing Tony, again holding onto the cell bars. Her face was still blushing, her eyes glazed, and her long red hair fell into her face. Steiner stood behind her, his long cock visible above her rounded ass-cheeks.

"You might wanna get your cock out, too," he said. "This should be good for jerking off to. Well, you can come all over her face, for all I care. Ready, baby?"

Adams nodded slightly. Her eyes met Tony's, but he didn't know what to make of the expression on her face. Sure, Steiner was an asshole, but maybe he'd got something right: Maybe she actually got off on the abuse and humiliation. Whatever game those two perverts were playing, this brutal kind of sex turned Tony on. He felt a huge hard-on throbbing in his pants.

Steiner grabbed his hard cock with one hand and guided it towards the entrance to Adams' pussy. Tony saw her close her eyes, as he entered. Steiner slid the entire length of his tool into her in one stroke, making her gasp for breath. Then he froze, holding his cock still inside her.

"Yeahhh," he groaned, savouring the sensation of her soft flesh around his cock. "That's good pussy!"

Tony watched, as Steiner pulled nearly all the way out, the hard shaft of his cock glistening with Adams' juices. The naked cop bent forward over his still uniformed female partner and whispered into her ear:

"I hope you're ready to get fucked."

The policewoman held on to the steel bars, gripping so hard her knuckles were white. She closed her eyes with anticipation.

"Yes," she whispered. "Fuck me, please."

"Right," Steiner said. "Here goes, baby."

He grabbed her hips with both hands and thrust hard and fast into Adams' pussy. He hammered his rigid cock into her again and again, as she held onto the steel bars for support. Tony watched her body shake with each powerful thrust, her breasts bouncing in time to Steiner's fucking rhythm.

"Oh God, yes," she whispered. She felt the hardness of her partner's cock poking the tender insides of her sex. She felt every inch, every swollen vein on the hard shaft probing her wetness.

Tony reached out between the steel bars, touching one of her breasts. She gasped as he began to massage it, squeezing and pulling the hard nipple, while Steiner was fucking her.

God, she was beautiful, Tony thought. Quickly, he unzipped his pants and pulled out his hard cock.

"Look at it," he whispered to her. And Adams watched with open mouth, as Tony began stroking his cock right in front of her. His cock was of just about average length, but he knew it was unusually thick, especially when he was as excited as he was now. The erect member swelled in his hand, as he shamelessly masturbated, letting the policewoman watch.

Steiner let his long cock slide all the way out of Adams' pussy, then buried the entire length in her with one hard thrust. And again: All the way out, and then all the way in. And out - and in. Tony watched his cock glisten and twitch, as Adams squirmed with unbearable pleasure.

"No, please," she whimpered. "Don't stop. Please. Fuck me hard."

Steiner slapped her ass again, hard. The smacking sound rang out in the concrete corridor. Then he resumed fucking her, even harder and faster than before. His hard cock hammered into her like a piston, over and over, making her sob and gasp for breath. Tony masturbated, turned on by the sight of their brutal sex act.

Now Steiner grabbed hold of Adams' hair, pulling her head back.

"Now suck that cock," he ordered her. "Suck the cock of that criminal scum."

Tony stepped up to the door, pushing his stiff cock out between two bars, waiting for Adams to start sucking it. And as Steiner slapped her ass again, she opened her mouth as wide as she could. Due to the size of Tony's cock, he was still just barely able to force his huge bulging helmet in between her lips.

"Ohhh," he groaned, as the soft wetness enveloped his cock. Adams started sucking it rhythmically, making loud smacking noises. Excited, Tony began moving his hips in time, fucking her mouth. Holding on to the bars, he slid his fat cock in and out between the policewoman's lips.

"Yeah", Steiner grunted, fucking her harder and harder from behind. Adams held onto the metal bars, making them jangle loudly in time with Steiner's powerful thrusts. They were both sweating from the strain. Tony smelt the sweet scent of female perspiration, as droplets formed on the policewoman's back, trickling down over her breasts.

As Tony pulled his cock out of her mouth, she gasped for breath and then looked up at him with glazed eyes. He inserted his thumb into her open mouth.

"Mmm," he groaned. "Open wide."

By now accustomed to the size of his meaty tool, Adams obediently opened her mouth as wide as she could. Looking him in the eyes, she let Tony feel her teeth and tongue with his rough finger.

"Yeah," he said. "Now suck this."

And slowly he slid his thick cock in between her lips again. Adams began sucking it harder, and Tony felt his erection growing, the veined shaft becoming stiff as a rod. He thought he could feel the policewoman drinking the clear fluid of excitement trickling from the tip of his cock.

"Unnnh," he grunted, as she sucked him with loud, wet noises. He forced his swelling tool ever further into her mouth and watched her perfect breasts bouncing, as Steiner relentlessly hammered into her pussy from behind.

"Yeah," Steiner said, suddenly pulling his long hard cock from Adam's slit. Tony saw the rigid shaft glistening with her wetness, as

the policeman slapped her ass hard with his stiff cock, leaving wet spots of pussy juice on her ass cheeks.

"Turn around," Steiner ordered.

Reluctantly, Tony pulled his cock out of her wet mouth, and she looked back over her shoulder at her partner. Her hair was a mess, sticking to her sweaty face, making her look even sexier to Tony.

"What?" she said.

"I said, turn around," Steiner roared, as he grabbed her by the hips and – clang! - pushed her ass hard against the steel bars of the cell. Pulling her hair, he made her bend over again, showing off her cute, shapely ass to Tony.

"Bet that criminal scum wants to fuck you, too," Steiner said, stroking his cock. "Open that pretty little pussy to him."

"Please…" she whispered.

Steiner slapped her face hard with his cock.

"Shut up!" he said. "Open your pussy. Looks like he's got a nice, thick one for you."

Cursing her partner, Adams stood with her legs wide apart. Using the fingers of both hands, she parted her pussy lips. The velvet, pink insides of her flesh glistened with the juice of her lust.

Tony was dying to feel his cock exploring her soft slit, but the sight of her open pussy turned him on. Fascinated, he knelt down behind her and drove a finger into the moist opening, feeling the intense heat of her pussy. She moaned softly with pleasure.

Turning his head, Tony flicked his tongue over her hardened clit, making her squeal. Licking her clit with the tip of his wet tongue, he drove his finger into her juicy slit again and again. Adams squirmed with pleasure, grinding her ass against the cold steel bars of the cell, approaching her climax.

"Yeah," Steiner grunted, stroking his cock. "That's the way: Make her come, then fuck her hard!"

Closing her eyes, Adams felt Tony pushing two fingers into her, rhythmically probing the tender insides of her sex, his tongue still teasing her erect clitoris.

With a loud scream of pleasure, the policewoman came again, her juices flowing over Tony's face and tongue. He lapped up the spicy liquid, as her entire body shook from her orgasm.

She was still trembling, eyes glazed, as Tony jumped to his feet behind her, pressing the bulging head of his cock against her labia.

"Oh, my God," she whispered, as he pushed forward, stretching her aching flesh with the thickness of his excited shaft.

"Give it to her," Steiner commanded, masturbating at the sight.

Still fully dressed, Tony the prisoner thrust into Adams, burying his fat cock in the wetness of her burning pussy. She was still gasping for air, as he started fucking her, sliding his hard tool in and out of the policewoman's yielding slit.

"Yeah," Steiner grunted, "fuck her."

Clear liquid dripped from the tip of his excited cock onto the concrete floor as he masturbated. As he stood closer to Adams, she willingly opened her mouth, expecting him to insert his cock. But grinning, he kept the throbbing tool fractions of an inch from her lips, still stroking himself with obvious pleasure.

"Tell me you want it," he hissed.

Tony grabbed her ass and hammered into her from behind, thrusting his thick weapon into her tight pussy again and again. Her body shaking in time to Tony's strokes, the policewoman looked up at her partner.

"No, please," she pleaded. Steiner grabbed her hair with one hand, still masturbating with the other.

"I'm gonna come in your mouth," he said, "but I wanna hear you beg for it first."

"Aaah!" she squealed, as Steiner yanked her hair, "Alright, alright! Come in my mouth, you bastard! I wanna drink your hot, thick cum!"

"Unnnh," Steiner groaned, as he slipped the tip of his cock in between the policewoman's lips. Holding onto her hair, he held her head still, only letting the head of his cock enter her mouth. As she closed her red lips around it, he kept stroking the rigid shaft, jerking himself off in her mouth.

Tony held on to the bars of the cell, pounding his bulging tool into Adams' pussy as hard as he could. The sensation of her wet pussy stretching around his bone-hard cock was irresistible, and Tony felt his orgasm approaching.

"Yeah, you fucking slut" Steiner groaned, masturbating into the policewoman's mouth. "I'm gonna fucking drown you. Ahhh, ahhh!"

Throwing his head back in ecstasy, Steiner climaxed. Tony saw the shaft of the policeman's cock swelling and jerking, as it fired jet after jet of hot, spicy cream into Adams' throat.

Steiner's body was shaking with pleasure, as thick sperm kept spurting from the tip of his twitching tool. Mad with lust, he kept masturbating, emptying himself for every last drop of semen, forcing Adams to swallow mouthful after mouthful of his boiling hot come.

Now Tony couldn't hold back anymore. Seconds before he came, he thrust the entire length of his cock into the policewoman's pussy and froze. Grabbing her ass hard, he savoured the feeling of his cock swelling inside her, it huge bulbous head growing even larger as he felt his boiling hot come bursting its way upwards through his cock. Until, finally, he exploded.

"Yeah!" he yelled madly, as he started ejaculating inside Adams. His cock unloaded its sperm in hard, powerful spurts, white-hot jets of creamy semen shooting into her aching pussy.

Tony felt her trembling, too. Had she come once again? Steiner finally pulled his limp cock from her mouth.

"Ohmigod," she gasped, out of breath, "ohmigod."

"Yeah," Steiner said, smiling at Tony, "she's a slut alright! Did you like that pussy?"

"Yeah," Tony gasped, "It was fucking great." He slowly slid his cock out of Adam's slit. It was still hard. Adams fell to her knees on the concrete floor, still out of breath.

Steiner had walked over to where his clothes lay and picked up the handcuffs.

"No," the policewoman whispered, as he walked over to her. "Please, no…"

"What do you mean, no?" he grinned. "It's what you want, isn't it? It's what you wanted all along."

Tony tucked his semi-erect cock into his pants and zipped up.

"No," Adams whispered, as Steiner cuffed her hands behind her back.

"Don't lie to me," he said. "You want it so bad, you can hardly wait, can you?"

He pulled his partner to her feet. Tony watched with amazement, as he unlocked the door to the cell.

"Don't do this to me," Adams protested, as Steiner threw her into the cell. Naked and handcuffed, she fell to the floor next to Tony.

Steiner locked the door and started putting his clothes back on.

"Well, honey," he said, buttoning his uniform trouser, "will 24 hours be enough for you? It may not be much, but this scumbag is a sex offender, and he knows this is his last chance to get pussy. So I think he'll let you have it in a big way."

Tony looked down at the beautiful, naked woman, sprawling at his feet, handcuffed. If Steiner was going to leave her here with him for 24 hours... He felt his cock swelling in his pants. It would soon be fully erect again. He might as well take his clothes of now. He pulled off his t-shirt, revealing his muscular torso.

"And you, scumbag," Steiner said. "You know what she likes."

Tony turned to face Steiner. The policeman was now completely dressed, while Tony was pulling off pants and shorts. Steiner looked at his erection and smiled:

"Yeah, that thing should keep her happy for a few hours."

Steiner picked up Adams' clothes from the floor.

"Okay," he said. "See you around."

His footsteps rang out in the corridor as he walked away.

Stroking his stiff cock, Tony turned to face Adams again. Her eyes were wide open, as she looked up at him. She was expecting him to do something, but he just smiled at her, still stroking his cock.

There was no hurry. He had plenty of time.

The Experiment

Part 1

"So," Dr. La Roche said, "if you'll just take off your clothes, I'll explain what we're going to do."

Smiling nervously, Katie looked around the laboratory. Like everything else in the clinic, it was very white and clean. However, the lights had been dimmed, making it feel a little less clinical. And thank God the doctor was a woman, too – otherwise she would probably have changed her mind. Dr. La Roche - in her white coat - smiled reassuringly. Katie sighed and began undressing.

The doctor stood holding a clipboard and a pencil next to something that looked vaguely like a dentist's chair: Wide, comfortable and probably adjustable in any number of ways. Except like an electrical chair, it seemed to have leather straps for the hands and feet.

On a small tray next to the chair was a selection of shiny steel objects – medical equipment, Katie assumed, although she didn't recognize any of them. They were all connected by electrical wires to a small table on wheels next to it. On the table was something like a control panel, the most striking feature of which was a huge red button – reminding her of a fire alarm.

"Once you're ready," Dr. La Roche said – ready being a euphemism for naked – "you'll sit down in this chair and get comfortable. Okay?"

Katie nodded. She was wearing only bra and panties now and was kind of reluctant taking off the rest. But Dr. La Roche smiled as if to say: I know how you feel. And she relaxed a bit.

"When you're comfortable," Dr. La Roche went on, "- in your own time, there's no hurry – I'll wire you up."

She put down her clipboard and pointed to the equipment on the tray.

"There's really two kind of devices," she said. "The stimulators – which are the ones we're testing. And a number of electrodes to check your response."

Katie stood naked in front of her. She was only 22 years old and had a body of classical beauty: She was of medium height, had long, slender legs and a shapely bust. Long, curly red hair framed her delicate features.

"Are you ready?" Dr. La Roche asked.

"I think so," Katie said, forcing a smile.

"You'll be fine," Dr. La Roche said. "You might actually enjoy it. In a way, that's the whole point, right?"

Katie sat down on the chair. It was covered with a synthetic fabric that felt slightly cold against her naked skin, but otherwise it was soft and comfortable. Dr. La Roche skilfully adjusted the chair, until Katie was half-lying, half-sitting. It was a very relaxing position – she'd easily be able to fall asleep like this. But she didn't suppose she'd get the chance.

Dr. La Roche picked up the first device: A plastic strap fitted with two rubber suction cups, wired to the control panel.

"Please sit up straight for a second," she said.

And quickly she strapped the device around Katie's chest, fitting the cups over her nipples.

"This," she explained, "is the mammarian stimulator. You'll feel it applies suction as well as vibration to your breasts."

Dr. La Roche picked up another device. It looked a bit like a thong bottom, except instead of a crotch it had two straps joined together by a round metallic object the size of a pillbox.

"This," she explained, "serves two purposes: These two straps are moisture sensors. And this" - she pointed to a round rubber button underneath the pillbox thing - "is the clitoral stimulator."

Katie nodded. She was blushing slightly, as Dr. La Roche fitted the straps around her back and thighs. The moisture sensors went against her labia, and the stimulator fitted over her clitoris.

The next device looked like a grotesque codpiece – two more straps with a huge metallic device in the middle. Katie frowned.

"Yes," Dr. La Roche said. "It looks a bit weird. But you might already have guessed what's inside."

She turned it over and indicated an opening, where the tip of some phallic, latex object peeked out: "This is the vaginal penetrator. Please lift up your bottom."

Dr. La Roche fitted the straps around her waist and upper thighs, strapping the thing to her crotch. Then, as Katie sat down, she picked up a fourth device. It looked exactly like the codpiece, except that it was only about one-fifth of the size.

"This," she said, "I will not use without your permission, okay? I'll be very much obliged if you try this out, too. And many women enjoy this stimulation immensely. But – and I really mean it – it's your decision alone."

"What is it?" Katie asked.

"The anal stimulator," Dr. La Roche said.

"No," Katie said, a bit louder than she'd planned. "I… I'm sorry, but I'm not into that kind of thing."

"That's okay," Dr. La Roche said smiling.

She put the device back on the tray and picked up a handful of electrodes, wired to the control panel.

"In that case," she said, "I'll just attach these and you'll be all set to go."

She quickly attached the electrodes to Katie's temples, breasts and thighs. Then she pushed the table with the control panel up against the chair.

"Are you okay?" Dr. La Roche asked.

Katie nodded.

"Fine," Dr. La Roche said. "I'll leave you to it then. I'll be in the control room. If you want anything, just call me. And this is important: If you want to abandon the experiment at any time – just push the red button. That will immediately switch off every device and every form of stimulation. Do you understand?"

Strangely, Katie felt herself getting aroused. Her mouth felt dry.

"Yes," she whispered. "I understand."

"And if you don't mind," Dr. La Roche said. "I'll just strap you down."

"Sorry?" Katie said.

"Of course, your right hand will be free to press the red button," she explained. "But for the sake of the experiment, we have to rule out the possibility of masturbation."

Dr. La Roche fastened the leather straps around her hands and feet.

"It's not too tight, is it?" she asked.

"No," Katie said. "It's… okay, I guess."

Dr. La Roche smiled.

"A bit weird, I know," she said. "You'll be fine. Just relax. And enjoy."

Katie forced another smile.

"I'll try," she said, as Dr. La Roche picked up her clipboard and turned around to leave.

She walked through a door, apparently into the control room. Next to the door, there was a huge smoked-glass mirror the size of a shop window. Katie guessed it was a two-way mirror, allowing Dr. La Roche to watch her. She'd try not to think about that.

The lights dimmed further – leaving the room in near darkness. Alone in the darkened room, she immediately felt more relaxed. Then she heard the slightly distorted sound of Dr. La Roche's voice through a loudspeaker somewhere in the room:

"Would you like some music?"

Katie almost giggled. Listening to music in this strange clinical setting was almost bizarre. But okay - it might help her relax.

"Um, yes…" she said.

"Classical? Rock? R'n'B?"

"You have some soft piano music?" she asked.

"Sure," the voice replied.

And moments later, the soft strains of Chopin filled the room. Sighing, Katie closed her eyes and relaxed – waiting for the experiment to begin.

"She's pretty," Jack said.

Dr. La Roche raised her eyebrows. He wasn't really supposed to talk about the test persons like this. However, it was somewhat sweet hearing a guy referring to a naked woman as merely "pretty".

"She chose no anal stimulation," she said. "And you know how much we need those data. Oh well. Let's get ready."

They sat next to each other at the instrument panel in the control room. Above it, through the big two-way mirror, they saw Katie lying naked, strapped to the chair.

"Let's start with clitoral stimulation at 2.3", Dr. La Roche said.

Jack turned two dials. This would turn on the vibrator in the strap above Katie's clitoris. All dials went from zero to ten, and the clitoral vibrator was now set at speed two, intensity three. This would massage her clit slowly and gently.

Katie twitched as she felt the device being turned on. Dr. La Roche watched the meter on the instrument panel, monitoring her excitement.

"Okay," she said. "She's responding. Go to 2.5."

Jack raised the intensity to 5, making the device massage Katie's clit with the same slow speed but with moderate force.

"Mmm," Katie said.

Dr. La Roche glanced at a meter slowly beginning to move.

"We have moisture," she said. "Mammarian stimulation 3.1.5."

The mammalian stimulator had three controls: One for suction, one for speed, and one for intensity. Jack worked the dials, activating the suction cups on Katie's breasts. Sucking gently, they vibrated very slowly, but with some force. Almost like a tender love-bite, he thought.

Katie was now moving about slightly in the chair, slowly getting aroused.

"Very good," Dr. La Roche said. "She's highly responsive. But I'd like more moisture before we penetrate. Increase clitoral stimulation to 5.5."

Jack turned a dial, keeping the force of the clitoral vibrator at the same level, but increasing the speed.

Through the window, they saw Katie squirming in the chair.

"Oh yes," she whispered. "Oh yes..."

Dr. La Roche inspected the meter and nodded, smiling slightly.

"Great," she said. "Let's go to penetration. Immobile to one inch - ever so slowly."

Carefully, Jack turned a dial for the vaginal penetrator. In immobile mode, he simply controlled how far into the woman's pussy the latex dildo went.

"One inch," he said.

Katie gasped loudly, as she felt the artificial cock entering her.

"Moisture is more than sufficient," Dr. La Roche said. "Go slowly to full length."

Jack turned the dial. Inch by inch the device pushed the dildo deeper and deeper into Katie's cunt.

"Oh yeah," she gasped. "Oh yeah. Oh yeah. Oh God."

Dr. La Roche looked at the meters and made a note on her clipboard.

"I think she's building towards a climax already," she said.

Jack had finally turned the dial all the way.

"Full length," he said. "Ten inches and immobile."

"Mammarian stimulus to zero," Dr. La Roche said.

Jack switched off all suction and vibration to Katie's breasts. She was now feeling only the dildo inside her and the vibration on her clitoris.

"Clitoral stimulation to 2.8," Dr La Roche said.

Jack turned two dials. The device now vibrated slowly against Katie's clit, but with great force. Dr. La Roche studied the meters carefully.

"And..." she said, "... orgasm!"

"Ahhh!" Katie cried from the room, her feet kicking helplessly inside the straps. "Ahhh!"

"Wow," Jack said. "Already?"

"Yes," Dr. La Roche replied. "This is promising. Penetration to mobile at 5.4."

Dr. La Roche wasn't going to give the woman a break. Katie was still in the middle of her first orgasm, but the doctor wanted to start the dildo thrusting into her. At 5.4, it would be thrusting half its length into her at a slow, but steady pace. Jack turned the dials and heard Katie crying out in the room."

"Ahhh! Oh yes! Yes!"

Dr. La Roche bit into her pencil. The woman's arousal had hardly dropped from the orgasmic level, and it was already building again.

"Penetration to 8.5," she said.

Jack turned the dials, making the dildo go almost full length, and just a little bit faster. Katie wriggled about in the chair, moaning aloud.

"8.5," Jack confirmed.

He tried to focus on his work, but he felt his cock swelling and rising inside his pants. Watching this young woman in sexual ecstasy was incredibly arousing. And on top of that, there was the feeling of power: Knowing that a touch of a dial would stimulate or penetrate her body, increasing her pleasure, even triggering one orgasm after another.

Before he started working for Dr. La Roche, Jack had considered himself an average guy - not attracted to power games at all. But now he was in control, and he was enjoying it. In fact, he had to admit it was giving him one hell of an erection.

Jack shifted in his seat, hoping Dr. La Roche wouldn't notice the growing bulge in his pants. But she didn't even look his way. She

was too busy following the meters in the control room and taking notes on her clipboard.

"Ohhh!" Katie cried. "Ohhh!"

They heard the heavy metal chair creaking loudly as her entire body jerked violently, her arms and legs pulling at the straps.

Dr. La Roche raised her eyebrows.

"Well, well," she said. "Another orgasm. Gradually increase penetration to 8.8."

Jack's hands were trembling slightly, as he adjusted the dials, making the latex cock pump into Katie's pussy in an ever-increasing rhythm. He almost felt sorry for the poor girl. He would have given her a break, but that was not for him to decide. As always, Dr. La Roche wanted to test her endurance.

"Oh God!" Katie cried, her body shaking with every thrust of the dildo.

"The moisture levels are impressive," Dr. La Roche said quietly. "Switch off clitoral stimulation. Mammarian stimulation to 5.8.8."

Jack turned the dials, giving Katie's clitoris a rest. Instead, her breasts were now sucked and vibrated with great force in a fast rhythm. The effect was like a lover biting into her nipples, then tugging at them by rapidly shaking his head.

Dr La Roche watched, as the meters showed Katie's arousal rising again, once more approaching orgasmic levels. Jack imagined seeing a reddish glow on Dr. La Roche's cheeks, and wondered how she managed to maintain her detachment.

When he lost focus and gave in to his excitement, he imagined being in the room with the Katie, sensing the smell of her skin and her excitement, touching her trembling body, controlling her pleasure up close.

But what could Dr. La Roche be thinking as she watched Katie driven from orgasm to orgasm? Was she imagining herself in her place? Was that what she'd like? To be the subject of the experiment herself?

"Ah! Ah! Ah!" Katie gasped, obviously heading for another orgasm.

God, she was gorgeous, Jack thought. A naked woman overcome by sensual pleasure had to be the most beautiful sight in the world. He shook his head, trying to snap out of it and focus on his work.

The latex cock kept thrusting into Katie's pussy in a relentless, mechanical rhythm. It could go on forever, and Katie knew that. She threw herself about in the chair, arching her back, tugging at the leather straps with all her strength.

"Aaah!" she cried – a deafening sound of animal lust. "Aaah!"

"And yet another orgasm," Dr La Roche said calmly.

Katie's face was red. Her entire body glistened with perspiration, strands of her red hair sticking to her sweaty face.

"Mammarian stimulation to 8.2.0." Dr. La Roche said.

Jack turned the dials, closing down the vibrations, instead applying powerful rhythmic suction at a slow pace. Katie moaned softly.

"8.2.0," he confirmed.

"Clitoral stimulation to 8.5," Dr. La Roche said without looking up from her clipboard.

Jack hesitated for a second. The experiment was clearly putting a great strain on Katie – he wondered if she could handle clitoral stimulation at this point. Of course, she could always use the red button to switch it all off, but what if she passed out? Would Dr. La Roche call off the experiment, if the test subject lost consciousness?

Jack turned the switches, making the device vibrate rapidly against Katie's clit with moderate force.

"No... Please!" Katie sobbed. "Stop it! I can't..."

Dr. La Roche pretended not to hear her.

"Vaginal penetration to 10.6," she said.

Jack turned the dials, making the latex dildo slow down slightly. Instead, it went in all the way with every thrust. All ten inches of the thing buried itself in Katie's pussy again and again.

"Stop!" Katie gasped. "Please stop!"

Her arousal levels were climbing again. Dr. La Roche moved to the microphone.

"If you want to stop the experiment, please press the red button next to you."

"Oh God!" Katie cried, as another climax hit her.

She fell back into in the chair and lay there trembling, tears streaming down her cheeks. The devices buzzed and shook all around her body.

"Ooh..." she whimpered, her right hand fumbling for the red button, "ooh..."

With trembling fingers, she found the button and pressed it. With a whirring sound, all machinery ground to a halt. Katie fell back in the chair, sweating, exhausted.

For a few seconds, all was quiet in the control room. The only sound was the Chopin piano music from the other room.

"Thank you very much, Katie," Dr. La Roche said into the microphone. "I'll be coming in to help you out."

Katie didn't answer. Jack could see her breasts rising and falling, as she tried to catch her breath.

Katie had gotten dressed, and Dr. La Roche paid her the fee, thanking her for her participation. Visibly embarrassed, the young woman nodded silently, then hurried out to the taxi.

Jack poured himself a cup of coffee and printed out the results of today's experiment: Several pages of graphs and statistics. Dr. La Roche collapsed in a chair beside him with an exasperated sigh.

"Damn!" she said. "She looked so promising."

"She was very responsive," Jack said.

"She refused anal stimulation," Dr. La Roche said. "And after three orgasms, she'd already had enough."

"Four," Jack said, consulting the printout.

"Okay," she replied. "But still. We should be able to do better than that. It's as if the test subjects get scared. They reach a level of pleasure they've never experienced before. Then they're afraid to lose control, and they push the damn button. If we could just persuade them to go on, God knows what results we might get."

She leaned back in her chair, stretching her body. Jack noticed the outline of her breasts beneath the white coat.

"I mean," she went on. "I think I could do better than that myself."

She paused.

"Do you want to help?" she said.

Jack stared at her.

"You mean..." he asked, "use yourself as the test subject?"

"Right," Dr. La Roche said, standing up. "Let's go."

Hesitantly, Jack followed her into the laboratory. He couldn't really imagine the doctor going through with this.

Dr. La Roche stood next to the chair and took off her coat. As she began to unbutton her shirt, she glanced at Jack.

"You're not embarrassed, are you?" she asked.

"Uh, no," he said.

He picked up the various devices, carefully wiping and disinfecting them. Still, he watched as Dr. La Roche swiftly undressed, slipping off her shirt, her white skirt and her white satin bra. She smiled self-consciously, as she finally pulled off her panties and placed them in the drawer next to the chair.

Jack looked at her. Her body was perfect, slightly muscular, with a light, even tan. Her legs were slender and her breasts were

fleshy, but elegant. Between her thighs, neatly trimmed hair framed her pussy - jet-black as the pageboy hairdo around her lovely face. Jack had never asked about the origin of her name, but there was something slightly exotic about her appearance - could it be her French genes showing? His cock had been semi-erect before – at the sight of Dr. La Roche's naked body he felt it stretching to a full hard-on inside his pants.

She sat down on the chair, making herself comfortable.

"Okay," she said with just the hint of a smile. "You know the drill."

Jack bent over her as he strapped the mammarian stimulator around her chest. He smelled the sweet scent of her skin and felt the softness of her breasts. Next, he fitted the clitoral stimulator around her waist, and strapped on the vaginal penetrator beneath it. The skin between her thighs felt soft and warm, and Dr. La Roche shivered slightly at his touch.

"You want anal penetration?" he asked casually.

"Of course," she said. "I intend to do this right."

Without a word, Jack picked up the anal penetrator. He applied lubricant from a small tube and strapped the device around Dr. La Roche's ass. Her buttocks were soft and round. He had to fight the impulse to slap them hard.

He didn't feel cautious anymore. As he fastened the leather straps around the doctor's hands and feet, he felt in control - and he liked that feeling. Dr. La Roche seemed to sense it, too. She looked up at him with an expression of curiosity - as if witnessing a new side of his personality.

Jack sat down by the mobile control panel. It was equipped with the same dials and meters as the bigger panel in the control room. He pulled the control panel towards him, placing it just out of Dr. La Roche's reach.

"Jack," she said. "I can't reach the red button from here."

"Oh," he said. "That won't be necessary, will it? I mean, I'll be right here. You just ask, and I'll switch it off."

There was just a hint of a smile on his face, and Dr. La Roche looked at him curiously.

"Right," she said hesitantly, "I'd like to..."

"I think we'll start with clitoral stimulation at 5.5," Jack interrupted and turned the dial.

Dr. La Roche twitched in the chair, as the device started massaging her clit at medium speed and intensity.

"I..." she gasped, "I have this experiment... planned..."

"Mammarian stimulation at 5.2.8," Jack announced, handling the controls. Dr. La Roche's breasts were sucked and vibrated vigorously at a slow speed - as if a lover chewed on her nipples with great force.

"Please..." she moaned, "I..."

Jack watched the moisture meters - she was getting wet already. Could she have been wet already, in anticipation of the experiment? He looked at her naked body, strapped down, subjected to the stimulation of the machinery. His cock grew to a powerful erection, pushing hard against the fabric of his pants.

"Vaginal penetration immobile to one inch," he said.

He turned the dial, pushing the latex cock just inside the mouth of Dr. La Roche's pussy. It seemed to go in smoothly, making her sob quietly.

"Jack," she whispered. "Please..."

"Vaginal penetration to 1.8," he announced.

As he turned the dial, the dildo began moving swiftly back and forth, but only just slipping in and out between her labia. The meters showed her arousal growing, and he saw her juices oozing out around the edges of the vaginal penetrator and flowing down the insides of her thighs.

"Oh, shit!" she gasped.

"Vaginal penetration to 8.5," Jack said calmly.

He turned the dials again, making the latex cock go slower, but deeper, thrusting into Dr. La Roche in a steady rhythm, almost burying the entire length inside her with every stroke. Her naked body quivered.

"Jack!" she cried. "I think I'm coming... Ahhh..."

He glanced at the meters – and sure enough: Her arousal levels were already building to a maximum. He watched, as the climax hit her, her back arching in the chair, her mouth open wide.

"Ohhh...." she moaned, "ohhh..."

But seconds later, still trembling, she looked over at Jack.

"Keep going," she gasped. "Cut the mammarian stimulation a bit. Otherwise, you're... doing fine..."

Jack cut the mammarian vibrators, keeping only a moderate suction, just letting her feel it.

"Clitoral stimulation to 8.8," he announced.

Turning the dials, he increased the speed of the vibrator massaging her clit. Buzzing wildly, the tiny device vibrated her love button at almost maximum speed. The meters showed her moisture increasing. Over the noise of the machinery, Jack heard the tiny wet sounds, as the latex dildo slipped in and out of her dripping pussy.

Fascinated, he watched the meters, trying to keep her arousal at a maximum at all times. Dr. La Roche sobbed quietly with pleasure in the chair.

"Yes," she moaned, "yes, that's it. Oh, my God..."

Inside Jack's pants, his cock was so hard, it was almost painful. He couldn't help thinking how good it would feel to simply unzip and let his hard-on jump out for Dr. La Roche to see. But no - first he had to focus on bringing her to another orgasm.

"Clitoral stimulation to 3.8," he said.

He gradually slowed down the speed of the vibrator, stimulating Dr. La Roche's clitoris, reducing it to a low, hard throbbing, so slow she could almost feel every beat.

"Mmm," she moaned, biting her lip.

"Clitoral stimulation to 8.8," Jack announced.

And just as slowly, he turned the vibration speed back up again, changing the low throb to a loud electric buzzing sound. Watching Dr. La Roche intently, he gradually changed the speed from fast to slow to fast, making her writhe with pleasure in the chair.

"Oh!" she cried. "I'm gonna come again! Aaah!"

Her juices flowed freely, as the orgasm surged through her body. She tugged at the leather straps, throwing herself about in convulsions of ecstasy.

"Ohhh yes!" she sobbed. "Ohhh..."

Breathing heavily, Jack unbuttoned his lab coat and threw it on the floor. Then - finally - he unzipped his pants and let his hard, throbbing cock out. Oh, that felt good. His erect member twitched impatiently, clear fluid dripping from its tip onto the floor of the laboratory.

Dr. La Roche gasped as she saw it.

"Jack!" she exclaimed. "What... what are you doing?"

Jack grinned, grabbing his cock.

"You like what you see?" he asked, taking a step closer to the chair. "I thought I'd improve the experiment a bit."

"You wouldn't dare!" Dr. La Roche hissed.

"Wouldn't I? You know, you're all tied up. What exactly are you going to do about it?"

As if she was only realizing it now, she began tugging at the straps. Her face was red – the latex cock was still pumping into her, the clitoral stimulator still running.

"Let me go!" she protested. "Stop it! Ah! Ah! Aaah...!"

And trembling and struggling, she succumbed to yet another orgasm.

Jack turned the vaginal penetrator off and clitoral stimulation all the way down to 2.2, just ever so slowly and gently teasing her, keeping her aroused. Then he undid the straps holding the latex dildo in place and slowly pulled it out. Its surface was wet and glistening. It almost made him want to lick her juices off it – taste her.

Then he stood between her legs, his erect cock pointing up at her dripping wet pussy. He knew very well that his cock was both longer and thicker than the latex dildo. And he could see from Dr. La Roche's eyes that she'd noticed it, too.

He pulled the control panel towards him.

"Jack, please..." she whispered.

He placed his cock at the mouth of her pussy. And with one swift thrust of his pelvis, he pushed the entire length of the shaft into her cunt.

"Ohmigod!" she cried.

Jack gasped. The sensation was amazing. Wet and hot, Dr. La Roche's pussy swallowed his cock, clenching it with her pulsating flesh. He began thrusting into her, his cock hard and throbbing with excitement.

"No, Jack," she moaned. "Don't..."

"Don't what?" he gasped. "Don't fuck you? Don't make you come? What?"

Jack reached for the dials, turning the clitoral stimulator slowly up to 8.2 – faster and faster, but still just the faintest touch. Dr. La Roche whimpered with pleasure.

"You wanted to know..." he panted, still fucking her, almost out of breath, "how much you could take... I'm helping you... find out..."

Dr. La Roche was sweating. Tiny drops of perspiration trickled slowly down her face, her breasts, her thighs. Jack thought it made her even sexier, made him want to fuck her deeper, harder. He

hammered his rigid cock into her again and again. Whenever he entered her, he could feel the slight throbbing of the clitoral stimulator on the skin of his cock.

Jack reached for the control panel and turned a dial he hadn't touched yet.

"You like that?" he gasped. "Now how about… anal penetration… immobile to half an inch."

"Oh!" Dr. La Roche cried, as the little latex dildo pushed into her ass.

Still fucking her at a steady pace, Jack kept turning the dial.

"One inch… two inches… three inches… is that good, huh?"

"Oh shit!" she gasped, writhing lasciviously around his cock, "oh shit!"

Four inches. Five inches. Like a small, rubbery finger, the miniature dildo pushed further and further into Dr. La Roche's anus. And over and over, Jack's swollen tool kept thrusting into her pussy.

Six inches. Seven inches. She squealed helplessly, tugging at the straps. With shaking fingers, Jack turned another dial, making the anal penetrator move slowly back and forth. He started at 3.3, making it move a few inches back and forth in a slow rhythm. Then, gradually, he increased it to 5.3, making it go deeper but at the same slow pace.

"Fuck yeah!" Dr. La Roche cried. "That's good, Jack!"

Jack looked into her eyes. She wasn't protesting anymore. All her objections had vanished and been replaced with pure, insatiable desire. Her eyes were gleaming, mad with lust.

Jack turned the anal penetration up to 8.6, making the little latex dildo fuck her ass deeper and a little faster. He was fucking her pussy in the exact same rhythm.

"Yeah, Jack!" she gasped. "Give it to me! Give it to me good!"

Grunting and sweating, Jack kept thrusting into her, finally pushing her over the brink.

"Aaah!" she cried as yet another climax hit her.

Gasping for breath, Jack held completely still inside her, feeling her pussy tightening around his excited cock. Dr. La Roche arched her back, shivering as she savoured the sensations of her climax. She looked up at him, her eyes glazed.

"That was amazing," she whispered. "Kiss me."

And Jack leaned over and put his lips to hers for the first time. They kissed greedily, their tongues eagerly lapping against each other – the kiss of two lovers, turned on by mutual attraction.

"Oh yes," she whispered. "Now let me go, please. I'm exhausted."

"Not yet," Jack said quietly. "I'm going to make you come again."

"No," Dr. La Roche sobbed, "I can't. Please."

Jack kept his cock perfectly still - the entire length buried inside her pussy. He felt the shaft twitching involuntarily every now and then. He turned the dial for anal penetration down to 8.2, making the little latex dildo fuck her anus just as deep, but slowly - slowly.

Dr. La Roche closed her eyes, moaning almost imperceptibly. Jack reached for the dial for the clitoral stimulator. Gradually he increased both speed and force. From 2.2 to 5.5…

"Oh!" she gasped.

Yes. It was working. Although she had thought she was finished, he managed to get her excited again. From 5.5 to 8.8. He could see the tiny device buzzing and throbbing, and he felt the vibrations on his cock.

Dr. La Roche bit her lip. Her nipples were hard as pebbles. Jack felt her juices flowing abundantly around his erect cock.

"Jack…" she whispered.

From 8.8 to 10.10. Relentlessly, the machine vibrated her clitoris at maximum speed and force. Dr. La Roche quivered in ecstasy, yet another orgasm approaching.

"Ohmigod!" she gasped. "Ah! Ah!"

Now Jack began thrusting into her, deep and hard. She was about to come, and he wanted to come with her, wanted her to feel – to watch – as he did.

He could hardly hold back anymore. The feeling of her soft, succulent pussy sucking his cock in – the sight of her naked body, strapped to the machine, subjected to the endless stimulations of the unfeeling devices – knowing that this was driving her to new heights of sexual pleasure – all this was enough to make him come any second.

"Jack!" she cried, writhing on the seat. "I'm coming! Ohmigod! I'm coming!"

Swiftly, Jack pulled out of her. His cock was jerking violently. He didn't touch it – he knew he was going to ejaculate anyway. He

just stood there, his hands on his hips, his twitching cock pointing straight at her, its head swelling, ready to come.

"Look at me!" he gasped.

Obediently, Dr. La Roche looked at him, her eyes still glazed over from her orgasm. And then he couldn't hold back any longer.

"Unhhh!" he grunted, as the first spurt of semen shot from his jerking cock. "Unhhh! Unhhh!"

Dr. La Roche stared at his cock as it kept ejaculating, jet after jet of thick sperm shooting from its tip. Long spurts of hot white semen spattered her naked body – her thighs, her belly, her breasts. A few drops even landed on her chin, and as she licked it up, she felt the machine once more pushing her beyond what she thought physically possible.

"Aaah!" she cried, arching her back in yet another powerful climax. "Jack! Please... stop it!"

Breathing heavily, Jack fumbled with the dials and finally decided to hit the red button, switching everything off at once.

The buzzing sounds slowed down and suddenly stopped, giving way to an unexpected silence. They hadn't noticed how much noise the machine was making. But now it was switched off, the laboratory was eerily quiet, making their heavy breathing sound savagely loud.

Jack looked at the naked, sweating woman in the chair. Tears were streaming down her cheeks. Whether it was from exhaustion or pleasure, he wasn't able to tell. Gently, he undid her straps and helped her get dressed. She was a bit unsteady, which didn't surprise him. He was impressed that she was able to stand up at all

An hour later, in the control room, Dr. La Roche studied the printouts.

"Six orgasms," she said calmly. "Not groundbreaking, I know. But quite impressive over such a short period of time."

"And notice," Jack said, pointing to a graph, "how each climax was stronger than the previous one."

"That is unusual," she said, nodding. Then she gave Jack a big smile. "We did quite well, didn't we?"

"I guess make a good team," he said.

"We sure do."

Dr. La Roche put the papers down.

"Why don't we get something to eat?" she said. "And then... are you doing anything tonight?"

"No," Jack replied.

Dr. La Roche grinned cheekily, running her hand through his hair.

"Oh yes, you are," she purred. "Yes, you are..."

Volume Two

The Kidnappers

"I said, I'm going downtown to arrange the ransom."

Frank spoke slowly, but the look on his brother's face remained blank. Sighing in frustration, he waited for the words to sink in.

"Okay," Billy finally said in his dull voice.

"Mmm!" the girl protested, squirming on the bed next to him.

"Shut up!" Frank snapped.

She was blindfolded and gagged, her hands cuffed above her head. She was dressed the way they found her – pink t-shirt, cut-off jeans, designer basketball shoes. Her braless breasts were clearly visible through the shirt, and Frank had to force himself to look away.

"I'll be back in an hour or so," he went on. "I'll take the car and make the call from the truck stop near…"

He paused. Billy wouldn't get any of this, anyway.

"I'll be back in an hour," he summed up. "Just make sure she's okay, right?"

Billy nodded slowly, seeming to understand.

Frank looked at the big oaf sitting on the bed next to the girl and sighed under his breath. Why did he even let him hang around? Well, two reasons: One – he was his brother and two – he was as strong as an ox. Which had in fact come in handy at the kidnapping. It had been a piece of cake dragging the doped girl from her dad's house while Billy had knocked out one bodyguard and held the other in a headlock.

The girl was quiet now. Five million, he figured. She would at least be worth that much. To her dad – the head of a huge investment firm – that kind of money was peanuts. And for his only daughter, he'd be willing to pay anything. This couldn't fail.

Frank opened the door.

"See you," he said.

"Bye bye," Billy said.

And as his brother closed the door behind him, he was alone in the cabin. It was small and grungy, but Billy liked it. He felt safe

here. His brother was here, taking care of him, handling the stuff he couldn't handle himself. Billy knew he wasn't smart. But Frank was.

Take the whole girl thing – that was Frank's idea. The rich guy paying them millions of dollars – Frank worked that out. That was the kind of thing he could do. Yeah, his brother was smart.

Billy looked at the girl on the bed next to him. She sure was pretty with her long, blonde hair. Her round, firm breasts moved up and down as she breathed rapidly. And the cut-off jeans showed off her long, shapely legs. Billy felt his cock growing hard.

He'd never had a woman. But he knew how. He'd looked through those magazines Frank sometimes bought at the truck stops. Magazines with pictures of sexy ladies getting fucked. The only thing Billy didn't understand was why the guys in those pictures always had such small dicks. Compared to his, they were tiny. But that was probably why they had to pose for magazines to get laid.

He bent over the girl's legs, inhaling her scent. Nice and sweet. He softly placed his hand on her thigh.

"Mmm!" she protested.

Billy grinned. The sound of her voice turned him on even more. He began to unbutton her shorts.

What the fuck is he doing?

Oh shit – it's the retard. I heard the normal guy leave, so this has to be the retard trying to get into my pants. Daddy is so going to kill these guys when he gets them!

The creep's unbuttoned my jeans – and now his fat fingers are inside my panties. He's touching my goddamn clit. Oh fuck, now he's stroking it – slowly, gently, masturbating me.

What the hell am I gonna do? My hands are cuffed, and I can't see or speak. He keeps going, teasing my clit. I don't want him to turn me on. But he does. I'm getting wet. Oh shit – please make him stop. But he just keeps stroking me. I feel my cunt oozing juice – excited as hell. Fuckhead!

"Mmm!" she cried, struggling on the bed. "Mmm!"

Billy was breathing hard as he pulled the cut-off jeans and panties down over her legs and threw them on the floor. His mouth watered at the sight of her long, slender legs and her naked pussy. She must have trimmed her pubes. Her pussy lips were clearly visible, and he could both see and smell the wetness he had caused by masturbating her.

Billy wondered what she tasted like – he actually felt thirsty for her juice. He placed himself between her legs and put his mouth against her wet slit. Gasping, the girl arched her back.

He began sucking at her pussy, greedily drinking the sweet, spicy juice that flowed from her pink flesh. The taste made his head spin. As he kept sucking, he pushed two fingers in between her pussy lips, moving them rhythmically back and forth. Slurping and smacking, he sucked her little, hard clitoris into his mouth.

Ohmigod. Ohmigod. His mouth is all over my goddamn pussy. I can't take it – I can't fight it. It just feels too fucking good. That retard is giving me the full royal treatment. Where did a jerk like him learn this shit?

Oh fuck – oh yeah – keep going, you horny bastard. Suck me, lick me, keep thrusting that finger into me. You're gonna make me come, if you keep that up. The heiress is going to come on your dirty mattress in your tumbledown shack.

I'm trembling like a leaf – out of control. I can't help myself. Ohmigod, he's got my clit in his mouth now, sucking it – and it feels so goddamn good.

Oh no – here it comes, here it fucking comes. Aaah!

"Mmm!" she cried as she came, her entire body squirming on the bed. "Mmm!"

Billy looked at her, fascinated, licking her juice from his fingers. He felt proud. He had made a girl come for the first time. And he felt pretty sure he was going to make her come again.

His cock was fully erect now, pushing hard against the inside of his jeans. It hurt. He quickly pulled off his jeans and boxers, letting his stiff cock spring out. Smiling, he admired his erection. He took it in his fist and stroked it a couple of times. It was thick and hard. The girl was going to like it, no doubt about it.

Billy crawled onto the bed, pushing her legs apart. He saw her pink flesh opening slightly. And he could just imagine how good that pussy would feel, wrapped around his cock. The thought itself made his hard-on twitch with anticipation.

He placed himself between her thighs, and guided the head of his massive cock towards her crevice. Pressing against her labia, the bluish helmet looked absurdly huge.

"Mmm!" she protested, louder than before. "Mmm!"

Billy felt himself drooling with lust. He pushed forward, feeling her pussy yield, slowly opening itself to his cock. Slowly, he forced

the tip of his member into her soft, wet sex. She thrashed about on the bed, kicking her heels into the mattress.

No! Stop! The retard is raping me.

No — there's no way I'm gonna stop him. I must try to relax — then it won't hurt so bad — I hope.

Fuck — that thing is huge! I can hardly believe it's a real cock. It feels like one of those outsized toys they have on display in sex shops to turn the guys on. Oh fuck — he's pushing it in deeper. Spread my legs — I have to spread them wide, or he'll never get it inside me.

Deeper and deeper. Inch by inch. Oh shit — that is the biggest cock I've ever had in my life. Never even seen a cock that big. The guy's a fucking mutant.

I feel my pussy stretching like it's never been stretched before. His shaft feels rough and veined. Another inch — and another. He must be inside me now. And what do I do when he starts fucking me? I don't think I can take it. I can't. Please…

"Aaah!" he gasped, burying the entire length of his cock inside her.

Damn, that felt good. Even better than he'd imagined. Soft and wet, tightly gripping his sensitive flesh. So this was what everyone was talking about. No wonder. Billy would do this all the time if he could. Push his hard cock inside some pretty young girl's pussy and just enjoy the sensation.

His cock twitched again, about to come already. Oh no, he didn't want that to happen. It wasn't supposed to be over so soon. He wanted to give the girl a long, hard fuck — make her come again…

He froze, holding his breath. After a few seconds, he slowly exhaled, fighting the impulse to ejaculate. That did the trick. His cock was still hard and swollen, but it had stopped twitching and felt completely stable. Oh yes, this was going to be great.

Billy felt the slick inside of the girl's pussy as he pulled back, just keeping the tip of his cock inside her labia. Then, in one powerful motion, he pushed forward, burying the entire length of his shaft inside her.

"Mmm!" she moaned.

He pulled back and thrust forward. Then back, then forward, then back… The rhythm felt so natural that after a few strokes, he didn't even have to think about it anymore. It was as if his body had

a mind of his own, driving his thick, bulging tool into the girl's pussy in deep, relentless thrusts. He felt like some kind of fucking machine. And it felt great.

Aaah! Take this gag off me – I wanna scream! He just keeps pumping into me with that great big cock of his. I don't know how my poor little pussy is gonna take it.

Oh shit, I'm so wet now. I can even hear the little, wet sounds my pussy makes as he fucks me. I spread my legs wide, wrapping them around his hips. I feel his muscles flexing in time with his strokes. As if he's using his entire body to thrust his cock into me.

Ohmigod… fuck me… fuck me, you bastard!

"Mmm! Mmm!"

The girl's muffled squeals seemed to rise in pitch. Yeah, that was it. He was fucking her to another orgasm. Billy enjoyed the feeling of control. He knew he wasn't too bright, and there were a lot of things he didn't do very well. But he'd just discovered that he knew how to fuck.

He pulled all the way out. His huge cock glistened with the girl's juice.

"Mmm!" she protested, screaming into the gag.

She thrust her pelvis upwards, impatiently, wanting to have his cock back inside her.

"Yeah?" Billy said, teasingly. "You want Billy's cock, now?"

"Mmm!"

He stroked the slippery shaft, watching the pretty girl writhing on the mattress.

"Want me to fuck you, huh? Yeah, that's what you want…"

"Mmm!"

"Yeah," Billy whispered, guiding his cock towards her pussy. "Here it comes, baby."

Slowly, he buried his cock inside her once more.

Oh yeah. Oh yeah. It feels so good. What a fantastic cock. Don't ever pull it out again. Just fuck me – make me come again.

Yeah, like that. In and out and in and… Deep, hard strokes. Just the way I like it.

He's moving faster now, his cock hammering into me like a piston into a cylinder. I respond to his motions, raising my hips and grinding in circles around his cock.

Faster and faster he fucks me. No. Please slow down. I can't…

Billy was sweating, drops of perspiration dripping from his face on to hers. He grabbed the girl's ass, pulling her up towards him. His thrusts weren't as deep now, just hard and fast. He felt her entire body trembling and twisting. She was out of control.

He kept going.

"Unh! Unh! Unh!" he grunted.

Her juices flowed abundantly around his pumping cock. And suddenly, she arched her back as the orgasm hit her.

"Mmm! Mmm!"

Her muffled cries were louder than ever. Billy felt her pussy contracting around his shaft, as she shivered in convulsions of violent pleasure.

The door swung open.

"What the fuck?" Frank asked, closing it behind him.

"I…" Billy gasped.

He could hardly think. His cock twitched and jerked inside the girl's pussy, and he couldn't stop thrusting.

Frank stared at him angrily. But Billy was about to come, and there was nothing he could do about it. At the last moment he pulled out and grabbed his cock in his fist.

Frank stared at his brother's huge tool, glistening and bulging. Then, seconds later, it began to ejaculate.

"Uhhh!"

Billy threw his head back, yelling like an animal. A long jet of white sperm shot from his huge cock, spattering the girl's t-shirt. Then it fired again, hitting her on her left cheek. She whimpered. Billy's cock kept jerking, pumping hot semen across her shirt and face.

Finally, his orgasm subsided and the last, thick drop of sperm oozed from his cock.

Frank was both shocked and impressed, but tried to maintain a façade of stern disapproval.

"Billy!" he said.

"I'm…" Billy stuttered, his cock growing soft in his hand. "I'm sorry."

"What the hell were you thinking?"

"She's... pretty", Billy said. "And... I think she liked it."

"You think she..."

Frank didn't finish the sentence. He sat down on the edge of the bed, next to the girl's head and thought for a few seconds.

"Well," he said. "You made a mess out of this. But since you did - we might as well enjoy it."

Billy shook his head, his face blank.

"What... what do you mean?"

"I mean," Frank said, "it's party time."

He turned around and untied the girl's blindfold. She blinked rapidly, accustoming her eyes to the light. Then Frank pulled out his knife. The girl froze at the sight.

"Mmm!" she cried.

Frank tugged at her t-shirt and cut it apart with the knife. He had to cut it in several pieces to get it off without opening her handcuffs. As he pulled the shreds away, the two men savored the sight of her shapely breasts. They were beautiful. Billy felt his mouth going dry.

"Okay," Frank said, getting up. "Up you go."

He pulled the naked girl off the bed, making her stand on the floor. Her legs trembled. Billy still lay on his knees on the bed, confused.

"Come on," Frank said cheerily, "it's time for a bath."

He pulled the girl into the next room. Billy stood up, only to realize that his jeans were still around his ankles. He kicked off his shoes and jeans, then followed behind Frank and the girl.

The room next door was a makeshift kitchen with a freestanding shower stall. Frank turned on the shower and pushed the girl in. He pulled a key from his pocket and opened the handcuffs. He wrapped the chain around the shower curtain rod, stretching the girl's arms above her head, and locked the handcuffs again. He grinned.

"You know," he said to the girl. "We're gonna make you scream. Would be a pity if we couldn't hear it."

He swiftly removed the gag. The girl immediately began screaming at the top of her lungs.

"Help!" she cried. "Help me!"

Frank laughed.

"Forget it," he said. "Do you have any idea where you are? It's ten miles to the nearest neighbor. You might as well relax and enjoy it."

He grabbed the shower head and pointed it at her pussy. She squirmed, her breasts bouncing as she tried to get away from the spray of warm water. Frank moved the shower in circles around her clit.

"No!" she cried, staring at Frank, her eyes open wide.

I don't think I can take anymore. Goddamnit, the normal guy is just as much of a pervert as that retard brother of his. The water gushes over my clit, tickling it. Oh shit. I try to move away, but it's no use. It feels just like when I'm masturbating with the shower myself. But no - I don't want him to turn me on. I don't want it, but... oh fuck, I can't help it. It just feels so goddamn good...

I'm standing naked in the grimy shower stall, arms above my head, my body exposed to those two creeps. I hear myself moaning out loud as I squirm with pleasure, pulling at the handcuffs. And that bastard just grins at me, teasing my pussy with the spray of water. He teases me with the shower, circling it around my clit. Oh, fuck yeah...

"Oooh," I whimper - like some slutty bimbo, but I can't help myself.

God, my nipples are so hard right not. Like they're pointing straight at the faces of those two horny guys. I can feel the juices flowing from my pussy, the shower washing them away. Oh shit, my legs are getting weak. I can't... Ohmigod, I'm going to come again. Oh shit, here it comes. Aaah...

"Aaah! Aaah!"

The girl threw herself about in the shower stall. If she hadn't been cuffed to the curtain rod, she would have collapsed from the power of her orgasm.

Frank turned off the shower. His cock had become stiff as a bone as he watched her come. Damn, she was a sexy little thing. He zipped down his black jeans, letting his hard-on spring out. He grabbed it in his fist and stroked it.

"No..." the girl whispered, still shaking from her climax. "Please don't. I'll do anything you say."

"Okay," Frank replied. "What I say is this: Let me fuck you."

The girl closed her eyes, whimpering. Frank stepped closer, still masturbating.

"But hey," he added. "Why should I even ask? I'm gonna fuck you anyway."

He stepped into the shower cabin, his long, hard cock brushing against her stomach. The handcuffs jingled, as she tried to take a step back. But instead she slipped on the wet surface, stumbling into his arms. Grabbing his cock, Frank maneuvered it in between her thighs, entering her pussy from below.

"Aaah! No!" she cried.

Grunting and struggling, Frank pushed upwards. His cock entered her smooth, slippery flesh, impaling her, and there was nothing she could do to stop it.

"Yeah," he gasped, his shaft buried deep inside her pussy. "Now ride it, baby. C'mon – up and down..."

No... I can't. He grabs my ass. I can feel those big, rough hands of hands around my ass-cheeks. For chrissakes, my entire weight is suspended from the damn handcuffs. My wrists hurt like hell. His cock twitches inside me, hard as fuck. I can't look at him – I have to close my eyes to escape the sight of his grinning, unshaved face.

"C'mon," he repeats, "up and down..."

I hear myself whimpering as I lift my legs off the floor and wrap them around his hips. Ohmigod – is this even possible? My legs are wet and slippery. But he's still wearing jeans and I'm able to get some traction from the rough fabric.

Using my legs and arms, I push and pull myself upwards. His cock slips out of my pussy, almost all the way out. Goddamn it, if I could only pull myself away from him like this – but I can't. My legs can't hold me up - I have to let go. And as I slip down, his hard cock plunges back into me - all the way up into my flesh.

"Ohhh!" I cry.

"Yeah," he gasps. "Do it again. Keep going."

I struggle to move up again – and slip back down. I move up again, then down again. I cry out in frustration. Fuck you – I don't want to do this, and it takes all my strength to do it. But he's in control, and I know it. Up and down, up and down, my pussy moving rhythmically around his shaft. The bastard is breathing hard – this is turning him on big time.

"Good girl," he grunts. "You're fucking me like a real slut. Look at me."

Fuck no – I can't. But I know I have to. I open my eyes and look at his face. It's red with excitement, and his eyes are gleaming with lust. Fucking animal! But I keep going, raising and lowering myself on his hard-on. And as I do, I feel his hand slowly moving across my left buttock, until his middle finger pokes my asshole.

"No!" I cry. "Stop it!"

"Shut up!" he shouts. "And keep going!"

Oh fuck – I'm almost crying now. This is too humiliating: Having to hump my kidnapper myself – while he drives his finger all the way into my ass. Please – make him stop... And more humiliating than anything: It's actually making me hot as hell!

Billy felt his cock swelling again. The sight of his brother fucking the girl was just so damn sexy. He stood watching them, wearing only his t-shirt.

The girl was sobbing and squirming, desperately riding up and down on Frank's cock. Frank buried his middle finger in her ass, twisting and turning it as her pussy slid rhythmically up and down over his shaft.

"Mmm yeah," he groaned.

"No!" the girl suddenly cried. "No! Aaah!"

Billy stared. Frank had made her come again. She threw her head back, her wet hair spraying drops around the shower stall. Her hips ground lasciviously around Frank's erect cock as a surge of sensual pleasure shook every fiber of her beautiful, naked body.

Billy stood next to them, slowly stroking his huge cock. Now that he knew how good the girl's pussy felt around his cock, he wanted to get inside her again.

Breathing hard, Frank finally pulled out. His stiff cock was deep red, slick with the girl's juices. As he let her go, she just hang limp from the curtain rod, her body trembling slightly from her climax.

"Ohmigod..." she whispered, "ohmigod..."

Frank looked at Billy.

"You want some?" he asked.

Billy nodded, still masturbating.

"Okay," Frank asked the girl. "Are you ready for my brother?"

She just moaned.

"Or rather," Frank went on, "you think you can handle the both of us?"

"No..." she whispered, shaking her head, "please..."

Frank grabbed her hair and turned her head to face him.

"You know," he said. "We're not really interested in your opinion, sweetie."

He kicked off his boots and then pulled off his jeans. Then he quickly stripped off his shirt and stood naked in front of the girl, his hard-on bouncing in front of him.

Fucking hell. What a hunk! He is an okay-looking guy with his clothes on, but naked, he's fucking amazing. Muscular, but not in that fake, pumped body-builder way. Damnit, now I think I understand what those nerdy girls in drama class mean. They always talk about some actor having a "powerful physical presence". This guy definitely has it.

Oh my god, I can't take my eyes off him — his broad chest, his muscular thighs, his long, beautiful cock. I try not to want him to fuck me, but I really, really do.

"Billy," he says. "Come here."

And the retard steps up, still wearing his t-shirt, with that gigantic cock of his in his hand. You know that clear liquid that comes out of a guy's cock when he's all hot and bothered? It just keeps dribbling out of his huge thing like water from a broken faucet, dripping on to the dirty floor.

The retard stands between my legs. Oh shit. He guides his great big cock towards my poor little pussy. He pushes up — oh fuck — up and into me. I cry out, yanking at the handcuffs. But I'm so wet, and I feel my pussy yielding as he keeps pressing his cock into me. God, it's so fucking huge. But he keeps pushing upwards, opening me wide, burying the entire length of his massive cock inside me.

Oh shit, he's fucking drooling. Now he grabs my hips and starts thrusting. Oh. Oh. Oh. He thrusts deep and hard. But who the fuck am I kidding? It's exactly what I want right now. Oh yeah, keep going. Fuck me harder. Do anything you want. Anything…

Frank stepped into the shower stall. The girl's body shook violently with every powerful stroke of Billy's cock. She had her eyes closed, groaning helplessly with lust.

He assumed the position behind her. Grinning, he grabbed her buttocks and spread them apart, revealing her cute little anus. He forced a thumb into her ass, making her scream.

"No! Don't!"

Her protests turned him on even more. He removed his thumb and guided his cock towards her rectum. She kicked and whimpered, pulling violently at the handcuffs, as he forced his hard cock into her ass.

She whimpered loudly, as he began thrusting into her. He was incredibly excited. The whole situation was too hot to believe: They had just kidnapped her for the money. But now, this young, beautiful girl was naked, strung up in the shower stall. And he and his well-endowed brother were fucking the hell out of her, fucking her pussy and her ass. And listening to her helpless cries, her screams of protest. Or screams of pleasure.

"Oh yeah!" she yelled. "Fuck me, you bastards. Fuck me!"

Oh, that feels so goddamn good. One's fucking my pussy, the other one fucking my ass. And I fucking love it! Give it to me! Harder! Harder! Ohmigod. Here it comes again. I... I think I'm gonna faint. Oh. Oh.

"Aaah! Aaah!"

The girl thrashed about in the shower stall as she climaxed once again. Frank and Billy struggled to keep their hard-ons inside her. They both grunted with pleasure, her body twisting and turning around their cocks. She kept moving in orgasmic spasms, her pussy and anus pulling and squeezing their shafts, irresistibly driving them towards their climax.

"Oh shit!" Frank gasped. "Billy, get the key!"

Billy's face was red. He was still thrusting his huge member into the girl's succulent flesh. He stared at his brother with a blank look.

"The key!" Frank yelled. "The key for the handcuffs, damnit!"

Billy pulled out, his swollen cock almost as red as his face. He stumbled into the other room and returned with the key. Frank had pulled out of the girl's ass, his cock twitching uncontrollably.

"Yeah," he said. "Get her down on the floor."

Billy unlocked the handcuffs. He lifted the girl out of the stall – she seemed almost weightless in his powerful arms – and placed her on her back on the floor. Frank stood next to him and began to masturbate, pointing his cock down towards the girl. Billy just stared at them.

"C'mon," Frank gasped hoarsely. "Let's jerk off all over her..."

The naked girl squirmed lasciviously on the floor, grabbing her young, shapely breasts.

"Yeah," she whimpered. "Let me have it."

Billy finally seemed to get it. His cock was pointing straight up, and he had to use some strength to force it down. Then he began stroking.

Frank was first to climax. He cried out with pleasure as a long, white spurt of semen shot from his cock, spattering the girl's breast. He spurted again, hitting her on the cheek. She opened her mouth.

"Unh!" Billy grunted.

His cock swelled in his fist and released the first jet of sperm, straight into the girl's mouth. She swallowed once, then stuck out her tongue provocatively. Grunting and masturbating, the two men kept ejaculating, attempting to spray their creamy semen into the girl's mouth.

Oh, fuck yeah. Give it to me! I find my clit with my right hand. Oh yeah, I want to touch myself while they jerk off all over me. I'm so fucking wet...

Mmm, yeah. I can't believe it. I'm lying on their dirty floor, catching their cum in my mouth like a total slut. Mmm. The normal guy's sperm tastes a bit salty, but not too bad, really. But the retard's has a strong, spicy flavor. I feel like it's burning my tongue with every spurt. But still I swallow, swallow...

The normal guy's done, now. He keeps jerking his cock, but it's starting to grow soft. Only little drops of sperm come out, dripping down on my tits. But the retard keeps going, pumping loads of his cum into my mouth. I can see his big, hairy balls contracting with every spurt. Mmm. I masturbate like crazy, but I haven't come yet.

"Mmm..." I hear myself whimpering.

Finally, the retard is done. His cock is growing soft. Oh fuck, it's still longer and thicker than any cock I've ever seen. I can taste their cum on my tongue. This is crazy. I keep stroking myself. I want to come again. Please, please. I'm shaking and sweating. Ohmigod.

The normal guy turns away and starts putting his clothes back on. No, come back. I'm doing this for you. Look at my little pussy. Look at me, when I come for you. Oh. Oh, shit. I wanna look at your big, lovely cocks when I come.

The retard is staring at me. Oh god, I look at his huge fucking cock and remember what it did to me. Oh yeah, I'm almost ready to come. I keep going, jerking off in a furious rhythm.

"Frank," the retard says. "Look at her."

And as Frank turns around, now fully dressed, I catch his eye. And at that precise moment, everything explodes inside my brain. Huge waves of animal pleasure rush through my body, making me scream at the top of my lungs.

"Aaah! Aaah!"

"Fucking hell!" Frank gasped, watching the girl orgasm on the floor. "She's one hot little number."

Billy just stood there, staring at her, like he'd never seen anything like it. But then again, he probably hadn't.

And, come to think of it, neither had Frank.

Two hours later, Frank burst in through the door, holding a sports bag triumphantly aloft.

"Are you ready?" he asked Billy.

Billy just nodded.

"Well, let's go then, for fuck's sake," Frank said, almost out of breath.

The operation had gone smoothly. They'd cleaned up the girl and dressed her, then Frank had driven her to the always-empty car park off the highway. The girl's wealthy dad had been there, alone as far as Frank could tell, with the money. And he hadn't detected anyone following him back to the cabin.

Billy followed behind Frank to the other car. Frank threw the sports bag in the back seat. They were about an hour's drive from the border. Then they'd be safe.

Billy got in and Frank started the car. He drove up the dirt road towards the highway – and that's where he saw the motorbike.

"Damn!" he hissed and hit the brake, throwing Billy forwards in his seat.

But who was it? It wasn't a police bike. And the rider was pretty small. Was it even a man?

Frank started the car again and drove slowly up to the motorcycle. As he approached, the rider removed the helmet and threw her long, blonde hair about, smiling.

"Shit!" Frank whispered, stopping the car again.

The girl went over to the driver's side and looked at Frank through the window. He just stared at her.

"Don't worry," she said. "I haven't called the cops or anything. I just followed you back."

"But... why?" came Frank's confused voice from inside the car.

The girl smiled wickedly.

"Why do you think?" she said. "You guys gave me the fuck of a lifetime. And, well... I want more, I guess."

Frank just stared at her. He couldn't believe it.

"So?" the girl asked. "Are you gonna let me in?"

Billy's mouth was open. He looked from the girl to Frank and back again.

"The door's open," Frank finally said.

The girl opened the door and sat in the backseat.

"Thanks, guys," she said.

Frank started the car and looked at her in the rear-view mirror. He was smiling, too.

"I think we're gonna have fun," the girl said, glancing at the sports bag.

"Yeah," Frank said, turning down the highway and speeding up. "I think we will."

My Naked Neighbour

For a guy like me, the flat was perfect.

It was located downtown on the third floor of an old house in a narrow street. Sure, it was small, but it was quite inexpensive and this area was simply where I wanted to live at the time.

Back then, I was in my mid-thirties and single. And I suppose my love life was rather average. I did bring girls home once in a while, but none of them ever became more than casual relationships.

And then there was porn. Since I was a teenager, I've been a great porn fan. And back then I spent a lot of time watching porn on DVD and masturbating,

For some reason, the flat had a vinyl floor. This meant I could ejaculate on the floor and just wipe up the sperm afterwards. You see, I just love watching myself shooting off. Probably because my ejaculations are quite powerful.

Anyway, I would watch porn DVDs in the nude and masturbate until my cock spurted semen several feet across the floor. Then I'd wipe the floor, pour myself another drink and wait until I was ready for a second round.

As I said, the street was narrow - and there was another flat directly opposite mine. This meant I could actually look right into the living room of my neighbour across the street.

After a while, I had my first glimpse of her: She was younger than me - in her mid-twenties, I guessed. A tall girl with short blond hair - a real beauty, in fact. Once, our eyes met across the street, and she gave a little nod, as if to say "yes. I know you can see me".

Of course, I didn't want her to witness my porn sessions. So every time I got the urge, I made sure the blinds were drawn before turning on the DVD.

And then there was that very special morning.

I'd just gotten out of bed, had my coffee and was getting ready for work. Absently, I looked out the window. Down in the street, cars and pedestrians were already on the move - city folk going

about their usual business in the cold morning air. And as I lifted my gaze to look at the window across the street, there she was. But this time she was naked.

I blinked. Yes, my neighbour was casually walking around in the nude. Her hair was wet, so I suppose she'd just stepped out of the bath. Fine. But why didn't she throw a bathrobe or a towel around her? Or - if she wanted to walk around in the nude, why didn't she pull the blinds or curtains?

I could have looked away, but I didn't. It was almost as if she wanted me to see her.

She was even more beautiful in the nude. She was slim, but not skinny. From where I stood, I could just glimpse her pussy: A neatly trimmed blond bush just above her labia. And her breasts were the kind you dream about: Not huge, just perfectly shaped. I stood there, imagining how they'd feel in my hands.

Suddenly, our eyes met.

She didn't flinch. She just stood there, naked, looking at me. Her attitude seemed to be saying "yes, I am naked. This is my body. I have nothing to hide - and nothing to be ashamed of."

As my neighbour looked into my eyes, I felt myself getting an erection. My cock felt warm and heavy against my thigh, slowly hardening - rising.

I walked away from the window. I had to get ready for work.

All day, I must have thought about that episode. It was funny how my neighbour's attitude made perfect sense. After all, what did she have to hide? What did anybody have to hide?

I thought about everything we do for that sole purpose - to avoid strangers seeing our naked bodies. All the clothes we buy, all the drawn curtains, blinds, closed doors... And we could all just as well do without it.

After the episode, my mind kept returning to my neighbour's naked body. Let's face it: We males are always on the lookout for a potential sex partner. And here was a gorgeous woman exposing her naked body right across the street from me. If that doesn't fuel a man's sexual fantasies, what will?

Anyway, I spent the next couple of days in a state of more or less constant arousal. And finally I decided I needed a good porn session. So on the way home from work, I went by my local sex shop and rented a couple of DVDs.

When I got home, I poured myself a whiskey, got naked and popped the first DVD in the machine.

The first movie was pretty hot: A cute young blonde joined the army, only to find herself surrounded by a number of very horny and well-endowed men - and the odd lesbian. Every training session soon developed into an enthusiastic sex act.

The heroine was a very sexy redhead, and I soon had a huge erection. And when the drill sergeant had the girl on all fours, pumping her fiercely, I started masturbating. I stroked my cock slowly at first, feeling it grow to its full size.

The girl on the screen shrieked loudly with pleasure, as the sergeant kept driving his huge cock into her pussy. Both actors were sweating, apparently completely engrossed in the pleasure of the act.

It was an incredibly sexy scene. I felt my balls tightening, my semen ready to burst from my cock.

Grunting with excitement, the drill sergeant pulled his cock from our heroine's cunt and turned her over on her back, pointing his hard-on straight at her face. Seconds later, the first jet of sperm shot from his cock, hitting the girl's pretty face.

I couldn't hold back any longer. I held on to my cock as the first powerful spurt of semen shot several feet across the vinyl floor. And as the sergeant spattered our heroine's sweaty body with his creamy spunk, I kept ejaculating.

Another spurt - and another - and finally I felt my orgasm subsiding. Trembling, I grabbed my drink and took a sip.

And that's when I saw it: I had forgotten to pull the blinds!

Through my window I saw my neighbour. She just stood there, naked, smiling at me. She must have seen it all. She must have watched me jerking off and ejaculating all over the floor. Damn!

Still out of breath from my climax, I jumped from my chair and stumbled towards the window. And just as suddenly, my neighbour was gone - and I found myself staring into an empty living room.

Had she even been there? Or had I just imagined it in some post-orgasmic hallucination? I couldn't be sure. I pulled down the blinds, wiped my semen off the floor and collapsed in my chair.

I emptied my whiskey and poured myself another one. Then I just sat there for several minutes, trying to catch my breath.

My mind was a chaos of conflicting reactions. At first, I just felt embarrassed. Of course I did: I had been caught in the most private situation I could imagine.

But then I recalled my neighbour's face - assuming I'd seen her at all, she'd been smiling. A friendly smile - as if we now shared a secret.

Maybe - the thought suddenly hit me - maybe she'd actually enjoyed it. Well, why not? Men enjoy watching women masturbate. And there had to be female voyeurs as well. Maybe my neighbour was one of them.

As I pondered this possibility, sipping my drink, I felt myself getting aroused again. My cock twitched between my naked thighs, slowly swelling to a semi-erection. I got up and put another DVD in the machine.

This one was even better: A group of young female fashion models were struggling to make it to the top. But behind the scenes of the glamorous industry they were all subjected to kinky sex acts.

Watching the movie, I still kept seeing my neighbour in my mind's eye, smiling. As the virile fashion photographers took turns fucking the models, one always snapping pictures of the scene, I masturbated again. Two more times I ejaculated on the floor of my flat before I crawled into bed, nearly comatose.

The next day I could hardly concentrate on my job. I kept seeing my neighbour's beautiful body, those perfect breasts, that cute little pussy. And her pretty face, smiling at me as I ejaculated like a beast.

You'd think I'd be drained after masturbating three times the night before. But I was still so aroused I had to lock myself in the bathroom at work and jerk off. But even that didn't help. A few minutes later, my cock was semi-erect again.

It was January, and darkness had fallen by the time I got home from work. I locked my door, undressed and took a shower. As I washed the soap off my body, my cock was already completely erect - hard as a rock. I dried myself, taking care not to rub it to hard and accidentally bring myself to orgasm. I wanted to save it.

I looked in the mirror. I've never been a fitness freak, but for some reason I was in pretty good shape. I've always been rather thin, but at the time I was all muscle. And between my legs, my nine inch cock stood up straight, twitching with excitement.

Naked, I walked into my living room. The blinds were up. Tonight, I wanted to be seen.

Standing by the window I looked across the street, into my neighbour's flat. She wasn't there. Her living room was dark, but I could see a light shining from another room. So she was home.

I waited, and soon a light went on and my neighbour came into view. Again, she was naked - and utterly beautiful in the soft lamplight.

She looked over at me - and as she saw me naked for the first time she froze in the middle of the room. I didn't move, and she didn't look away.

I was acutely aware of her gaze on my cock. It felt strangely exciting, and I felt it twitching, slapping against my stomach.

I noticed that today she wasn't smiling. Absently, she brushed her hair away from her face and bit her lip, still staring at my erect cock.

With a graceful movement she crawled on to a small table in front of the window, giving me a perfect view of her naked body. She knelt on the table top, spreading her thighs. Beneath the blond tuft of pubic hair I could just make out the pink flesh of her labia.

As she looked straight into my eyes, her fingers found her pussy. Gently she began stroking herself with one hand - masturbating for me. My cock was so hard it was almost painful. She massaged her clit, slowly at first, then gradually increasing the rhythm.

Her nipples were hard, poking out from her perfect breasts. She opened her mouth, breathing hard as she stroked her cunt.

Shivering with excitement, I cleared a table and placed it in front of the window. Then I crawled up, kneeling on the table top like her. Staring into her eyes I grabbed my cock and began masturbating.

I had to stroke myself slowly and gently, otherwise I would have ejaculated immediately. Clear fluid trickled from the tip of my cock. I spread it over the shaft, making it wet and slick.

Slowly, my neighbour slipped two fingers inside her cunt. I gasped at the sight. Carefully, she moved them back and forth, exploring her own flesh. Then with a delicate movement, she put the fingers in her mouth, closing her eyes as she savoured the taste of her juice.

I grabbed my cock in my hand. I had almost come at the sight.

My neighbour looked me in the eyes, licking her own juice off her fingers. Then she repeated the procedure - probed her pussy

with the fingers, then sucked the wetness off them. With her other hand she grabbed her breast, gently squeezing its soft flesh.

I moved close to the window pane, letting my cock graze it. The clear liquid trickled down the glass.

My neighbour imitated my move. Moving forward, she pressed her pussy against her windowpane. As she slowly pulled back, I saw a steamy patch of her moisture on the glass. I could just imagine how that sweet, wet pussy would feel wrapped around my cock.

And just as I thought I couldn't take any more, she reached down behind the table and pulled out a latex dildo. It must have been about the size of my own member - nine inches long. The mere thought of her fucking herself with that thing made my hard-on twitch in anticipation.

She lifted up her left leg and let the tip of the dildo slip inside her. She looked down at her cunt, apparently wanting to watch her labia stretching around the latex toy. Slowly, she pushed it in deeper. Her mouth was open - I could just imagine her gasping with pleasure as she felt the thing entering her sensitive flesh.

Fluid dripped from my cock. The pressure was so great, small globs of semen mingled with the flow, already anticipating a massive ejaculation.

My neighbour looked into my eyes and began moving the dildo in and out of her cunt, fucking herself. Her face was flushed, and droplets of sweat were appearing on her skin, making her glisten in the lamplight.

I couldn't keep still anymore - I felt my pelvis thrusting back and forth as I masturbated. As if my brain was subconsciously forcing my body to fuck.

As my neighbour masturbated with her dildo, love juice flowed down her thighs, wetting the sex toy, wetting her fingers, everything between her legs wet and slippery.

We were teasing each other, whipping up a sexual frenzy across the darkened street. This was foreplay without touching, sex without any physical contact. And we were both turned on far beyond the point of no return. We couldn't have stopped now if our lives depended on it.

I kept stroking my cock, grunting like an animal in heat.

With great force, my neighbour thrust the dildo into her cunt again and again. She was still looking at me, but her eyes were glazed, unfocused. I could tell she was on the verge of coming.

And suddenly she froze, her face transformed by a wild rush of pleasure. Trembling all over, she had a powerful orgasm before my eyes. As I watched her coming, I couldn't control myself. I grabbed my cock with both hands, as I began ejaculating.

I yelled out loud with lust, as the first spurt flew several feet up in the air, hit the window pane and slowly began trickling down the glass. My neighbour watched intently as jet after jet of creamy white semen shot from my jerking cock, spattering the window in front of me. I kept masturbating, wanting my orgasm to last forever. But finally it subsided, and I squeezed the last thick drops of sperm from my cock.

I was dizzy. I had to hold on to the window frame to steady myself. Across the street, my neighbour slowly slipped the dildo out of her pussy, dripping juice on to the table top. She was gasping for breath, utterly exhausted.

I didn't want it to be over yet. I held the head of my cock between my thumb and index finger and gently kept stroking it. Slowly, carefully, I massaged it, making it swell, maintaining my erection. Soon, the shaft was as hard as before, and I began masturbating again.

Watching me, my neighbour bit her lip. She turned a switch on the dildo, making it vibrate. As I stroked my cock vigorously, she let the tip of the vibrator touch her clit.

This time we managed to maintain eye contact all the way through. My mouth was dry. I would have loved to kiss her, to feel her tongue against mine as we worked our way to another simultaneous climax.

I felt my balls contracting, as my second orgasm approached. Like a madman, I heard myself shouting unintelligible obscenities, urging my neighbour to masturbate and come for me.

I watched her shiver uncontrollably, tears of joy streaming down her cheeks as she came again - another rush of animal pleasure.

I came at the sight. Once more my stiff cock began ejaculating. Powerful spurts of semen shot from its tip, spattering the window. I noticed the liquid was clearer this time, less milky white. I had almost emptied myself of sperm and was now just pumping fluid.

Still, my ejaculation was almost as strong as the first one. As the contractions ceased, I held my cock in my fist, finally allowing it to soften. It was bright red and burning hot from the strain.

Naked and sweating, my neighbour and I sat there for a while, just looking at each other. We were both exhausted - and utterly satisfied.

I looked down into the street. People in winter coats were rushing by on the sidewalk, cars slowly making their way through. Had anyone seen us? If they had, I didn't care.

My neighbour smiled at me - a tired, happy smile. Then she slowly crawled off the table and disappeared into the shadows.

After that night, I often saw her naked and I often walked around naked myself. But we never did "that thing" again. It remained a fond memory of a random act of uncontrollable lust.

My neighbour moved out a few months later. I stayed in the flat for about a year. But it remains one of my favourite sexual memories.

Every now and then, I think back on that night. I recall the beautiful sight of her naked body, quivering in orgasm, my cock pumping thick jets of hot sperm across the window. And as I wonder where she is now, I imagine her recalling it, too. I imagine her reliving that night, aroused, vigorously masturbating to the memory.

And that thought never fails to make me come...

The Maid

Sylvia had been working as a maid at the Savoy hotel for six months now, and was beginning to get into the routine. She had even gotten to like the maid's uniform she had to wear. Not because it looked good, but because there was something inexplicably kinky about it.

At 3 p.m., Sylvia was working her way through the eleventh floor. Most of the guests were away at this hour, and she liked that. It meant she could just move from one room to the next, do a bit of cleaning, change the sheets and towels and know that the entire floor would soon be finished for today.

Sometimes she would even have some time left to spend in an empty room, lying around on a big double bed with the television on. But God forbid the management ever found out what she was really doing in those rooms...

Room 1106. No "do not disturb" sign on that doorknob either. Great. Sylvia unlocked the door and pulled her trolley through the doorway and got ready to check the bathroom.

"Oooh. Yeah, baby."

Sylvia froze as she heard the muffled voice coming from the bedroom. It was a man's voice, deep and husky. She liked the sound of that voice.

"Yeah, like that. That's so good."

Sylvia left the bathroom. She knew what she was supposed to do now. Just get the hell out of there, and leave this man and whoever was with him alone.

The door to the bedroom was ajar, but she couldn't see anything from where she was standing.

Yeah, she really should leave now. That would be the right thing to do. But she didn't move.

"Oh, yeah. Mmm, keep going."

Oh God, that voice! No, she would leave, but first she had to see what that guy looked like.

Slowly, careful not to make a sound, Sylvia closed the door behind her. Then she tiptoed towards the bedroom door. Just a few steps, and there — she saw them.

The man stood naked in the middle of the room. He was dark, medium-height and very muscular. Sylvia noticed that he needed a shave — there was dark stubble on his chin and his cheeks.

Kneeling on the soft carpet in front of him was a naked woman, sucking his cock. The woman had long red hair and big, voluptuous breasts, and — she was blindfolded.

Sylvia watched them, spellbound. The woman held her head still, as the man slowly moved his hips back and forth, sliding his cock in and out of her mouth. It was long and hard, glistening with saliva. He buried the entire length of the shaft in her mouth with each stroke. Sylvia was amazed that the woman didn't once pull back, but seemed able to take it all.

The man was loving it, too. Breathing heavily, he looked down at the woman's face as he fucked her mouth. Then he grabbed her by the hair, and holding his hips still, pulled her head slowly back and forth, making his erect cock enter her mouth over and over.

"Yeahhh," he whispered, absorbed in his own pleasure. Sylvia could see and hear the wetness as he repeatedly entered and withdrew from the woman's mouth. She could imagine what this long, hard cock would feel like in her mouth, veined and swelling with excitement.

The man pulled all the way out. His hard erection twitched in front of the woman's face. She opened her mouth and tried to catch it, but because of the blindfold, she merely snapped at the air.

Finally the man grabbed his cock and guided it back into her mouth. Now, she started sucking hard on the swollen head of the cock, making loud smacking noises. The man threw his head back, grunting with pleasure.

Sylvia stared at his cock, watched the thick, hard shaft twitching and swelling as the woman sucked it like a piece of candy.

"Ahhh yeah," he gasped. "Unnnh..."

And suddenly, he struggled to pull his cock from the woman's vigorously sucking mouth. With a loud, wet, popping sound he yanked the stiff tool out from between her lips. Her saliva dripped from the hardened shaft on to the carpet.

He had been about to come, Sylvia thought. That had to be it. He had been about to ejaculate into the woman's mouth. The thought excited her. She wished he had, so she could have watched.

The man looked down at the woman, breathing deeply, composing himself. He was obviously planning to make the sex last for as long as possible.

Sylvia thought for a second. She didn't have time to watch it all. But she could stay just a little longer.

Tiptoeing back to the door, she locked it, again careful not to make a noise. Then she tiptoed back to where she could watch the couple in the bedroom.

The man was stroking his cock, smiling.

"Get on your back!" he ordered.

And the woman obeyed. Naked and blindfolded she lay down on her back on the soft, thick carpet. The man got down on all fours, spread her legs wide, exposing her neatly trimmed, dark red pubes. Then he placed his unshaven face between her legs and gave her pussy a big, wet kiss.

"Oh," the woman gasped.

The man's hands gently stroked the inside of her thighs, getting ever closer to her pussy. The woman lay completely still, breathing faster and faster.

Just as his hands were about to reach her pussy, he started licking the same area: The inside of her thighs, the thin, sensitive skin close to her sex. The woman dug her fingernails into the carpet.

Sylvia watched as he licked the woman's thighs, then bared his teeth and bit gently into the soft, pale flesh of her thighs.

"Aaah," she gasped.

The man kept going, gently nibbling at the sensitive skin of first one thigh, then the other.

"Oh please," the woman pleaded. "C'mon. Do it!"

"Do what?" the man whispered.

"My pussy," she whispered back. "Do it to my pussy. I want it so bad..."

And gently, the unshaven man placed his mouth over the woman's pussy, slowly kissing and sucking it. He pressed his lips against her labia, massaging her pussy with her mouth. Moaning loudly, the woman arched her back, throwing her head back on the carpet.

"Yeees," she cried, grabbing her breasts with both hands.

Sylvia could almost feel what the woman felt: The man's lips sucking her pussy, his stubble scratching the tender skin of her thighs. Sylvia felt herself getting wet. Slowly she reached under her skirt and pushed the crotch of her panties aside to feel her flesh.

Oh yes, she was even wetter than she thought, her labia all slippery with juice. She wanted to touch herself, wanted to masturbate as she watched the couple in the bedroom.

"Ohhh," the woman moaned, writhing on the carpet.

Sylvia watched as the man drove his thick, wet tongue in and out of her pussy. Moving his head up and down, he let his tongue enter her wet flesh again and again. Then he began flicking his tongue up and down as he continued the motion, licking her. Licking her labia, licking the inside of her pussy, licking, licking...

The woman was gasping uncontrollably, her ankles clasped around his shoulders.

Sylvia felt her cheeks burning. She just couldn't leave. Not yet. Slowly, quietly she removed her panties and dropped them on the floor. She reached under her skirt again, gently touching her naked pussy. Just touching her slippery slit made her fingers all wet.

On the bedroom floor, the man kept driving his tongue into the woman's pussy, faster and faster.

"Oh yes," the woman cried, "oh please, oh yes."

The man held on to her thighs, digging his fingers into her flesh. His face was red and sweaty from the strain, but he kept going, flicking his tongue, fucking the woman with it, harder, faster...

"Aaah," she screamed, throwing herself about on the carpet as she came. "Aaah!"

The man strengthened his hold on her thighs, his mouth firmly planted on her pussy, as she thrashed about on the floor, swept away by her powerful orgasm.

Sylvia gently began stroking her own pussy, slowly massaging her wet labia. It felt so good. She closed her eyes and almost moaned out loud, but she bit her lip, struggling to keep quiet.

Breathing hard, the woman was recovering from her orgasm.

"Oh God," she whispered. "That was so good."

The man was kneeling between her legs now, masturbating. Sylvia watched him stroking his cock, making it stiffen and grow. And as she watched him, she masturbated herself, rhythmically rubbing her pussy, feeling her juices flow.

The man didn't say a word. He looked around the room as if searching for inspiration. Then he got up and lifted a footstool into the middle of the bedroom. Then, gently, he placed the woman face down on the stool, her side towards Sylvia.

As he knelt down behind her, his eyes met Sylvia's.

Sylvia almost screamed, but she managed to keep quiet. Oh God, what would happen now? Would he throw her out of the room? Yell at her? Complain to the manager?

But the man did nothing. He even smiled. Kneeling behind the woman, he kept stroking his cock, which was now long and hard as a rock.

"Are you ready?" he said, looking Sylvia in the eyes.

"Yes," the woman whispered, her face quivering beneath the blindfold.

The man smiled at Sylvia as he guided his erect cock towards the woman's succulent pussy. Using two fingers, he parted her wet labia as he brought the tip of his cock up close to her inviting slit.

"Ohhh," the woman cried, "let me have it! Please!"

Sylvia spread her legs as she stroked her pussy, staring at the man's cock, long and hard and veined. She masturbated, relishing the sensations of pleasure, starting from her pussy and rippling through her entire body, making her nipples hard.

Finally, the man entered the woman, burying his cock in her moist slit with one powerful stroke.

"Aaah," she cried, gripping the fabric of the footstool with both hands, trembling all over. The man started hammering his cock into her in a hard, relentless rhythm.

"Yeah," he hissed, grabbing her hair. "You like that, don't you?"

"Yes," the woman gasped. "Fuck me!"

Sylvia felt her legs trembling underneath her and got down on her knees in her corridor. Watching the fucking couple, she kept excitedly massaging her wet flesh, applying ever more force. Her rhythmically stroking fingers gradually pushed her labia apart and found their way into her tender pussy.

Oh, yes. That felt good.

"Yeah," the man grunted, driving his erect cock into the woman over and over, "I'm gonna fuck you hard. Can you feel it? Can you feel my hard cock fucking your little pussy?"

"Oh yes!" the woman gasped. "Talk to me! Keep talking dirty to me! Ahhh, yes! You know I love it!"

The man smiled, looking over at Sylvia.

"Oh yeah?" he said. "Well, get this: We are not alone."

"Ohhh," the woman moaned, as the man's stiff cock slid in and out of her pussy. "Yes, I like that. We're being watched? Ohhh. Tell me more!"

Stunned, Sylvia stared at the man. He was telling the truth, but the woman had no way of knowing that it was anything more than just a dirty fantasy. The man winked at Sylvia and continued:

"Yeah, the maid just walked in. She's watching us right now."

Hearing herself mentioned in the story excited Sylvia even more. Parting her labia with one hand, she began fingering her tiny, hardening clit with the other. Oh, it felt so good. It made her want to cry out with pleasure. But no, she kept quiet, masturbating, watching and listening.

"Ohhh yes, the maid," the woman said, her entire body shaking with every thrust of the man's cock. "What does she look like? Ahhh. Yes! Is she pretty?"

The man looked at Sylvia again. She looked him deep into the eyes. And still fucking the naked, blindfolded woman in front of him, he began describing Sylvia:

"Oh yes, she's beautiful. Young - short, black hair. She's wearing that maid's uniform, you know."

"I bet that turns you on," the woman whispered.

"Can't you feel it?" the man asked, hammering his long, hard cock into her. "Can't you feel how hard I am?"

"Ohhh," the woman cried.

The man grabbed hold of her ass-cheeks and decreased the rhythm. He kept driving the entire length of the shaft into her with every stroke, but now he slid it slowly back and forth, back and forth, teasing her.

"And you know what else?" he whispered. "She's masturbating. Yeah. The maid is watching us fuck, and she's stroking her cute little pussy at the same time."

"Oooh," the woman whimpered. "It turns her on to watch you fucking me."

"Yeah," the man grunted. "I bet she likes the sight of my cock."

And Sylvia watched the hard, glistening cock poking the woman's pussy. She knew just what the woman felt now, the stiff shaft stretching her lusty flesh as the drove his hard tool into her again and again.

Sylvia could hardly take her eyes away from the couple fucking before her eyes. But by now she was dying to feel a cock in her pussy, and she knew what to do.

She got up and stumbled towards the trolley. Her legs felt weak, and she almost fell. But no, she couldn't make a sound, and she just barely stayed on her feet.

Sylvia reached in between some flannel towels on the trolley and found her flesh-coloured latex vibrator. This was the one she sometimes used, when she lay all alone on a double bed in one of the rooms. She would take all her clothes off, find a porno movie on the hotel network and slowly, lazily masturbate herself to orgasm. Just thinking about that now turned her on even more.

She knelt down again. The woman was whimpering now, her entire body shaken by the violent thrusts, as the man kept driving his cock into her pussy. Sylvia saw the muscles of his thighs and ass flex with each stroke.

She gently opened her labia with the fingers of one hand. God, she was wet. She felt her love juice trickling down the insides of her thigh. And then, with the other hand, she placed the dildo at the mouth of her pussy. With a light motion of her hand, she slid the rubbery tool upwards, filling her hungry flesh.

"Tell me more!" the woman gasped. "What's she doing now?"

The man turned his head towards Sylvia and smiled.

"She's got a big rubber dildo," he said. "And she's fucking herself."

"Oh God," the woman gasped. "Is she really so hot? From watching us fuck?"

"Yeah," the man said, pulling his cock all the way out of the woman's slit. "She likes it, when I do... this!"

And in one brutal thrust, he buried his cock inside the woman's pussy, making her cry out loud with shock and lust.

"Aaah!" she screamed. "Yes! Do it again!"

Sylvia started moving the dildo up and down, massaging the insides of her aching flesh. She wanted to cry out with pleasure, but no. She had to keep quiet.

Again the man pulled out of the woman's pussy. Sylvia saw his glistening, erect cock twitching with lust before he once more hammered the entire length of his shaft into the woman again.

"Aaah, yes!" she cried. "I bet she likes that!"

"Yeah," the man said, now fucking her in a moderate, insistent rhythm. "She loves it. She's taking her clothes off. She wants to get naked now."

The man looked into Sylvia's eyes as he said it. Sylvia was fucking herself faster and faster with the dildo and didn't want to stop now. And she shouldn't even be here in the first place. Watching the couple was bad enough. Masturbating at the sight was even worse. No, she could get naked. Not here.

But somehow, she felt obliged to. The blindfolded woman had no idea what was really going on, but it was as if she had an understanding with the man: He had allowed Sylvia to stay and watch, and now it was her turn to repay him.

Looking the man in the eyes, she pulled the dildo out of her pussy and laid it, dripping wet, on the floor. Then she undressed, still keeping her eyes fixed on his. He smiled approvingly as he saw her naked body, her young, shapely breasts pointing little hard nipples straight at him, her moist pussy freshly shaved.

It felt strange to be naked in the hotel room, uninvited, watched by a strange man in the act of fucking. It turned her on, and she showed her pussy off to him, parting her labia, allowing him a glimpse of the wet, pink flesh inside.

Excited, the man drove his cock deeper and deeper into the woman, pushing her body back and forth across the footstool.

"Oh yes," she gasped. "Is she naked now? Is she beautiful?"

"Ah yes," the man grunted. "A pretty, young thing: Nice tits, shaved pussy. God, I'd love to fuck her."

Sylvia grabbed the dildo and slid it back inside her pussy. It felt so good. As she started moving it back and forth, she realized she was about to come. Her thighs were quivering with pleasure.

"Pretend I'm her," the woman cried, her voice trembling. "And fuck me the way you'd fuck her. Fuck me, like you were fucking the maid."

"Yeah!" the man yelled, driving his hard tool deep into her pussy again and again. "Take that, you randy little maid. Can you feel that?"

Kneeling naked on the floor, Sylvia fucked herself with the vibrator. Faster and faster – her head was spinning.

She saw the man forcing the tip of his thumb into the woman ass, making her whimper.

"Oooh yeah, make me come," she howled, as the man's cock kept pounding into her. "Make me... come!"

The man's unshaven face was red from the strain, and finally Sylvia heard the woman scream as the orgasm hit her. She held on hard to the footstool, as she cried out loud with pleasure:

"Ohhh! Ohhh! Ohhh!"

Sylvia felt like screaming, too. But even in her excited state she was able to keep quiet. Even as she climaxed. Oh, God. Trembling all over, she almost fainted.

Driving the rubber toy deep into her twitching pussy, she bit her lip hard as her orgasm sent wave after wave of lustful sensations through her body. She was gasping for breath.

Through misty eyes she saw the man pull his cock from the woman's pussy. Holding it tightly in his hand, he roared like a wild beast, as he started ejaculating:

"Ahhh!"

Sylvia saw the head of his cock swelling, as the first jet of white, creamy semen shot several feet into the air, spattering the woman's back. As the man grunted and yelled, his cock kept twitching, pumping out spurt after spurt of hot semen. Finally, his orgasm subsided, and he lazily kept stroking his cock, until his erection started wearing off.

"Oh baby," the woman whispered, as he bent down to kiss her.

Sylvia felt a strange urge to tiptoe into the bedroom to lick his cum of the woman's back. She smiled quietly at the thought.

Now she had to put her clothes back on and get out. Quickly, before the woman took her blindfold off. She knew the man would try his best to make her wait, but for how long?

Her panties and her maid's uniform lay in a heap on the floor. Sylvia picked them up. This would not be easy. For one thing, she was still weakened by her orgasm, and furthermore she had to dress without making a sound. But she had to be quick, before...

Sylvia froze, as she heard the sound of a key in the lock.

The doorknob turned, and the door opened. Sylvia was sure it would be the manager, catching her red-handed. She would be fired

immediately. She would never work in this city again. Damn it! Damn it!

A man entered. Sylvia was confused. She'd never seen this guy in her life. He was blonde, thickset with piercing, pale blue eyes that looked at her briefly, before he rushed past her into the bedroom.

"You slut" he shouted to the woman. "You fucking, no-good slut!"

"No, please!" Sylvia heard the woman cry. "I'm sorry! I'm so sorry!"

"You're sorry?" the blonde man sputtered. "You promised me that it was over between you and him. But you're nothing but a slut and a liar! This time it's over! I'm gonna fucking divorce you right this second!"

Sylvia was still paralyzed. She just stood there naked, holding on to her clothes in a bundle. So this was it: She had been watching a wife and her lover. And what was her husband going to do now?

Suddenly, the husband stood there looking at Sylvia.

"And what's this?" he asked. "The fucking maid? That's what turns you perverts on? Making the maid watch as you fuck? Come here!"

And the husband grabbed Sylvia's hand and pulled her into the bedroom.

"No, please," she protested. "I..."

He threw her on the bed, naked.

"Shut up!" he shouted. "This'll teach you not to screw up other people's marriages."

"But..." his wife protested, "I didn't know..."

"Yeah, right!" her husband laughed. "You think I'd buy that?"

The lover had fled to the farthest corner of the room and was quickly putting his clothes back on. The husband didn't even seem to notice him. His piercing blue eyes were fixed on Sylvia's naked body lying on the bed.

Now he unhooked his belt and zipped down his fly.

"No," his wife protested. "Please..."

The husband crawled on to the bed and pulled out his cock. Sylvia was amazed to see how hard it already was. Huge and swollen it pointed straight at her face, twitching slightly as she watched it. It was as long as the lover's, but thicker than any cock she'd ever seen.

"Spread your legs," the husband commanded. "Spread'em. Now!"

Hesitantly, Sylvia opened her legs. He smiled, gently stroking his big cock as he crawled towards her on his knees.

"Please..." she whispered.

Over the husband's shoulders she saw the lover running out of the room. The wife stood by the bed, leaning against the wall, motionless, watching them. But her husband seemed to have forgotten all about her – his pale blue eyes were fixed on Sylvia's wet, hairless pussy.

"Yeah," he whispered. "I'm gonna fuck you good."

Sylvia still didn't understand how he had gotten an erection so soon. Had discovering his wife with her lover actually turned him on? Was this just some sort of game?

"No," Sylvia whispered.

Indifferently, the husband steered his cock towards Sylvia's pussy, resting it on her trembling labia. As he applied the slightest pressure, the tip of the head just slipped into the mouth of her moist pussy. And then, breathing heavily, he let go of his cock and grabbed her wrists with both hands.

"Unnnh," she groaned, struggling to break free. But the husband was too strong, and she felt his huge cock slowly penetrating her. Grunting with lust, he drove the thick tool into her, stretching her wet, tender flesh around it, until finally, he had buried the entire length of the shaft in her pussy.

He lay still for a few seconds. Sylvia gasped, as she felt his cock throbbing and swelling inside her. He held on tight to her wrists, and then, suddenly, the fucking began. The husband thrust his rigid member into her pussy again and again, making her throw her head back and scream out loud.

"Yeah," he shouted at her over her cries. "How do you like that, you little bitch? How do you like my big, hard cock in your pussy?"

The mattress squeaked and bounced beneath them, as the husband kept hammering his stiff pole into Sylvia's aching slit.

"Oh God," she cried. "Oh God!"

And then, above the sound of the husband's animal grunts, she heard the sound of a woman moaning. And as she looked up, she saw the wife, still naked, masturbating as she watched them.

Shocked, Sylvia started struggling again, trying hard to get out of the husband's grip. This was sick! Those people were crazy! But it was no use. The husband pressed her wrists down into the mattress

with his entire weight, as he kept ramming his hard cock into her flesh.

"No!" she cried. "Stop!"

"You dirty little bitch!" he shouted, almost out of breath from the strain, "Feel my cock! I'm gonna fuck you hard!"

"Oooh," his wife moaned beside them. Watching them intently she was vigorously rubbing her clit with one hand and kneading her soft, fleshy breast with the other.

The sight of the lusting woman pleasuring herself, made Sylvia realize that she, too, was getting excited. The husband's hard cock kept pounding into her soft, succulent flesh, massaging the insides of her sex with irresistible force. Each violent thrust drove her closer to another climax, making her moan louder and louder.

Sylvia heard the wife screaming – a loud cry of pure, overwhelming lust. Had she already come?

The sound seemed to turn the husband on. Sylvia felt his fat cock swelling inside her, as he seemed to drive it even deeper into her tender, wet pussy. He was sweating now, dripping little droplets of salty sweat onto her naked body.

Gasping, she felt her orgasm approaching.

"Oh yes," she gasped. "Keep going. Make me come."

Roaring like an animal, the husband thrust his thick tool deep into her flesh. And again. And again. Until finally she felt the waves of pleasure wash over her as she came once more:

"Aaah!" she cried. "Aaah!"

Moments later, the husband pulled out of her. Sylvia saw his huge cock swelling wildly, as he grasped it with both hands. And suddenly, the first spurt of burning, white cream came shot out of the twitching tool.

"Ahhh!" he yelled. "Yeah!"

Sylvia watched in amazement, as the giant cock kept ejaculating, pumping jet after jet of thick sperm on to her naked body. Long spurts of semen hit her belly, her breasts, even her face, as the husband kept stroking his cock, grunting with excitement.

Finally, his orgasm subsided, and he took some deep breaths, smiling peacefully. Sylvia lay back on the bed and closed her eyes.

When she awoke, she was alone in the room. She was still naked, but someone had pulled a blanket over her.

She got up, dressed and looked at her watch. Thank God, she had only been asleep for a few minutes. She would have to hurry, but she would still be able to finish her work on time.

As she pulled the trolley out of the room, she shook her head. What had she been thinking? She promised herself never to do anything like this again. Ever.

But as Sylvia walked down the corridor, she turned her head to look once more at the room number.

1106.

She would try to remember that.

The Hangover

I didn't wake up until after one in the afternoon. And even by then I felt too dizzy to get out of bed right away.

It had been a wild party last night. But as I looked out over my apartment, it didn't really look too bad: Lots of empty bottles, ashtrays that needed emptying – and of course, the floor needed a thorough cleaning. But nothing seemed to be broken or ruined.

God, I was thirsty.

I simply had to get up, if only for that reason. As I sat up in bed, my head started spinning. I couldn't even begin to estimate how much I had drunk the night before. What the hell.

A few seconds later, I felt better and got out of bed. I was naked. Nothing weird about that: All summer, I sleep in the nude – I was more surprised that I had even bothered to get undressed. Maybe I hadn't been so drunk after all.

I walked out of the bedroom and through the living room. Sure, it was a mess, but nothing I couldn't handle. The only thing I didn't like to see was the messy pile of cds in front of my stereo. That would be the first thing I'd pick up.

I walked towards the kitchen, and that's when I saw her: One girl hadn't made it home after the party, and now lay sleeping, curled up on the couch. I stopped to look at her. Strangely, I didn't remember who she was. I knew I'd seen her at the party, but hadn't talked to her. She must have been someone's friend.

She was a pretty young thing – in her early twenties, I'd say: Short, dark brown hair, a slender body and cute, rounded breasts wrapped in a black t-shirt. Without thinking, I touched my cock. It had swelled slightly at the sight of the sleeping girl. I held my cock in my hand and stroked it a few times, back and forth, feeling it bulge and grow.

Then I stopped. What the hell was I thinking? She could wake up any second – and then what would she think? I wasn't some kind of leering pervert, jacking off at the sight of a sleeping girl.

Or was I?

I headed towards the kitchen. Okay, so I had it in me. But I could control it. I reached into the fridge and got out a cold can of cola, popped it open and drank. Whew, that was better. I rolled the cold can across my forehead, and my headache subsided slightly.

I took another sip of the cola and looked back at the girl. No problem: I'd just let her sleep it off, and when she woke up she'd say bye-bye and go home. But it didn't look as if she'd wake up any time soon. I had plenty of time to get dressed.

I finished the cola and looked around the kitchen. It was a mess, all right – but nothing disturbing. You know how they say that all parties end up in the kitchen? Apparently, last night people had been too busy dancing around the living room to go sit in the kitchen.

By now, I was feeling okay. A little dizzy, a slight headache. But I knew that a few more cans of cola and one of Ahmet's kebabs from the shop next door would make me feel a lot better.

I looked down at my cock. Oh yes, and one more thing: A hangover always makes me horny.

Gently, I touched my cock. It felt warm and heavy. I have a rather long cock, even when it's soft. And when it's erect, it gets quite thick. Most girls seem to like it. My ex-girlfriend couldn't stop telling me, how "beautiful" she thought it was. That is, until she didn't even want to look at it anymore.

The blood was pounding in my cock, and I watched it jerk and bulge, growing semi-erect. I held it in my fist, squeezing it. Yeah, that felt good. I was getting more excited by the second.

I stroked my cock a few times. It grew harder and harder, its bluish head swelling, as I felt the shaft throbbing in my hand. Mmm, yeah...

There was no turning back now. I was too excited to stop. I would have to jerk off, probably shooting my load into the kitchen sink. And so what? I massaged my cock slowly, feeling it stiffen and grow. Breathing hard, I savoured the sensations of pleasure, masturbating until my cock was long and hard.

My head filled with scenes of lust: Girls I had fucked, girls I had longed to fuck. Ahh, yes. I imagined my cock sliding into the moist holes of girls I'd known, supermodels, movie stars, every desirable female I could think of.

I could almost hear them begging for my cock, as I fucked them, slowly, teasing them, making them come again and again. Oh,

yeah. I stroked my cock faster, as I imagined pulling out of a beautiful celebrity's slit to let her watch me masturbate, while she screamed at me, demanding to be fucked. Mmm...

Stroking my shaft vigorously, I felt my orgasm approaching. Damn, it felt good. I slowed down, wanting to enjoy the sensations for a bit longer. Mmm, yeah...

But still, coming would feel good, too. And I could always masturbate again later. I moved towards the sink, pointing my rigid cock downward, getting ready to shoot.

"Wow!"

I turned my head, and there she was: The girl had woken up and stood in the doorway looking at me.

Shit.

I let go of my cock and, without thinking, turned to face her. And, really - what could I do? Not only was I naked, my cock was fully erect. I had been seconds away from ejaculating, and now my tool pointed straight at the girl, long and hard, twitching with excitement.

'Wow', she'd said. 'Wow'? Really? Was that the best she could think of? How about 'I'm sorry'?

I looked her over: Yes, she was pretty - with her dark brown hair and her clear blue eyes wide open. She had the breasts of a young girl: Round and firm – they really looked good in that tight t-shirt. And though she was about medium height, she had long, slender legs in her flared jeans. Cute little thing, all right.

And she just stood there, looking at me. I don't know. I've never been in this situation before, but you'd think that a girl that walks in on a strange man masturbating would back off and leave.

Unless...

"Come here," I said.

I held my rigid cock in my hand. Mostly to keep it from jerking and twitching, but also to show it off to her. I wanted her to look at my cock, to see how long and hard it was.

Slowly, she walked towards me. I don't know if I'd really expected her to obey, but she did. She came towards me slowly, hesitantly, and finally stood right in front of me, staring at my erect cock.

"You like what you see?" I asked.

She nodded. "Mmm..."

It was a strange feeling – an exciting feeling – to be standing, naked and aroused, in front of a young girl I didn't even know. Fuck, it turned me on. I'd been excited before, but now I was out of my mind with lust.

"So – what do you want me to do?" I asked.

She didn't even look me in the eyes anymore – her gaze was fixed on my cock.

"I don't know," she said.

"Oh, I think you do," I said.

Stroking my cock with one hand, I held her chin with the other.

"Look at me," I said. "Do you want to watch me masturbate? Is that it? You want me to jerk off in front of you?"

"Yeah," she said, smiling. "Why not?"

I smiled, too.

"Say it," I ordered.

"I want to watch you masturbate," she whispered. "I wanna watch you come."

I let go of her face and began stroking my cock, laughing quietly.

"My, you are a naughty little thing, aren't you?" I said, masturbating nice and slow, right in front of her face.

Her eyes grew even wider, as she squatted down on the floor, staring intently at my cock. I looked down at her pretty face as I kept stroking myself, rhythmically massaging my hard shaft, until the clear liquid of lust trickled from the tip of the head.

"Is that good?" I asked, almost of breath. "Do you like that?"

"Yes," she gasped. "Keep going. Shit, it's huge."

"Ahhh," I groaned. I was masturbating faster now. The sensations of pleasure were almost unbearable.

"You wanna watch me come?" I grunted, stroking my cock in a steady rhythm.

"Yeah," she whispered and lifted up her t-shirt, exposing her breasts. "Come on my tits."

I gasped for breath at the sight. Her young, firm breasts were lovely. And in my excited state I thought they were the most beautiful breasts I'd ever seen. Staring at them, I kept masturbating, feeling my excitement grow. The head of my cock was bulging madly, ready to ejaculate.

"God, I'm gonna come," I whispered hoarsely.

"Yes," she said, squeezing her breasts together. "Let me have it."

I forced my bone-hard cock downwards, pointing it at her breasts. I kept stroking the shaft, harder, faster, feeling my climax approaching.

"Unh,unh," I grunted, in time with my strokes. "This is fucking great."

She smiled, licking her lips nastily.

"Yeah," she purred. "Come on. Show me what that big fat cock can do. Blow your load all over my tits."

Her sexy voice almost brought me over the edge.

"Uhhh," I yelled, masturbating feverishly, feeling the pressure build up from my balls, up through the shaft.

"Uhhh..."

I could have fainted. Jerking off, looking at her lovely face, her shapely tits. Yeah. All I needed was a few more strokes.

"Ahhh..."

I yelled like an animal. One more stroke - and I came. Came harder than I have ever come before.

"Oooh," she cooed.

The semen began squirting from my cock, long white jets, spattering her breasts, as I cried out in ecstasy. The girl stared at my cock, amazed at the force and amount of my ejaculation.

"Yeeeaaah..."

Sperm pumping from my cock, I stood there, shooting spurt after spurt across the young girl's breasts. I clenched my swollen cock in my fist, feeling my ejaculation decrease in force. One more squirt - and another – and finally, the last few, thick drops dripped from the tip onto her breasts.

"Mmm, yeah," she said, approvingly. "That felt good, huh?"

"Fuck, yeah," I gasped. "Come here."

My legs were trembling, but I had to do it. I pulled her up and lifted her up on the kitchen table, resting her ass next to the sink.

"Oooh?" she gasped.

"Take your jeans off," I ordered.

Her breasts were glistening with globs of my white sperm. She unbuttoned her jeans and quickly pulled them off.

"Panties, too," I said. "I wanna see your pussy."

"Okaaay," she said, deftly pulling her panties off. "You know what you like, don't you?"

"You bet," I gasped as I caught sight of her pretty, young pussy – an inviting, pink slit, crowned with a small tuft of dark brown hair.

I knelt down, spread her legs and let my tongue graze her labia. She sighed deeply. I gently began licking her pussy lips – up and down, up and down, making them nice and wet. I felt her thighs trembling next to my face.

Thirstily, I kissed her pussy, sucking at her tasty crevice. I sucked rhythmically at her slit, massaging her soft flesh with my lips.

"Oh God," she whispered, almost out of breath.

I forced my tongue into her slit, savouring the taste of her wetness. This was one tasty young pussy. Slurping loudly, I wriggled my tongue around the insides of her flesh, drinking her spicy juice.

"Yeah," she gasped, "oh yeah."

I licked her as hard as I could. Moving my head back and forth, I thrust my tongue into her cunt over and over. She was wet now, really wet – and I heard her helpless moans rising in pitch, as my tongue action drove her closer and closer to orgasm.

Just as she was about to come, I pulled back. Instead, I slipped two fingers into her dripping wet slit.

"Are you coming?" I asked, sliding my fingers back and forth in her soft, wet pussy.

She bit her lip, trembling.

"Yes," she whispered, eyes closed in ecstasy. "Please... don't stop."

"Don't worry," I grinned. "I'll make you come so hard, you'll never forget it."

I pulled my fingers out of her cunt. She whimpered in protest. But instead I grabbed the shower attachment that I use for washing dishes in the sink and turned on the tap. As the warm gush of water hit her tender pussy, she cried out loud.

"Aaahhh! Fuuuck!"

Trembling and kicking, she immediately had a violent orgasm. I had to hold on to her hard to keep her from falling off the table. But all the time I kept the jet of water directly pointing at her cunt.

"Ohmigod!" she squealed. "Ohmigod! Aaahhh!"

She just seemed to keep on coming, crying out with pleasure, as I slowly moved the jet in circles around her flesh. Breathing deeply, she tried to compose herself.

"Oh fuck!" she whispered, still trembling from her powerful climax. "Oh fuck..."

I grinned at her, slowly sliding a finger into her slit, as I kept the gushing shower aimed directly at her cunt. She was gasping for breath now, her gaze fixed on her own pussy. Finally, I saw her body tensing up, as she muttered under her breath:

"I'm gonna come again. Fuck, I'm gonna come again."

She grabbed hold of my hand – the one holding the shower – and pulled it towards her slit, as she came.

"Aaahhh!" she cried, gripping my wrist with all her might. "Yesss!"

As I watched the struggling girl thrashing about on my kitchen table, I felt my cock starting to swell. Hot and throbbing, it began to grow and stiffen. Soon, she would feel it inside her, long and hard, pounding into her pussy. But first... I had to taste her again.

Still showering her pussy, I put my head between her thighs and licked at her labia. I tasted water, I tasted soft, female flesh and the spicy flavour of her juices. Wrapping my lips around her flesh, I sucked away at her pussy, as the water gushed across my face.

Slurping loudly, I licked her tender cunt, as the water kept pouring over it. I swallowed mouthfuls of water, savouring the faint taste of love juice. She whimpered helplessly, as my thirsty tongue flickered over her hot, drenched pussy lips.

"Ooooh!" she cried.

My cock was now completely erect. I'd have loved to lick her to yet another orgasm, but I was so excited that I wanted to fuck her right then and there.

I stood up and turned off the tap. I noticed the girl still had her t-shirt on, pulled up over her breasts. Apart from that, she was naked, of course. She looked at me, eyes open wide, watching as I stroked my long, rigid cock.

"Mmm," she purred. "That thing sure is hard again..."

"Yeah," I said, massaging my hardened shaft. "And you know what that means, don't you?"

She didn't answer - just pulled off her t-shirt and threw it on the kitchen floor. Then she sat there smiling cheekily at me. Damn, she was cute.

"Come here," I said, and grabbed her arm.

I pulled the girl down off the kitchen table and into my living room. She stumbled after me, her legs apparently still weak from her orgasms. I pulled up a leather armchair and pushed her forward.

"Heeey!" she yelled, losing her balance.

She landed on her knees, her upper body bent over the arm of the chair. She looked back over her shoulder at me with mock annoyance.

"Be careful," she said. "I might break."

I looked at her, admiring her cute little round ass. Noticing my glance, she wiggled it inviting at me. My cock twitched at the sight.

"I don't hope you break that easily," I said, slowly stroking my cock. "You're in for a rough ride."

"Mmm," she purred. "I like the sound of that."

I knelt down behind her ass and slowly slid a finger into her juicy slit. I moved it back and forth a few times, feeling the heat of her excited flesh. She was incredibly wet, and my motions made her ass wiggle again.

"Ah yeah," she whispered.

I kept going, slowly slipping my finger in and out, in and out of her dripping cunt, teasing her. Her body shivered.

"C'mon..." she whimpered impatiently. "Please. You know what I want."

"No," I lied. "Tell me."

She sighed.

"For fuck's sake, you bastard," she said. "I want your fucking cock. Get it? I want you to fuck me good with that big, hard cock of yours."

I pulled my glistening finger out of her slit and stood up.

"What?" she cried. "No. Don't stop. Fuck me!"

I pulled out a drawer in my desk and got my handcuffs. I went back to the girl, and quickly locked her hands behind her back. She gasped.

"Jesus!" she said. "You really are a kinky bastard, aren't you?"

I knelt down behind her again, my cock now hard as bone, twitching with desire. I grabbed it and aimed it straight at her pussy. As she felt the head of my cock touching her labia, she sighed.

I pushed forwards gently, feeling her flesh yield to my erect tool. Inch by inch I drove it into her, guiding my shaft into the soft wetness of her cunt.

"Ohhh," she moaned. "Push it in. I want that thing inside me!"

And finally, it was. I held still for a moment, letting her feel the length and thickness of my excited cock. Then I took a deep breath and pulled back, almost all the way out of her pussy.

"Okay, baby," I sneered. "This is it."

Grabbing hold of her hair with one hand, I thrust forward, impaling the handcuffed girl on my cock.

"Aaah!" she screamed. "Aaah!"

Again and again I plunged my shaft into her cunt with deep, powerful strokes. I fucked her as hard as I could, hearing her scream out loud with every thrust.

"Fuck! Yeah!" she shouted. "Give it to me hard!"

By now I was sweating from the strain. I felt droplets of perspiration running down my face and my body. My slippery cock pumped in and out of her juicy cunt, and I felt her trembling as her orgasm approached.

"Come for me," I commanded. "Now!"

And, incredibly, she did.

"Ahhh!" she screamed, jerking uncontrollably. "Fuck! Yesss!"

As she shuddered in the throes of her climax, I showed her no mercy, but kept on hammering my cock into her in a hard, relentless rhythm.

"S-stop," she shuddered, yanking at the handcuffs. "Please... I can't..."

"What?" I sneered, thrusting away. "Can't handle a good fuck?"

"Oh, please," she gasped, out of breath. "Just wait a second..."

Slowly, I slid my cock out of her moist, pink slit and stood up. Just as well, I thought. I had been just about to blow my load, too — and I didn't want that. Not yet.

"You crazy bastard," the girl said. "You wanna kill me with that thing?"

I didn't answer. Walking back to the desk, I opened the drawer where I'd taken the handcuffs.

"Well," I finally said. "If you don't want my cock — let's try this instead."

I pulled out a large latex vibrator and dangled it in front of her face. She gasped. The thing was even bigger than my cock.

"No!" she protested. "Don't! Please!"

Ignoring her cries, I knelt down behind her and placed the tip of the toy against the mouth of her cunt.

"You see," I said, "the cool thing is: Not only does it fill out your pussy..."

I pushed the dildo deep into her wet flesh.

"Ohhh," she gasped.

"...it also stimulates you. And I think you need that, don't you?"

I turned on the vibrator at the slowest speed. It started buzzing, teasing the tender insides of the girl's excited cunt. She shivered.

"Please," she gasped, "turn it off. I can't... ahhh..."

And she came again. Hands cuffed behind her back, the latex toy vibrating inside her pussy, she threw herself against the arm of the chair, delirious with pleasure. And I stood right next to her, watching, stroking my hard, swollen cock.

"Oh God," she sobbed. "Make it stop!"

"Yeah," I said, masturbating at the sight. "That's good, huh? Just the thing for a randy girl like you. Makes you come really hard, doesn't it?"

She was shaking all over, yanking helplessly at the handcuffs. She looked back at me, cheeks flushed, eyes open wide.

"Please," she whimpered. "I'll do anything. Just take that thing out... Oh, God!"

I couldn't believe it. Once again, she succumbed to orgasm. She cried out in ecstasy, her body shaking convulsively. The sight made me incredibly horny. My cock was as hard as it had ever been, clear fluid dripping from the tip onto my carpet.

I had to fuck her again. I pulled the vibrator out of her slit and turned it off.

"Open your mouth," I said.

She obeyed, and I put the slippery wet dildo between her lips.

"Mmmm!" she protested.

"Yeah," I said. "Like the taste of your own pussy, don't you?"

Quickly, I unlocked the handcuffs. Then I pulled the girl down from the chair, placing her on her back on the soft carpet. I pulled her arms up over her head, and quickly cuffed her again. Now she lay stretched out on the floor, her cute breasts pointing their erect nipples straight at me. I removed the vibrator from her mouth.

"Spread your legs," I said.

She spread her legs wide, and I assumed the position between them, guiding my erect cock towards her slippery cunt.

"Yeah," she whispered, "fuck me again."

I sank my tool into her flesh, making her gasp. Then, resting on my arms, I began fucking her. Slowly, deliberately, I drove my cock in and out, in and out of her wet, burning sex.

"Aaah," she cried.

I moved the entire length of my shaft into her with each thrust, and then withdrew almost completely, every time I pulled back. In and out, in and out.

Gradually, I increased the tempo, plunging into her faster and faster. I could hardly breathe from strain and excitement.

I was about to come. But I wanted to make her come again. I thrust into her deep and hard, making her cute breasts jiggle in time. She closed her eyes, focusing on her growing sensations of pleasure.

"Yes, yes, yes," she whispered frantically, "keep fucking me. Make me come. I wanna come with that big cock inside me. Yes! Yes!"

I could hardly hold out any longer. Thinking only of my own pleasure, I plunged deep into her as hard as I could: One, two, three... And then she came again.

"Aaahhh!" she cried, stretching out on the carpet, pushing her pelvis against mine.

"I'm coming, too!" I cried, feeling my sperm forcing its way up through my cock.

"Show me," she purred. "Squirt all over me."

At the height of my excitement, I pulled out. Grabbing my cock in my fist, I felt my ejaculation starting.

"Unnnhhh," I roared.

A long jet of semen shot out of my cock, splashed across her body and hit her on the cheek. Another spurt spattered across her breasts. Grunting and masturbating, I kept coming, shooting hot creamy spunk across the handcuffed girl's naked body, as she lay there, still dazed and trembling from her last orgasm.

I don't think I've ever spurted so much sperm before. But finally, my climax subsided.

I was completely exhausted. I unlocked her handcuffs and got two colas from the fridge, one for her, one for me.

We sat there, naked, chatting, sipping our colas. Her name was Melissa, and she was the friend of a girlfriend of a friend of mine.

Later that night, she dressed up as a hooker, while I dressed up as a policeman. Then we went down to the parking lot, where I fucked her across the hood of a car until she screamed.

I still see her once or twice a week. She's cute and great fun to be with.

And of course, we fuck like animals.

The Nurses

"I think the patient in room 9 is waking up," nurse Karen said. "I think we should pay him a visit."

"Hmm," Nurse Gina said. "Don't think I've heard of him."

"Nothing much," Karen said. "He was brought in yesterday after a minor traffic accident. Suspected concussion. But he seems to be okay now."

Karen, the tall blonde, opened the door to room 9 and went in. Gina, the just as tall brunette, followed her, and then froze as she saw the figure on the bed.

"Karen, Please!" Gina exclaimed.

The patient was still unconscious. One end of his bed was raised slightly, so that he was half-lying, half-sitting. He seemed to be naked, covered up to his waist by a blanket. What could be seen of his torso was impressively muscular. But his hands... His hands were raised above his head and fastened to the bedposts with leather straps.

Also, he appeared to have an erection.

"What were you thinking?" Gina said. "We have to untie him immediately!"

"Why?" Karen asked quietly. "Before we have a chance to enjoy ourselves? By the way, keep your voice down. You might wake him up."

"Ohmigod," Gina sighed. "You can't do a thing like this. When he wakes up, he'll sue the hospital – and we'll be fired!"

"Sue?" Karen asked, smiling wickedly. "I guess that depends on how well we treat him."

"Treat him?" Gina said. "Now, listen to me. You can't..."

Ignoring her, Karen stood by the bed, pulling the blanket off the patient.

Gina swallowed. He really was amazingly muscular. What was he? Some professional athlete? Those legs, that chest, those arms. And between his legs, a big, hard cock was pointing straight at the ceiling. Gina felt herself blushing at the sight.

"Mister?" Karen asked. "Excuse me, mister. Time to wake up."

The patient stirred slightly, without waking up.

"Mister?" Karen said. "Hello?"

Suddenly, the patient opened his eyes, making Gina take a step back.

"Oh," he said in a muffled voice. "Hi."

"Hi," Karen grinned. "Feeling okay?"

"Um, yeah," he said. Then, looking down at his huge erection, he gasped. "Oh, I'm so sorry!" he added.

God, Gina thought, he is so dazed, he doesn't realize he's tied up.

"Oh, that's alright," Karen said. "Don't you worry about..."

"Hey!" the patient shouted, looking at his tied hands in confusion. "What's this?"

"It's okay," Karen said in a calm, professional voice. "We had to..."

"No!" the patient shouted. "It's definitely not fucking okay! You've tied me up for no good reason. And now you're gonna untie me, alright?"

"Sure," Gina said, "I'm very sorry, but..."

Karen stared at her angrily.

"It's our professional opinion," she said, "– though my less experienced colleague might disagree – that your personal safety would be jeopardized, were we to untie you."

"Hey!" the patient shouted. "You fucking untie me, you hear?"

Karen didn't answer. She simply produced a pair of latex gloves from her pocket and put them on. Then she knelt down between his legs and touched his cock.

"What are you...?" he gasped. "Jesus..."

Slowly, Karen began stroking his erect shaft. Gently, she moved her hand up and down, caressing his hardening cock.

"You're crazy," the patient said, his tied hands tugging at the straps. "Let go of me. You have no right..."

"Relax," Karen whispered. "It's okay."

She kept masturbating him, her gloved hand gently squeezing his bulging tool.

Exasperated, the patient threw his head back.

"Oh, fuck..." he exclaimed.

Karen winked at Gina, who just stood here, frozen in amazement.

"Come here," Karen said, and Gina slowly walked to the bed, staring incredulously at the patient's cock.

As she approached, he looked at her pleadingly.

"Please," he hissed, "make her stop!"

"Aw, come on," Karen said, smiling. "It's just sex. Enjoy it."

The patient was breathing hard, his huge muscles flexing, as she kept massaging his cock.

"Ahhh..." he moaned.

Karen smiled at Gina.

"See?" she said. "He loves it. Men always do. Now let's see how he likes this."

Karen bent over and guided the twitching cock into her mouth. Closing her lips around the shaft, she began sucking it, slowly moving her head up and down.

"No!" the patient yelled. "Fucking bitch! Stop it!"

Then the sensations of pleasure seemed to overpower him again, and he fell back on the bed, panting with excitement.

Gina just stood there, staring at them. She could feel herself getting excited. The situation was absurd, and Karen was obviously insane, but Gina was a healthy young woman with natural sexual urges. And she definitely felt her pussy getting wet.

"Karen..." she whispered nervously.

Karen let the patients cock pop out of her mouth and looked over at her colleague.

"Oh sure," she said. "Go ahead and play with yourself. It's okay."

Gina gasped. She hadn't even thought about it. But now that Karen mentioned it, she realized how badly she wanted to touch herself. Oh, God, even the thought of masturbating made her shiver.

Karen now had her tongue out, licking the patient's stiff cock. Slurping loudly, she moved her tongue around the shaft, making it twitch and swell even further.

"Ohhh," the patient moaned.

His eyes were closed, and his hips began to move up and down in a fucking motion. As Karen once more took his cock into her mouth, his movements made it slide in and out, glistening with saliva.

Gina stood right next to them and let her fingers slip into her panties, caressing her clit. She almost cried out with excitement at

her own touch. But she bit her lip, remaining calm. Gently, she began massaging the base of her clit. God, that felt good. Whimpering slightly, she masturbated as she watched Karen sucking the patient's cock.

He was no longer fighting the sensations, no longer tugging at the straps that held him. Karen's treatment had won him over, had finally made him give in to excitement.

Instead, his face was now hard with determination, as he kept moving his hips up and down, slipping his rigid tool in and out of Karen's mouth. Up and down, up and down, while she obediently sucked his cock, making smacking sounds.

"Yeahhh..." the patient whispered. "Oh, that's so nice..."

Still stroking herself with one hand, Gina unbuttoned her nurse's uniform with the other, then reached inside, fondling her breast.

"Ahhh..." she gasped.

Gina was dizzy with excitement. Masturbating and kneading her shapely breast, she felt pleasure washing over her body, making her tremble.

"You want some?"

Gina opened her eyes. It was Karen talking to her. She had pulled the patient's cock from her mouth and was holding it in her gloved hand, pointing it towards Gina.

"Karen..." Gina gasped.

"Go ahead," Karen said. "Suck his cock. It's really nice. And I'm sure he won't mind. Will you, mister?"

The patient fell back on the bed, moaning.

"Oh, God..." he said.

Licking her lips, Gina knelt down next to Karen. Up close, the patient's cock looked even bigger. Dripping wet from Karen's juices it stood straight up, its bluish head bulging with lust. Gina swallowed once, then she opened her lips and let her mouth engulf his throbbing tool.

"Ah!" the patient shouted.

This time he lay still on the bed, letting Gina move her head up and down. She ran her lips all the way up and down his shaft, swallowing it as far as she could, then let it pop out of her mouth with every stroke.

The patient breathing got harder, and he threw himself about on the bed, yanking at the straps.

"That's good, Gina," Karen said. "Keep going."

"Fuck!" the patient yelled. "That bitch is gonna make me come!"

"I'm glad to hear that," Karen said, smiling. "That was the general idea..."

Gina kept sucking his cock in a steady rhythm, slurping loudly. Suddenly, the patient's entire muscular body became tense, pulling at the straps with all his might.

"Aw, shit!" he cried. "Here it comes!"

Gina let the jerking cock slip out of her mouth and grabbed it with both hands as the patient ejaculated. The first powerful spurt shot several feet into the air, spattering the flushed faces of both nurses.

"Unhhh!" he yelled, pumping his pelvis up and down in his climax. "Unhhh! Unhhh!"

The tip of his rod kept squirting semen, while Gina held it firmly with both hands. Long, white jets of piping hot sperm pumped from the patient's cock, landing on the women's faces and white uniforms.

Finally, his orgasm subsided. Exhausted, he fell back on the bed.

"Ahhh..." he whispered, eyes closed, savouring the afterglow.

The room fell silent. Gina looked from the patient to Karen in disbelief. She couldn't believe what had happened.

Then, eventually, Karen broke the silence.

"Good job," she said to Gina, wiping the patient's semen from her cheeks. "I don't think he will sue us now. Will you, mister?"

"Not if you untie me, no," the patient said weakly. "I mean, fun's fun, and I actually enjoyed that. But, come on..."

Karen laughed.

"Untie you?" she said. "Hell, no, we're just getting started."

"Started?" the patient cried. "No. This is it. You untie me. Right now!"

Karen shook her head.

"And miss the best part?" she said. "Surely not."

She pulled a small table on wheels over to the bed. On it was an electronic device, about the size of an old radio receiver, with wires attached, and a hypodermic filled with a yellowish fluid.

The patient stared at the table, his eyes wide from fear.

"No, please!" he said, his voice trembling. "I can't! You know, I just came. I won't be of any use to you, until you let me rest. Might as well untie me. Look."

He nodded towards his cock, which was already quite soft. Still rather big, but soft.

"Oh, don't worry about that," Karen said, picking up the hypodermic. "We're professionals."

The patient stared in disbelief, as she picked up his limp cock and quickly gave it a shot.

"Ow!" he cried as the needle pierced the tender skin.

"Yeah," Karen said. "That hurt a bit. But I assure you, it's worth it."

The patient let out a deep sigh of frustration.

"Fuck. You're crazy!" he sneered.

"Mmm," Karen said, glancing at her wristwatch. "Now, let's see..."

A few seconds later, the patient's cock began swelling again. Slowly, but surely, it grew and hardened, eventually becoming completely erect. The patient himself just stared at it, amazed at the sudden transformation of his own cock.

"What the..?" he exclaimed.

Gina once more had her hand between her thighs, slowly masturbating at the sight of the man's hard-on.

"So," Karen said calmly. "How does that feel?"

The patient shook his head. His cock was throbbing eagerly.

"Great," he said. "Um, yeah, pretty good, actually."

Karen smiled and picked up the wires attached to the electronic device. They ended in a narrow ribbon, made of a dark material with a golden sheen.

"That's nice," she said. "We'd better make sure it stays that way."

The patient wriggled about on the bed, his eyes fixed on the wires.

"No!" he said. "Fuck, no! You're crazy!"

"Shhh," Karen said, fastening the ribbon around the root of the patient's cock.

Then she turned to face the device, rotating a dial about ten degrees clockwise. A faint buzzing sound was heard, and the patient squirmed on the bed.

"Ahhh!" he shouted.

Shocked, Gina stared at him. Was he in pain? But as she heard him breathing heavily, she realized that it had been a cry of pleasure. His cock was hard as a bone, twitching vigorously at the electric stimulation.

Karen kept her hand on the dial and looked over at the patient. "More?" she asked.

"Oh fuck, yeah," he gasped. "Give it to me. I can take it."

Karen turned the dial a little bit further, making the patient arch his back, sticking his stiff cock out at them. Clear fluid trickled from its tip, wetting the purple head.

"Aaah!" he yelled. "Aaah! That's fucking great!"

Karen stood up, licking her lips, looking down at the bulging erection.

"But really, mister," she said, "we can't just leave you like that, can we?"

Slowly, she unbuttoned her uniform, and opened her white coat. Inside, she was naked except for her panties. The patient gasped at the sight. She was beautiful, long and slender, but still with a distinct hourglass figure, emphasized by her perfectly rounded breasts. Visibly excited, her nipples were hard as pebbles.

"I mean," Karen went on, her voice becoming hoarse, "you need... treatment."

Next, she pulled off her panties, exposing her pussy, her inviting, pink labia crowned by a neatly trimmed, blonde bush. Then she crawled onto the bed, her knees on either side of the patient's legs. Pink and moist, her labia glistened invitingly.

"And I think I know what's good for you," she whispered. "Don't resist."

"Oh, please," the patient gasped, his cock twitching with anticipation. "Please. Let me have it!"

Karen touched herself, gently massaging her cunt. Then, very slowly, she lowered her abdomen, her juicy pussy closing in on the patient's cock.

He almost screamed with desire.

"Oh!" he cried. "Yes! I want to fuck you!"

As her labia made contact with the head of his cock, they let out a deep sigh in unison. Then, as Karen lowered herself inch by inch, his cock slid into her moist crevice, opening her, stretching her soft, warm flesh.

"Ahhh," she moaned, grabbing her breasts, massaging them lustfully, as the patient's tool penetrated her cunt.

Gasping for air, the patient began moving his pelvis up and down, thrusting up into her again and again, as he tugged at the straps, mad with excitement.

"Oooh, yes," Karen whispered, "fuck me. Fuck me good."

Gina moved closer, still masturbating. Fascinated, she watched the patient's hard, swollen cock sliding into her colleague's pussy. Wet and slippery, the throbbing shaft first appeared, then disappeared again into Karen's succulent cunt.

"Yes! Yes!" the patient yelled in time with his strokes.

Over and over, Karen's slick crevice swallowed his hard pole. Gina masturbated shamelessly at the sight. Then Karen let out a mad scream of lust.

"Aaah!" she cried, writhing in orgasm, "Aaah!"

She had come already. Beneath her cool posture, she had been excited as hell. Now her entire body shivered with the climax, her pussy impaled on the patient's pumping cock. It kept thrusting into her, swelling madly, obviously ready to come.

"Turn it down," Karen gasped, sweating from the strain.

Gina let go of her own cunt and stumbled towards the electric device.

"Just a little bit," Karen said. "I don't want him to come just yet."

"Oh, God!" the patient yelled, throwing his head back on the bed.

Gina turned the dial back a notch, and the buzzing sound became even fainter. The patient kept thrusting into her, slowing down slightly. Karen placed both hands on his huge chest.

"Wait," she whispered in her husky voice.

The patient stopped moving, relaxing on the bed.

"Now what?" he said.

Karen slowly raised her abdomen, exposing his glistening cock. Red and swollen, it had obviously been close to ejaculating.

"This," Karen whispered, "is where I fuck you!"

And slowly, she lowered herself again, impaling her cunt on his tool. The patient gasped, as her pussy engulfed him. Then, slowly, she began moving up and down, his cock slipping in and out of her, making little wet sounds with each motion.

Gina began stroking herself again. That cock was just so big and hard and beautiful, and now she wanted it, too.

Yes, she realized, her initial apprehension had all gone. Now that she was excited, she was simply jealous of Karen. Gina wanted that thing inside her, too, wanted it to fuck her, deep and hard. She fantasized about that as she kept masturbating.

Karen's cute little ass moved rhythmically up and down, as she fucked the bound patient.

"Is that good?" she whispered to him. "Do you like it?"

"Ohhh..." he groaned. "I'm coming... I'm fucking coming."

"Mmm," Karen purred. "He's gonna come again. You wanna see?"

"Yeah," Gina gasped. "Please..."

Elegantly, Karen slid off the patient's cock and stood next to the bed. The rigid shaft jerked with anticipation, wet and slippery from Karen's juices. She turned to the device and turned it up slightly, making the buzzing sound increase. Gina watched in fascination, as the patient's cock swelled towards orgasm.

The effect was instantaneous.

"Aaah!" the patient yelled, yanking at the straps. "Aaah!"

He ejaculated with amazing force. Long, white spurts squirted from his twitching cock, shooting several feet into the air.

"Fuuuck!" he shouted.

White-hot semen kept pumping from his rhythmically contracting rod. Gina caught some drops on her fingers, licking it up. Finally, the swollen tool gave one last spurt. It kept twitching slightly, as thick sperm trickled down the shaft, but the patient's ejaculation was finally over.

"Wow," Gina whispered.

"Yeah," Karen said. "And get this: It doesn't go soft."

Gina stared at the patient's cock, and it was true: It looked reddish and sore from fucking, but it was still hard.

"Well, mister," Karen asked. "Are you ready for more sex?"

"Hell, yeah!" the patient shouted. "I wanna fuck! I want the dark-haired bitch!"

Gina jumped at the words. Karen smiled at her.

"I believe he means you," she said.

Gina looked at the muscular man, tied to bed, his huge cock pointing straight at her. She had wanted this to happen. But now she felt a little bit scared. The patient was so excited – and his voice

so demanding. Still, she realized that she would regret it if she didn't just do it.

Slowly, she unbuttoned her uniform.

"Yeah," the patient said. "Take it off. I want you to be naked."

Gina pulled off her white coat and her panties. Her body resembled that of Karen's, but her skin was a slightly darker hue, and her breasts were bigger and heavier, with darker nipples.

The patient grinned lustfully at the sight of her.

"Come here," he ordered. "I wanna fuck the hell out of you!"

Hesitantly, Gina crawled on to the bed, her eyes fixed on the patient's twitching cock. Clear fluid leaked from its tip, trickling down the swollen head. Trembling with excitement, Gina positioned herself so that her thighs were on either side of his legs, his cock pointing straight at her cunt.

She grabbed the erect tool with both hands and began lowering her abdomen towards it, when the patient interrupted her.

"No!" he cried. "Turn around! I wanna fuck your ass!"

Gina hesitated, didn't know what to do. She had tried anal sex with her boyfriend a few times, and the result had been the same every time: After some initial pain and discomfort, she'd been overcome by the most violent orgasms she'd ever had. And the thought of going through that with a strange man – and in front of her colleague – made her feel extremely embarrassed.

"No, please," she said. "I... I can't..."

Naked and shameless, Karen now sat in front of the device, slowly stroking her cunt.

"Oh God, Gina," she whispered. "Let him do it. I would love to watch that."

"Yeah," the patient growled, his cock twitching with anticipation. "Listen to your filthy friend. I'm ready for your ass, baby!"

"Please, Gina," Karen said pleadingly.

Gina sighed and turned around on the bed, sitting with her back towards the patient's face. He grinned viciously as she fulfilled his wish.

Next, Gina grabbed his rigid cock with one hand – it felt wet and slippery from Karen's juice and the patient's own semen. She sighed again, as she guided it towards her anus. Relaxing her muscles, she slowly lowered herself, allowing the stiff cock to penetrate her ass.

"Ohmigod!" she cried.

It was slightly painful, but most of all - it was exciting. She felt her tender ass muscles stretching around the patient's hardened cock. Watching them, Karen masturbated slowly, moaning with pleasure. Gina stared at her wet pink slit, fascinated by the sight.

"Oh, yeah," the patient said, almost drooling with pleasure.

His eyes were fixed on Gina's perfectly rounded ass and on his own cock, half of which was buried inside it.

Then, he pushed his abdomen upwards, penetrating Gina's ass completely, making her scream. Quickly he fell down on the bed, pulling out, then immediately thrust upwards again. He kept going, rhythmically pumping his erect tool into Gina's ass.

Her hands grabbed hold of the bedstead, and she kept her body almost still, while the patient relentlessly kept fucking her ass. With every thrust she gave a shriek of pain and pleasure.

"Ooh!" she cried, "Ooh...! Yes...! Aah...!"

Karen slipped one finger into her moist cunt, then two. Rhythmically, she began fucking herself, watching the bound patient abusing her pretty colleague.

The patient pulled at the straps, his muscular body glistening with sweat. His face was a grimace of strain and lust as he kept pounding his cock into Gina's tight ass.

"Come on," he ordered. "Play with yourself. Masturbate for me."

Gina shivered at the thought. She knew that if she obeyed, she would climax almost immediately. But still, she gently stroked her moist labia.

"Mmm," she moaned, as she began massaging the base of her clit.

She felt the patient's rigid cock thrusting into her ass, driving her ever closer to a powerful orgasm.

And then she couldn't control it anymore.

"Oooh!" she squealed, as she came. "Oooh!"

Her body tensed up, shuddering uncontrollably. As her orgasm washed through her, she felt hot juice squirting from her cunt. The sensation of pleasure was incredible.

Eyes wide open, Karen stared at her colleague. She masturbated slowly now, apparently wanted to delay her own climax.

As the patient felt Gina ejaculating over his thighs, his cock grew even harder.

"Ahhh!" he shouted, still thrusting his cock into Gina's ass. "I'm gonna come!"

Gina kept masturbating feverishly, her hand massaging her wet flesh in a fast, frantic rhythm. She felt the patient's cock bulging, pumping into her ass, and wanted to make herself come again.

She closed her eyes, as she felt the patient's cock begin to squirt inside her ass.

"Unnnhh!" he yelled, thick semen spurting from the tip of his cock.

Gina fell forwards, as she climaxed again. The violent surge of pleasure almost knocked her unconscious. Her head was swimming, as she felt the patient's jerking cock pumping its sperm into her ass.

Karen had come, too. Eyes closed, she fell back on her chair, moaning quietly

Grunting, the patient thrust a few more times into Gina's ass, completely emptying himself into her.

For a few seconds, they were all quiet. But through the daze of her orgasm, Karen heard the buzzing sound and realized that the device was still running.

"Gina," she gasped. "Get off him."

Slowly, Gina got up, the patient's cock slipping out of her ass. It was still erect, the metal ribbon buzzing around its root. Reddish and bulging, it kept jerking, as if about to come again.

They all just stared at the cock – the two women fascinated, the patient slightly alarmed.

"Um, girls," he whispered out of breath, "I don't think I can go on anymore... Could you please... turn that thing off?"

Karen nodded and reached for the dial. But instead of turning it off, she gave it a fast twist to maximum power. The buzzing increased, making the patient scream.

"Nooo!" he cried. "Stooop! Aaah!"

Immediately, he came again. His cock and balls began contracting rhythmically, pumping his semen out in long, white jets. Karen and Gina stood over it, catching globs of sperm on their tongues.

"Mmm," they purred in unison.

The patient threw himself about on the bed, still ejaculating.

Finally, Karen switched of the device. The patient gave a deep sigh of relief.

"Fucking hell," he gasped. "You girls are crazy!"

Smiling, Karen removed the ribbon from his cock. His erection was subsiding now, his red, tender cock finally growing soft.

The two nurses quickly got dressed. Karen pulled the blanket over the patient.

"Thanks," he mumbled, exhausted.

Seconds later, he was asleep.

"Aren't you going to untie him?" Gina asked.

"What?" Karen laughed. "We might be back later, you know."

Gina shook her head. Karen turned out the lights and the two women left the room.

"Poor man," Gina said as they walked down the corridor.

"What do you mean?" Karen asked. "He just had the best fuck of his life. Never heard a man complain about having too much sex. Have you?"

"Yeah, but..." Gina said. "That machine. You could have killed him."

"Well, yeah," Karen said. "Killed with pleasure. Sounds kinda nice, though, doesn't it? Wouldn't you like to be killed with pleasure?"

Gina smiled shyly, blushing.

"You know," she said. "He almost did."

Yes, My Darling - Tonight

I walk up the stairs from the subway into the cool night air. And there in the distance I see the apartment block where you live - a huge, concrete structure towering against the night sky.

This is a working-class area. I wouldn't come here if it wasn't for you, my darling. This part of town is as alien to me as my rich suburban home is to you.

I walk up to the building and look up at your window. Your lights are on - you're home tonight. Good.

I take the elevator, its walls of smeared with obscene graffiti. A lot of lowlifes live around here. But you, my darling, are not one of them.

Stepping out of the elevator at the eighth floor, I pause in front of the door to the left – your door. Even as I read your name below the doorbell, I feel myself getting excited: I can't help recalling your beautiful face, your perfect body, your soft, succulent flesh. And standing there outside your door, I already feel my cock throbbing inside the pants of my business suit.

I don't knock or ring the doorbell. I simply grab the handle of your door and open it. You never lock your door. You really should be more careful, my darling.

I step into your apartment. It's small, but neat. You've decorated it with cheap, but tasteful furniture and you keep it perfectly clean. Another thing I like about you.

Where are you? I close the door behind me, locking it, and look around. Haven't you heard me enter?

But then I see you. Slowly, you move towards me from your living-room. Your eyes are wide open, just looking at me. You recognize me, of course, from the last time, and the time before that, and all the countless times I have come to pay you a visit.

You're beautiful, my darling: Dressed in a short black skirt and a pale pink blouse I don't remember seeing before, but which shows off your shapely breasts quite nicely. And your dark blond hair is

still cut in that pageboy hairstyle I love so much. Standing just a few feet away, I believe I detect the sweet scent of your lovely skin.

How old are you? I've never bothered to find out, but you must be in your early twenties. Yes, you are only half my age. And of course that adds to my excitement.

You stop in the doorway. I know you can't decide whether you should run past me or back off into the living-room again. You should know by now that neither will do you any good.

Oh, you're trembling, my darling: Your lovely, slender legs are shaking slightly as you stand there, staring at me.

"Please," you whisper. "Not tonight."

I don't say a word. I never do. I just watch you as you stand there, trembling, pleading:

"Not tonight. Please. Don't."

Slowly, I walk towards you, my cock swelling in my pants. I grab your hand and pull you towards your bedroom. Yes, I can smell you now: The sweet, intoxicating odour of female flesh. Whimpering quietly, you try to put up a fight, but you're no match for my strength, and I drag you into your own bedroom.

Your bedroom is neat, too: Pastel colours, soft carpets and a big, soft bed. As I throw you onto your bed, you let out a small shriek of surprise. Sprawled on the bedspread, you look at me.

"No," you sob. "Please don't."

You are so beautiful now, my darling. My erection has grown too large to fit inside my pants, and I have to zip down to let my cock out. You stare at my cock: Even half-erect, it's huge.

I stroke my cock. I like touching myself while you watch, and soon I have masturbated myself to an impressive erection: A big, swollen cock, all ready for you, my darling.

Walking up to your bed, I grab your panties and quickly pull them off. I sniff them greedily, savouring the smell of your lovely, young pussy. Then I throw them on the floor.

I kneel down and spread your legs.

"Nooo," you whisper.

But I lean forward, and as I lift up your skirt, I can see your pussy: Your beautiful, young pussy, a soft, inviting slit crowned by a tuft of blonde hairs. I can even smell it: A spicy, delicious womanly scent.

I have to taste it, and I lie on your bed, my face between your legs. As my lips touch your labia, you gasp. My tongue starts licking

your flesh, and the taste of young pussy makes my mouth water. Slurping and dribbling, I lick your slit vigorously, exploring your fleshy lips with my tongue. I drink the taste of your pussy, making your labia all wet and glistening with my saliva.

You struggle feebly, my darling. One arm across your belly is all it takes to hold you down, as I keep licking away at your lovely, tasty crevice. I make my tongue hard and force it in between your labia like a tiny, soft cock. You moan uncontrollably. Moving my head up and down, I slide my tongue in and out of your pussy. In and out, in and out, yes, my darling, fucking you, fucking you with my tongue.

"Nooo," you whimper, "nooo."

The sound of your pleading voice makes me even more excited. My cock is swelling with lust, but I want to make you wait. Instead I pull my tongue out of your tight crevice and slowly insert a finger into your pussy. Slowly, carefully exploring the soft insides of your tender flesh. Then I slide it back out. And in. And out. Slowly fucking you with my finger, rhythmically massaging the moist walls of your sex.

You're writhing on the bed, my darling. You're trying to fight the sensations of pleasure, but it's no use. My finger keeps moving in and out of you. I hear you gasping with every stroke, louder and louder. I feel you getting wet, deliciously wet - allowing me to slip another finger into the yielding wetness, fucking you deeply and thoroughly with two fingers. I look up at your face. Your eyes are closed, your face flushed, you lips parted, trembling. My darling, you are more beautiful than ever.

"Oh, please, no," you cry. "Ohmigod."

Still sliding my fingers in and out of your moist flesh, I kiss your pussy. I lick your labia, sucking gently at your tiny pink clit, making your hips jerk violently on the soft bed.

Sensing you're about to come, I increase my efforts. I poke my fingers rhythmically in and out of you, sucking and smacking at your succulent flesh. I feel your fingers grabbing the back of my neck, forcing my face into your pussy. I lick and lick at your slit, finger-fucking you at a mad, relentless pace.

"Ohmigod," you scream. "Aaah! Aaah!"

Yes, my darling. You have come. Your body lies writhing on the bed, shaken by a powerful orgasm. And slowly I let my fingers slide out of your hot pussy, dripping with your juice.

I lie on my knees between your thighs, watching your beautiful face transformed by ecstasy. As you finally open your eyes, I begin playing with my cock again. You're still breathing heavily, recovering from your orgasm. Your pretty little mouth hangs open as you watch me stroke my rigid shaft.

Yes – I will fuck you soon. Nothing you do or say can stop me now. Watch me masturbate, my darling, and imagine what it will feel like to be fucked by my cock.

I like to tease you – to prolong the wait. But now I cannot wait any longer. My cock is fully erect, and your sweet, succulent pussy is only inches away – wet and inviting.

Slowly, I guide my cock towards the mouth of your pussy, letting the bulging head rest against your labia.

"No," you whisper. "Please, no."

But your hoarse, pleading voice only excites me more, and I let my bulging cock plunge into your slit.

You whimper, as I bury the rigid shaft inside your tender flesh. The size of my excited cock stretches your pussy, filling every inch of your sex.

Again, you try to struggle away from me. Oh no, my darling: With both hands, I pin your wrists to the bedspread. You won't escape. I hold still for a moment, letting you feel your helplessness, before I start fucking you.

Ah, yes, my darling: I gasp with pleasure, as I feel my cock ploughing through your soft, velvety flesh. I fuck you slowly, savouring the sensation: In and out, in and out, letting you feel every inch of my hard shaft.

Do you feel me, my darling? Do you feel me piercing your moist slit, fucking you in a slow, but insistent rhythm? You're writhing beneath me, sobbing loudly as I keep thrusting into you.

You are beautiful, my darling: Your sweet face grimacing slightly from the strain, eyes shut. Like an animal, I lick your face, tasting your sweet female skin. I lick your breasts, suck on your little, hardening nipples, then I bite into one of them.

"Aaah!" you shriek, wincing slightly from the pain.

I increase the tempo slightly, hammering the entire length of my cock in and out of you with every thrust. Your breathing increases, too, until you're gasping for breath in time with my strokes. Yes, my darling, despite yourself, another climax is approaching.

You dig your fingers into the bedspread, and I let go of your wrists. You won't run away. Not now, when I'm fucking you to an orgasm.

I withdraw completely and look down at my cock: It is hard as steel and glistens with your love juice.

Impatiently, you raise your pelvis towards me, offering your hot, yielding pussy to my cock. Again, I want to tease you - and again I can't resist. I cup my hands under your ass and force my erect member into you again, making you scream out loud.

I'm grunting like an animal, as I fuck you hard and fast. You tremble uncontrollably, as I plunge into you over and over, letting you feel the power of my thrusts.

"Oooh," you whimper, "oooh."

Yes, feel me, my darling, feel my cock. Feel how much I lust for you, how hard you make me. Oh yes, I want you to feel every throbbing vein on my rigid shaft, as I fuck and fuck and fuck.

"Oh, my God," you moan. "No, please..."

It is time, my darling: A few more violent thrusts of my hard tool, and you will come. I can't hold out much longer either: I feel my cock swelling, ready to discharge. But I will control myself until I've made you come again. I hammer my cock into your sopping slit, counting every stroke: One, two, three, four...

"Aaah!" you scream, as you climax, kicking your feet beneath me. "Aaah! Aaah!"

Never have you been more beautiful: Your perfect body tensing up with pleasure, your face reflecting the ecstasy you feel. Just a few more thrusts, and I, too, will give in to orgasm. In hard, fast strokes, I bury my cock inside you again and again, until I finally feel myself coming.

Ahhh. Ahhh yes. Ahhh.

As my huge cock starts contracting, I pull out. You open your eyes in time to watch the first spurt of semen pumping out of my swelling cock. I grab it hard with my hand, as my cock starts jerking wildly, spraying your naked body with piping hot sperm.

I love to watch my cock ejaculating over you, my darling, spattering your skin with the liquid of my ecstasy. My gift to you, a thick, creamy gift, brought on by your beauty and my lust for you.

Ah, yes, my darling. Feel my cock. Feel my stiff tool penetrating your ass, as I begin fucking you. Slowly, I pull all the way out and then back in – and out – and in – slowly, slowly, fucking your ass.

You sob helplessly, your ass muscles stretching around the girth of my huge cock, as I plunge into you over and over.

I hear from your breathing that you're getting excited, too. You're gasping for breath, turned on by some sinful combination of pain and pleasure.

"Ah. Ah. Ah," you pant in time with my strokes as I fuck your ass.

I feel the bulbous head of my cock swelling madly, your rectum tightly clenched around it, as I drive my cock back and forth. I grab a fistful of your hair and increase my rhythm, plunging into your ass faster and faster. It's so tight. So incredibly tight. And by God, it feels good.

I'm sweating from the strain and the excitement, the sweat running down my body, lubricating my cock even more, as I keep hammering into your ass. Your lovely tight little ass, my darling.

You're whimpering and sobbing uncontrollably, your face pressed into the bedspread. It could be just from pain, but I sense you're getting excited, too. And sure enough: As I look down, enjoying the sight of my huge cock impaling your ass, I see your little hand, trembling between your thighs, as it slowly begins massaging your juicy slit.

Ah yes, masturbate, my darling. Masturbate for me while I fuck your ass. Make yourself come – with my cock deep inside you. Maybe we can come together tonight. Maybe you'll feel me spurting my semen into your ass,while you masturbate yourself to orgasm. How would you like that, my darling?

The thought turns me on, drives me mad with lust. I keep going, relentlessly hammering my rigid tool into your tight little hole. You're gasping for breath now, eagerly stroking your swollen labia.

I could climax any second, but I want you to come, too. I didn't only come here for my own satisfaction. No, I want to pleasure you, as well. I want to make you scream out loud in ecstasy, while my raging cock explodes inside your ass. You may feel it's wrong, you may feel ashamed. But that's what I want. And I will make it happen.

Yes, my darling, keep going. Masturbate for me.

Your moans of pleasure are getting louder. You're stroking your moist flesh frantically, my swollen cock poking into you again and again. And I can't hold out much longer, either.

Now - come for me, my darling. Feel my stiff shaft stretching your tender ass and come for me.

"Aaah! Aaah!"

You scream out loud, as the climax hits you. With both hands I pin your shoulders to the bed, as you wriggle about, trembling with the pleasure of your orgasm. The ecstasy surges through your struggling body, shaking you for several minutes, making you sob and whimper helplessly.

Yes. I did it. I held out until you came again, But the sight of your violent orgasm is just too beautiful to behold. As I feel the semen bursting out through my swelling shaft, I force my cock deep into your ass, holding still, savouring the unbearable tension, before I explode inside your clenching tightness.

"Unnnh!" I yell. "Unnnh!"

I know, my darling: Usually, I never make a sound when I'm with a woman. I let to let her do the moaning (and I do love the sound of female moans). But when I'm with you, my darling, feeling your flesh, watching your lovely body squirming beneath me, smelling the excitement on your young skin, it all gets to much. And I roar like an animal, my hot semen spurting into your ass.

You gasp out loud, my darling. Yes. Can you feel it? Jet after jet of piping hot sperm pumps out of my jerking cock, squirting deep into your ass. Dizzy with pleasure, I'm also amazed to feel the power of my second ejaculation tonight, as my cock keeps on going, spurting and spurting my sticky cream into you.

Ah yes, my darling. Finally my orgasm subsides. And slowly, slowly, I slide my still semi-hard cock out of your ass. You lie there, exhausted, breathing hard, face down on your bed as I zip up.

I look at you one more time before I turn and leave your bedroom. Yes, you are beautiful, my darling. And when I get home I will still fantasize about you. Maybe I will even masturbate.

But you know I have to leave. Yes, I could spend the night with you, but that would change everything. It wouldn't be the same, then, the next time I came to see you, would it, my darling?

No, I must be the stranger who comes without warning, uninvited The stranger who fucks you hard in your own bedroom. The stranger who makes you come against your will.

You know I'll be back, my darling. And you may be afraid. And you may feel ashamed. But you'll be waiting.

Won't you, my darling?

Volume Three

The Bank Robbers

As soon as Kelly woke up, she reached for the book.

Last night she'd dozed off right in the middle of the best part, and she couldn't wait to read it now. She blinked her sleepy eyes and yawned, as she leafed through the pages to find the spot.

"The leader of the Black Knights held Lady Stephanie in a tight grip, looking her over. Her feminine curves were clearly visible through the thin silk nightgown. Her breasts were rather large, and her nipples had grown stiff in the cool air of the dungeon. The Black Knight laughed fiendishly as she squirmed in his grip. 'Let me go!' she protested."

"Let me go," Kelly whispered as she read.

"Another knight reached under her nightgown, and Lady Stephanie felt the icy cold of his armoured glove touching her thighs, moving further up towards her sex. 'No!' she gasped."

"No!" Kelly whispered, smiling to herself. She lay on her stomach, and her hand quickly found her clit, gently massaging it as she kept reading.

"The Black Knights moved in closer. Lady Stephanie looked from one to the other, only to find their faces hidden by the iron helmets. Through the visors she saw only their eyes, gleaming with sick and unnatural desires. As one knight lifted up her nightgown, she felt the heat of his hardened manhood against her skin. She struggled helplessly, but the other knights tightened their grip, allowing him to stand between her legs."

"Oh yes," Kelly murmured, still touching herself, "give it to her…"

"Horrified, she felt her soft flesh yielding, as he pushed into her. His erect staff filled her female crevice, making her cry out loud in the darkened corridor. The knights grunted with pleasure at the sound of her distress. Her assailant began moving in and out of her, his rigid pole penetrating the moist depths of her tender flesh."

Moaning softly, Kelly masturbated, increasing the rhythm. She felt her juices flowing abundantly over her fingers.

"The knight pulled out of her, only to be replaced by another, his tool even more massive than the previous one. Lady Stephanie screamed in vain, as the perverted knight raped her with deep, savage strokes. And now – oh, the humiliation – she sensed her young body responding against her will to the abuse. Her flesh grew dripping wet, and she felt a tiny spark of pleasure quickly growing towards an inevitable climax."

"Oh yeah," Kelly gasped. "Fuck her. Fuck her good."

She could smell her own excitement – a scent that never failed to turn her on even more.

"Lady Stephanie whimpered, as the knight pulled back and let yet another knight take his place. She struggled violently as a third member thrust vigorously into her succulent sex, pushing her over the edge with stroke after powerful stroke. 'Aaah!' she cried, as the surge of carnal ecstasy washed over her trembling body."

Kelly gasped with excitement. She, too, was only seconds from coming.

"The knight froze inside her, his stiff manhood bulging and twitching. And then it came – a hot explosion of cream, shooting with great force into her aching flesh. Again and again the knight's tool erupted, filling Lady Stephanie with his thick juice. Grunting, he held onto her hips, until he'd emptied himself into her. And then, another knight took his place."

"Oh yeah!" Kelly cried, massaging her clit feverishly, making herself come. "Oh fuck! Oh yeah!"

She fell face down on the pillow as she climaxed, pushing the book aside. The orgasm surged through her, making every fibre of her body tingle with pleasure.

Oh yes. Minutes later, Kelly rolled over on her back and put the book back on the nightstand. It might not be great literature, but it sure did its job, and did it well.

Her fingers were wet and slippery with her own juice. She looked at the clock – she had plenty of time. She could shower and have a decent breakfast and still make it to work on time.

Kelly got out of bed – she always slept in the nude - and looked at her naked body in the mirror. She wasn't thin like some of those anorectic fashion models you see in the magazines. She had feminine curves – rounded hips and full breasts. Her long, dark hair reached down to her nipples.

Yes, she liked her body – in the fifties she could have made it as a pinup girl, she always thought. Too bad she didn't have a boyfriend at the moment. But hey, you never knew what the day might bring.

Smiling, Kelly stepped into the shower.

At half past eight, she entered the bank through the staff entrance. As she walked into the lobby, towards her counter, she was greeted by a familiar, high-pitched voice.

"Hiii Kelly," Gina squealed. "Looking hot today."

Kelly smiled unconvincingly. Yeah, right. Gina stood in her path, tossing her long (fake) blond hair around, giggling in that annoying way she had. And as usual, she was wearing something very tight and very pink, showing off her boobs.

"Hi Gina," Kelly said.

And she knew it was only a matter of time before Gina would start bragging about her love life.

"Boy," she said. "Am I tired today…"

Kelly stood by her till, getting ready to open.

"Oh yeah?" she said.

"Didn't get much sleep last night," Gina giggled. "I met this really cool guy…"

Kelly didn't really listen. She'd heard similar stories before: Gina meets "really cool guy", he comes on to her, she's like "no way", but for some reason changes her mind (the stories were always kind of unclear at this point) and ends up having hot sex all night long with the really cool guy. And somehow she always expected Kelly to be impressed.

Kelly couldn't help wondering what the guy in the story was telling his friends right now: "I met, like, this totally whacked-out slut…" Kelly had met a couple of those "really cool guys". They'd looked like something the cat would complain in writing about having to drag in – and had been unable to form one coherent sentence between them.

"Sounds like you had a good time, then," Kelly said calmly, placing her purse on the counter and switching on the computer.

"Sure did!" Gina replied, beaming with joy. Then she stepped up close and whispered into Kelly's ear: "And it was, you know, at least ten inches!"

She had another giggling fit, and Kelly turned away. Amazing, wasn't it? Thousand of decent, careful, intelligent women are raped and mistreated every day, and this little peroxide slut – an open invitation to danger and abuse - went through life unharmed. Good for her, of course, but still sort of unfair. Kelly almost hoped that one day she would get a nasty surprise. Might teach her a lesson.

"And how was your evening?" Gina asked.

Kelly wished she'd had the guts to tell her "well, I stayed at home with only a bottle of Chablis, a dirty book and my own clitoris to keep me entertained." But what would be the point of that? Gina wasn't even smart enough to know sarcasm when it hit her straight on her cute little nose.

"Oh, nothing much," she said. "Dinner with friends – an early night."

"Hmmm," Gina replied with an absent smile.

The bank's manager, Mr. Denham, walked briskly through the lobby, his shoes clicking on the marble floors. He passed the huge, dark green leather sofas that lined the walls. He was a tall man in his fifties with steel grey hair and actually quite nice underneath his façade of military efficiency.

"Good morning," he said to no-one in particular. "All set?"

Kelly nodded. They bank would open in five minutes, and she was ready. She heard a nervous giggle and shuffling of paper beside her and knew that Gina wasn't. Really!

"Very well," Mr. Denham said. "Walter, let's go. Have a good day, everyone."

Walter, the bank's chief guard, walked to the heavy, wooden entrance doors and unlocked them.

And then...

Afterwards, Kelly would be unable to account for what happened in the next thirty seconds. She only remembered the door being flung open, a chaos of loud noises and general confusion.

She saw Walter lying on the floor, knocked down. And she saw three men dressed in black, wearing black gloves and black ski masks running through the bank, brandishing their guns. One of them jumped on to one of the sofas and stood there, waving his gun and shouting orders.

She was too confused to make sense of the words, but eventually she guessed that they wanted all employees to gather

behind the counter. She joined her colleagues, and sat on the floor, while the bank robbers kept shouting at them.

One of them leaned over her and asked her a question. Kelly could hardly breathe.

"I'm… I'm sorry," she gasped. "What?"

And finally she was able to make out what the robber was saying.

"The safe!" he barked. "Take us to the fucking safe!"

Quickly, Kelly found the keys in her drawer and led him towards the elevator. She noticed that one more robber followed them, the third one stayed behind. Her faculties were slowly returning to normal – she was able to figure out that the third man was going to watch over the hostages.

On the elevator ride down to the basement, Kelly sneaked a look at the two men. One was tall and lean, the other short and muscular. She tried to keep calm, reminding herself that behind the ski masks they were just ordinary men. If she dealt with them in a respectful manner, she would probably make it out alive. After all, they just wanted the money.

The elevator reached the basement floor, and the door slid open. Kelly led the two armed men through the corridors towards the huge underground safe. She unlocked the gate with iron bars and stepped into the chamber in front of the safe.

"This way," she said, and the robbers followed her.

Kelly turned the dials on the safe door. She'd known the code by heart for years, but ironically, this was the first time she used it. As the last lock clicked into place, she turned the handle and opened the safe. The robbers peeked into the safe. There were stacks of bars of gold, silver and platinum, bags of bills and shelves piled with stocks and bonds. The contents of the safe were worth millions of dollars – Kelly couldn't even begin to imagine how many.

The bank robbers murmured among themselves. They obviously weren't prepared for this much loot. Looking at them, Kelly relaxed. And not only that. There was something else going on inside her that she couldn't quite figure out.

With a loud metallic clang, the iron gate swung shut behind them. The two men in ski masks looked over at her, and as her eyes met theirs, the strange emotion got even stronger.

What was it? Kelly leaned back against the walls of the chamber and tried to grasp what was happening to her. And suddenly, images

from the dirty novel flashed through her mind. The vault became the castle, she saw herself as Lady Stephanie. And the bank robbers could almost be a contemporary version of the Black Knights.

Kelly couldn't believe it. Was this in fact turning her on? No, it couldn't be.

But as he tried to banish the thought from her brain, she realized another thing: Without thinking, she had placed herself in a provocative pose – hands behind her back, one leg propped coyly against the wall behind her, and her breasts pushed out. Her body was practically offering itself to the two bank robbers.

And - she was getting wet, as well.

"We're going back up", the tall robber said.

Kelly looked at them, smiling.

"What's the hurry?" she heard herself purring.

And slowly she raised her short skirt, revealing her black panties. The two men stared at her in disbelief. She pulled the crotch of the panties aside, letting them glimpse her neatly trimmed pussy – a moist, pink slit, crowned with a tuft of dark hair.

"We have to go," Shorty said, moving forward. But his partner held him back.

Kelly couldn't believe she was doing this. She felt as if she were watching it all from a distance, looking at some sultry actress in a silly porn movie. Slowly, carefully, she began to massage the base of her clit, feeling the wetness on her fingers. She moaned quietly to herself.

"Okay," the tall one said. "Show us what you got, honey."

Kelly was incredibly turned on. A bit scared, too – what were they going to do to her if she kept leading them on? – But somehow that just added to the excitement. Masturbating, she looked over at the robber, making sure he had a clear view of her pussy at all times.

"You like that?" she gasped.

"You know what?" the tall one said to his partner. "We sure chose the right fucking bank."

Both men laughed, their laughter echoing in the vault. Kelly could see the bulges in their pants swelling as they watched her touching herself. She shivered with pleasure.

The tall robber stood in front of her.

"Okay, baby," came his voice from inside the ski mask. "Let's see what you can do."

Kelly heard the sound of the man unzipping his pants, and immediately his half-erect cock sprang out. It was rather big and quite thick.

"Suck it!" he ordered.

Kelly dropped to her knees on the marble floor and opened her mouth. Slowly, the tall guy pushed his hot, throbbing cock in between her lips. He groaned with pleasure as s closed her mouth around his shaft. She began to move her head back and forth, slurping and salivating, feeling his cock hardening as she sucked it.

"Yeah!" the tall robber gasped, looking over at his partner. "You too, c'mon. Get your cock out."

Slightly surprised, but fascinated, Shorty zipped down and released his stiffening cock. Kelly noticed that it was of medium girth, but slightly longer than the one she had in her mouth now.

Unexpectedly the tall robber pulled his cock from her mouth, the suction causing a loud popping sound.

"Now you try," he said to his partner. "She's fucking great!"

Shorty took his cock in his gloved hand and guided it in between Kelly's lips. Then he thrust forward with great force, driving its entire length into her mouth. She could hardly breathe. Grunting, he pulled out, then thrust it all the way back in. Again and again, he slipped his erect tool in and out of Kelly's mouth.

"Mmm!" she protested, almost gagging on his cock.

"Yeah!" he gasped. "Like that! You like that, huh?"

Shorty grabbed her hair, still fucking her mouth with savage energy. His partner stood next to them, masturbating at the sight, his gloved hand stroking his cock.

"My turn!" he finally said, his erect cock twitching in front of him. He grabbed his partner by the shoulders and tried to pull him away.

His cock still buried deep inside Kelly's mouth, Shorty turned his head and hit his partner on the jaw.

"Ow! Fuck!" he cried.

Then Shorty slipped his cock from her mouth. Kelly gasped for breath. The tall robber aimed a fist at his partner's gut, but his opponent grabbed his arm in mid-air, twisting it. Cursing and panting, the robbers wrestled, their erect cocks bouncing in front of them.

Oh my God, Kelly thought, still kneeling on the floor. They're actually fighting over me. I can't believe it. She was so wet...

Eventually, the two men gave up the fight. For a while they just stood there looking at each other, their stiff cocks sticking out of their pants, twitching.

"What the fuck was that about?" Shorty asked. "Sure, we both wanna fuck her. But I'm pretty sure she can handle both of us. Right, honey?"

Kelly looked at them, biting her lip.

"Yeah," the tall robber said, not even waiting for her to reply. "Just look at her. She wants it. She wants it bad. Well, honey – today is your lucky day. We're gonna fuck the hell out of you. Come here!"

They placed Kelly on her hands and knees on the cold marble floor of the chamber. She felt Shorty lifting up her skirt and pulling down her panties, heard him breathing hard as he saw her pussy for the first time. Then she felt his gloved finger touching her labia, probing her, slowly slipping all the way into her slit. She gasped.

The tall one offered his wet cock to her mouth. She eagerly took it in, feeling it swell and throb on her tongue. At the same time, Shorty's gloved fingers found her clitoris and began to massage it slowly, teasing her. Kelly shivered as he touched her. She felt her juices beginning to trickle down the inside of her thighs.

Shorty knelt down behind her, and she felt the tip of his cock pushing against the entrance to her pussy. She wiggled her hips impatiently, wishing for him to enter. She could almost feel her flesh opening up, begging for his penetration.

And finally, Kelly felt his hard shaft pushing into her pussy. He entered her slowly, inch by inch. She felt every move, felt the hardened tool filling her eager flesh, felt her muscles clenching around his cock.

"Mmm!" she moaned, the tall robber's cock filling her mouth.

Both men began thrusting into her. They fucked her mouth and her pussy, making her body shake. Their rhythm was gentle at first. But gradually they increased the pace, fucking her with greater and greater force. Kelly felt her arousal growing, her juices flowing, soaking the pumping cock inside her.

She moaned with pleasure. The men hardly made a sound. The only noises heard in the vault were their heavy breathing and the wet, rhythmic sounds of sex, as their cocks slipped in and out of her mouth and her pussy again and again. Kelly shivered on the marble floor, feeling their excitement, their concentration, their

determination. They had come to rob the bank, but the only thing on their minds right now was fucking her brains out.

Kelly felt her orgasm approaching, and knew it was going to be a powerful one. She trembled uncontrollably on the floor. The tall one grabbed the back of her neck, as Shorty held onto her hips. That way they could hold her in place, letting her feel the full force of their thrusts.

"Mmm!" she cried, her cries stifled by the tall robber's cock. "Mmm!"

One more thrust, and another, and another. And then Kelly's climax washed over her, like an electric shock tingling through every fibre of her body. Sobbing helplessly, she sucked even harder on the tall robber's cock. She grabbed his buttocks, feeling his muscles tensing up beneath the denim. Tears flowed down her cheeks.

"Unh, yeah," he grunted. "Here it comes, baby!"

His cock twitched in her mouth, swelling slightly. Then, with a violent jerk, he began to ejaculate. Kelly tasted the first spurt of semen, hot and salty, as it shot into her throat with great force. Contracting rhythmically, his cock squirted long, hot jets of sperm into her mouth.

Gasping with pleasure the tall robber pulled out. He held his cock in his gloved fist, still ejaculating. She watched, out of breath, as the semen kept coming, splashing onto her cheeks and her lips.

"Yeah..." the robber whispered through the ski mask.

He grabbed his cock and shook off the last, sticky drops. Then he stood up, his legs trembling slightly. He tucked his cock away inside his jeans and just stood there watching his partner fucking Kelly from behind.

Maybe the sight of his partner coming had turned Shorty on. She felt him increasing his force, thrusting deeper and harder into her tender pussy. She heard him grunting savagely, seconds from orgasm.

"Oh yes," she whispered. "I want to feel you come."

"Ahhh!" Shorty yelled, unable to hold back anymore.

He pulled his cock from her pussy and pushed her skirt aside, as the first spurt of sperm shot from its tip. Kelly felt his white-hot cream landing on her ass.

"Uh, uh, uh!" Shorty grunted.

He masturbated, his cock jerking wildly. Long jets of semen kept pumping from its tip, spattering Kelly's naked ass with thick globs of spunk.

"Ah!" he shouted as his orgasm subsided. "Yeah! Fuck!"

Kelly felt the last, thick drops falling on to her ass. She purred.

Then the two robbers just stood there, looking at her. Shorty zipped up, too. Having satisfied their lust, they now seemed somewhat amazed that this had happened at all. And finally, Kelly got up as well. She felt dizzy - but she felt great. She found some napkins in her purse and wiped the semen off her skin.

"Thanks, guys," she said, smiling. "That hit the spot. So… I guess this is where you take the money?"

"Yeah, well…" Shorty said.

"Well, maybe," his partner said. "And maybe not…"

"What the hell you talking about?" Shorty asked.

"It wouldn't be right just keeping her to ourselves," the tall one said. "Take your clothes off!"

"You mean…?" Shorty asked.

"Take her upstairs, yeah," his partner said. "Now take off those goddamn clothes, honey!"

"Oh, he's gonna love that," Shorty said.

Kelly slowly undressed. She understood. They were going to take her upstairs so that the third bank robber could do her as well. And they wanted her to be naked from the start.

"Yeah," the tall robber said. "He always likes a good piece of ass. Kind of a sick bastard, though…"

"Oh, yeah," Shorty grinned. "You're in for a rough ride, honey."

The robbers looked at her, standing naked in the vault. Her figure was perfect – and the nipples on her shapely breasts stood out, hard and excited.

"That's a good fucking pair of tits, honey," the tall robber said.

"And a sweet little pussy as well," his partner added. "Well, come on. Let's go."

Shorty picked up her clothes and her handbag from the floor. Then they grabbed her arms, led her into the elevator and pressed the button for the lobby.

They stood close in the small car – Kelly could smell the sweat on their skin. Going up, she felt their eyes all over her naked body. But strangely, they didn't try to touch her.

As the elevator reached the lobby, the two robbers dragged the naked Kelly from the car. She saw the rest of the staff still sitting on the floor behind the counter, the third robber keeping watch over them with a sub-machinegun. The eyes of the hostages widened as they saw her coming towards them naked – especially the eyes of the men.

"We brought you something," Shorty said.

The leader turned around and looked her over.

"Nice," he said slowly. "Number One, you take this and keep the hostages in check."

He passed the machine gun to the tall robber – evidently known as "Number One" – who took over the task of guarding the hostages.

The Leader turned to Kelly. She could see his eyes gleaming through the ski mask.

"Hold her," he said to Shorty.

Shorty dropped Kelly's clothes and purse on the floor. Then he swiftly pulled her arms behind her back and held them there. Kelly felt her breasts standing out, exposed to the Leader's gaze.

"She's all yours," Shorty said.

"Looks good," the Leader responded, walking up to her. "Now the only question is: Does she taste as good as she looks?"

He knelt down in front of her and Kelly felt his wet mouth against her pussy. She gasped. The rough fabric of his ski mask scratched the inside of her thighs, as his lips gently sucked her labia, tasting her wetness. She squirmed, but Shorty tightened his grip, making sure she could not get away.

Kelly felt her juices flowing from her excited cunt. The Leader placed his thumbs on either side of her flesh and pulled her labia apart, opening her.

"Mmm," he murmured, his deep voice making her pussy vibrate.

My God, she thought, he's making me so hot. If he starts using his tongue, I'm gonna faint.

And sure enough, next she felt the soft wetness of the Leader's tongue pushing into her sensitive flesh.

"Ohhh!" she cried, her voice echoing in the lobby.

She felt everyone looking at her. What was she doing? While the rest of the staff cowered in fear, she'd willingly let two of the robbers fuck her to orgasm. And now the third one was about to

bring her off once more. She moaned. The thought made her even more excited.

The Leader jerked his head back and forth, poking his tongue in and out of her pussy in a fast, irresistible rhythm. As Kelly panted with excitement, his gloved hands found her breasts. His leathery fingers squeezing her hard nipples, he kept fucking her with his tongue.

"Oh yes!" Kelly cried, mad with excitement. "Make me come! Aaah!"

The orgasm hit her hard, almost knocking her unconscious. Thankfully, Shorty held onto her and kept her from collapsing, as her entire body shivered with pleasure.

The Leader stood up and kissed her, pushing his tongue through the ski mask. Kelly could taste herself on his tongue and almost fainted again. Thirstily, still in a daze from her violent climax, she sucked her own juices from the robber's mouth.

Then, he pulled back. She could see a huge erection bulging and throbbing inside his black jeans. She was turning him on as well.

"Right," he said, his voice cool and steady. "Let's have some fun here. You…"

He pointed to Gina.

"Come out here, where we can see you."

Shaking and whimpering, the blonde staggered forward in her high heels and stood in the middle of the floor, anxiously staring at the robbers.

What are they going to do to her? Kelly wondered. Granted, Gina was an annoying airhead – but she didn't want to see her hurt. But well, on the other hand, perhaps just a little bit…

"Who's the manager here?" the Leader asked.

"I am," Mr. Denham answered, trying to keep his voice calm.

"Okay. You come out here, too."

Mr. Denham stepped forwards, standing next to Gina. He gave her a slight, reassuring nod.

"So," the Leader said. "This little babe works for you?"

"She does, yes."

"Well, today she's going to do some very special work for you. Take your pants off."

"No!" Mr. Denham protested. "This is madness!"

The Leader grinned.

"Jesus," he said. "Well, Miss. I guess you'll have to do it for him, then."

Gina didn't dare object. Wide-eyed, she slowly unbuckled Mr. Denham's belt and unbuttoned his pants. Then she pulled his zipper down.

"Gina…" he began.

Trembling, Gina pulled down his pants and boxers. His cock hung long and semi-erect, visible beneath his shirt-tails. Gina swallowed once, staring at her boss' member.

"Now," the Leader ordered. "Suck his cock."

Gina seemed to be in a daze of fear and confusion. Without arguing, she took the manager's cock into her mouth and began sucking.

"Gina!" Mr. Denham gasped. "No. Please."

But Gina kept going. She began moving her head back and forth, letting his hardening cock slip in and out between her lips. Fascinated, Kelly watched, as the manager's long, veined shaft stiffened, its rough surface glistening with Gina's saliva.

"Oh yeah…" she whispered, wriggling lasciviously in Shorty's strong grip.

The Leader looked at her, grinning.

"You like that, huh?" he asked. "I knew you were a nasty little slut."

Yeah, Kelly loved it. The whole situation was so outrageous. Standing naked at her place of work, watching a colleague giving her boss a blowjob. And with the rest of the staff watching as well. Oh yes, this was making her hot as hell.

The Leader turned to Gina and Mr. Denham. The blonde was still vigorously sucking her boss' cock, which was now completely erect. The manager closed his eyes, breathing rapidly, apparently fighting the impulse to come in her mouth.

"Okay," the Leader said. "Now, honey – stand up and take off your clothes."

Gina let the manager's cock slip out of her mouth with a loud popping sound. Slowly, shaking, she stood up.

"You're crazy," she sobbed. "Crazy."

"Yeah, yeah," the Leader mocked her. "We just want to see your tits and your pussy. Now get those clothes off!"

Sniffing and whimpering, Gina tore her clothes off and stood naked on the marble floor. She was thin and long-legged with

impressive breasts. Kelly wondered whether her breasts were fake, but they looked convincingly real. The sight of her body made Mr. Denham's cock twitch impatiently. The Leader grinned.

"Get on your knees on that couch," he said.

Obediently, Gina placed herself on all fours in one of the sofas. Kelly could guess the rest.

"And you, sir," the Leader said. "Get over there and fuck her!"

"No!" Gina and Mr. Denham cried in unison.

The Leader raised his gun, pointing it at each of them in turn.

"Shut up!" he said. "You two are now in the entertainment business, okay? You're here to show us what we like to see. And what we like to see is a hot, sexy babe getting a good, hard fuck. So when we tell you to fuck, you fuck. Okay?"

Mr. Denham stood behind Gina, his fingers feeling her pussy.

"I'm sorry," he said.

Gina just shook her head, tears rolling down her cheek. Having determined that she was wet, Mr. Denham grabbed his cock in his fist and guided it towards her slit. He thrust his hips forward, burying the entire length of the shaft inside her pussy.

"Ah!" she cried.

Mr. Denham grabbed her hips and began fucking her. Over and over, he drove his cock in and out of the naked blonde's juicy cunt. Kelly stared intently at the scene. She could just imagine what that long, hard cock would feel like, banging into her pussy. How she wished Mr. Denham had been forced to fuck her instead.

The Leader was getting excited as well. He zipped down his jeans, released his cock, and began stroking it with his gloved hand. His cock was hard and thick. Kelly moaned at the sight of it, but he didn't seem to hear her.

"Yeah," he said, his gaze fixed on Gina and Mr. Denham. "Fuck her. Fuck her good."

Clear fluid trickled from the tip of his member, dripping onto the marble floor. Kelly squirmed in Shorty's grip. She stared at the Leader's cock, wanting it – just to touch it would be enough.

Fascinated, the entire staff just sat there, staring as Mr. Denham kept thrusting his cock into Gina from behind. You could tell they wanted to look away - but they just couldn't take their eyes off the sight of their elderly boss fucking his young, sexy employee. Kelly bet that some of the guys were getting erections now. She shook her

head – why couldn't she think about anything but cocks? Damn, she was so hot…

"That's good," the Leader said to M. "Now turn her around. And fuck her like you mean it."

Mr. Denham pulled his cock from Gina's pussy and swiftly placed on her back on the couch. She was trembling now, her face flushed, obviously aroused against her will. Mr. Denham, too, was breathing hard, his cock twitching as he assumed the position between her legs. Gina's eyes widened, as he grabbed the shaft and slowly slid it in between her labia.

"Mmm," she moaned.

Without waiting for further commands, Mr. Denham began pumping his cock into the blonde on the couch. He fucked her in a rough, demanding rhythm, making her whimper. He grabbed her ankles, placing them on his shoulders, allowing his cock to penetrate her even deeper.

The Leader masturbated at the sight, his eyes gleaming inside the ski mask.

"Look at him," he told Gina.

Reluctantly, the couple looked into each other's eyes. It was as if this made the act even more outrageous – like they were now actually lovers and not just strangers forced to perform a sex act by some perverted criminal.

Gina was gasping for breath. As Mr. Denham kept thrusting his rigid tool into her, she shivered with pleasure, as the orgasm hit her.

"Ohhh…" she cried. "Ohhh…"

She dug her fingernails into Mr. Denham's buttocks, as he drove his cock into her again and again.

"Holy fuck…" Kelly whispered.

The Leader laughed.

"What a filthy slut!" he said. "She just loves it. C'mon mister, keep going."

Mr. Denham held Gina down, fucking her with deep, hard strokes. She struggled in his grip.

"No…" she gasped, "wait…"

"Shut up!" the leader shouted. "Don't listen to her, mister. Fuck her as hard as you can."

Gina squirmed beneath her boss, whimpering. Kelly wanted to touch herself, but Shorty held her arms firmly behind her back. She

stared at the couch, where Mr. Denham was fucking Gina with relentless energy.

"Yeah!" Kelly shouted, out of her mind with lust. "Fuck her. Fuck her ass!"

The Leader turned his masked face towards her, nodding in approval.

"Alright," he said. "You heard her, mister. Fuck her ass."

Without a word, Mr. Denham pulled his slippery cock from Gina's pussy and guided it towards her anus.

"No!" she cried. "Don't!"

Grunting with lust, the bank manager pushed forward, forcing the head of his cock into Gina's ass.

"Aaah!" she screamed. "No!"

Mr. Denham kept pushing. Inch by inch he buried his erect cock inside the blonde's tight little ass. She struggled helplessly, as he began thrusting into her anus in deep, slow strokes.

"Play with your pussy," the Leader ordered, stroking his cock.

"I… I can't," she sobbed.

But she still obeyed the command. Her trembling fingers found her clit, and as Mr. Denham kept pumping his cock into her ass, she began to masturbate. Juiced flowed abundantly from her pussy, trickling down over the manager's cock.

"Ohmigod!" she gasped, massaging her clit, "Ohmigod! Aaah!"

And with her boss relentlessly fucking her ass, Gina brought herself to another orgasm. Her entire body quivered uncontrollably on the couch, as her cries of pleasure echoed through the bank.

"Unh!" Mr. Denham gasped. "Fuck!"

He pulled his twitching cock from Gina's ass and held it tightly in his fist, as he began to ejaculate. The first jet of sperm flew several feet across her body, spattering her face and her left breast. With incredible force, Mr. Denham's cock released spurt after spurt of creamy semen, leaving hot white trails across Gina's naked flesh.

Mr. Denham masturbated vigorously, forcing the last drops of sperm from his cock, and finally Kelly saw it beginning to soften.

"Okay," the leader said. "Now you two go and sit with the others."

Mr. Denham zipped up his pants and staggered towards the staff. Several seconds later Gina got to her feet and joined him, naked, trails of his sperm trickling down her skin.

The Leader turned towards Kelly.

"Okay," he said, his excited cock jerking in front of him. "Let's do it."

Kelly looked at him in disbelief. Was he finally going to fuck her?

She spread her legs wide, as he assumed the position between her thighs. The Leader grabbed his thick cock in his gloved fist and placed it at the mouth of her pussy. She whimpered, as she felt its swollen head pushing against her flesh.

Then he swiftly thrust his pelvis upwards, burying the entire length of the shaft inside her.

"Aaah!" she cried.

In her excited state, the sensation was almost enough to make her come. Shorty held her arms tightly.

"Yeah?" the Leader grunted, as he began to thrust rhythmically into her pussy. "You like that? Huh?"

"Oh yeah," Kelly whispered. "I love it. Fuck me. Fuck me hard."

She felt his cock ploughing through her quivering flesh, entering her again and again. The sensation was incredible. Every thrust of his massive tool triggered a surge of pleasure, unlike anything she'd ever experienced.

The leader's eyes were gleaming inside the ski mask. She felt his hot breath on her face, as he kept fucking her. She could feel the eyes of the entire staff on them, watching their every move.

And suddenly, without warning, a powerful orgasm hit her. Caught by surprise, Kelly screamed with pleasure, her savage cries echoing among the marble walls of the lobby:

"Aaah! Aaah!"

Her entire body shivered in ecstasy. As the climax washed through her, she felt the Leader's cock, still relentlessly pumping in and out of her pussy. This was so wrong, and it felt so good. He was raping her, and she came like she had never come before. And she didn't care who saw it. In fact, she wanted them to watch – that just turned her on even more.

Kelly's naked ass wriggled against Shorty's crotch. And through the fabric of his jeans, she felt his cock growing long and erect. And within seconds, she heard the rustling noise of his belt being unbuckled and his zipper pulled down.

"No!" she whispered.

Shorty let go of her arms and instead grabbed her hips, eagerly pushing the head of his cock against her anus. Kelly struggled helplessly, feeling the pain as he entered her inch by inch. His cock felt wide, stretching her rectum as he steadily penetrated her ass. She closed her eyes and tried to relax.

She could smell their sweat. Grunting like animals, the two robbers thrust into her pussy and her ass. Gradually, they synchronized their movements, fucking her in unison. Throwing her head back, she moaned loudly. She let them have their way with her, feeling the amazing force of their erections hammering into her tender holes.

They were mad with lust for her. And she herself was hot as hell, turned on by those two brutes and their vigorous fucking. As Shorty's cock kept thrusting into her ass, the pain was now indistinguishable from pleasure.

This time she felt it coming. The pleasure built up slowly, making every fibre of her flesh tingle as if electrified. And then - the release. The overpowering rush of a violent orgasm, sending her entire body into uncontrollable spasms.

"Ohmigod!" she whimpered. "Ohmigod!"

Quivering in ecstasy, she felt their cocks still thrusting into both her tender openings. Tears of joy flowed down her cheeks. She felt like Lady Catherine must have felt, raped by the black knights in the castle dungeon. Like any woman had felt throughout history, when brutal men had vigorously fucked her to incredible orgasms.

"Yeah!" Shorty said. "I'm gonna blow!"

The men both pulled out. Through a haze of pleasure she saw the Leader's cock twitching, red and swollen, about to ejaculate.

"Get down on the floor!" he commanded, grabbing his cock. "On your back!"

Kelly almost collapsed onto the cold marble floor of the lobby and spread out on her back. The two masked men stood above her, their gloved hands stroking their erect cocks. Clear fluid dripped from their tips onto her naked breasts.

"Oh God," she whimpered, writhing.

And then they came. Shorty's cock went first, releasing a long, white spurt of hot semen that landed on her face. Before he fired a second time, the Leader let out a yell, as he, too, began to ejaculate. A jet of creamy sperm shot from his jerking cock, hitting her across the breasts.

Kelly opened her mouth. Grunting and yelling, the two bank robbers aimed their cocks at her mouth, pumping spurt after spurt of semen at her face. She tasted the spicy drops on her tongue, licked them from her lips and swallowed load after load of their abundant sperm. They seemed to ejaculate forever, masturbating, emptying themselves of every drop of creamy semen.

And finally, it was all over. Panting exhaustedly, the two men stood above her, their cocks slowly growing soft. They tucked them into their pants and zipped up.

"Yeah," the Leader whispered.

Kelly just lay there, feeling the flecks of sperm turning cold on her naked skin.

She heard the tall robber giving orders to the hostages, telling them to remain calm and not to use the alarm for the next half hour.

The leader bent down to help her up.

"We're leaving now," he said gently. "We're taking the money and making a run for it."

Kelly found some paper napkins in her purse and used them to wipe the sticky stains of semen off her body. Then she picked up her clothes and got dressed.

"Yeah," Shorty said. "Make sure your colleagues keep quiet, okay?"

Kelly looked over at the staff, huddled on the floor behind the counter. Gina caught her eyes. Her gaze was scared, but there was something else, as well. It was almost as if she was... jealous? Yeah, that was it. Kelly was sure of it now. Gina – naughty, sluttish Gina – would have loved the treatment the robbers had just given her.

Well, it had been pretty hot. But to be perfectly honest, Kelly didn't think Gina could have coped. Kelly was a bit sore, but she felt great. Not only had she endured the rough desires of the three bank robbers. She had actually discovered that it gave her an immense pleasure – a pleasure greater than she'd ever imagined.

Yes, she felt great. Previously, she'd been convinced that Gina was the naughty one – the one with the wild sex life and that she was a bit on dull side herself. But in fact, Kelly was the one with the raw, savage sexuality. She wouldn't have thought she could ever do this: Letting three masked men fuck her raw, driving her from climax to climax. While in fact she had been the one wearing them out, letting them have their way until they'd finally succumbed to their lust for her, emptying their balls of all their pent-up juices.

She felt proud – she felt like a real woman. Not afraid of her desires, however dark and twisted her fantasies. Today she had faced her sexual demons, bringing incredible pleasure both to herself and the three men.

"Are you okay?" the Leader asked. "You'll keep an eye on them for us, right?"

Kelly, now fully dressed, straightened her hair and smiled at him.

"On them?" she giggled. "Hell no, boys. I'm coming with you!"

The three robbers laughed. Then they led her through the lobby and out the doors to their car. On the way out she felt the Leader's gloved hand grabbing her ass.

She was in for a rough time with these guys.

Hopefully.

The Gas Station

In her dream, she is naked.

She is all alone, naked except for her high-heeled shoes.

She's standing at a gas station in the middle of the desert. The midday sun is high in the sky, and the air is burning hot.

She looks around. Behind the gas station steep mountains reach for the sky. In front of it the highway stretches out for miles. But there's not a car in sight.

She walks back and forth in front of the gas pumps, but still there is no traffic.

Even the gas station itself looks deserted. The pumps are rusty, the windows dirty. It looks as if no one has been here for years.

How did she get here? And why? What happened to her clothes?

She has no recollection. But for some strange reason she's perfectly calm. She has a feeling that it's okay. She's supposed to be here. And it's okay to be naked. It's too hot to wear clothes, anyway.

She looks out towards the highway again. Something has happened. There's still not a car in sight, but now a man is standing in the middle of the road.

He is naked, too. A muscular man with a deep tan, wearing only a pair of black boots. He just stands there, looking at her. She can't help but look at his cock. It's long and semi-erect.

Slowly, she walks towards him. He watches her intently, studying her naked body as she walks along the highway. She feels her breasts bouncing gently with each step. She feels exposed to his lustful gaze, but that's okay. Keeping her eyes fixed on the man's rising cock, getting closer and closer, she has a feeling that this is it. This is why she has come here.

Now they're standing face to face. She in her high-heeled shoes, he in his boots, his long cock swelling and growing. A blanket is lying on the road in front of him and he nods at her. But she already knows: It is for her.

Obediently, she kneels down, sensing the burning heat asphalt through the blanket. His twitching cock is inches from her face. She opens her mouth wide, and he skilfully steers his cock in between her lips.

She starts sucking the man's cock. The salty taste of his rigid member excites her: This is it. Now it has begun. And somehow she knows there is no turning back.

The highway is silent. As she lies on her knees in front of the naked man, all that can be heard are the wet, slurping sounds she makes as she sucks his cock.

Grunting, the man grabs hold of her hair and starts moving his hips back and forth. Wet and stiff, his cock slides in and out of her mouth. Teasingly, she moves her wet tongue around the shaft, feeling the veins swelling, as the man's cock grows even harder.

Excitedly, he increases his speed, fucking her mouth with deep, eager strokes. He's very excited now, and she swallows repeatedly, letting him have his way with her mouth.

Suddenly, he pulls his cock out of her mouth and helps her get up. Taking her hand, he walks with her toward the gas station.

From behind one of the pumps another man appears. He, too, is naked, wearing only sunglasses. And he, too, has a huge erection.

She hesitates. But somehow she knows it's no use. What will happen here today is beyond her control. There is nothing she can say or do that will change it.

The newcomer stands between to gas pumps, his erect cock pointing straight at her face. Gently, the other man grabs her shoulders, bending her over. She opens her mouth and lets the man in front of her slip his cock in between her lips. She begins sucking it. It is warm and hard and has a slightly different taste from the one before.

The first man stands behind her now, gently fingering her cunt. She is wet. She is very wet. His finger pokes her slit, slowly exploring the wetness inside her. She is trembling with pleasure, as he slips it back and forth, making tiny wet noises.

The second man's cock fills her mouth. He moves his hips slowly back and forth, as if he's savouring the sensation. She can feel every inch of him in her mouth, her tongue exploring his hard, veiny shaft.

The first man slips his finger out of her cunt. But then she feels him pulling her labia apart ever so slightly with his thumbs. She

knows what is coming now. Something warm and bulging touches the mouth of her pussy, and she knows it is the head of his cock.

She salivates around the second man's tool, slurping excitedly, while the first man's cock is slowly stretching her cunt muscles. Inch by inch he pushes forwards, filling her completely with his rigid meat.

The second man grabs hold of her hair and increases his rhythm. With steady thrusts, he keeps sliding his hardened cock in and out of her mouth. The first man holds still, his cock swelling and throbbing inside her flesh.

She knows than soon he will start fucking her. The wait is unbearable. But finally it happens. The first man pulls his tool all the way out of her cunt and immediately rams it back. The thrust almost knock her off her feet.

Now, both men grab her, holding onto her as they pump their cocks into her - one into her mouth, the other into her pussy. Again and again, she is poked by their excited rods. They fuck her in a fast, demanding rhythm, making her think they want to bring themselves off. But soon she realizes how wrong she is. They don't want to come themselves – they want her to come.

With unfaltering strength, the first man keeps pumping his cock into her wet cunt, driving her closer and closer to her climax. Tears of joy run down her cheeks. The pleasure builds inside her, sending ripples of electricity through her entire body, brought on by the hard cock hammering into her flesh.

Gratefully, she sucks the second man's cock, shivering with lust. The first man pulls out of her, then buries the entire length of his shaft inside her cunt, then pulls out again. Over and over, he repeats this long sliding motion, the width of his cock stretching her moist labia. With each thrust she feels every inch of his rock-hard member.

Now she can take no more. Swallowing hard, almost choking on the second man's cock, she feels the orgasm overpowering her. Her cunt muscles clench around the magnificent cock that has brought her off. Trembling in ecstasy, she feels her juices flowing down his erect shaft.

He doesn't stop. Neither of them do. She is about to faint with pleasure, but they show her no mercy. They just hold onto her hard, pumping their ever-rigid cocks into her mouth and pussy.

But then, the second man pulls his cock from her mouth. Panting, out of breath, she looks up at him. Seeing the excitement on his face, she grabs his wet cock with both hands and begins masturbating him. The shaft feels hot, throbbing with excitement in her hands. She wants to make him come, as if that would somehow stop the first man's cock relentlessly hammering inside her pussy.

But it's no use. The second man just grins at her, enjoying her treatment, while the first man keeps fucking her, sliding his cock in and out of her cunt in deep, rhythmic strokes. Sighing, she bends over and takes the second man's cock in her mouth again, her lips closing around his hardened tool. Gently, she begins sucking it, feeling it swell, and tasting the liquid oozing from its tip.

She closes her eyes, once more giving in to the sensations of pleasure. She feels the long cock sliding in and out of her cunt, teasing her, driving her towards another climax.

But suddenly, the first man pulls out, leaving her pussy feeling empty. The second man, too, pulls his cock from her mouth. Then he takes her hand and leads her away. The first man follows behind.

Her head is spinning. She still doesn't understand what is going on. She just comes along, letting the two men use her as they please.

Behind the gas station, in the midday sun, the man pulls her towards an old, abandoned bus. By now, it is no more than a rusting wreck. The second man climbs into the bus, pulling her with him.

Inside the bus, the heat is unbearable. The sun beats down on the wreck, making the air inside so hot it almost burns her skin. The first man enters the bus, too, and they make her stand in the aisle between the seats. Now, the first man, who has just fucked her, stands in front of her, and the second man behind.

Before she knows what's happening, the second man's cock slides into her slippery cunt. It feels somehow different, stretching her soft flesh, letting her feel its rough surface. As he begins pumping it into her, she feels every inch of it as it slips in and out.

The first man stands in front of her, his tool standing at attention, pointing straight at her mouth. He looks at her, demandingly, as if he doesn't even have to ask. As if she's supposed to know what is required of her.

And she does know. Without a word, she takes his cock into her mouth. Its taste is different now, and she realizes why: It's the taste of her own pussy. Somehow, this turns her on, and she

greedily sucks the juice off the first mans cock, licking up the taste of her own excited cunt.

Sensing her excitement, the second man increases the depth of his thrusts. He doesn't speed up, but buries his cock up to the root with each thrust, completely filling up her yielding cunt. Feeling his power, she's excited, and her juices flow copiously, soaking his hardened tool. Invitingly, she lifts her leg, placing one foot on the seat next to her, allowing him to penetrate her even deeper.

Her mouth is watering, her saliva drenching the first man's cock as she sucks it noisily, slobbering rhythmically around his erect shaft. As the second man's cock keeps moving inside her pussy, she feels another climax approaching. Her legs are trembling, and the man fucking her grabs her hips, holding her up. She relaxes, letting the lustful sensations of pleasure overwhelm her. And finally, she comes again.

"Mmmm! Mmmm!"

Her screams of pleasure are muffled by the huge cock filling her mouth. But both men sense her climax. She is momentarily drained of all energy, feeling like a helpless rag doll in their hands. And she just knows that they love it.

Both men pull out of her, their reddened and excited cocks dripping juice onto the floor of the bus. Their hard-ons are as huge as they've ever been. How can they go on? she wonders. Will they never come? Will they just keep fucking her forever and ever? And will she be able to take it?

The man she was sucking sits down in the middle of the wide back seat of the bus. Then he pulls her towards him, making her sit on his lap. As she does so, he parts her ass-cheeks with both hands, guiding his wet, erect cock towards her rectum,

She gasps and frantically tries to pull away from him, but his strong hands keeps pulling her down onto his cock. The other man, too, steps up and pushes her hips down. And now she feels it happening: Wet and thick, the head of the seated man's cock forces its way into her anus.

She gives up the fight, instead trying to relax, as the entire length of his cock slowly slides up into her, filling her ass. The man then holds her still, his tool throbbing inside her tight canal.

The other man is visibly excited, masturbating at the sight. He pushes her thighs apart and positions himself between her legs. His

erect cock is pointing straight at her pussy. She looks at him, incredulously. No, she thinks. He wouldn't...

The other man grabs his cock, guiding it towards the entrance to her cunt. She feels the bulging head pushing against her labia, the seated man's cock filling her ass. As the standing man pushes forward, she looks into his eyes. His face is expressionless, but she sees his pupils dilating as his erect shaft slides all the way into her succulent cunt.

Her ass and pussy are both penetrated by their massive cocks. She can't believe this is happening. And what about the men? Were they really expecting her to give in to them in this way? Now she is at their mercy. And she senses how excited this is making them.

The man in front of her grabs her hips and lifts her up. She feels both cocks sliding out of her body, out of her ass and her pussy. Then, he lowers her, letting them penetrate her holes to the root. Again he lifts and lowers her sweating body, up and down, up and down, allowing their bone-hard tools to fuck her tight openings.

Her head is swimming from the dry heat inside the bus and from the powerful stimulation of her sensitive holes. She struggles as she feels her climax approaching, pushing against the muscular torso of the man in front of her. But it is no use. Relentless, he raises and lowers her helpless body, increasing the rhythm. The two cocks impale her tender flesh over and over until she loses control.

"Aaah!" she cries.

Throwing her head back, she comes. She almost faints from pure pleasure, as a violent climax washes through her body. Her love juices gush from her spasming cunt, drenching the cock that's poking her pussy. The man in front of her keeps lifting her up and down, faster and faster. She hears the men breathing harder and harder and feels their long cocks swelling inside her holes.

Suddenly, the man in front of her lifts her up by the shoulders, letting both cocks slip out of her with a wet sound. He forces her down on her knees on the floor of the bus. The men stand above her, pointing their erect cocks at her, ready to blow.

Still dazed from her orgasm, she takes a cock in each hand and begins stroking them. The men gasp, thrusting her hips back and forth as she masturbates them. Clear fluid drips from the tips of the cocks onto the floor. She keeps going. The men tremble as the bluish heads of their cocks swell in her hands.

And then it happens. The first long, hot spray of sperm shoots from one cock, hitting her naked breast. Then the first spurt shoots from the other, spattering her cheek. She keeps masturbating them, as they ejaculate, shooting semen onto her face and breasts. Squirt after squirt of thick, piping hot spunk keeps pumping from the two men's excited cocks.

Still, even in the throes of orgasm, the men hardly make a sound. Only their laboured breathing accompanies their powerful ejaculations. And finally, they too subside. She keeps stroking their cocks, squeezing the very last drops of sperm out of them. Then, slowly, their erections wear of, and the cocks feel soft and hot in her hands.

Still kneeling on the floor, she watches, as the men quietly turn around and exit the bus. She wipes a drop of semen from her breast, tasting it. It is very salty.

Slowly, she gets up and looks out through the dirty windows of the bus. The men are gone. But where did they go? How could they disappear so quickly?

And that is when she realizes that it has all been a dream.

Sheryl was still shivering as she woke up.

It took her a few seconds to recognize her own bedroom - and to realize that it had all been a dream. There had been no gas station, no broken down bus - and no men.

She was wet. She must have come in her sleep – perhaps more than once.

As she looked at the clock on her nightstand, she realized she was already late for the appointment. She ran into the shower.

Minutes later, Sheryl was in her car, heading for the appointment. Soon, she was several miles out of town in an area she didn't know and had to check with the map. Yes, she was on the right way.

But somehow, the landscape seemed strangely familiar: The desert, the highway, the mountains in the distance.

As Sheryl saw the abandoned gas station ahead, she shivered in the desert heat. She slowed down and drove up in front of the gas pump. Yes. She recognized it all: The dirty windows, the rusty pumps.

Hesitantly, Sheryl got out of the car.

She unbuttoned her blouse, letting it drop to the ground. Then her skirt, her bra and panties. Finally, she was completely naked. And naked, she walked towards the gas station.

The Warehouse

Tanya could hardly concentrate on her work. Her thoughts kept returning to the proposal - the proposal made to her by the men in the warehouse.

And every time, she was enraged and had to get up from the computer, annoyed. What were they thinking? What the hell were they thinking?

About 10 p.m. one of her co-workers had told her, that the guys in the warehouse wanted a word with her. Tanya had wondered about that - usually she wasn't in touch with the warehouse at all.

So, leaving her office and crossing the yard to the big warehouse building, she was a little bit curious.

I was a big, chilly room, with cardboard boxes stacked all the way to the ceiling along every wall. And seated around a tiny desk in one corner, the men sat drinking coffee. There were three men working there today, and she just barely knew their names: The young, skinny apprentice was named Johnny, the handsomely built guy in his mid-twenties was named Rick, and sitting at the head of the table was the oldest of the men: The stout and somewhat grumpy looking Sven.

Rick had spoken, and Tanya hadn't believed her ears. They wanted sex with her - all three of them.

"I know it sounds rude," Ricky quickly added. "But please let me explain."

Tanya leaned against the huge metal door, listening. The men looked at her curiously, as if judging whether she could be persuaded. Raising her chin, she looked at them with quiet contempt.

"You can say no and leave," Rick said. "Actually we're already out of line here. If you want, you could get us fired."

It hadn't occurred to her. She wondered why Rick would even mention it.

"And don't think we disrespect you," he went on. "A lot of girls fantasize about sex with several men. And - well, we thought you might be one of them."

In a flash, Tanya imagined herself lying naked on the table, surrounded by the three men. She imagined their erect cocks, tasting one on her tongue, feeling one in her pussy. The men's hands caressing her naked body. Herself climaxing on the table, the sound of her screams echoing between the boxes in the storage room.

Confused, Tanya shook her head. Where did she get those ideas, anyway?

"But if you're not into that kind of stuff," Rick went on. "We're very sorry, and of course you're free to leave. But if you should change your mind the offer still stands."

Tanya hadn't thought of anything to say. Silent and confused, she'd left the warehouse and returned to her seat in the main building.

What the hell were those jerks thinking? She was seething with rage, but even so the images of sex with the three men kept returning, distracting her even more. The more she tried blocking them out, the more vivid they got.

Now young Johnny was pumping her strong, powerful cock into her. Then Rick's beautiful cock was fucking her. And then the thought of Sven brutally attacking her pussy made her shiver with lust.

Damn! Couldn't she think of something else? Tanya looked out the window. The sun was shining on the parking lot from an almost cloudless sky. ("A lot of girls fantasize about sex with several men.)

Tanya didn't really fantasize much about sex at all. She was single at the moment - and why get all hot and bothered about something that wasn't going to happen? Or was she repressing some desires? Had the men's rude proposal brought them out into the open?

Whatever. Maybe fantasizing about sex with several men was fun. But she knew one thing about fantasies: Never try to live them out. It was bound to be a disappointment - never as exciting as the fantasy.

("But if you should change your mind the offer still stands")

Tanya got up quickly and went to the restroom. There was something to be done about this.

She locked the door and stood in front of the mirror. She saw her hard nipples poking the fabric of her shirt, and without thinking she gently caressed her breasts with both hands. Oh, that was wonderful. Moaning, Tanya closed her eyes. She kneaded her breasts, pressing them together, massaging them hard. She was getting hotter every second.

Then she unbuttoned her jeans, pulling them off along with her panties. Tanya studied her pussy in the mirror. Her juice made the labia glisten and the curly hairs stick to her skin. Parting her wet pussy lips with two fingers, she exposed her tiny, swollen clit. She caressed it hesitantly and shivered with lust. Then she started masturbating.

Yes, that was wonderful. And now - finally - she allowed herself to think of the men in the warehouse.

One by one she saw them pull out their cocks: Johnny, Rick, Sven. Stiff, throbbing cocks just getting ready to fuck her. Mmm, yeah. Tanya rubbed her pussy, overcome by desire.

In her mind they came towards her. She was lying down and they stood around her, showing off their erect cocks. "Yes," she whispered. "Fuck me."

She lay there watching them calmly masturbating. The laughed at her, softly. "What was that?" Rick said.

"Fuck me," Tanya repeated. "Fuck me, all three of you. Please fuck me."

But suddenly a distinct voice cut through her fantasy. She thought it sounded like Sven.

"No," the firm voice said. "Not here. Not here, Tanya. Only in reality."

Letting go of her pussy, Tanya jumped away from the mirror. She looked around, confused. What was happening here?

Out of breath she sat down on the toilet seat and wiped her dripping wet fingers with a paper towel.

She pulled up her jeans. What the hell was going on here? She couldn't even masturbate anymore? Apparently, that damn fantasy had taken over completely. Well, okay - only one thing to do then.

Tanya left the restroom, passing the reception on her way out.

"I'm just going over to the warehouse," she said.

- - -

The huge metal gate of the storage room slammed shut behind Tanya, startling her. The men looked up in surprise and saw her.

Again they were sitting at the small table, studying something. A porn magazine?

Either way, there was an air of hot lust about the men. They had been waiting. They had been fantasizing about her, too, ever since she'd left.

Their desire made Tanya brave, devil-may-care. She locked the door so that no one could come in and interrupt them. Johnny and Rick stood up. Sven remained seated at the head of the table, staring at her.

No one said a word. No one came over to her. Tanya took a deep breath. She didn't dare. Yes, she did ... she had to ... she couldn't help it. And trembling with excitement she did what she had been dreaming about:

Tanya pulled of her jeans and panties, exposing her dripping wet pussy to them. Leaning against the cold metal gate, she masturbated in front of the men, like she had been masturbating alone. But this turned her on so much more. Madly, she rubbed her tender clit, panting with lust. Then she pressed two fingers inside her pussy and started fucking herself with them.

The men watched her attentively and she heard them grunting approvingly. This turned Tanya on, making her shameless with lust. She spread her shapely legs wide, thrusting her outstretched fingers in and out of her soaking wet pussy.

"Oh, oh, oh," she moaned loudly in time with her finger-fucking.

She looked at the three men. Cocks were swelling in Johnny's and Rick's workpants. Young Johnny stared at her with wide-open eyes, gasping for breath. But Sven just sat there, not moving a muscle - utterly unmoved by Tanya's sexy performance.

She was about to come. But she felt like waiting a little. Slowly she let her fingers slide all the way out of her pussy. Then she put them to her lips, licking her own hot sex juices. Rick moaned deeply at the sight and she caught his eye, as she teasingly let the tip of her tongue lick her fingertips.

She hadn't noticed that young Johnny had joined her. He knelt down, sniffing the smell of Tanya's hot pussy. And suddenly she felt his wet tongue between her legs.

Tanya moaned loudly, as Johnny's thick tongue poked its way in between her labia. She clenched her pussy muscles around it, but Johnny kept pressing and squeezing his tongue further and further

inside her. All the way, letting the tip of his tongue explore the velvet folds of her cunt.

"Ah, ah," she sang out, her legs trembling beneath her. But his amazingly strong arm grabbed her, holding her pressed against the cold metal door.

Slurping greedily Johnny tasted the love juice flowing down his chin, as his twisting tongue slid in and out of her pussy. Tanya felt his hot breath against her abdomen as he panted with excitement.

She was trembling all over from desire. She grabbed the back of Johnny's neck, pressing his face against her slit. She her Johnny grunting, as his tongue thrust all the way into her red-hot slit. And then she climaxed.

"Aaah!"

She nearly passed out with ecstasy. And just like in her masturbation fantasy Tanya's screams of orgasm echoed in the storage room. Shamelessly slurping, Johnny drank her juices as her body squirmed in orgasm.

"Oh," Rick moaned lustily, squeezing his swollen cock through the fabric of his work pants. Without further ado, Sven stood up and started clearing away coffee cups and porno magazines from the small table.

Johnny stood up. He still had to hold on to Tanya, who was completely exhausted. Now Rick joined them. And as Sven gave a sign, the two men lifted her up and carried her to the table.

They placed her on her back on the table and stood around her. Rick unbuttoned his pants, letting his erect cock jump out. It must have been well over eight inches long and stood vibrating in front of Tanya's face. She gasped at the sight.

Panting, Johnny, too, fumbled with his work pants, finally getting his cock out. It was long and rather thin, but already hard as a rock. The foreskin was rolled tightly behind the huge bluish helmet, swelling madly before her eyes.

At the head of the table, Sven sat smiling fiendishly.

Without a word Rick grabbed his cock, slamming it repeatedly against Tanya's red lips. She immediately opened her mouth, letting the stiff, hot cock slide in. She sucked it gently, and Rick gave a loud gasp.

Johnny stood between her legs and parted her pussy lips with two fingers, making Tanya squirm with pleasure. She was about to

talk to him, beg him to fuck. But at that moment, with great force, Rick pressed his cock deep into her throat.

Tanya choked and swallowed, as Rick brutally started thrusting in and out of her mouth. She could tell that Sven was enjoying the sight.

Young Johnny was getting hot, too. He let go of her pussy with one hand and instead slid his long cock into her. Tanya pulled her mouth away from Rick's cock. She just had to cry out with lust, as Johnny thrust deep into her: "Oh yes. Oh yes."

Johnny's cock got wet and slippery from her hot juices, and rhythmically he started pumping in and out of her cunt.

Grunting impatiently, Rick grabbed the back of her head. The only thing on his mind was his own cock and how to use Tanya's soft, wet lips to satisfy his desires.

Obediently, she licked the stiff, trembling member, the tip of her tongue playing teasingly around the helmet, tasting the clear liquid starting to flow from the tip. Then, finally, she took it into her mouth, rhythmically sucking his swelling cock. Rick gave a deep moan of excitement.

Johnny fucked her in a steady rhythm, getting ever more aggressive. His long, rock hard cock thrust into her tender pussy, over and over. Tanya spread her legs for him, twisting with pleasure. Servicing two men at once turned her on. To be available – their sex toy. It turned her on like nothing she'd ever known. And Sven watched it all unperturbed: Watched them fucking her, savouring the sight of her helpless lust.

Johnny's cock swelled madly in her pussy. "Ohhh," he yelled. And suddenly he froze between her legs - and his cock started ejaculating. Climaxing, Johnny yelled out loud, as Tanya felt his member spitting hard jets of hot sperm way up into her pussy.

Rick pulled his cock out of her mouth and nearly pushed Johnny out if the way to get at her pussy. He was almost drooling with lust, as he placed his swelling cock at the mouth of her pussy. But with intense concentration, he inched his hips ever so slightly forward, letting only the exposed head of his cock slip inside her – and then he held it still.

Gasping, Rick let his bulging helmet feel the burning heat of Tanya's pussy. Then he bent over her.

"Do you want it?" he snarled. "Do you want my cock?"

"Mmm, yeah," Tanya begged. "Give me your wonderful cock. Fuck me."

Sven grunted with satisfaction. He enjoyed watching Tanya humiliated by her own lust.

"What do you want?" Rick barked. "What? What?"

She saw Sven unbuttoning his workpants. And she shivered at the sight: His cock was enormous - a monstrous, thick member, blue veins swelling beneath its rough skin.

"Say it," Rick whispered to her. "Say it again."

"Oh fuck me," Tanya sobbed. "Fuck me with your big cock."

Sven held his giant cock in one hand. And slowly he began jerking off.

"I'll fuck you hard," Rick hissed. "I'm gonna give you my cock till you scream."

And with one wild stroke he rammed his hard cock into her. All the way, making her gasp out loud. Again and again it thrust into her, as Rick sweated with the strain.

The clear fluid slowly flowed from Sven's cock as he stood next to Tanya's face.

"No," she whispered out of breath.

"Suck his cock," Johnny ordered. This young man already had a hard-on again.

"No," Tanya gasped, "I can't..."

And she came again. The orgasm gushed through her body, even more violent than before. For a moment she thought she was going to pass out.

But their mad lust had made the men merciless. Sven just laughed satanically at her helplessness, showing off his erection to her. Rick's hard cock pounded her cunt relentlessly. And Johnny commanded, as if nothing had happened.

"Do it! Suck his cock, you filthy little whore!"

And reluctantly, Tanya opened her mouth to the huge, bluish-red head of Sven's cock. Sven slowly let his hard cock slide over her wet tongue, letting her taste his hot lust.

"Ohhh," he groaned - a deep animal noise, making Tanya even hotter. She immediately started sucking his fat cock, making loud, smacking sounds.

Tirelessly, Rick was pumping her pussy, his rock hard cock tightening to the limit with each thrust into her warm, slippery crevice.

Johnny stood beside the table, masturbating at the sight.

"Well," he hissed, "You're getting fucked? Are you?"

Sven's huge cock swelled in Tanya's wet mouth. The helmet was bulging, his semen boiling in his bursting balls. Then he pulled his cock out of her mouth, dripping with saliva, and held it in his hand.

"Ohhh," he moaned in his deep voice. "Let me fuck her."

Rick thrust one more time into Tanya's pussy - hard and deep, making her shriek. Sven smiled wickedly and slowly Rick slid his cock out of her. Sven then turned her onto her belly and stood behind her ass.

His cock pointed straight up, trembling with lust.

Rick and Johnny stood around the table, expectantly massaging their cocks.

"Now fuck her," Rick said.

"Let the bitch have your fat prick," Johnny panted.

Grunting, Sven slid a thick finger up into Tanya's cunt. She felt so hot and wet, she thought she was going to come again.

"Make her beg for it," Johnny said.

Sven's finger slipped in and out of her dripping wet pussy, making her squirm and sob with lust.

"Is it Sven you want?" Rick whispered into her ear.

"Mmm," Tanya whimpered.

"Say it," Johnny ordered.

"Tell him to fuck you," Rick whispered.

Sven laughed fiendishly. With one hand he stroked his monstrous cock. With the other he was finger-fucking Tanya, slowly and thoroughly, her round ass rotating before him.

"Fuck me," she whispered. "Please fuck me."

"Say the word," Johnny yelled.

Sven's treatment made Tanya gasp. No. Now. Now she was about to come again. He closed her eyes in unbearable lust.

"You know how," Rick said teasingly. "And you won't have his cock, until you say it."

Tanya whimpered. Then she took a deep breathing and yelled into the storage room:

"Fuck me, Sven! Give me your fat cock! Is that what you want to hear? Fuck me, goddamnit! Sven, fuck me with that giant cock of yours!"

Sven grabbed hold of her hair, pulling it hard. Then he let out a yell, pressing his huge cock up into her pussy from behind.

"Yeah, yeah," he grunted. But she didn't have even half the huge cock inside her yet.

"All the way up," Johnny grunted. "Fuck her." He and Rick were masturbating like mad.

"No. Stop," Tanya gasped.

Sven thrust as hard as he could. His giant member pressed into her stretching pussy, making her sob.

"Well," Rick whispered viciously. "That's what I call a cock, isn't it?"

And with one last, brutal thrust Sven buried his cock in Tanya's aching pussy.

"Oooh," she whimpered.

"Fuck her," Johnny gasped.

And Sven started fucking. The huge cock was wet and slippery from her juices, and Sven slowly slid it in and out of her. Oh, that was wonderful. It filled the entire width of her pussy, and with each stroke she felt its hardness. Felt every fold, every vein on the rugged, stone hard cock. The entire tender inside of her pussy was caressed, massaged and teased by Sven's incredible sex tool.

"Mmm, delicious cunt," he snarled.

Eyes glazed, Tanya looked up at Rick and Johnny. Panting and sweating they watched her getting fucked. And before her eyes they stroked their rock hard cocks.

"Ohhh, I'm gonna shoot off," Sven murmured.

And quickly he pulled his cock out of her. Johnny and Rick turned her onto her back, and the three of them stood around the table, masturbating.

"Come on," she gasped. "Let me have your delicious sperm."

Here Tanya lay. On the tiny wooden table, a few yards away from her workplace, while three lusty men stood around her jerking off.

God, she was hot. Her fingers found her soaking wet pussy and her swollen, aching clit and she began to masturbate.

"Yeah, play with your pussy," Johnny whispered.

And at that moment Tanya climaxed for the third time. Already utterly exhausted she just lay there, letting the waves of lust wash over her, emitting low wailing sounds.

The men, too, sensed her orgasm, and that set off their own ejaculations.

Rick was the first one to come.

"Ahhh," he shouted angrily, long jets of sperm shooting from the tip of his cock, splashing hot across her cheeks. He spurted again and again, and the sight of his ejaculation set Johnny off, too.

Johnny let go of his cock, and Tanya watched it jerk madly, as he came.

"Yes," he shouted, as the first spurt of his lustful cream flew through the air. His cock was pumping wildly, jet after jet of boiling hot semen hitting Tanya's burning face and breasts.

She thought he'd never stop, but finally his ejaculation subsided, and he squeezed the last sluggish drops of sperm onto her skin.

Sven was in control to the end. Grunting he masturbated his giant, swollen member, watching his to workmates spraying Tanya with their semen.

"Now you get my load," he snarled.

"Spray me," she whispered. "Do it."

"Ohhh," Sven yelled, letting go of his load.

It was incredible. The huge cock spurted like a fountain. Two foot long jets of thick, warm sperm shot over Tanya's naked body. Opening her mouth, she tasted his strong, salty drops on her tongue.

Slowly the three men settled down, pulling away from her. Tanya lay on the table, her breasts and her face covered in their sperm. She shivered, eyes closed, savouring the feeling of being bathed in their semen.

They brought her a clean, white towel, and slowly she wiped off the semen and got dressed.

The men poured coffee. Tanya had a cup, too. Now they were completely calm, relaxed. The animal savagery from a few moments ago had disappeared. Even Sven seemed like a nice, normal guy.

"Thanks," she finally said.

"Well, you're welcome," Rick laughed.

"You were fucking great," Johnny exclaimed.

"So were you," she whispered.

They sipped their hot coffee in silence for a while.

"Well," Rick said. "I guess you have to get back to work.

"Yeah," Tanya laughed and got up. "I think I'd better."

"Very well, Sven said."But if you should change your mind, the offer still stands."

Tanya was silent for a moment. Then she laughed out loud. And the men laughed along with her.

The Elevator

At a few minutes to five, Michael switched off the computer on his desk. It had been a dull day, and he'd passed the time surfing the web, especially the porn sites. He'd found a clip of a couple having sex in an elevator, and for some reason that had really turned him on.

As he left his office and walked down the corridor, he still felt his member bulging in his pants. Feeling horny at work was such a frustrating feeling. Now all he wanted was to get home as fast as possible, preferably not talking to anyone on the way. Get home and wait for that lusty feeling to wear off, or if didn't, he could just masturbate and get it over with.

As he stood in front of the elevator door, the pictures he'd seen on the web flickered through his mind. Hot, hot, hot. Damn, he had to try to think of something else. He pressed the button, and a few seconds later the little bell rang, and the doors opened.

The car was empty except for a tall blond woman dressed in a dark jacket with a matching short skirt with a handbag slung over her shoulder. Michael recognized her as an executive from the 18th floor – Maria something. Due to her high status, she'd never really paid any attention to him, but as he entered the elevator she nodded politely. The doors closed, and the elevator started going down.

Maria smiled to herself, and Michael wondered if she'd noticed the bulge in his pants. It was not big enough to be really embarrassing, but he knew that if his mind ever drifted back to those porno pictures, it would grow to a bona fide erection that he couldn't possibly hide. God, he looked forward to getting home.

Still, he couldn't help glancing at Maria – her long blond hair, her long, slim legs revealed by the short skirt. And suddenly, as she adjusted the strap of the handbag, something shiny fell out and rolled across the elevator floor.

It took Michael a moment to realize that it was a steel vibrator. Flustered, Maria bent down to pick it up, but the dildo rolled across the floor and didn't stop until it hit Michael's right shoe. Now he

bent down and picked it up. The metal felt cold and smooth in his hand.

Maria stared at him, speechless. The whole situation was absurd. Here he was, all hot and bothered because of that elevator story, himself in an elevator face to face with a hot female executive who was afraid to ask for her dildo back.

Michael knew he was about to do something, he might live to regret, but to hell with that. He slammed his palm against the emergency stop button, and the car stopped with a loud noise and a violent jerk, which almost knocked them off their feet.

"What the hell do you think you're doing?" Maria shrieked.

Slowly, Michael walked towards her holding the vibrator.

"I think you need this," he said.

"That's none of your fucking business," she hissed.

"What if I make it my business?" Michael asked.

He now stood next to her, almost touching her. Maria glanced at the vibrator in his hand.

"Alright," he said. "Show me your pussy."

"What?"

"You heard me."

Maria didn't answer right away. Michael examined the sex toy, turning it on. It started vibrating between his fingers with a buzzing noise. He switched it off again.

"You've got some fucking nerve, asshole!" Maria finally said.

"Hey," Michael said. "We're stuck in this fucking car, and you'd probably like to get off. Am I right? Okay, so now show me that pussy."

Cursing, Maria pulled off her white silk panties and lifted up her skirt. Her pussy was shaved, completely hairless, showing off her pink labia. Michael felt his cock throbbing in his pants.

"Happy now, creep?" she asked.

Without a word, Michael spun her around, making her face the wall. Then he put one arm around her and held her tight, pressing his torso against her back and grabbing her right breast hard.

"Oh," she muttered.

Michael turned on the vibrator and let the buzzing steel toy graze Maria's labia. She struggled in his grip, as he moved the vibrator up and down her pussy lips. Now he placed the tip right next to her clit, letting the buzzing toy vibrate her love button.

Maria gasped for air, her whole body jerking wildly. But Michael held on tight.

"Spread your legs," he whispered into her ear.

And as Maria stood with her legs spread wide on the elevator floor, Michael slid the vibrator up and down her labia, pressing it against her pussy.

"Oooh," she sobbed, as the pressure of the toy opened her pussy lips slightly, letting it vibrate the soft insides of her slit.

"Wider," Michael ordered.

And moaning, Maria spread her legs even more, opening her moist flesh to the buzzing toy. Michael kept sliding it up and down, massaging the inner surface of her tender sex.

She felt herself getting wet and held her breath, trying not to give in to the pleasurable itch she felt between her legs. But Michael watched with satisfaction, as Maria's juices formed sparkling droplets on the shiny surface of the vibrator.

Now his cock was hard as rock in his pants. He pressed his crotch against her ass, letting her feel his erection through the fabric. Then Michael put the dildo to her mouth.

"Lick it," he whispered into her ear. "Taste your own pussy."

And Maria licked the buzzing toy, savouring the spicy taste of her own love juice.

Next, he slid the wet, slippery vibrator up into her pussy like a cock. Maria gasped, as she felt the hard steel object buzzing inside her, teasing the depths of her hot, excited flesh.

She was trembling now, as the vibrations of the sex toy sent waves of pleasure through her body. And still, Michael held her tight, pressing her against the wall of the elevator with his entire weight.

"Oh, shit!" she hissed, banging her hand against the wall in excitement and frustration. "Shit!"

Michael held the vibrator still inside Maria's pussy, and watched as she started wriggling her ass, grinding her pelvis against his hand, making her wet flesh slide up and down the length of the vibrator.

"Yeah?" he said. "You like that?"

His cock was fully erect now, stretching downwards inside the leg of his pants, feeling hard and burning hot next to his thigh.

"Oooh!" Maria cried out as she suddenly climaxed.

She pressed her forehead against the wall of the elevator, sobbing uncontrollably, shaken by a powerful orgasm. Ever so

slowly, Michael pulled the vibrator out of her, and watched the juices trickled down the insides of her trembling thighs.

He let go of her, and Maria slowly sank to her knees, still leaning against the wall. She was breathing deeply, her jacket and skirt slightly ruffled by the sex act. Michael dropped the wet, glistening vibrator on the elevator floor.

"Take your clothes off," Michael ordered.

She didn't answer.

"What's the matter?" he grinned. "Never been naked in an elevator before? Well, there's a first time for everything."

Maria got up, looking at him, confused.

"No, please..." she whispered.

"Do it!" he shouted. "I want you naked right now!"

And slowly, Maria started undressing. Her jacket and shirt came off, revealing her bra. She looked glumly at Michael as she unhooked it and threw it on the floor. Her breasts were of average size, but perfectly shaped, bouncing gently as she moved, her little, dark nipples stiffening as he watched.

Finally, she unbuttoned her skirt and let it fall to the floor. She stood naked in front of him, there in the elevator, naked except for her high-heeled shoes.

She was beautiful. Her body was slender and slightly muscular - and Michael couldn't take her eyes off that shaved pussy.

Michael, however, did not undress. Instead, he only unzipped his fly and carefully guided his huge, stiff cock out of his pants. It stuck out horizontally from his body, pointing straight at Maria. He had often been told that he had a big cock, and today his erection was extremely hard – almost painful.

"Over there," he said. "Back against the wall."

Staring at his cock, Maria pressed her back against the wall.

"Touch yourself," he said. "Play with your pussy."

Maria obeyed. Leaning against the wall, she started stroking her labia, closing her eyes as her finger massaged the base of her clit. Michael smiled approvingly, masturbating at the sight. Slowly, he walked towards her, eventually standing so close that his cock almost touched her skin.

"Open your pussy," he whispered.

Hesitantly, Maria used two fingers to pull her pussy-lips apart. Michael looked with pleasure at the pink, glistening wetness he was about to enter.

Grabbing the base of the shaft with both hands, he steered his rigid tool towards her pussy. And as Maria opened her flesh to him with trembling fingers, she felt the bulbous head of his cock penetrating her sex.

"Unnnh," she groaned.

Michael bent his knees slightly, allowing his cock to enter her from below, slowly, slowly sliding up into her pussy, stretching her wet love muscle with his erect rod.

Maria closed her eyes, her cheek resting on the elevator wall, her face flushed with excitement. Michael pushed forward, filling her slit with the entire length of his cock and pressing her back up against the wall. Then he skilfully lifted up her legs and placed her calves on his shoulders. She was now suspended in mid-air, held in place by the elevator wall and Michael's cock.

It felt dangerous, but she had already broken all the rules. She almost felt like she wasn't herself anymore, but some other woman, a creature of pure lust, naked, getting fucked by a fully dressed man in an elevator in an office building.

Michael placed his hands under Maria's ass – and then he began to fuck her.

He moved his hips back and forth, up and down, driving his erect tool into her again and again. She gasped with each thrust, her wet flesh opening itself to him, feeling his bulging cock slide in and out of her tender slit.

Maria wrapped her arms around his neck, and to her surprise, he kissed her passionately. Greedily, she opened her mouth to his, sucking at his lips and mouth and letting his wet, wet tongue meet hers.

Michael thrust his bone-hard cock into her pussy faster and faster, deeper and deeper, as their wild tongues flicked playfully at each other in their mouths. His hands grabbed her ass-cheeks hard, then his fingers curved around her thighs, pulling at her labia, opening her sex even wider to his attack. Out of breath, Maria let go of his mouth.

"Oh God, oh God," she whimpered, as she felt her second orgasm approaching.

Her hands grabbed frantically at the smooth surface of the elevator wall, searching for something to hold on to. Eventually, she grabbed hold of Michael's upper arms, feeling the muscles flex

through the fabric of his business suit, as he relentlessly hammered his cock into her succulent pussy.

"Ahhh," he yelled, sweating from the strain, his powerful fucking driving her ever closer to the brink.

Maria dug her nails into his sleeves, as she came. Throwing her head back, she cried out loud with pleasure, her pussy muscles pulsating around Michael's thrusting cock.

"Yeeeaaahhh!" she cried. "Yeeeaaahhh!"

There was a loud banging on the ceiling of the elevator car. Michael wondered what it was, but he couldn't stop now. Sweating and panting, he drove his erect cock into Maria's wet sex over and over and...

The banging came again. Maria was limp, exhausted, but Michael kept on fucking her, slamming her back up against the elevator wall with each stroke. His cock was swelling madly, ready to blow, its skin hypersensitive with excitement.

"Oh no," she moaned, "please..."

A trapdoor opened in the ceiling of the elevator and a man's face appeared. He showed a mixture of shock and amusement as he watched the fully dressed Michael fucking the naked Maria up against the wall. Michael's cock was about to explode. Still thrusting into Maria, he looked up at the newcomer.

"What does it look like we're doing?" he hissed. "Aaah, aaah, shit!"

Michael began ejaculating wildly in Maria's pussy. He felt his balls contracting, shooting spurt after spurt of piping hot cream into her sex. Trembling as he came, he gently lifted Maria's legs onto the floor, letting her stand by herself. His cock jerked a few times more, emptying itself of every last drop of semen.

"Yes," he sighed, as his orgasm subsided. He held his cock still inside Maria's sticky slit, and to her surprise it stayed hard.

A metal ladder came down from the roof, and a repairman in bright orange overalls climbed down into the car. For a few seconds he just stood there, looking at the couple by the wall.

"So that's why you hit the emergency stop?" he said, grinning at Michael.

Michael pulled his cock out of Maria's pussy. It was bright red from fucking, but still stood straight out.

"Yeah," he said, nodding towards Maria. "You know what it's like."

"Yeah," the repairman said. "And I see you're not finished with her. Mind if I join you?"

"No. Be my guest," Michael said.

And quickly, the repairman went over to the naked Maria. She shrieked, as he put his arm around her waist and carried her off. Grinning, Michael began undressing, his erection still jutting out from his body.

"No!" Maria screamed, as the repairman dragged her towards the ladder. "Put me down!"

"You're gonna like this," the repairman said to Michael.

Maria was kicking and cursing, as the repairman lifted her up the ladder. She fought as hard as she could, but she was no match for his strength.

As the naked woman was halfway through the open trapdoor, he put her down. Her feet on the ladder, she rested her hands on the roof of the elevator car.

"Shit! It's dirty up here," she said.

The repairman stood right behind her on the ladder. Now he unbuttoned the fly of his overalls and pulled out his erect cock. Michael – who was now standing naked on the floor - saw that the repairman's cock was not quite as long as his own, but considerably thicker; especially the swelling, bluish head looked huge. Knowing how tight Maria's pussy was, he knew this was going to get rough.

The repairman slid the head of his cock in between Maria's pussy lips from behind. Michael could hear the wetness, as the fat member forced her labia apart.

"Oooh," she whispered.

The repairman pulled back slightly, then in again. He moved his hips up and down, just inching the head of his cock in and out of Maria's succulent pussy. Unable to keep still, she wriggled her ass lustfully, as the repairman kept penetrating the outer folds of her slit.

Michael heard her moans of pleasure echoing from the elevator shaft above the car. She was getting ever wetter from excitement, her juices trickling down the massive shaft of the repairman's cock. When he found she was wet enough, he thrust upwards, driving the entire length of his cock into her.

"Aaah!" Maria cried out.

The repairman grabbed her hips and began fucking her, poking her tight crevice again and again with deep, powerful strokes. Michael masturbated at the sight, his long cock hard and ready.

The men heard the sound of Maria letting herself drop onto the roof of the car.

"Unnnh, Mmm, unnnh," she panted, as the repairman slid his rigid cock into her tender flesh over and over.

She felt the fat tool growing even fatter, turned on by the sensations of her soft, moist pussy.

"Yeah, it's big, isn't it?" he grunted. "But I bet you like having a big cock inside your pussy. Don't you?"

The men heard Maria gasping for breath, as the repairman kept fucking her, his thrusting cock glistening from her juices.

Maria whimpered quietly, as he suddenly pulled out of her.

"Okay," he said to Michael. "Let's get up on the roof."

And within seconds, the repairman had disappeared through the trapdoor, carrying Maria with him.

Michael followed up the ladder, naked, stroking his hard cock. Climbing up through the trapdoor, he looked up into the tall, darkened elevator shaft, thick steel cables disappearing far above him.

The repairman stood on the roof of the car, behind the naked Maria, making her bend over. His cock stuck out from the fly of his orange overalls, and he carefully guided it towards her slit.

"Spread your legs," he whispered.

And sighing quietly, Maria stood with her legs apart, as the repairman slowly slid his hardened cock into her moist pussy.

Michael masturbated at the sight, and enjoyed having her watch as he massaged his swelling tool. Drops of clear liquid oozed from the tip of his excited cock, dripping onto the dirty roof of the elevator car.

The repairman grabbed hold of the thick steel cables.

"You better hold onto something, too," he said to Maria. "I wanna fuck you hard!"

Her arms were shaking, as she reached out to find some cables to hold on to.

"Please..." she whispered, as she heard the repairman breathing heavily behind her, getting ready to fuck.

In one swift stroke, the repairman pulled his cock nearly all the way out of Maria's pussy. Her tender flesh was stretched so tightly around his cock, that the movement of his thick, hard meat made her gasp.

And then he pushed forwards. She cried out loud, as the repairman impaled her on his swollen cock. He pulled back, only to penetrate her again and again, her cries echoing through the darkened elevator shaft.

Michael grabbed her hair and pulled her head down towards his erect cock. Obediently, she parted her mouth, letting the hard tool enter her mouth. And there, naked, on top of the elevator car, Maria let him feel how she sucked a cock:

Slowly, she slid her lips up and down the shaft, letting it slip out of her mouth occasionally, to lap at the exposed head with her soft, wet tongue. Savouring the sensation, Michael's body trembled with lust.

"Unnnh," he grunted, already close to orgasm.

Meanwhile, the repairman was hammering his cock into her tight pussy. Over and over, he drove the entire length of his bulging tool into her yielding wetness in a mad, relentless rhythm.

When it almost slipped out of her pussy, he slowed down and entered her again slowly, letting her feel the pressure of his rigid cock on her tender, pink labia. Then he resumed his frenzied rhythm, impaling her again and again with deep, powerful thrusts.

Maria felt both men pulling out of her simultaneously; then heard their hurried footsteps across the roof of the elevator. And suddenly, it was the repairman standing in front of her, offering his fat, bulging cock to her mouth.

At that moment, Michael groaned with pleasure as he drove his long, stiff cock into her pussy from behind.

"Yeah," the repairman said. "Fuck her!"

Maria felt Michael's cock beginning to thrust into her aching slit, burying the entire length inside her with every stroke. God, it felt good! The long, hard tool probed the depth of her sex, massaging the soft folds of her flesh, making her wet and driving her ever closer to another orgasm.

The repairman slapped her face with his thick, swelling cock.

"Suck it!" he ordered.

As Maria opened her mouth, the repairman guided his cock in between her lips. But due to its size, she could only fit the huge, swollen head in her mouth. The repairman panted with pleasure, as she sucked his bluish helmet. She felt it bulging with lust, burning hot on her wet tongue.

Still driving his cock into her, Michael was ready to let go. Gasping, he felt Maria's love juice flowing from her succulent pussy, drenching his cock and trickling down the insides of her thigh. He fucked her harder and faster, wanting to make her come before he did.

"Mmm! Mmm!"

She tried to cry out, but the huge head of the repairman's cock filled her mouth, stifling her voice. He grinned.

"Got something to say?" he asked, pulling the cock from her lips.

"Ohhh God!" Maria screamed, as Michael thrust hard into her again.

"Yeah!" the repairman yelled, stroking his cock in front of Maria's face. "Make her come!"

"Ahhh," Michael cried.

He held onto the steel cables, as he drove his cock into Maria's pussy. Out of breath he kept going, in and out, in and out, but he couldn't go on much longer. His cock was swelling madly, ready to ejaculate.

Maria, too, clung to the steel cables, as the orgasm washed over her.

"Aaah!" she screamed. "Aaah!"

Her cries of lust echoed through the elevator shaft, as the climax shook her naked body. She almost fainted with pleasure. And at the height of her ecstasy, she felt her lover's cock exploding inside her overflowing pussy.

"Yeeeah!" Michael yelled, as his long cock started contracting inside her.

Jerking wildly, it spurted jets of hot semen into her pussy - hard, powerful spurts filling her aching slit with thick sperm.

"Open your mouth," the repairman grunted.

Still wearing his orange overall, he was masturbating, his fat tool only inches from her face.

And she obeyed. As Michael held his twitching cock still inside her pussy, the repairman jerked himself off, pointing his cock at Maria's open mouth.

"Get ready for a big load," he grunted. "Watch this! Yeah!"

Its head was swelling grotesquely before her eyes, as the first long, hard spurt of white semen shot out of the twitching cock. It hit Maria's tongue, letting her taste his spicy cream.

"Unnnh! Yeah!" he yelled, still masturbating. "Swallow my cum!"

Jet after jet of thick, boiling sperm spurted from the repairman's cock, as he jerked of wildly. Maria let him see how she swallowed his semen, licking her lips as she looked into his eyes.

"Uhhh!" he shouted, as his ejaculation finally subsided.

The last drop of sperm fell onto the roof of the elevator, as Michael pulled his limp cock from Maria's pussy.

There was an embarrassed silence. It was as if they couldn't believe what had just happened. And only now did they notice how cold it was up here.

The repairman zipped up.

"Well," he said. "I guess I'd better get this elevator started."

Naked, Maria and Michael climbed down the ladder into the elevator car, followed by the repairman.

A few minutes later, they stepped out of the elevator on the ground floor. The repairman waved and left. Maria and Michael looked at each other.

"Well," Maria said, almost regaining her superior attitude. "I guess we won't be seeing each other again?"

Michael grinned.

"I guess not," he said. "Unless..."

And triumphantly, he pulled the vibrator from his pocket.

Maria looked around, making sure the lobby was empty.

"You..." she stuttered, "you wouldn't..."

"Of course I would," Michael said quietly. "Tomorrow at eight? My place?"

Without awaiting her reply, he walked off.

Oh yes, he thought. This was going to be good. He was going to stay up all night, surfing the web, looking for new stuff they could try – next time.

And what else? Oh yes, batteries. He'd better buy lots of batteries...

Her Best Friend

Cathy's in the kitchen when I come home. I try to catch my breath before I enter. Yes, I'm late, I know it. As I walk by the dining room, I see the candles on the table; they've almost burned down by now. Cathy's upset.

"Where have you been?" she asks me, her dark eyes looking straight at me. "If you were working late, why didn't you call me?"

"I'm sorry," I say, still out of breath from exhaustion.

"I've been so worried," she says.

"I know," I say. Cathy's standing by the sink, her cute little ass resting on the edge of the kitchen table.

"But... I wasn't working late," I say.

She stares at me, shocked.

"What?" she gasps. "Then where were you? Why don't you tell me what happened?"

I smile, still trying to catch my breath.

"Don't worry," I say. "I'll tell you everything."

I'm standing in the doorway, looking at her. She really is beautiful – not tall, not short, her short hair shiny black, her breasts small, but perfectly rounded, bulging under the red silk blouse she's wearing. She's also wearing a short black skirt, black silk stockings and those red high-heeled shoes I really like. And just a bit of make-up - her quivering lips are bright red.

As for me, I'm in my jeans and t-shirt.

"I met your friend Karen on the way," I say.

Cathy's eyes are wide open. An idea is forming in her mind. She's afraid of what I'm about to tell her.

"She's really pretty," I say. "I guess most men find her attractive. You know: Tall, blonde, big tits..."

"So," Cathy interrupts, "you met Karen, and then what?"

"Well," I say. "We just talked. You know, she's single and all that."

"I know she's single," Cathy said. "She's my best friend. So?"

"You know," I say, "I've tried to set her up with some guys from work. I wanted to hear what had happened."

"In detail, I guess?" Cathy sneers.

"Sure," I say. "And she's certainly not shy. Told me some great stories. Some of those guys are real animals. Fucked her in all kinds of strange ways. Luckily, Karen's really into that sort of thing, so she had had some great sex."

"So Karen told you stories of great sex for two hours?"

That makes me laugh. "Oh no. No, I told her I had something to tell her, and that I'd rather tell her in private."

Cathy looks confused.

"What did you have to tell her?" she asks.

"Nothing," I say. "I lied."

"You lied to my best friend?" Cathy cries. "Why the hell did you do that?"

"Oh," I say. "That's not all I did to your best friend. Far from it, in fact. Okay, so we decided to go back to her apartment."

Cathy stares at me. Now she's almost certain what she is about to hear.

"But actually," I say, "we didn't really make it all the way."

"Why not?"

"Well," I say, "listening to all those stories had really turned me on. Well, you know. So I was following her up the stairs, looking at her cute little ass. And it really is cute. I just couldn't wait any longer. So I grabbed her arm and made her stop."

"Right there – on the stairs?" Cathy says.

"Sure. She turned around and looked at me. And that's when I asked her."

"Asked her what?"

I'm looking Cathy in the eyes as I say: "I asked her if she wanted to see my cock."

Cathy gasps: "Oh, my God. I can't believe you really said that."

"I did," I say. "A pretty girl like that. I really wanted to show it to her."

"And what did she say?" Cathy whispers.

"She just looked at me. So I asked her again: 'Do you want to see my cock?' And she smiled and nodded."

"And then," Cathy says, "then you went to her apartment?"

"Oh no," I say. "I didn't have time for that. I just opened my pants then and there and pulled out my cock."

Cathy is silent for a moment, still leaning against the kitchen table. Then she looks at me again.

"So... was it hard?" she asks.

"Pretty damn hard," I say. I'd been walking around with a hard-on from all her sexy stories. And when I stood there with Karen looking at it, it got hard as a rock. I let her watch, as I stroked it, making it stiffen. She seemed to like that."

"Really?"

"Oh yeah. 'Keep going,' she said. 'I wanna watch you masturbate.'"

Cathy's blushing now.

"Karen said that?" she asks.

"Sure," I say. "That's one nasty friend you've got there."

"So what... what did you do?"

"I masturbated," I say. "I stroked my cock and let her watch. 'Look at it,' I said. 'Look how hard my big cock is.' Oh, she loved it."

"Did she touch herself?" Cathy asks. "Did she masturbate?"

I know why she's asking. This is turning her on, and Cathy wants to masturbate herself. I smile at her.

"Not at first," I say. "She sat down on the steps in front of me, just looking at it. I just stood there on the stairs, stroking my cock. It felt great having a pretty blond girl watch me as I masturbated."

"Oh God," Cathy moans, "I don't want to hear this."

"No?" I say. "Well, I don't think you have much of a choice, do you? And in fact, I think you do want to hear it. Don't you, Cathy?"

She doesn't answer. She keeps adjusting her skirt and her stockings, just dying to touch herself.

"Then what happened?" she finally asks.

"Well," I say, "I got so hard, I was ready to shoot off. But I didn't want that."

"No," Cathy whispers. "You wanted to fuck her, didn't you?"

"She is an attractive girl," I say. "But first, I told her to get down on all fours and show me her pussy."

"No, please," Cathy wails. With trembling fingers, she pulls up her skirt and touches the crotch of her black silk panties. She moves her hand up and down, stroking her pussy through the fabric.

"It's okay," I say gently. "Touch yourself as much as you want."

I hear her panting with lust, her eyes closed.

"So," I go on. "Karen got down on all fours on the steps in front of me, and I lifted up her skirt to see her pussy. She didn't wear any panties. And she'd shaved her pussy. Did you know that?"

Cathy doesn't answer. I watch her masturbating, enjoying the sight of my beautiful girlfriend stroking her pussy.

"I knelt down on the steps behind her," I say, "and put my face next to her pussy. It smelt nice and hot. Karen must have felt my breath on her pussy lips, 'cause she wriggled her ass just a little bit. 'Do you want me to touch it?' I asked her. 'Do you?'"

Cathy is gasping loudly. She has pushed the crotch of her panties aside and is vigorously rubbing her wet slit.

"Please tell me she said yes," she whispers.

"She did," I say. "She was dying for me to touch her flesh, tease her pussy and make her really, really wet."

"Oh God," Cathy gasps.

"So," I say, "I licked my middle finger and slowly drove it into Karen's pussy. Oh, she loved that. She cried out loud as I buried my finger in her pussy. Then I started fucking her with it, sliding it in and out, in and out..."

"Was it tight?" Cathy whispers. "Does she have a nice, tight pussy?"

"Oh yes," I say. "Her flesh even fit so tight around my finger. I could feel her pussy muscles contracting as I probed her. She was moaning with pleasure as I thrust my finger into her. But I just had to pull it out to lick it and taste her juice."

"Oh yes," Cathy says.

"Mmm. Karen has the sweetest pussy," I tell her. "She's your best friend. Don't tell me you never tasted her pussy?"

Cathy shakes her head: "No... I haven't."

"But I want you to," I say. "I'll invite her over. And then you're going to lick that sweet little pussy of hers."

Cathy's moaning as I tell her this.

"Anyway," I go on, "I slid my finger back into Karen's pussy, pumping it back and forth. Her flesh felt so soft and wet. And I couldn't wait to feel my cock inside her."

Cathy has grabbed one of her breasts now, tweaking one hard, little nipple with one hand, as she keeps stroking her pussy with the other.

"Yeah," I say. "Keep going, honey. Make yourself come."

Cathy throws her head back, whimpering with lust, as I continue my story:

"I pulled my finger out of Karen's pussy again. This time I put it to her mouth, telling her to taste it. And she did. She licked her own spicy love juice from my finger. Seemed like she just loved the taste of pussy. Does she? Do you know? I'd like to see her lick yours one day."

"Ohhh, ohhh." Cathy moans, rubbing her clit fiercely.

"Then," I say, "I parted her labia with my fingers, looking into her pussy. God, it was beautiful: Soft, pink flesh, already juicy wet with lust. I wanted to get my cock inside her. I wanted to feel that tight, slippery slit stretched around my fat cock."

"Oh yes," Cathys gasps. "Oh, yes. She really deserves your cock. I hope you let her have it!"

"I told her to stand up and spread her legs," I say. "And soon she was standing bent over in front of me. I slapped her cute little ass - just once. Then I stroked my cock again, making sure it was hard as a rock."

Cathy's smiling now, massaging her breast and her clit, no doubt visualizing the scene.

"I placed my cock at the mouth of Karen's pussy, pressing it hard against her flesh. But she was so tight that I didn't enter her. When I pushed harder against her, it only made her whimper. Instead, she put a hand in between her legs, pulling her pussy lips apart, opening herself to my cock. Oh, that felt good."

"Oh yeah," Cathy whispers. "I bet it did."

"I slid my cock all the way up into Karen's pussy. It felt soft and wet, wrapped around the skin of my cock. I felt my cock grow even bigger, swelling inside her tight pussy. And she loved it. I heard her moaning with lust, because she loved to feel my big, fat cock inside her."

"Oh, baby," Cathy sobs, "who doesn't?"

"Then," I say, "I began fucking her. I grabbed her hips and thrust my cock into her as hard as I could. And I kept going, driving it into her again and again. Karen gasped and held on to the handrail – otherwise I would have knocked her over."

"Ohhh," Cathy whispers, rubbing her clit vigorously, "I hope you fucked the hell out of her. Ohhh, ohhh..."

Leaning back against the kitchen table, Cathy's entire body stiffens up as she comes. Shaking all over, she breathes hard,

savoring a powerful climax. It's been a while since I last watched her masturbate herself to an orgasm, and I just love the sight.

Flushed and still trembling, she looks over at me. I unbutton my pants and take my cock out. It's very hard, and I let her watch as I start stroking it. Cathy smiles and lights a cigarette.

"You mean, you really fucked her right there on the stairs?" she says. "Didn't anybody see you?"

"Well, not at first," I say.

Cathy opens her eyes wide as she looks at me. But I haven't come to that part of the story yet.

"But I did worry a bit," I say, "'cause Karen was really making a noise. I went a bit wild, fucking her as hard and fast as I could. And she was screaming her head off."

"What did she say?" Cathy asks.

"She kept saying 'fuck me'," I tell her. "'Fuck me with that big, hard cock!' And I just kept pounding it into her. She was loving every second."

I'm still stroking my cock, as Cathy watches, smoking her cigarette.

"Then," I say, "I pulled out of her and made her sit down on one of the steps. We were still almost fully dressed, so I pulled her clothes off. She looks great naked – nice body, big, beautiful tits. Then I got naked myself. 'Spread your legs wide' I told her, 'then play with your pussy.' And she did. I watched Karen as she sat naked on the steps, rubbing her sweet little pussy."

"I bet you loved that," Cathy says.

"Oh yeah," I say. "My cock got so hard, I just had to fuck her again. Then I lay down between her legs and drove my cock into her again. She was so wet, she just opened herself to me, and the entire length of my cock slid into her. I started fucking her again – slowly this time, pulling my cock out of her, then sliding it back in, over and over, letting her feel every inch of the hard shaft."

"Mmm, yeah," Cathy purrs.

She has put out her cigarette, and now she pulls of her panties and starts stroking herself again, her little tuft of black pubes glistening from her juices.

She's so beautiful. I could just walk over and fuck her now. But somehow – I don't know why – I'm enjoying this even more. I just want to stand here in the kitchen, watching Cathy masturbate herself to yet another orgasm.

"I looked down at Karen's pussy as I fucked her," I say. "I saw her clean-shaven labia stretching around my cock. I saw my cock, wet and slippery from her juices, as it slid all the way out and then buried itself in her pussy again. I wish you'd been there to see it. You'd have liked that, wouldn't you?"

Cathy's stroking her pussy again.

"Karen was screaming so loud," I say, "telling me to fuck her harder. And finally I felt her coming. She dug her nails into my back, and I felt her tight flesh clenching my cock. She cried out, shaking all over. I thought she was about to faint."

"And you?" Cathy asks. "Did you come too?"

"No," I say. "My cock was still hard as a rock. I waited for a few seconds, till her orgasm had subsided. Then I started fucking her again."

"Oh God," Cathy says. "I bet she was all sore. How did she take it?"

"Oh, she sobbed and told me to wait," I say, "but her pussy felt so soft and wet, I just had to fuck her. And after a while, she was loving every stroke. By the way, that's when I noticed him."

"Who?" Cathy asks.

"I don't know," I say. "Probably some man who lives in the same building. About fifty. Wore a suit."

"Did he watch you?" Cathy asks.

"You bet he was watching us," I say. "He just stood there, grinning, as I drove my cock into Karen's pussy. I think he got really hot, listening to her moaning. 'Do you see him?' I whispered to Karen. 'Talk to him'. Karen just stared at me at first, but then she started talking, as I fucked her."

Cathy's rubbing her little pink clit now, trembling with lust.

"What...?" she gasps, "What did she say?"

"She asked the man if he liked it," I say. "'Do you like to watch us fuck?' she said. I could tell he was really excited. There was a huge bulge in his pants, and he kept touching himself through the fabric. Then I whispered to Karen: 'Tell him to get his cock out'."

"And did he?" Cathy asked.

"Oh yeah," I say. "And it was huge. A big, wide cock pointing straight out. And he started stroking it, as he watched me fucking Karen. She was staring at the man's cock, like she'd never seen anything like it."

"But..." Cathy asks, "was it bigger than yours?"

"Yeah," I say. "It was so thick. I don't know how he could ever fuck a woman with that thing... But anyway, I pulled out of Karen's pussy and told her to get up. Then I sat on the step, my cock pointing straight up at her, and told her to sit down on my dick. And she did. I guided my cock into her soft, wet pussy, as she lowered herself down over me. 'Ride me,' I said."

Cathy's masturbating harder. "Oh God," she pants. "I wish I could have been there."

"That felt great," I say. "Karen was really hot. She rode me in a fast, frantic rhythm. I felt my cock sliding in and out of her slippery pussy, swelling, ready to burst. The man was still stroking his cock, but now he came over to us and put his huge tool against Karen's lips."

Cathy is sliding two fingers into her pussy, gasping with excitement. I'm masturbating, too, drops of clear liquid dripping onto the kitchen floor.

"Karen opened her mouth as wide as she could," I say. "But the cock was so big, only the head fit in her mouth. But the man grunted with pleasure, as she started sucking on the big bulging head of his cock. Karen was still riding me, her big, shapely breasts bouncing in time to the fucking. I wanted to fuck her even harder, so I started thrusting my hips up towards her, over and over, making my cock enter her even deeper."

Cathy is doubled over, fucking herself with two fingers, breathing heavily. I walk over to her, stroking my cock as I watch her driving herself ever closer to another orgasm.

"I knew Karen was about to come again," I say, "And I grabbed her thighs, pressing her down hard onto my cock, filling her out as she came. I think she came even harder this time. Her body jerked wildly, as I held her tight. The man pulled his cock out of her mouth and let her scream so loud, everyone must have heard her. God, she was beautiful. And now none of us were able to hold back."

"Oh yesss," Cathy whispers, trembling with desire, rubbing her tender pink clit.

"The older man came first," I tell her. "I saw he was getting ready to ejaculate. And I told Karen to open her mouth. I wanted to see her tasting his cum. He started yelling as he came. His big cock swelled even more, and long, white jets of sperm shot out into

Karen's mouth. He kept coming, pumping spurt after spurt of creamy semen onto her tongue."

"Oh God," Cathy moans.

I'm standing right next to her.

"Get down on your knees," I tell her.

And she does, keeping her legs spread, stroking her wet pussy as she looks up at me.

"Finish the story," she whispers. "You came inside her, didn't you? You came inside my best friend."

"I kept thrusting my cock up into her pussy," I said, "until I couldn't hold back any longer. I just lay back on the stairs, feeling the sperm bursting its way out through the shaft. She moaned as she felt the first, hard spurt shooting into her flesh. And I kept coming, squirting my thick, hot sperm into her pussy."

Cathy looks up at me, as I point my bulging cock at her face.

"Yes," I gasp. "I came inside her, and now I'm gonna come all over you."

I freeze, grasping my cock. I see Cathy's eyes glazing over as the orgasm hits her. My cock seems to stiffen even more in my hand. And in a split second, it happens.

"Aaah," I yell as I start to ejaculate. "Fuck, yeah!"

My twitching cock starts pumping hot sperm at Cathy's face. She whimpers quietly, savouring her own climax, as jet after jet of thick cream hits her cheeks, her lips, her tongue.

I keep masturbating, emptying myself. Then I kneel down in front of her and kiss her, even tasting my own semen.

As we get up, she asks:

"But then, what happened next?"

"Oh yeah," I say, "I forget to tell you, we talked to the man. And he and Karen are coming over later tonight."

Cathy is puzzled.

"But... why?"

"What do you mean?" I laugh. "I suppose he wants to fuck your brains out. Come to think of it, we all want to fuck your brains out."

Cathy shakes her head, wondering whether I'm telling the truth.

But I won't tell her.

I'd rather let her find out.

The Construction Site

Taylor almost tripped on the wooden planks on her way to the trailer. What had she been thinking, she wondered, wearing high heels at a construction site?

She looked around. The site was huge, and now that night was falling, lit by dozens of floodlights. It seemed quite chaotic: Huge piles of earth, concrete slabs and heavy machinery, all utterly deserted by now. And of course the trailer, where she was going to do her interview. She knocked on the door.

"Come in," a male voice answered.

She opened the door.

At the small table the foreman sat, a balding man in his fifties. He didn't seem tall and was slightly overweight, but seemed remarkably fit.

He didn't get up as Taylor entered. She walked over to him and shook his hand.

"Welcome," he said. "Coffee?"

"Yes, please," she said, sitting down by the table.

The foreman got up to get the coffee. The trailer was quite neat. Not surprisingly, she noticed the usual nudie calendars — rather explicit, in fact — on the walls, but everything seemed to be in its place: Next to the sink was a coffee machine, and next to that a bottle of some sort of clear liquid — some kind of hand cleanser, probably.

But no dirty coffee mugs, no piles of paper on the floor. She was probably prejudiced anyway: A construction project of this magnitude demanded something close to military discipline.

The foreman returned with the coffee, and Taylor pulled out a note pad and a pen.

"Shall we get down to it?" she asked, smiling.

"I sure as hell think we should," the foreman said.

Taylor didn't like the tone of his voice. In fact, she didn't like the way he looked her over.

"So," she began, "what is the biggest challenge you're facing on this project?"

"Well," the foreman drawled, sitting down opposite her. "The worst thing is - there ain't no chicks 'round here. Know what I mean?"

Taylor smiled.

"Ah," she said, "the lack of female company?"

"Company?" he laughed. "It's the lack of fucking pussy, that what it is!"

Taylor felt herself blushing.

"I think..." she said.

"But what the hell," the foreman went on. "I shouldn't complain. Now you're here."

She could almost physically feel his eyes on her legs, her crotch, her breasts. He stood up and walked over to Taylor, standing right in front of her.

"Yup," he said. "Problem solved."

Suddenly, she felt his hand on her breast, squeezing it.

"Stop that!" she ordered.

The foreman just grinned.

"Nah," he said quietly. "I don't think so."

Taylor jumped from the chair and ran for the door. But the foreman grabbed her wrist, pulling her back.

"Let me go!" she hissed, struggling in his grip.

"Now don't disappoint me," the foreman said, pulling her towards the table. "I've been saving myself for you."

He forced her down on her back on the table. Holding her down with one hand, he lifted up her short skirt with the other. Again she tried resisting, but he was too strong.

The foreman pushed Taylor's panties to the side, and she felt his rough fingers touching her labia.

"No!" she cried. "No! Don't!"

Slowly, his thick fingers began massaging the mouth of her pussy. Taylor gasped, realizing she was helpless. Holding her down seemed to require no effort on his part.

He stroked her flesh rhythmically, moving his strong fingers toward her clitoris. Taylor squirmed on the hard tabletop. As the foreman masturbated her, she felt her labia getting moist. He kept going, stimulating the flow of her female juices.

Eventually, she was wet enough for him to push two fingers inside.

"Ah!" she cried.

She felt the foreman's rough fingers probing her, wriggling deep inside her sensitive pussy. She'd given up resistance now. If she let him have his way, she reckoned, it would soon be over. She hoped.

His fingers slipped out of her cunt, then pushed back in again. Then out again and in again, fucking her ever so slowly, her pussy making tiny wet noises with each stroke. The foreman bent down between her legs, touching her cunt with his tongue.

"Oooh!" she gasped.

Taylor felt his lips sucking at her pussy, thirstily drinking her juices. He slurped loudly, sucking and licking, his fingers thrusting in and out of her soft flesh.

And then she felt it: The pleasant tingling sensation, spreading from her cunt like electricity, making her entire body tremble with anticipation. If the foreman kept this up, she was going to have an orgasm right there on the table. Taylor bit her lip. She didn't want it to happen. Not here, not now, please...

But suddenly he stood up, slipping his finger from her pussy. He looked at her, grinning. He knew. Sadistic bastard, he knew.

The foreman unzipped the fly of his overalls and his erect cock sprang out. It was hard and thick, its reddened head bulging with excitement. A tiny drop of clear liquid dribbled from its tip. He took the stiff tool in his hand, pointing it guided it towards the mouth of Taylor's cunt.

"Oh no," she whimpered, "no..."

"Forget it!" he gasped. "Take your clothes off! You know you want it!"

Did she? Taylor could hardly think straight anymore. The whole situation was humiliating — and she hated the sight of the fat, elderly man and his lascivious grin. But then again, her body was in a state of excitement that needed to be satisfied with an orgasm.

She hated the man, but she yearned for the cock. It was really quite simple. Wasn't it?

Taylor knew that if she thought it over, she would change her mind. Instead she undressed as quickly as she could, throwing her blouse, her bra, her skirt and her panties on the floor of the trailer.

Then, trembling, she lay back on the table. Her nipples were actually hard. She couldn't believe it.

The foreman stood between her legs and grabbed hold of her thighs. He placed his cock at the mouth of her pussy and pushed forward with a loud grunt. She felt her soft flesh stretching around his shaft, as he drove his tool into her dripping wet cunt.

She could tell the foreman was excited now. Before, he had been calm, teasing and fingering her - but now he thrust into her in a fast, energetic rhythm. Over and over, he plunged his cock into her tender pussy, grunting like an animal in heat.

And as he moved inside her, probing her flesh, she felt her climax approaching.

"Shit!" she exclaimed.

It was horrible: The dirty old man raping her to orgasm on the table in his trailer. And yet it was totally wonderful. Her pussy opened wide, inviting him to push deeper, deeper. Her juices flowed abundantly, lubricating his pumping cock, almost drowning it. And then...

Taylor held on to the table. Held on hard. Her vision flickered — she almost fainted as she came.

"Aaahhh!" she cried. "Aaahhh!"

She threw herself about on the table, overcame by a powerful climax. Moaning uncontrollably, Taylor felt unbelievable sensations of pleasure washing through every fibre of her body. It was incredible. This could even be the best orgasm she'd ever had...

"Yeah!" The foreman yelled, thrusting into her.

She felt his cock swelling inside her. His eyes were wide open, as he approached his climax. As he came, he pulled out and grabbed his throbbing cock in his fist.

"Unnnhhh!" he yelled.

A long spurt of semen shot from his cock, flying several feet across her body. And another one, hitting her face with a glob of burning hot spunk. And again. And again. Masturbating, the foreman made his cock keep pumping, showering her face and body with thick, sticky sperm.

"Aaah yeah," he grunted, squeezing the last drops from his reddened cock.

Breathing hard, Taylor tried to compose herself. Now he would let her go, she thought. He had gotten what he wanted.

Clumsily, the foreman put his cock back into his overall and zipped up. Then he turned around, opened the door to a locker and took something out. Dazed, Taylor couldn't quite make it out. But as he turned to face her, she realized what it was.

A length of rope.

"What... ?" she gasped.

She tried to sit up, but she was still too exhausted. The foreman quickly grabbed her wrist and tied it firmly to one leg of the table.

"No..." she whimpered. "Please..."

The foreman's face was still red from the strain. He went round the table, expertly tying her other wrist to another leg, then both her feet. Seconds later, he was finished — and Taylor couldn't move. The foreman looked her over, admiring his work.

"Bet you thought I was finished with you?" he said. "Oh no, honey. The best is yet to come."

"Fuck!" Taylor shouted, yanking at the ropes. "Let me go!"

The foreman grinned, enjoying the sight of the naked woman struggling helplessly on the table.

"You know," he said. "You'll only tighten the knots when you do that. But, by the way, I know someone who's just dying to meet you. I'll only be a second. Don't go anywhere."

And with those words, the foreman left the trailer, leaving Taylor naked, tied to the table.

She let out a loud, exasperated grunt. What was he going to do now? She felt his sperm on her face and body. Taylor stuck out her tongue and tried to lick some of it off her cheeks and chin. It had a salty, powerful taste.

The door opened again, and two construction workers entered the trailer, dressed in overalls, boots and helmets. One was a big, muscular man, with dark, Mediterranean-style hair and complexion. The other was blond and thin and had piercing, pale blue eyes that made him look like a psychopath. Taylor was scared of him.

Both men looked at Taylor dispassionately. They smiled wickedly as they saw the tiny pile of her clothes on the floor. Behind them, the foreman, too, entered the trailer.

"Here she is, boys," he said. "Let's get to work."

He grabbed a towel and wiped his own semen off her body.

"There," he said. "As good as new."

The dark man kicked off his boots and unbuttoned his overalls. He swiftly pulled it off, standing naked except for the construction

helmet. His semi-erect cock bounced in front of him, as he moved. It was long, longer than the foreman's, and about the same thickness. Taylor gasped.

Now, the dark man put his boots back on. And naked, wearing boots and helmet, he walked towards Taylor. His heavy footsteps made the trailer rock.

Instinctively, Taylor tried to pull away, only to realize she was tied up. The dark man placed two fingers on her labia, then spread them, opening her pussy. He smiled at the sight. With his other hand he grabbed his cock and began stroking it, slowly masturbating himself to a full erection.

"Let her have it!" the blond man said.

"Shut up!" the dark man hissed.

Then he bent down and put his face between Taylor's thighs. Spreading her labia, he stuck out his tongue and pushed it into her pussy.

"Oh God!" Taylor gasped.

The dark man wriggled his tongue around inside her, exploring her soft flesh. He moved his head back and forth, fucking her with his tongue and sucking at her juicy pussy. The lustful sensations made Taylor tremble all over.

Then he pulled back and stood up, still holding on to his erect cock.

"Okay," he said. "Let's fuck."

Taylor was so wet it was almost embarrassing. She felt the juice trickling down the insides of her thighs.

The dark man placed his cock against her labia and Taylor felt the wide head bulging against her flesh. Shivering, she realized that his cock was even bigger than the foreman's.

"Oh God," she whispered.

Slowly, the dark man pushed forward. Taylor felt her wet pussy stretching around his swollen shaft, as he buried his cock inside her. She closed her eyes, whimpering with pleasure.

"Yeah," the blond man said, visibly excited at the sight, "you love it, don't you honey?"

"She sure does," the foreman said, grinning. "Fuck her good, buddy."

And the dark began thrusting into her, making her gasp out loud. He drove his cock in and out of her slippery cunt in a steady

pace, from the tip to the root with every stroke. Taylor tugged at the ropes, writhing lasciviously on the table.

"Keep going!" the blond man commanded

He was breathing heavily now, and as Taylor opened her eyes, she saw the bulge growing inside his overalls. The blond man began touching himself, stroking his cock through the rough fabric.

"Unh," he grunted. "Yeah..."

Taylor looked up at the man fucking her. His face was determined, unemotional. She felt his massive cock pumping rhythmically into her, massaging the sensitive insides of her cunt, driving her ever closer to another orgasm.

"Shit!" she gasped.

But there was no stopping it now. One more thrust of the dark man's cock. And another. And another...

"Aaahhh!" Taylor cried. "Aaahhh!" Her body exploded in convulsions of pleasure, throwing her about on the table. The dark man held on to her thighs, fucking her relentlessly. Almost losing consciousness, Taylor felt his swollen cock hammering into her, over and over, wet and slick with her abundant juices.

"Stop..." she whispered helplessly."Please... wait..."

The blond man stepped up to the table. He had zipped down his fly. His long, slender cock stood straight out, fully erect. He stroked it slowly, watching the dark man fucking the almost lifeless Taylor.

Then the dark man pulled out, his hard cock dripping juice onto the floor of the trailer.

"You want some?" he asked his mate.

"Don't mind if I do," the blond man replied, assuming the position between Taylor's legs.

Staring straight at her with his pale, piercing eyes, he thrust three fingers into her cunt and started massaging her pink clit with his thumb.

"No..." Taylor moaned. "I... I can't..."

Closing her eyes again, she gave up. Sprawled on the hard tabletop, she surrendered to the feelings of pleasure. Vigorously, the blond man thrust his fingers into her cunt, his thumb circling her stiffened clitoris.

"Damn!" he whispered. "That's one fine pussy you got there, honey..."

With a wet, squishy sound, he pulled his glistening fingers from her sex. Then he grabbed his cock and stroked it, covering it in Taylor's juices. Soon she felt his wet, bone-hard cock poking the mouth of her pussy.

Taylor was exhausted. She was no longer sure how long she had been in the trailer. And now the third man — the third cock — was about to fuck her. Lying there naked, tied to the table was utterly surreal - she had never experienced anything like it. But although she was scared, somehow she wanted them to go on. They obviously intended to fuck her senseless, and she found the thought outrageous — and terribly exciting.

In one smooth motion, the blond man thrust the entire length of his rigid cock into her tender slit. Taylor let out a loud gasp. She felt the rough fabric of his overalls against the skin of her thighs. And swiftly, in long smooth strokes, he began fucking her, still staring into her eyes with those intense pale eyes.

"Yeah..." the foreman said, a bulge growing inside the crotch of his overalls."Fuck her good!"

Holding onto Taylor's slender thighs, the blond man kept hammering his cock into her flesh in fast, powerful thrusts. She was gasping for air.

The foreman kicked off his boots and quickly undressed. His cock was semi-erect again. Taylor wondered whether it was normal for a man his age to get ready again so soon.

Grinning, he walked around the table and stood behind Taylor's head. Grabbing his hair, he pulled her head back over the edge of the table, her face upside down. Then he put his cock to her lips.

Taylor tried to spit it away, but he pushed against her lips. And finally she gave up and opened her mouth to the foreman's cock. She could still taste her own juices on its skin.

As the blond man kept fucking her, the foreman grabbed her shapely breasts, squeezing them gently, massaging them. Taylor sucked on his cock, sucked it as hard as she could. He tried to pull back, but was not prepared for the powerful suction she applied.

"Yeah!" he gasped, wriggling his hips. "Suck it good, little lady!"

Finally, with a loud popping sound, the foreman managed to pull the cock from Taylor's mouth. It stood red and erect in front of her face.

"Suck it again!" he ordered, ramming his hard tool in between her lips.

Taylor kept sucking, as the foreman began moving his hips violently. Still kneading her sensitive breasts, he pumped his cock into her mouth with hard, fast strokes. At the same time, she felt the blond man's long tool thrusting deep into her cunt.

She was at their mercy. Naked, tied to the table, while they fucked her mouth and pussy. Taylor hadn't been aware how excited she was, but suddenly it hit her again.

"Mmm!" she cried, her screams muffled by the foreman's cock. "Mmm!"

She came again. Her bound legs kicked helplessly as the climax sent waves of pleasure through her flesh. She felt both cocks swelling inside her mouth and cunt — the men were obviously turned on by the sight of her orgasm.

"You like it, huh?" the blond man sneered. "Huh? Huh?"

He thrust deep into her pussy with every word, making Taylor sob in unbearable ecstasy.

"My turn!" the dark man grunted.

And the blond man slipped his cock from her cunt, letting the dark man take his place. She recognized the feeling of his thick tool, stretching her labia as it entered her flesh. He began pumping her vigorously, burying the entire length of his cock inside her with every stroke. The blond man stood next to them, masturbating slowly, clear fluid dripping from the tip of his cock.

The foreman slipped his cock from Taylor's mouth and stood there, his hard-on bobbing up and down in front of her face.

"Tell me you want it," he gasped, his voice hoarse with lust. "Say it!"

"Oh God!" Taylor cried, the dark man's cock hammering into her tender slit. "Yes! I want it! Give it to me."

Grunting like an animal, the foreman once more forced his throbbing cock into Taylor's mouth. She sucked it greedily, slurping loudly, as he slid it back and forth between her lips. The blond man watched them intently, masturbating at the sight. The head of his long, erect cock bulged as he stroked it rhythmically with his fist.

Taylor hadn't quite recovered from her last orgasm. She was in a state of heightened sexual sensibility. Every touch, every move the men made, triggered sensations of pleasure, making her shiver,

making her juices flow around the dark man's erect rod. She could climax again at any moment.

Suddenly, the foreman pulled his cock from her mouth, making a loud popping sound.

"Let's untie her," he said.

And both men quickly untied the ropes, throwing them on the floor.

Taylor was confused. Had they changed their minds? Were they going to let her go? The two workmen hadn't even come yet.

The foreman lay on his back on the floor of the trailer, his stiff, wet cock pointing straight up. The blond man lifted Taylor off the table and carried her to where the foreman lay. Grunting, the foreman grabbed his cock and guided it into her pussy, as the blond man slowly lowered her, making her sit on his lap. Moaning with pleasure, Taylor felt his erect rod entering her flesh from beneath.

The dark man stood in front of her and grabbed her chin. Obediently, she opened her mouth and let him push his cock in between her lips.

"Yeah," he said. "Suck it good."

His cock was considerably bigger than the foreman's — she could only fit the swelling head in her mouth. She began sucking it, once more tasting her own juice on a man's cock. Taylor held it by the root with one hand and took his hairy balls in the other, gently caressing them, making him gasp.

She began moving her hips up and down, making the foreman's cock slip in and out of her pussy. She wriggled around in circles on top of him, letting his erect tool explore every inch of her slippery crevice. Moaning with pleasure, the foreman just had to lie there - Taylor took care of the fucking.

The blond man grabbed the bottle beside the sink. Squeezing it, he poured the oily liquid over his stiff cock, making it bounce. Then Taylor felt the cold spray hitting her ass.

Surprised, she pulled her head away from the dark man's cock.

"What... ?" she gasped.

But the dark man grabbed her hair, pushed his cock back into her mouth and began thrusting in and out between her lips. Underneath her, the foreman began moving his pelvis up and down, fucking her pussy.

And then she felt the blond man's fingers, slick with oil, forcing their way into her anus.

"Mmm!" she protested, her mouth filled with the dark man's swelling cock. "Mmm!"

The blond man assumed the position behind her ass, his rigid cock pushing hard against her rectum. As he grabbed her hips, Taylor felt the head of his cock forcing its way into her ass.

She struggled in the grip of the three excited men. Exasperated, she banged her hands of the floor of the trailer.

"Mmm!" she cried.

But slowly, the blond man buried the entire length of his hardened shaft inside her rectum. Then he pulled back and thrust into her again. And again.

Pain gave way to pleasure, and soon Taylor felt herself wriggling her ass against him, encouraging him to go deeper.

Taylor felt herself quivering uncontrollably. They were having their way with her, fucking her savagely in every orifice. She was the object of their animal lust, their anonymous sex toy. And she loved it. It was filthy, shameless, outrageous...

And as they kept hammering their cocks into her in a hard, relentless rhythm, she once more gave in. The dark man seemed to sense her orgasm approaching and pulled his cock from her mouth, letting her cry out on ecstasy.

"Ohhh!" she yelled. "Ohhh!"

Grabbing his cock in his fist, the dark man came, too. A thick spurt of semen shot from his cock, spattering Taylor's flushed face. And once more — a long jet of sticky sperm sprayed into her open mouth. Masturbating, the dark man pointed his cock toward her breasts. Still trembling in her climax, Taylor arched her back, letting him pump his semen onto her naked breasts. Grunting, he squeezed every last drop from his cock.

Inside her, the foreman was the next to come.

"Unnnhhh!" he cried. "Unnnhhh!"

Kicking his heels against the floor of the trailer, he ejaculated inside her cunt with incredible force. Taylor felt his cock contracting, spurting shots of hot semen into her tender pussy. His orgasm seemed to go on forever, sperm pumping from his jerking tool.

Even before the foreman's ejaculation had subsided, the blond man pulled his cock from her ass. Taylor felt the first jet of his semen shooting across her naked back.

"Yeahhh!" he shouted. "Fuck yeah!"

The foreman pushed Taylor away, rolling her onto her back on the floor. Ejaculating, the blond man towered above her, his cock protruding from his overalls, pumping hot sperm all over her naked body.

"Take that!" he gasped, masturbating vigorously. "Take it! Yeah!"

Spurt after spurt of his semen shot from his cock, landing all over Taylor's body.

And then, suddenly, it was all over.

The foreman and the dark man put their clothes back on without a word. The blond man merely had to zip up.

For a few seconds they just stood there looking at her, as she lay sprawled on the floor, exhausted, gasping for air.

Then, quietly, they left the trailer.

All alone, Taylor wiped herself with the towel, then put her clothes back on.

Outside, there was no trace of any of the three men.

She stood in the cold night air, looking out over the construction site, bathed in harsh floodlights.

They were gone. She would just have to go home.

Taylor picked up her cell phone and dialled her editor. She got his answering machine.

"Hi," she said after the beep. "This is Taylor. About the interview: Something came up. I didn't get to speak to anyone. I'm sorry, but I will have to go back once more. To the construction site."

Volume Four

Bedfellows

"I'm sorry, Miss," the receptionist said. "But there's really nothing I can do."

"But we did make a reservation for two single rooms," I protested.

"So you told me. But I don't see that reservation anywhere. All I know is that I have a double room available for you."

"And you're telling us," Steve said, trying to control his anger, "that you can't change that reservation now?"

"I would if I could," the receptionist said, exasperated. "But we're fully booked. There's a conference in town, you know."

"Yes, I know," Steve snapped. "That's why we're here."

"We'll take the room," I sighed. "We'll work something out."

The receptionist handed us the key and Steve took it.

"I'm really very sorry," the receptionist said.

"Yes, I think you mentioned that," Steve said.

We rolled our suitcases to the elevator and got in. Steve pushed the button for the fifth floor.

"I don't know," he said. "Of course, it's possible that my secretary made a mistake. But she never did before."

"We'll be okay," I said. "Don't worry."

We got out on the fifth floor and rolled our suitcases across the soft carpet to the room.

I'd been working with Steve for five years, and we had always had some kind of harmless flirt going. We were attracted to each other, but he had been married the whole time, and I didn't want to cause any trouble. So at every office party we'd drink and laugh and dance – and then leave it at that.

Steve unlocked the door and opened it.

"Oh, shit!" he exclaimed.

We'd probably both been hoping for a double bed that could somehow be separated into two parts. But this one was a real king size double bed. And due to the size of the room, there was no couch, no folding bed, nothing.

"Well," I said. "Um..."

"This won't do," Steve said.

"Look," I said. "This is all we can get. The hotel is full. Of course we could run around town looking for another hotel. But how much do you wanna bet they're fully booked, too? And it's late, and we have to get up early tomorrow. We're adults. We can work it out. Right?"

Steve closed the door behind him and sighed.

"You're right," he said. "Of course we can. Nothing we can do about it now, anyway."

I sat down on the bed and looked at him. He actually is quite handsome in a classic way. You know, the broad-shouldered, dark-haired, square-jawed type.

When word got around that we were going to the conference together, there had been some giggling among the girls in the company. They all had the hots for Steve, anyway – and of course they were joking that we wouldn't be able to keep our hands off each other for a whole weekend. I wonder what they'd said if they'd seen that bed.

Smiling nervously, Steve turned towards the mini-bar.

"Care for a drink?" he asked. "God knows I could do with one."

"Oh, yes please," I said. "Any white wine?"

He opened the door and looked.

"It's your lucky day," he said and produced a small bottle of white wine and a miniature bottle of whiskey for himself.

He sat down in an armchair across from me, and we poured our drinks into plastic glasses, Steve adding an ice cube from the freezer. We sipped quietly for a while. The white wine was pretty awful, but a pinch of alcohol helped to relieve the mood.

We chatted casually for a while, until Steve finally brought up the big question:

"So, where do you sleep? Pick a side."

"Um, left," I said.

"Left it is," he replied, finishing his drink. "Ready to call it a day?"

I nodded.

"Okay," Steve said, standing up. "I suggest the following: I go to the bathroom first. Then, when I come out, you go, while I get ready for bed."

"And when I come out?" I asked.

He smiled.

"I promise I won't look," he said.

I rolled my eyes, grinning.

"Whatever," I said. "It's a deal."

Steve slipped into the bathroom and I heard the water running. I turned on the little lamps over the headboard, then switched off the other lights in the room. Suddenly, the anonymous hotel room really looked quite cosy.

I sat down on the bed again. The mattress was quite soft – a bit softer in fact, than I liked it. But so what – it was only for two nights. From the bathroom came the sounds of Steve brushing his teeth. And then he came out.

"Okay," he said. "It's all yours."

"Great," I said. "I'm dead tired. Aren't you?"

"Yeah. Going straight to bed."

I slipped into the bathroom and got ready for bed. Through the door I heard the faint rustling as Steve undressed. I stared at his toothbrush on the bathroom shelf. And suddenly I realized that it was true: We were going to spend the night in the same bed.

Take it easy, I told myself. I wasn't going to seduce him – I wouldn't mess with his married life. And he sure as hell wasn't going to seduce me, either – he loved his wife too much for that to happen.

I took a deep breath as I went back into the room. Steve was in bed, his lamp already switched off. He certainly wasn't looking. Maybe he was already asleep. I changed into my night clothes: A pair of panties and a big t-shirt. Then I crawled into bed, pulling the sheet over me.

"Goodnight," Steve mumbled beside me.

"Goodnight," I answered, switching off the lamp.

I lay there for a while, waiting, the scent of his skin tickling my nostrils. It was kind of arousing, but no – I would not allow myself to get turned on.

A few minutes later, I heard Steve's breathing becoming slow and deep, with a slight snore. He was asleep.

Actually, I prefer to sleep naked, and now I seized the opportunity. Without making a sound, I slipped off my t-shirt and then my panties, throwing both on the floor next to the bed. Tomorrow, I would work out a way to put the clothes back on without him noticing.

The sheets felt cool and sexy wrapping around my naked body. And breathing the unfamiliar scent of Steve's skin, I drifted off to sleep.

It was dark when I woke up. I lay face down, my arms wrapped around the pillow, my face turned away from Steve's side of the bed.

At first, I wondered what had woken me. But then I felt it – the mattress was rocking. A slight, rhythmic motion, making the entire bed shake and squeak. The rhythm was somehow familiar. And suddenly, I knew what it was.

Steve was masturbating.

I froze in position. He obviously thought I was asleep, and I wasn't going to reveal that I wasn't. The embarrassment would be enough to kill us both.

The bed kept rocking and squeaking. I heard Steve grunting softly. Damn, how I would have loved to watch him masturbate. Just turn my head and get a good look at his cock. But no – I resisted the urge and forced myself to just lie there and wait for him to get it over with.

Rocking, squeaking, panting – his rhythm was increasing. He must be about to come – and I realized that the thought of Steve ejaculating was beginning to make me wet. Oh, God. Good thing I was pretending to be asleep – that was saving us both a lot of embarrassment.

Suddenly, I felt a chill, as the sheet was lifted off my naked back. From the movements of the mattress I figured he now sat astride me, one knee on either side of my legs, masturbating to the sight of my naked ass.

And I couldn't move! I just didn't have the nerve to simply turn around, look him in the eyes and watch him come. Although the thought of it did turn me on – a lot.

His breathing grew louder. The rocking motions increased in speed and intensity. Until suddenly they stopped.

"Mgh!" he grunted.

And I felt the first spurt of semen landing on my naked back.

I shivered, and tears welled into my eyes. Just imagine: His secret lust for me was so great that he couldn't help jerking off at the sight of my naked body.

He kept ejaculating – squirt after squirt of burning hot sperm spattered my naked back. I was so hot now, I could have screamed out loud. I could have begged him to fuck me – I just didn't care

anymore. But somehow, I managed to control myself and kept absolutely still.

Steve's orgasm subsided. I felt him gently pulling the sheet back over me. Then, carefully, he climbed back to his side of the bed and lay down.

I was beside myself with lust. But knowing men, I figured he would soon be fast asleep.

I waited. And a few minutes later, his heavy breathing had quieted down, becoming slow and relaxed. He was asleep.

As quietly as possible, I slowly reached down between my legs, touching my clit. I sighed deeply at my own touch. I ran my fingers ran over my labia, feeing the wetness of my flesh. Slowly, without a sound, I began massaging my clit. All the tensions seemed to evaporate from my body, leaving me calm and relaxed.

I closed my eyes, feeling the sensations of pleasure washing over me. Laying flat on my belly and moving my fingers ever so slightly, I could still apply pressure to my clit. The mattress hardly moved, as I masturbated with almost imperceptible strokes. I caressed my clit faster and faster, gasping under my breath.

I spread my legs, my thighs trembling slightly with pleasure. Juice flowed over my fingers, as I buried my head in the pillow, sobbing helplessly as I felt my climax approached. I could smell Steve's sweat, his semen on my back, mixing with the hot scent of my own excited flesh.

"Mmm..." I moaned, masturbating myself towards orgasm. "Mmm..."

But suddenly I felt it: Another finger touching the mouth of my pussy.

I froze. Afraid to move, I opened my eyes wide in the darkness. Steve had woken up. And now he was touching me.

I had stopped masturbating – and now his finger slowly entered my dripping wet slit. He slid it slowly back and forth a couple of times – then slipped it out completely.

My breathing was hurried, apprehensive. I couldn't believe this was happening, but at the same time I felt there was no turning back. By masturbating, I'd somehow become part of the game – leading him on. And besides, it was too late to admit that I'd been awake the whole time. Now I had to keep pretending.

He changed his position – and then I felt it: The head of his cock pushed against my labia, hot and hard. Gradually, my pussy

yielded to the pressure, letting him enter. As he buried his tool inside me, I felt my juices flowing around his thick shaft, making it wet and slick.

He pulled back and entered me again, letting me feel the entire length of his erect cock. I closed my eyes, trembling with pleasure as he began fucking me. He thrust into me in a steady, sensual rhythm. Over and over he buried his rigid shaft inside me, making my pleasure grow, pushing me closer and closer to an orgasm.

Suddenly it dawned on me: He was raping me. This was how he would fuck a helpless, defenceless female. But in that case, I would have imagined a brutal, painful violation. To my surprise, he was pleasuring me as well as himself, stimulating my sensitive flesh with every thrust of his hard cock.

And then I couldn't hold back any longer. I came hard – an explosion of lust that burst through every fibre of my body, making me shiver. I bit into the pillow to keep myself from screaming out loud with pleasure.

Steve kept going, his cock pumping into my pussy like a piston. Had he noticed my orgasm? If he had, it hadn't necessarily called my bluff: I could have climaxed in my sleep.

With a grunt, he pulled out of me. And then, a few seconds later, I once more felt the pressure of his cock.

But this time it was pushing against my rectum.

I wanted to cry out, to make him stop. But by now it was too late. I had played along, and now I was going to get my punishment.

Steve forced his slippery cock into my ass, my anus slowly opening itself to him. I whimpered into the pillow as tears filled my eyes. But the pain merely added to the pleasure. In fact, I knew right there and then that if he fucked my ass, he would make me come even harder.

Slowly, his thick cock buried itself inside my ass. He held still, letting me feel it throb with lust. As he began fucking me, I couldn't suppress a cry:

"Ah!" I shrieked.

He didn't care. His hands grabbed my hips, as he kept going, thrusting his erect tool in and out of my ass.

He must have been insane with lust. Fucking a sleeping woman was one thing. But how could he even imagine fucking my ass without waking me up? In his excited state, he was obviously past caring.

And then Steve surprised me once more. His right hand found my clit and began massaging it. I sobbed uncontrollably, as my arousal built towards another climax. Again and again, he hammered his cock into my ass. Juices flowed from my excited cunt, wetting his finger and trickling down the insides of my thighs.

His breathing grew louder, and I felt his cock twitching inside my ass. And finally, he thrust deep into me and held still. His tool swelled inside my narrow passage, stretching my tender anus even more. And finally he came.

As the first powerful spurt of semen shot into me, I came too. I screamed loudly into my pillow, screamed again and again. My entire body trembled, as waves of sexual electricity surged through me. Inside my ass I felt Steve's cock contracting, pumping long, powerful jets of white-hot sperm into my tight little hole.

Our orgasms seemed to last forever. His cock stayed hard inside me.

Finally, he pulled out. I heard him quietly slipping into the bathroom. When he returned, he cautiously pulled the bedspread over me and climbed into bed beside me.

I heard him sighing with satisfaction, and soon he drifted off to sleep.

My mind was spinning. I thought I'd be lying awake for hours. But the two powerful orgasms had worn me out, and in fact I feel asleep a few minutes later.

As I woke up, he was getting dressed.

"Oh," he said. "Good morning. Did you sleep well?"

I looked at him. He wasn't going to talk about what happened. And why should I?

"Yeah," I said, pulling the sheets around me, as I realized I was still naked. "Fine."

"No bad dreams?" he asked.

He had some nerve. But I couldn't help smiling.

"Oh no," I said. "Quite the opposite, in fact."

He laughed.

"That's good," he said. "We've got time for breakfast before the conference starts."

"Okay," I said. "I'll be ready in a minute."

We didn't talk about what had happened that night. And we never have since.

Steve went back home to his wife. And of course that's where he belongs.

But I had him once. Just for one night, I had him.

We can pretend it never happened. But neither of us will ever forget.

The Tourists

Nikki never knew that sand had a taste.

But after driving around for more than a week in this godforsaken desert, she knew. Riding on the back seat of Jack's stupid scooter, she imagined she could even learn to distinguish the various parts of the desert by the taste of sand that constantly blew into her mouth.

But why bother?

She hated it here. Jack had promised the trip would be exotic and fun, but she didn't get it. She hated the heat, the sand, the food – and not least, she hated the goddamn Arabs. Scruffy, unshaven bastards, leering nastily at her wherever they went. As if they hadn't seen a pretty American blonde before. Come to think of it, they'd probably never seem any woman before – at least not without that stupid sheet over the head.

Oh sure, Jack kept telling her it was a "different culture" and that she should be "open to new experiences". But nothing she'd seen so far had challenged her conviction that this was a hopelessly backwards country, inhabited by horny towel heads.

But she didn't complain much anymore. Lately, Jack had began to act annoyed. He'd tell her to shut up, and that he didn't care – that this was a great holiday destination – and why hadn't she brought proper clothes, anyway?

Nikki had no idea what he meant: She knew they were going to a hot place, so she'd brought her little tops and short skirts. And how was she to know that you couldn't walk in desert sand in high heels? After all, she wanted to look her best – and that included sexy shoes. But as usual, Jack didn't have a clue.

They sat in the closest thing to a restaurant in this tiny desert town, the scooter parked outside. Jack had savoured the grilled something with horrible sauce like a gourmet meal. Nikki had been starving, but only managed to eat a few mouthfuls.

"It's disgusting," she declared.

Jack reached for his wallet, then froze.

"Fuck!" he said.

"What?"

"I left our money at the hotel," he sighed. "You don't have any, do you?"

Nikki shook her head.

Slowly, the waiter came over to the table. He was a tall, young guy with dark skin and dark eyes. Nikki didn't care for him, but didn't find him quite as repulsive as the other Arabs she'd met.

"Sorry," Jack explained to the waiter. "I'll have to go back to our hotel for the money, okay?"

He pointed to Nikki.

"She'll stay here until I get back."

The waiter nodded, grinning.

"What?" Nikki shrieked. "You're gonna leave me here?"

"What else am I going to do?" Jack said. "You don't know how to drive the scooter. Anyway, it's only half an hour to get there and back."

He stood up and kissed her on the cheek.

"Love you, Nikki," he said. "See you soon."

And with those words, he left and drove off on the scooter.

Nikki shifted uneasily on the uncomfortable chair. The young waiter went into the back room, leaving her alone in the otherwise empty restaurant. She heard him talking to another man in a muffled voice. And soon, an elderly Arab man came through the door and walked over to Nikki's table.

Oh God – he was exactly the kind she couldn't stand: Greying stubble on his cheeks and a lustful gaze. He almost drooled at the sight of the young blonde sitting alone in his restaurant.

Nikki turned to look out of the window, but felt him stepping up close to her. She shivered, as she felt him stroking her hair.

"Hehe," he grinned. "Hehehe."

His hands moved down over her body, stroking her breast, squeezing it.

"No," she whispered. "Please..."

The old man's hands stroked her thighs, found their way up under her short skirt. He pushed her panties aside, his fingers poking her pussy lips.

Nikki turned and slapped his face hard.

He let go immediately, staring at her in a state of shock.

"Abdul!" he cried.

The young man came from the backroom and joined them at the table. The old man explained the situation in Arabic, and Abdul frowned at Nikki. Then he stood behind her chair and grabbed her arms.

"What?" she cried.

Abdul spoke to the old man. And whatever he said, it lit up the old man's face in a lusty grin. As Abdul held Nikki's arms, the old man pulled down his loose linen pants. His dark-skinned cock hung semi-erect between his legs.

"No!" Nikki cried. "Let me go!"

She struggled frantically, but Abdul was too strong for her.

The old man held his cock in his fist with one hand and forced Nikki's mouth open with the other.

"No, please," she protested, as he pushed his cock in between her lips, "pl... Mmm... Ngh..."

Nikki felt the old man's cock throbbing in her mouth, tasting faintly of spice and desert sand. His bony fingers grabbed her hair, as he started thrusting back and forth, fucking her mouth.

"Ah," he groaned. "Ah. Unh."

His thick member swelled and hardened with each thrust. Nikki gasped and gagged, as wet, slurping noises filled the room.

She tried struggling again, but Abdul held her even harder, letting the old man plunge his erect cock in and out of her mouth. Outside the window, a couple of veiled women stopped to watch. They seemed to be giggling, pointing their fingers at the pretty American girl giving a blow job to an old Arab man. Humiliated, Nikki closed her eyes.

The old man was moaning louder now, thrusting his bone-hard cock into her mouth. And finally, she felt it swelling and twitching, ready to come. He froze, throwing his head back in ecstasy. Nikki tried to pull her head away, but it was no use. The old man pushed his erect cock even deeper inside her mouth, as he began to ejaculate. For a second, Nikki noticed how – regardless of cultural differences – all men look the same when they orgasm.

"Huhn!" he yelled. "Ahhh! Hunh!"

A long, hot spurt of spicy semen exploded into Nikki's throat. Frantically, she tried swallowing the first creamy load, but another one followed immediately after, filling her mouth with salty spunk. And another – and another. Gulping and choking, Nikki felt the old

Arab's sperm running down her chin and her neck, as his cock kept jerking and spurting between her lips.

Then, finally, his ejaculations subsided. Breathing heavily, he held his cock inside her mouth, savouring the sensation as it slowly went soft. As he pulled back, Nikki saw the dark skin of his shaft glistening with semen and saliva.

The old man gazed at her almost lovingly, as he swiftly pulled up his pants. Nikki tried swallowing the rest of his spunk – but it was still the only taste in her mouth.

She felt Abdul loosen his grip, and realized she could now move her arms. Abdul said a few words to the old man, and he disappeared into the back room. Then Abdul stood in front of Nikki, still frowning.

"You don't humiliate my uncle," he said in a hoarse voice with a heavy accent.

Nikki was somewhat impressed that he knew the word "humiliate".

"I... I'm sorry," she said.

He shook his head.

"Not good enough," he said.

Suddenly, he grabbed her, lifting her up and placing her on her back on the table.

"Hey!" she cried.

Swiftly, Abdul lifted up her skirt. Then he bent down, pushed her panties aside, and put his mouth between her legs. She felt his wet tongue poking her pussy lips.

"No..." she cried, struggling.

But Abdul grabbed her thighs with his hands, pinning her down as he pushed his tongue into her cunt. She felt his hot breath on her belly, as he began moving his head back and forth, thrusting his tongue in and out of her pussy. He pushed it all the way in, holding it still, then wriggling it around, exploring the wet, sensitive depths of her flesh.

Nikki moaned helplessly, feeling her juices starting to flow. Perhaps even the attack by Abdul's uncle had turned her on a little bit – but Abdul's tongue action sure was irresistible.

He pulled his tongue from her cunt, and licking from side to side like a snake he slowly moved towards the base of her clit.

"Oh no," she gasped. "Please..."

He licked her clit rhythmically, circling it with his salivating tongue. Nikki squirmed with lust on the wooden table, involuntarily pushing her pussy against his face.

Abdul kept going, gasping with excitement, licking around and around Nikki's tiny, hardening clit. She banged her fists on the table, crying out loud with pleasure.

"Yes! Yes!"

And finally – inevitably – the orgasm surged through her. Nikki trembled in ecstasy, her juices gushing as she felt the climax pumping through every fibre of her body. It seemed to go on forever, while she whimpered and moaned on the wooden table.

In her post-orgasmic daze, she vaguely sensed Abdul's wet tongue letting go of her pussy. He stood in front of her, undressing completely. He was fit, not too muscular – his skin dark, his cock long and almost fully erect. In fact, Nikki thought to her own surprise, he was a bit of a hunk. But no, she couldn't be thinking that – must be the orgasm talking...

Abdul grabbed his long, hard cock in his hand and began masturbating, staring at Nikki with his intense dark eyes.

"Your clothes – off!" he commanded.

Nikki's head was spinning. Still on her back on the table, she slowly pulled off her skirt and panties – and then her top. When she sat up to unbuckle her high-heeled shoes, Abdul stopped her – heels evidently turned him on – and she lay back on the table again.

He stood between her legs, his erect cock pointing straight at her face. Forcing it down, he guided it toward the opening of her cunt.

"No..." Nikki whispered, as the tip of Abdul's cock made contact with her pussy lips. "Please. Please don't..."

Breathing heavily, she lay there staring at the Arab's hardened tool. Her breasts quivered – there was no way she could hide her excitement.

Grunting, he slowly slid his cock into her. Nikki gasped, her mouth open wide. She felt his erect shaft forcing her pussy open, entering her flesh inch after inch.

Abdul was breathing harder now. Having buried the entire length of his cock inside her, he held still, letting her feel it grow to an even harder erection.

Then he grabbed her thighs with both hands. And suddenly, Nikki felt the first powerful thrust.

"Ah!" she cried.

He plunged the entire length of his stiff cock into her. Then he pulled out, only to thrust again – as deep as before. And again – and again – back and forth, in a steady rhythm, pumping her cunt with relentless energy.

"Ohhh..." Nikki whimpered, "ohhh..."

Abdul fucked her savagely, his long cock stiff as a pole. But when Nikki looked up at him, his face did not reveal his excitement. It remained an expressionless mask, his jaw clenched in intense concentration.

This frightened her slightly – it was so unlike Jack, who was always yelling and drooling when he fucked her. And she'd always sort of liked to sense Jack's excitement. Being impaled by this unfeeling Arab fuck machine was rather frightening – but in a really sexy way...

Abdul grabbed her wrists, pinning her to the wooden table, as he kept thrusting into her. Nikki heard an evil cackle nearby. As she looked around, she saw that the old man – Abdul's uncle – had come back into the restaurant and was now watching them. He grinned lustfully at the sight of his nephew fucking the American girl. As he watched them, she saw him fingering his old cock through his loose pants. She closed her eyes to avoid the sight of the leering old man.

Abdul vigorously kept plunging into her excited pussy, moving his hips around, varying the angle of entrance ever so slightly, letting his erect cock stimulate every surface of her sensitive flesh.

Nikki felt another climax approaching. She couldn't believe it. For all her hate of Arabs, there was no denying that Abdul just fucked her so good. So goddamn good.

Juices gushing from her pussy, Nikki felt her body beginning to tremble again. She opened her eyes and met his piercing gaze. He was sweating from the strain, drops of perspiration running down his face and breast. But his dark eyes were completely focused, as if evaluating the effect of each thrust of his cock, following Nikki every step of the way towards another orgasm.

"No..." she gasped, her body jerking uncontrollably. "No... Ohmigod. Ohmigod..."

Using all his strength, Abdul managed to plunge even harder and deeper into Nikki's slurping wet cunt. And once more, she succumbed to an overpowering climax.

"Aaah!" she cried, "aaah!"

Abdul held still inside her, as her pussy contracted violently around his erect cock. Then, ever so slowly, he let it slip out. And once more he knelt between her legs, licking the juices from her labia. Nikki shivered with pleasure, her orgasm seemingly prolonged by the stimulation.

"Abdul..." she whispered deliriously, "you're crazy. Stop that. I can't go on... Oh, God..."

With both hands, she tried to push his head away from between her legs, but it was no use. He forced his mouth towards her crevice, licking thirstily at her succulent pussy with the most obscene slurping and lapping sounds. Slowly, he slid two fingers into her cunt, moving them around and back and forth, making her whimper softly. Then – finally – he let go of her pussy and stood up.

"Come here," he ordered, grabbing her wrist.

Nikki got off the table. Abdul's uncle still stood there, staring at her. He wasn't touching himself anymore, but his erection was clearly visible inside his loose pants.

She stood naked in front of Abdul and just looked at him – dark-skinned and muscular, his long, erect cock pointing straight at her, still dripping from her juices. He really was quite a hunk, wasn't he?

Nikki still couldn't believe she thought that. A fucking Arab – a hunk? Yes, right now she was horny as hell. But she wasn't attracted to towel heads – not in a million years.

No, it had to have something to do with the heat – the relentless heat of the desert. Driving around for days and days, all that heat must have accumulated inside her. And Abdul had just released it all – turning her into an insatiable whore. She'd just wanted any – any – hard cock inside her, even if that cock happened to belong to a disgusting Arab.

Abdul pulled her towards the door. Her legs still trembling after two orgasms, Nikki stumbled after him.

"No!" she said, as she realized he was pulling her out into the street. "Stop!"

What the hell was the matter with him? She wasn't going to be walking around naked in the middle of this goddamn shithole of a town. She struggled furiously, but he grabbed her wrists harder and pushed her out of the door.

Outside was another little rickety wooden table, bearing the marks of countless sandstorms. Abdul made her bend over, face down, her ass in the air. His uncle had followed them and now stood grinning lustily at her.

"Oh yeah," Nikki whispered under her breath, "you piece of shit. Go ahead and play with your dirty old dick. Bet you've never seen a naked woman before. Ah!"

Nikki jumped, as she felt Abdul's fingers between her legs, grabbing her labia and pulling her pussy wide open. She felt the hot desert wind blowing against her sensitive flesh.

Holding her gaping hole open, Abdul slowly pushed his rigid cock in between his fingers. Nikki felt her cunt stretching wide, as he buried the entire length of his tool inside her. Finally, his fingers let go of her cunt, and her soft, elastic flesh slammed shut around his shaft.

Abdul grabbed her hips and pulled back. His first thrust was so hard, it made her scream.

"Aaah!"

Abdul began fucking her in a mad, frantic pace. It was as if someone had pulled a switch, starting some powerful, unstoppable engine. His cock hammered relentlessly into her quivering slit like a piston, poking her with mechanical precision.

"Aaah! Fuuuck!"

Nikki held on to the table, her entire body shaken by the force of each powerful thrust. Abdul's uncle finally pulled his pants down, letting him watch as he stroked his dark-skinned cock, which had now risen to a full erection.

"No-o-o!" she cried, her voice broken up by the rhythm of his Abdul's fucking. "Ab-du-u-ul! Sto-o-o-op!"

Nikki thrashed about on the wooden table, her legs kicking helplessly. Abdul held her down, his cock plunging deeper and deeper into her tender flesh. She cried out, as she felt the tip of his thumb entering her anus.

"Nuuuh!" she protested.

Her body trembled with a curious mix of pleasure and humiliation. Slowly, Abdul forced his thumb into her ass. And somehow, this strange sensation turned her on. Really? Was she losing her mind? She was too horny to think straight anymore – the cock in her pussy and the thumb in her ass just kept pushing her to new levels of excitement.

Nikki's juices flowed from her cunt, lubricating Abdul's cock with her wetness. She was getting more and more excited, sure – but strangely not approaching orgasm. But – she was going to climax eventually, wasn't she? Or was it just going to be like this forever – ever-increasing levels of pleasure? She wasn't sure she could take it – could almost feel her abdomen clenching up in pain, desperate for the release of orgasm.

Nikki whimpered helplessly, as Abdul kept fucking her vigorously, his thumb buried deep inside her sensitive anus.

Then, hearing a familiar noise, she raised her head.

An engine. The scooter. It was Jack finally coming back from the hotel.

This was it, she thought. She had to struggle out of Abdul's grip, get inside and get her clothes back on. Letting Jack see her like this was simply out of the question.

As the scooter clattered down the street, Abdul kept fucking her, his uncle drooling at the sight. And with each thrust, Nikki felt more sensual, more lustful, more delightfully filthy.

Fuck it, she thought. Let him watch.

Whenever he was really horny, Jack would talk about how he'd like to see her get fucked by other men – by complete strangers in the middle of the street. And now he'd finally gotten what he wanted. Nikki moaned loudly at the thought.

Jack parked the scooter outside the restaurant and stumbled towards them, his eyes open wide.

"Wha...?" he stuttered.

Abdul held still inside Nikki, his erect cock twitching inside her clenching pussy.

"We fuck," Abdul said.

"Yeah," Nikki purred. "We're fucking. And you can watch. You always wanted that, remember?"

"Nikki..." Jack protested. "I..."

"Yeah," she went on, using her huskiest voice. "You can watch as Abdul fucks me. Take your cock out, honey."

"Take my...?"

"You heard me. Take it out, so you can jerk off. Watch us fuck. Yeah, c'mon, Abdul – I'm ready."

Abdul grabbed Nikki's ass and brutally thrust into her slit, making her scream out loud:

"Aaah!"

Jack stood right next to them, watching Abdul's cock plunging into his girlfriends pussy.

"Yeah," she whispered. "Look at that. You like that, huh? You like that?"

"You filthy slut," Jack hissed. "You dirty, dirty whore."

He unbuckled his belt and pulled down his pants. His thick cock was half erect. Nikki gasped at the sight.

"Yeah?" he said. "Is this what you want? Is it?"

Jack grabbed his cock and began masturbating right in front of her. Abdul fucked her fiercely from behind, making the small wooden table wobble and squeak in time to his rhythm.

"Oh, yes..." Nikki whispered.

She held on to the edges of the rickety table, as each of Abdul's powerful thrusts threw her back and forth. She felt the entire length of his stiff tool plunging into her slippery pussy again and again, driving her ever closer to another orgasm.

Gasping for breath, Jack masturbated, watching them fuck. His fist vigorously stroked the veined shaft of his cock, making it swell to a full, throbbing erection. A drop of clear fluid began to ooze from its tip.

"Fuck her harder," he said to Abdul. "Fuck her till she screams."

Incredibly, she felt Abdul applying even more force to his deep, relentless thrusts. Juice squirted from her slit, running down the insides of her thighs.

"Ah!" she cried. "Ah! Ah! Ah!"

The table creaked and shook, as Jack masturbated at the sight, his eyes dark and mad with lust. Nikki screamed out loud as she came again.

"Aaah! Aaah!"

Abdul held on to her hips, as she threw herself about on the table, waves of pleasure coursing through her trembling body, until she thought she would faint. Her pussy twitched around his cock, squeezing its swollen head. As he slowly pulled out, she once more felt her juices gushing from her snatch. Never before had she felt so excited, so overcome by lust.

"Right," Jack said hoarsely. "We're not done with you yet."

To Nikki's surprise, he sat down in the sand next to the table, his stiff cock pointing straight up.

"Come here," he ordered.

Nikki staggered towards him on unsteady legs, but he swiftly grabbed her ass and pulled her down to him. He made her sit on his lap, facing away from him, and then guided his cock in between her labia.

Nikki gasped, as she felt her boyfriend's cock enter her dripping wet pussy, and she immediately began moving up and down over it, letting it slip in and out, making little, wet sounds.

She knew Jack had been mad at her for fucking Abdul – and for enjoying it so immensely. But now, she figured, he was so horny he didn't care anymore. He just wanted to feel her pussy again – and she was going to give him the ride of his life. So maybe there was a bit of a randy slut inside her, but she was also a good little wife that could show her man a good time – and she was going to fuck his brains out now.

"Stop!" Jack said. "Don't move!"

Confused, Nikki froze, Jack's cock still hard and throbbing inside her as she sat on his lap.

"But..." she protested.

"You!" Jack called to Abdul. "Come over here."

Abdul walked towards them, his erect, dark-skinned cock bouncing with every step.

"Put your cock in her pussy," Jack said.

Nikki stared incredulously, as Abdul knelt down between Jack's legs, guiding his cock towards her pussy. She struggled to get away, but Jack grabbed her arms and held her down. He still had his cock inside her – and now Abdul, too, tried to force his tool in.

She whimpered, as Abdul's cock pushed down on Jack's. As Abdul applied force, she felt the head of his member stretching her labia, forcing her cunt open.

"Nooo..." Nikki cried.

Abdul grit his teeth, pressing forward. Ever so slowly, he managed to squeeze his cock into her yielding flesh. She felt the two bulging cocks throbbing, rubbing against each other inside her tender cunt.

"Yeah, like that!" Jack roared.

Nikki knew that voice. Jack always sounded like that when he was beside himself with lust. And in that state he was liable to do anything – anything at all – to achieve satisfaction. Which would invariably be a very loud and powerful ejaculation.

"No, please," she sobbed. "Stop it. Don't..."

"Keep going!" Jack shouted. "Get that cock inside her!"

Inch by inch she felt Abdul's cock forcing its way into her pussy, stretching it wide open.

"Yeah," Jack whispered into her ear. "You feel that, honey? Two fat cocks inside your dirty little cunt. And now we're gonna fuck your brains out..."

"Nooo..." Nikki yelled, but it was too late.

"Let's fuck!" Jack ordered, and the two men began thrusting savagely into her pussy.

"Aaah!" she cried. "Aaah!"

She had never felt anything like it. Now the two cocks moved in sync, feeling like one gigantic member – now they alternated – one plunging in as the other slipped out, each cock stimulating a different area of the insides of her tender, moist flesh. She felt each thrust stretching her cunt, forcing her open wide – again and again.

Abdul was sweating, his perspiration dripping on to her naked body. She caught drops of sweat on her tongue – it tasted spicy, a bit like she'd imagine his semen would taste. And all the time the two cocks hammered away brutally inside her wildly expanded pussy.

"Ohmigod," Nikki cried, as she felt yet another climax approaching. "Ohmigod. Ohmigoood..."

She threw her head back as she came. It was a violent orgasm, making her entire body jerk in convulsions, as hot juices squirted from her quivering cunt. Again she struggled, but Jack held her down, letting himself and Abdul thrust into her pussy again and again.

"Yeah," Jack yelled. "Fuck yeah. I'm gonna come!"

He plunged his cock into the depths of Nikki's flesh and froze, his shaft bulging and throbbing. Abdul kept pumping in and out, his cock rubbing violently against Jack's. And finally, Nikki felt Jack starting to ejaculate.

"Unhhh!" he yelled, as his cock jerked spasmodically, squirting spurt after spurt of burning hot semen deep into Nikki's cunt.

His think spunk filled her jam-packed pussy, seeping slowly out of her, as it kept pumping into her. Abdul gave a few more violent thrusts, the pulled out and grabbed his cock in his fist. He yelled something in Arabic, as he, too, began to ejaculate.

Dazed, Nikki felt the spurts of hot semen hitting her face, her cheeks, her breasts. She stuck out her tongue and savoured the taste

of Abdul's sperm – it was pretty much like the spicy taste of his sweat, only more concentrated. Abdul kept ejaculating, jerking off like a madman – until finally he had emptied himself, and one final thick drop of sperm dripped onto Nikki's tongue.

Abdul took a few deep breaths, steadying himself. Then went inside and came out fully dressed.

Nikki felt Jack's cock still throbbing inside her, until it went soft and slowly slid out of her dripping wet slit.

"Ahhh..." he sighed.

Nikki got up. Jack just lay there for a while, smiling at her.

"Now there's a good little whore," he murmured.

"Did you..." Nikki asked, "did you get the money?"

Abdul had brought Nikki's clothes for her. She nodded politely and began dressing.

Jack sat up and swiftly pulled up his pants.

"Oh yeah," he said. "I forgot."

He stood up and took out his wallet.

"The money," he said to Abdul. "How much do we owe you?"

To his surprise, Abdul also brought out a leather purse and began taking money out. Jack stared at him, confused.

"No, no," he said. "The lunch. How much?"

Abdul laughed and shook his head.

"Lunch is on the house," he said, then pointed to Nikki:

"But the girl. We keep the girl. How much?"

Superficial Damage

As a woman, I'm sick and tired of all this talk of "woman drivers". I believe I'm a perfectly decent driver, and I pride myself in taking care and staying safe.

On the other hand, that begs the question: What the hell happened last Thursday night? I have no idea.

That's not entirely true. I have an idea. Sex happened. That's what.

I was driving home through the city late at night, I was bored, and my thoughts turned to sex. They say men think about sex every seven seconds. I don't know how they handle that – but they must be able to switch off again immediately, or they'd never get anything done. Because once I start thinking about sex I seem to get stuck in that mode. And that's what happened last Thursday night.

It had been a long day at work – meeting after boring meeting, and I'd hardly been able to concentrate. Towards the end of the last one my head was already full of kinky fantasies. And when I got in my car to drive home, I was wet and horny – and couldn't wait to get inside and lock my door.

It was dark, and the neon lights were out as I drove through the deserted city centre. Boy, it would be nice to be home. I'd get into bed with a good book (you know the kind), maybe play with my favourite pink vibrator (which was sitting in my purse on the passenger seat), and finally – finally release the lustful tension pent up inside my body.

Maybe I drove a bit too fast, maybe I wasn't thinking clearly. For whatever reason, I didn't see the black sports car turning onto the street in front of me, before it was too late.

I braked immediately, my tires squealing as they slid across the asphalt. And I tried frantically to turn away – but it was no use.

With a loud crash my sedan smashed into the side of the black sports car. Both vehicles came to an abrupt halt – and as the crash and the small tinkling noises died out, we just sat there. Out of

breath, I looked around and felt myself, trying to figure out if I was okay – which to me surprise I seemed to be.

My car door was ripped open.

"What the fuck are you doing?"

The driver of the black sports car stood outside, fuming with rage. He was a stocky man with stubbly, reddish beard and hair, and his face was red with anger.

"You should be kept off the streets!" he sputtered.

"I... I'm sorry," I said.

"Sorry's not good enough," he said.

He grabbed my arm and pulled me out of the car. I stumbled out, unsteadily.

"Look at that," he said, indicating the damage too his car.

I'd hit him rather hard – but I was surprised to see that the damage was relatively superficial: Some indentations, some paint scratches. It should be relatively easy to repair.

"Look," I said, "I'm sorry. But of course I'll pay. I have insurance. I'll give you..."

"Insurance," he scoffed, shaking my arm.

His grip hurt quite a bit, but I didn't want to protest.

"Do you know how long that will take?" he went on. "And you don't expect me to drive around... like that, do you?"

"But..." I felt my voice breaking, tears welling up in my eyes, "what do you want?"

"You got money?" he asked.

I hardly ever carry cash with me.

"A little," I said. "But I can go to the nearest ATM and get more."

He let go of me – then reached into my car and took my purse.

"ATM," he said sarcastically, going through my purse. "What have we here?"

He pulled out a few bills, counted them and stuffed them into his pocket. As he reached deeper into my purse, he froze.

"What the hell?" he said quietly.

Slowly, he pulled my pink vibrator out and brandished it in my face.

"What's this?" he asked. "Not only are you a lousy driver – you're also a goddamn pervert."

I could hardly look at him – it was too embarrassing. First the accident, now this. I just wanted to run far away and hide – but I was afraid to even move.

He was silent for a few seconds.

"Right," he finally said, his voice deep and determined. "Take off your clothes."

"What?" I gasped.

We were in the city centre. The pavements were deserted, and so were most of the buildings around us – almost all of them offices. But still – we were standing in the middle of the street.

"You heard me, baby," he said. "Strip for me."

No. There was no way out. I just knew that.

I unbuttoned my blouse, then pulled it off – and then my skirt. The evening breeze felt cool on my skin. Next, I unhooked my bra and threw it on the ground. Finally, I slipped out of my black satin panties and stood before him naked except for my high-heeled shoes.

He smiled fiendishly.

"Lie down on the hood of my car," he said. "On your back."

Slowly, I did as I was told, feeling the heat of the engine through the metal. He handed me the vibrator.

"Play with your pussy," he said.

I stared at him, quietly shaking my head. We were out in the open – in public, for God's sake. What was he thinking?

"Do it," he insisted, raising his voice.

I didn't like the look of him. Big and burly, with that stubbly beard and hair, making him look rough and unkempt. It was no use. I just had to obey.

I licked the fingers of my right hand, and with a sigh I slid them towards my clit. I had been wet in the car, and I still was. My pussy lips were swollen, and as I gently caressed them, it was as if they wanted to suck my fingers inside.

Closing my eyes, I began stroking myself, my fingers circling my clit. I felt the cool breeze on my pussy, smelt the fumes of the big city, and listened to the sounds of distant cars and trains. I was masturbating in the middle of the street – and to be honest, it felt pretty good. Juices flowed from my slit, wetting my fingers.

"Now – use that thing," he demanded.

As if the big, strong man was afraid to use the word. Of course, he meant my vibrator, which I still held in my left hand. This was

getting weirder by the second. Masturbating in public was pretty wild – but for some reason I felt that using the vibrator was an even more personal thing – something I only did behind closed doors all alone – or once in a while with a particularly imaginative boyfriend.

I fumbled hesitantly with the pink rubber toy. Eventually, I managed switched in on and heard the familiar buzzing noise.

I only meant to graze the hood of my clit with the vibrator. But either my hands were unsteady, or my clit was sensitive as hell. Whatever the reason, a jolt went through my body, as I felt the rubber buzzing madly against my love button.

"Oh!" I cried, throwing my head back.

The shock didn't put me off. On the contrary. Now I wanted more.

I sat upright on the hood of the car, watching intently as I moved the tip of the toy slowly around my clit. Shivers of excitement ran through my body, giving me goosebumps in the cool night air. My juices flowed down my thighs, glistening on the car's metal. I breathed heavily, my mouth wide open.

"Mmm," a deep voice said. "Yeah. Like that. Keep going."

I looked op. The driver had zipped down his pants and pulled out his erect cock. It was long and thick, with a swelling, bluish head. As he watched me, he masturbated, making it grow and stiffen. I heard myself whimpering with pleasure and felt my naked legs shaking uncontrollably. The driver smiled fiendishly. Still stroking his cock, he looked up at the buildings around us.

"And look," he said. "They're all watching."

I, too, looked up. Lights were on in several windows, and I could distinctly make out silhouettes in many of them – men, women, couples – all looking down at us. Were they getting excited now? Were they masturbating, too?

I held my breath as I guided the tip of the vibrator in between my dripping wet labia. Feeling it buzzing inside my cunt made me moan with lust. Slowly, I moved it back and forth, my slippery pussy muscles clenching the vibrating rubber toy. I was about to come.

"Oh, God," I sobbed. "Oh, God."

The driver stared at me lustfully. Clear fluid leaked from the tip of his cock and trickled down the shaft, wetting his stroking fingers.

Once again, I lay down on the hood of the car, then used both hands to bury the entire length of the vibrator inside my pussy.

Closing my eyes, I felt it purring away at the insides of my flesh, finally bringing me to orgasm.

"Aaah!" I cried, arching my back as my juices gushed around the rubber toy. "Aaah!"

My cries echoed between the buildings in the cool night air, as the climax ripped through every fibre of my body, almost making me faint with pleasure.

Gradually it subsided. I lay flat on my back, breathing deeply, savouring the afterglow.

"Yeah," the gruff voice said.

I felt the vibrator being pulled from my pussy by his strong hand. As I looked up, he was spreading my legs apart and guiding his hard, swollen cock towards my slippery hole. Still dizzy from my orgasm, I put my hands on his hips and tried to push him off me.

"No..." I gasped.

"Shut up!" he replied, easily brushing my hands away.

I felt the bulbous head of his cock pushing hard against my labia. There was no stopping him now – he was stronger than me, and horny as hell.

My flesh yielded to his cock, and I felt my cunt muscles stretching around his girth as he entered. Inch by inch his massive tool forced its way into my tender crevice.

He grabbed my upper arms and held me down.

"Look at me," he ordered.

His face had been red with anger, now it was just as red with lust. He was sweating. In the glare of the street lights, droplets of sweat glistened in the stubble on his head and his chin.

I gasped involuntarily, as he began thrusting. Just the sensation of being filled with such a huge cock was incredible. But I couldn't have imagined what it felt like moving inside me. In a hard, steady rhythm he thrust in and out, in and out, sliding his rough, veined shaft back and forth against the succulent walls of my pussy.

Over and over his cock plunged into my flesh, sweat dripping from his face on to my naked breasts. I spread my legs as wide as I could, letting him enter deeper – deeper. Again my fingers found my clit, and I masturbated vigorously as he kept fucking and fucking.

"Yeah," he grunted. "Play with your sweet little pussy. Hunh! Hunh! Hunh!"

Tears of joy began to flow from my eyes. Again I looked up at the buildings around me. This time I imagined I could see a man

masturbating as he watched. And in another window a couple fucking, watching us. It was as if the whole city was in heat.

I felt another climax approaching. Besides myself with lust, I believe I heard my own voice mumbling wild obscenities, urging the driver to use me, abuse me and do whatever he liked with me.

I cried out loud with pleasure, as I came again, even harder than before.

"Aaah! Aaah!"

I threw myself about on the hood of the car, but he held me down, still thrusting his swollen cock into my orgasming pussy. I wanted him to stop – to take a break – but he just forced my thighs apart with both hands and kept fucking me.

"No..." I gasped. "Please..."

He grunted like an animal, almost drooling with lust. His fat tool plunged in and out of my tender slit, making wet, slippery sounds.

He picked up my vibrator, still wet from my juices. His eyes gleaming madly, he forced the rubber tool deep into my anus and switched it on.

"No!" I cried. "Aaah!"

The sensation was unbearable. The vibrator buzzing inside my ass, while his big, fat cock kept hammering away at my ravaged pussy. I had already come twice – and I was going to come again.

And he could feel it. I saw it in his eyes.

"Yeah?" he said. "You like that?"

"You bastard," I gasped. "Mmm..."

A few more thrusts, and I couldn't hold back any longer. Another orgasm exploded inside me, making me throw myself about on the metal hood.

"Ohhh. Ohhh..."

I thought it would never stop. Dazed and trembling, I felt the driver's cock swelling inside me, ready to ejaculate. Frantically, he pulled out.

He stood between my legs, masturbating. I switched off the vibrator, and pulled it out of my ass. Then I looked him deep in the eyes, letting him watch as I buried three fingers inside my pussy.

And then he came.

"Yeah!" he yelled. "Fuck yeah."

His hairy balls contracted and hardened, as he clenched his cock in his fist. The bluish head swelled – and finally, it fired the

first, long white spurt of semen. Hot and sticky, it landed on my belly. His fat, veined cock jerked and twitched in his hand, as jet after jet of spunk shot from its tip, spraying my breasts and my face.

Grunting, he kept masturbating, until the last, thick drops of semen oozed from his cock, dripping onto the black asphalt.

His cock remained erect. And once more he buried it inside my pussy.

"Oh!" I gasped.

Breathing hard, he began thrusting. Faster this time, as if he knew his time was almost up. His big hands grabbed my breasts, squeezing them hard in time with his rhythm.

"Play with your pussy again," he panted.

His cock was still hard. I couldn't believe it. Fat and swollen, it hammered into my tender flesh again and again. Whimpering, I masturbated, my abundant juices flowing over my fingers. If he kept going a little longer, I could make myself come again.

"Aaah!" he yelled. "I'm gonna come again! Open your mouth!"

His cock slipped out of my pussy and he stumbled to the side of the car, offering his cock to my mouth. It was red and sore, dripping with my juices. I opened my mouth wide and closed my lips around the massive tool.

The sensation made him come immediately.

"Unnh! Unnh! Unnh!"

He ejaculated into my mouth with just as much force as before. I swallowed again and again, as the huge, jerking cock shot long, hot jets of spunk into my throat. It was impossible to drink down all of it – I felt some of it dribbling hot and slimy down my chin.

And as I tasted the salty, animal flavour of his semen, I masturbated myself to one more orgasm.

"Mmm!" I purred, my mouth still filled with his squirting cock. "Mmm!"

I didn't come quite as hard this time. Not so much an explosion, more like a wave of sensual pleasure washing over me, leaving me writhing lasciviously on the hood of the car.

The driver's orgasm subsided and he pulled his cock from my mouth. I just lay there, licking up the last drops of semen.

He zipped up and just stood there looking at me.

"Grab your clothes," he said.

I climbed down off the hood and picked my clothes up off the ground.

"You're coming with me," he added.

I stared at him, incredulously.

"You think I'm done with you?" he asked. "No way. Get in."

He opened his car door. I began pulling my panties on.

"No," he said. "No clothes. Get in there – naked."

Obediently, I got into his car and sat there in the nude. He got into the driver's seat and started the engine.

"Where... where are we going?" I asked as we drove off.

He smiled.

"Where do you think?" he said. "Back to my place, of course."

He accelerated, driving the car through the empty city streets.

Naked, I leant back in my seat, trying my best to relax.

Revenge

An sudden noise woke me up. It took me a few seconds to realize it was the phone.

My bedroom was dark. I turned the light on and looked at my watch. It was one AM. I don't know anyone who calls me at one AM.

The phone rang again, and I picked it up.

"Get over here!" a gruff voice shouted. "Get over here right now, you piece of shit!"

I don't have friends who call me at one AM, and I certainly don't have friends who call me at one AM to yell at me.

"Who is this?" I said.

"Who do you think? It's Ed, your fucking neighbour. Now get over here right now!"

He hung up.

I'd lived next door to Ed for five years now. He was a short, but quite muscular guy with pale red hair. I never liked him much, though I wasn't sure why. There was just something about him – he seemed not too smart and a bit too aggressive.

I got dressed and went over to Ed's house. He was standing in the driveway, his face bright red. His right hand was clutching a bottle of bourbon.

"Oh, there you are, you fuck!" he shouted as I approached. "Happy now?"

"Ed," I say quietly, "calm down. What's the matter?"

"Calm down?" he yelled. "Oh, that's a good one. Come in here, for fuck's sake!"

I followed him into the house, and he closed the door behind me.

"What's the matter?" I asked.

"As if you didn't know. You got busted, that's what's the matter."

"Busted? What did I do?"

- 256 -

"How long has it been going on? Tell me that."

I stared at him. And somewhere in the house I thought I heard a muffled voice:

"Mmmf!"

"Going on?" I asked. "Has what been going on?"

Ed rolled his eyes.

"Don't play the fucking innocent with me," he sputtered. "How long have you been fucking my wife?"

So this was about Gianna. But who ever put that idea into Ed's head? Sure, I liked Gianna – who wouldn't? She was a beautiful, sexy woman with dark skin, jet-black hair and fiery, dark eyes. Sometimes I wondered how she'd ended up with a guy like Ed. But of course I'd never made a pass at her – she was married to my neighbour, after all.

"Ed," I protested. "I swear to you, I never..."

"She told me," he said triumphantly, taking a swig of the bottle.

"Told you?"

"In her sleep. She was dreaming – and I distinctly heard her say 'Mike'. I woke her up, and the goddamn slut was all wet. Because she'd been dreaming about fucking you!"

None of this made sense. But Ed was so worked up, there was no way I could convince him.

"Ed, please," I said. "That's not..."

"Shut the fuck up, you bastard! Come in here!"

I didn't dare disobey, but followed Ed into the bedroom.

"Now look what you've done!" Ed said.

Gianna lay on the bed stark naked, tied up and gagged. Her hands were bound together and fixed to the rail with duct tape. Her legs were spread apart and duct taped to the bed posts. She was gagged with more duct tape, wrapped around her head. At least Ed had taken care to get her hair out of the way first. On her belly he'd written "Filthy whore" in lipstick – and "Slut" across her breasts. I couldn't help noticing that penmanship wasn't Ed's forte.

"For God's sake, Ed," I said, "why did you do that to her? Please..."

Ed took another swig of the bottle.

"Take your clothes off," he said.

"What?"

I saw Gianna writhing on the bed, pulling at the tape. Her lovely breasts bounced slightly with every motion.

"You take your fucking clothes off – now!" Ed shouted.

I didn't know what to do. Ed was the kind of guy that was liable to pull a gun on you at any moment, so I really felt I had no choice.

I unbuttoned my shirt and took it off. Gianna seemed to run her eyes over my naked chest.

Next, I kicked off my shoes and pulled off my socks. But when I unbuckled my belt, it got a little awkward: I was starting to get an erection.

"Fuck!" I cursed under my breath.

Really – I'm not that kind of guy. Or at least until that night I thought I wasn't. My neighbour's wife, naked and tied to a bed should make me sad and furious – not horny. What the hell was wrong with me?

"Go on," Ed said.

I pulled off my pants and shorts and stood naked in Ed's and Gianna's bedroom. My semi-erect cock stuck out in front of me, pointing straight at Gianna. She stared at it – but quite calmly, in fact.

"Now what?" I asked.

"Now," Ed said slowly, "you fuck her!"

"Mmmf!" Gianna cried.

"What?" I said.

"Aw, c'mon," Ed said, as he pulled up a chair and sat down. "It's not like you haven't done it before. You should be pretty used to it by now. Only this time – I wanna watch. Fuck her!"

I couldn't believe this was happening. But I didn't see any way out. I was going to have to fuck Ed's wife. My first, frantic thought: To make sure she was wet – to give her as little discomfort as possible.

Hesitantly, I walked over to the bed and knelt down between Gianna's legs. Her jet-black pubes were neatly trimmed, her dark labia clearly visible. The scent of her flesh teased my nostrils.

I gently ran my fingers over her bush, then leant forward and let my tongue touch her clit. She sighed behind the gag, and I applied gentle pressure. Then – slowly – I began moving my tongue in circles around her pink love button. I tasted the spicy flavour of her juices – and the taste made my cock throb and swell.

"What the fuck..." Ed muttered

I kept licking rhythmically at Gianna's clit, then slowly slipped two fingers into her pussy. I felt the inside of her flesh – soft and wet. And as I moved my fingers back and forth, her juices trickled over my fingers, making them wet and slippery. I thrust my fingers deeper and deeper into her juicy pussy – and I felt Gianna moving – grinding her pelvis against my hand.

But why? Did this turn her on? Did being tied up turn her on? Did forced sex with a strange man turn her on?

Looking up, I saw a vibrator lying on the night stand. It was clear latex, with all sorts of ribs and knots. It looked very a state-of-the-art – and probably expensive. The thought of Gianna playing with that when she was alone turned me on quite a bit. Well, of course, they could be playing with it together – but somehow I couldn't see Ed being that adventurous.

I stood up, took the vibrator, then once again knelt between her legs. Gianna's eyes opened wide.

I put the tip of the vibrator against her clit, then turned it on.

"Mmm!" she cried, struggling, pulling at her ties, "mmm!"

Fascinated, I sped up the toy, then slowed it down, making Gianna writhe with pleasure on the bed. I felt my cock swelling at the sight.

Ed banged his bottle on the floor.

"Enough of that shit!" he shouted. "You get to the action. Now!"

I reached for my cock to check my erection. It already felt long and completely hard in my grip. I stood up, showing my cock off to Gianna. She stared at it, gasping behind the gag.

"I'm sorry," I whispered, as I crawled on top of her. "I'll be gentle."

Taking the shaft in my hand, I placed the head of my cock at the entrance to her pussy – right beneath the words "Filthy" and "slut". Then I pushed forward, slipping the swollen head in between her labia. Another push, and I slowly penetrated her – feeling her soft flesh yield to me as I buried the entire length of my cock inside her pussy.

"Mmm!" she moaned.

"Yeah, that's it," Ed said, taking another swig of bourbon. "Now fuck her good."

It felt so good – her soft, moist flesh wrapped around my bone-hard cock. Slowly, I began to move my cock in and out of

Gianna's pussy. I felt awkward – like a robot going through the motions. In, out, in, out.

"Faster!" Ed said. "Harder and faster. Make her feel it."

I increased my pace, fucking the bound Gianna relentlessly. Part of my brain didn't want to enjoy it – but I couldn't help it – that tight little pussy just felt so damn good clenched around my thrusting cock.

And Gianna seemed to feel it too. Her cheeks flushed, her body began writhing beneath me, moving against my thrusts. Eagerly her pelvis started pushing against me, making me go deeper and deeper into her wet slit.

"So," Ed exclaimed. "What's it like, huh, Gianna? Do you like that? Do you like it when your filthy lover fucks your filthy cunt?"

"Mmm!" Gianna moaned, "mmm!"

"Um, Mike," Ed said, wiping his mouth, "could you, um... could you remove the gag? I like to hear her moaning and screaming, when you fuck her."

Still thrusting into Gianna, I carefully pulled layer after layer duct tape off her cheeks and the back of her neck, until finally her mouth was free.

"Oh, God," was her first words, "oh, God..."

"Oh, yeah," Ed grunted, stroking his crotch.

He was clearly beginning to get an erection.

I caught Gianna's gaze. She looked right back at me with her piercing dark eyes – with no fear, no remorse, just fascination. It was as if she had accepted her fate, and now wanted me to show her what I could do – how good a fuck I could give her.

That gaze turned me on – made me want to drive her mad with pleasure. I felt my cock growing even stiffer and bigger, as I kept thrusting deeper and harder into her, covering my shaft in her juices.

Breathing heavily, Ed finally unzipped his pants and pulled out his erect cock. I noticed it was not particularly big. About average, I suppose – but nowhere as big as mine. Grunting like an animal, Ed grabbed his cock and began masturbating. His eyes were fixed on his wife's pussy, watching as I thrust into it again and again.

"Oh," Gianna whimpered "Oh, keep going. Don't stop."

I was sweating now, fucking her with all my strength. With every thrust I pulled my cock almost all the way out, watching it glisten from her juices. And then, with a hard, fast motion, I buried every inch inside her again. And out – and in – and out.

Gianna whispered in my ear: "Get ready. When he comes, we can take him."

"Okay," I gasped.

"When he comes," she whispered, "untie me – and we can both grab him and tie him up."

Ed had no idea what his wife had planned. He was almost drooling, masturbating at a furious pace.

"Unh, unh," he grunted.

I pulled out of Gianna, my wet cock jerking, dripping with juice.

"I'm sorry, Ed," I said. "But I have to untie her arms – I want her to jerk me off."

"Yeah, yeah," said Ed, stroking his cock. "Whatever."

Gianna smiled almost imperceptibly, as I ripped the duct tape of her wrists. Then she sat up and grabbed my cock with both hands, masturbating it. I gasped. It felt so good, it almost made me come.

"Okay," I gasped. "That's enough. Lie down."

Gianna lay down, and I once more slipped my cock into her soft, succulent hole, thrusting into her in a relentless rhythm. She gasped helplessly, her entire body trembling beneath me.

She looked up at me, incredulously. I could tell I was about to make her come. She hadn't expected that to happen so soon, and wasn't sure how to react.

I pulled out again.

"Ohhh," Gianna cried, exasperated, her pussy muscles quivering like a sea anemone.

"Ed," I gasped. "I wanna get her legs around my ears. I have to untie her feet, too."

"Unh, unh," Ed panted, jerking off like a man possessed. "Yeah – you do that. Okay."

I ripped the duct tape off Gianna's left foot, then the right. And she was free.

I lifted her ass off the mattress and let my cock enter her pussy in a downwards angle.

"Oh fuck!" she cried.

Holding her shapely ass in my hands, I thrust into her hard and deep, again and again, making her whimper helplessly, until finally...

"Aaah!" she cried, as the orgasm hit her. "Aaah!"

I held Gianna still, as she threw herself about on the mattress, her juices gushing around my erect cock. Her cries of pleasure filled the bedroom.

As I looked over at Ed, the first spurt of semen shot from his swollen tool.

"Unhhh..." he grunted, "unhhh..."

"He's coming," I whispered to Gianna. "Quick!"

I pulled out, my hard cock dangling in front of me, and swiftly made a jump for Ed. I grabbed his hands away from his cock, and it kept pumping away on its own – squirting little white jets of hot spunk across the bedroom floor.

"Huh? What...?" he said.

Naked and sweating, Gianna grabbed the roll of duct tape from the night stand and joined us. As I held Ed's arms in place, she began pulling off long strips of tape. And cursing under her breath, she vigorously wrapped it around his wrists and the chair – then tied the chair to the radiator.

When she was finished, he couldn't move – he just sat there, breathing hard, staring at us in disbelief, the last drops of semen oozing from his still semi-hard cock.

Gianna stood there for a while, looking at him.

And suddenly it struck me: I couldn't remember ever having seen a woman that beautiful. Stark naked, sweat running down her face, her shapely breasts, her legs. Her jet-black hair was a gorgeous mess, and her dark eyes glowed with righteous anger at her paranoid and violent husband.

She reached down and grabbed Ed's bottle, then slowly poured the bourbon over his head. The smell of liquor filled the room, almost making my eyes burn.

"No..." he whimpered.

"Shut up!" she shouted. "You and your fucking booze. Don't you think you've had enough now? Can't you see how it fucks you up?"

"But I thought..." he protested.

Gianna brushed her hair away from her face.

"Listen," she said. "I have not. Been. Fucking. Mike. Okay? But..."

She grinned fiendishly.

"Now that I've tried it..." she went on. "you know – I quite like it."

Gianna looked over at me, smiling lasciviously, stroking her shapely breasts. Damn, she was beautiful. My erect cock stirred, still dripping wet from her juices. I grabbed it with my fist and slowly began masturbating.

Ed looked from me to his wife and back again, his hair soaked with bourbon. Whatever mind he had left was obviously racing.

"I'm sorry..." he whimpered.

"No, you're not!" Gianna shouted back. "You don't know how to be sorry. You never did. Well, guess what, asshole – you brought this upon yourself!"

She stepped right up to me, gently rubbing her body against mine. I grabbed her ass and pulled her in close. My cock brushed up and down her sweaty belly, growing hard as a rock.

"I want more," she mock whispered, making sure Ed could hear.

"Well, you're in luck," I said. "Because you're gonna get it. Turn around."

Gianna turned her back to me, spread her legs and bent over, until her hands rested on the floor. I grabbed her ass again, kneading it hard. Spreading her ass-cheeks, I stared at her cute little anus and the soft folds of her dripping wet pussy. I could smell her excitement – and my erect cock jumped again.

I put my thumb against her anus and slowly pushed it inside.

"Ah!" she cried.

I gently turned the finger around, feeling the squeeze of her ass muscles. Then, slowly, I began to move it in and out, in and out, fucking her ass with my thumb.

"Yeahhh..." she groaned. "Oh, that's it."

With my other hand, I grabbed my cock and guided it toward her pussy. I thrust forwards and shivered with pleasure, as I once more felt her succulent flesh wrapping around my shaft. Grunting, I began to fuck her in a steady rhythm.

"Oh yes!" Gianna cried. "Ed – are you watching? Mike is fucking my goddamn brains out, Ed – and I love it! Aaah..."

Ed just stared at us, his mouth wide open.

I almost didn't care anymore. Mad with desire, I just kept hammering my erect cock into his wife's soft pussy – over and over and over, my thumb still buried inside her anus.

Gianna gasped loudly, her body trembling with pleasure.

"Oh, Mike," she whimpered. "My ass. Fuck me in the ass."

I pulled my cock out of her pussy and spreads her ass-cheeks apart. I spat into her anus and onto my cock for lubrication. Then, I grabbed the shaft and placed the head of my cock against her rectum. Gently, I pushed forward, my hard, wide tool stretching her ass as I penetrated her. Gianna screamed.

"Aaah! It's... it's so fucking big! Keep going. Fuck me!"

It almost felt impossible. But I forced my cock deeper into her, feeling her ass muscles tighten like a vice around the shaft. Grabbing her hips, I began pushing back and forth, thrusting my cock in and out of her incredibly tight hole.

"Ed," she giggled, "are you watching? Mike's fucking my ass..."

She licked her fingers seductively, then reached between her legs.

"Okay, Ed," she teased, "is it okay with you if I masturbate? You know – I just have to play with my pussy – because Mike is fucking my ass so damn good..."

She gasped loudly, as she began stroking her clit. I thrust deeper and deeper into her ass, feeling my cock swelling, ready to ejaculate.

"Gianna..." I gasped.

"Wait," she said. "Keep going. I'm nearly there..."

"Aaah!" I yelled, fighting back my climax, thrusting into Gianna's ass again and again.

Until finally, I felt her entire body shaking uncontrollably.

"Fuck!" she screamed. "Aaah! Hold me!"

As the orgasm hit her, she started shaking uncontrollably. I reached around and grabbed her breasts, holding her up. And as tremors of pleasure coursed through her body like electricity, she cried out in ecstasy again and again.

"Aaah! Aaah! Aaah!"

Ed said nothing. I couldn't tell if he had been crying.

I felt my balls tightening, ready to spurt.

"I'm gonna come, too," I whispered.

"Okay," Gianna gasped. "Just a second."

As she took a step forward, my cock slipped out of her cunt, twitching. She smiled at me, then stood right behind me, reached around, and grabbed my cock. She aimed it straight at Ed's face.

"What?" I said. "No..."

"Do it," she ordered. "Come in his fucking face."

She began stroking my cock vigorously.

"Aaah!" I cried. "Gianna, please... Aaah!"

I couldn't hold back any longer – I came so hard, it hurt. A thick jet of semen spurted from my cock, hitting Ed on the cheek, as Gianna kept masturbating me. My legs trembled, as I squirted again – this time into his right eye. Again and again, I ejaculated – long, hard jets of spunk into Ed's face.

Until finally, my orgasm subsided. Ed just sat there, helpless, my thick spunk running down his cheeks, dripping from his chin.

"Right," I whispered, out of breath. "That's it."

"No," Gianna insisted, still masturbating me. "You go again."

"I... I can't," I protested. "I'm spent. No more!"

She held the ridge of my helmet between her thumb and pinkie, gently massaging it, while her other hand fondled my balls. My erection never really subsided – and after a minute I felt my cock growing harder still.

"Oh, Gianna," I gasped, "you're amazing!"

"Mmm," she purred. "You're a big boy. You can come again."

My cock swelled madly, as she stroked it. As she leant against me, I smelled the sweet scent of her sweat.

The sensations of pleasure were unbelievable. My vision flickered, as Gianna masturbated me toward another climax. Finally, I felt my hard shaft contracting with such force, I almost fainted.

"Aaah!" I screamed. "Fuuuck!"

I came even harder than before. The semen burst from my cock, splattering Ed's face with another creamy spurt. As Gianna kept stroking my shaft, I ejaculated again and again.

"Oh yes," she whispered. "Get it all out. Empty those lovely balls."

Grunting, I shook the last, thick drops off in Ed's face, and finally, Gianna let go of my cock. Then I took her hand and led her to the bed.

"Lie down," I said.

She lay on her back. I lay on top of her. My erection was subsiding, but my red, swollen cock was still hard enough to slip into her moist pussy one last time.

"Mmm..." she moaned, as I pushed it in deep.

We lay on the bed for a long time, savouring the afterglow of our mutual ecstasy – kissing and stroking each other's sweaty, trembling bodies.

Gianna slept at my house that night. And the next day, Ed was gone. In fact, no one has seen him since then.

Gianna has filed for divorce. When she sells the house, she's moving in with me.

And of course, we make love as often as we can. Just like that night. Except now, I don't have to tie her up.

Unless, of course, she wants me to.

The Plumber

Christy lit a cigarette and leaned back on the couch, brushing her wavy, red hair aside. She could hardly wait. Her expensively furnished apartment was still empty, but soon... Soon he would be here.

Only last week, she had been visiting a friend, when this young, handsome plumber had come over to fix something. Christy hadn't been able to take her eyes off him, his tall, muscular body, his blonde, ruffled hair, his rough, unshaven face. As soon as he had gone, she had asked her friend for his phone number.

She had conjured up some fictional plumbing problem, and he had agreed to come over. Today at two PM. It was already ten minutes past, and Christy was growing restless.

She was prepared to reveal her intentions straight away. She had put on make-up, her pink negligee and her high-heeled shoes, and on the table stood a bottle of her favourite champagne in an ice cooler. She glanced at her watch. Where the hell was he?

Christy felt aroused. She had always hated that word "aroused", but that was how she felt – aroused. She wanted that man. And she didn't think he would turn her down. He had felt her eyes on his body that day. And she was a good-looking woman in her early thirties, long legs, rather big, shapely breasts and quite a pretty face, often lit up by a cheeky smile. Oh yes, she was gonna have him.

And then her doorbell rang. Oh, yes.

Christy got up from the couch, fixed her hair, straightened her negligee and took a deep breath. Then she went to the door and opened it. Outside...

... were two men.

Christy gasped, unable to speak. Two?

"We understand you have a problem here. Can we come in? "

It was the young plumber she had called, but she realized now that he was just an apprentice. He was accompanied by another, older man, probably the owner of the business. Both of them were

dressed in overalls. The older man was short and husky, with small, piercing eyes. As Christy just stared at him, he smiled.

"Hello? " he said sarcastically. "Can we come in? "

"Oh, " she responded. "Oh yes. Please. "

And grinning at her, the plumbers stepped into her apartment.

"Where is it? " the apprentice asked.

Christy didn't know what to say. What would happen when they found out she had lied?

"In... in the bathroom. "

They nodded.

"Expecting company? " the older man asked, indicating the champagne on the table.

"No. Yes," she stuttered.

The plumbers smiled at each other and went into her bathroom, closing the door behind them.

Christy sat down on the couch again, cursing herself. What the hell had she been thinking? And how was she going to get out of this mess? She heard the plumbers laughing in the bathroom, mocking her. Then the door opened, and they came out.

Naked.

The apprentice was lean and muscular, and Christy found his cock beautiful. The older plumber wasn't fat, just squat, and his cock was long and thick. He still carried his toolbox in one hand. As the men watched her, their cocks started swelling.

"No," she whispered. "No, please... "

"We discussed the situation," the older man said. "And we figured you probably had the hots for my young friend here. Well, today's your lucky day. Two for the price of one. "

"I..."

Christy got up and started moving away from the two men. But the apprentice grabbed her arm and pulled her back towards the couch.

They made her bend over the armrest as the apprentice knelt down behind her. He lifted up her negligee, pulled her lace panties aside, and she felt the tip of his wet tongue touching her labia.

"Oh God, " she sobbed quietly, as the apprentice slowly started licking her pussy.

His thick lips sucked at her tender flesh, greedily kissing the soft skin of her slit. Now his fat tongue began probing Christy's

pussy over and over, massaging her pussy lips and wetting them with his saliva.

"Yeah. Lick that pussy," the older plumber grunted.

She buried her face in the seat of the couch, as the apprentice grabbed her ass-cheeks, spreading them apart and pressing his face against her pussy.

Then she felt the older plumber pulling her up by the hair.

"Come here, baby," he mumbled.

Stark naked, he put his toolbox down on her coffee table and sat on the other armrest of the couch, facing her. Holding onto her hair, he pulled her face closer and closer to his heavy, swelling cock. He grabbed it with his free hand, softly stroking it and showing it off to her.

"No," Christy whispered.

"Open your pretty little mouth and suck my cock," he said.

And she obeyed. As she opened her mouth, he pulled her face towards her and guided his semi-erect cock in between her bright red lips. Pulling on her hair, the plumber moved her head quickly up and down, letting his cock slide in and out of her wet mouth. It grew quickly, and Christy felt the veins throbbing hot on her tongue.

"Yeah," he grunted. "Make it wet. Make it really wet, honey."

The shaft of his cock was already glistening, but Christy salivated even more, until her spit ran down the entire length of the plumber's cock, dripping onto the couch as he groaned with lust.

The apprentice was stroking her labia with a finger, and carefully started probing her moist slit. He wriggled the finger back and forth between her pussy lips, teasing her for several minutes. But finally he let his finger slide slowly all the way into Christy's steaming hot pussy.

Then he pulled it out and instead slid two fingers inside her. Twisting his fingers around her pussy, he felt the soft insides of her sex muscle before he started pumping his fingers back and forth, fucking her.

"Oh yeah," the older plumber yelled. "Work that pussy good!"

His cock had grown hard and thick in Christy's mouth. He was still holding onto her hair, but had slowed the rhythm down in order to savour the sensation of each stroke. Staring down at her pretty face, he forced her mouth slowly up and down the stiffening shaft, the tip of his cock poking the back of her throat.

The apprentice's fingers thrust into her a few more times, then pulled out. After giving her pussy a wet kiss, he got up and stood in front of the couple on the couch.

He took the champagne from the ice bucket and drank a few sips directly from the bottle. Sucking away at the older plumber's cock, Christy glanced at him out of the corner of her eye. His cock, too, was now long and erect, and he was masturbating, watching her sucking the plumber's cock.

Now the older man pulled out of her mouth, his thick cock dripping with saliva. He pointed to the apprentice.

"Suck him," he ordered.

And Christy knelt down on the seat of the couch, and took the apprentice's cock in her mouth as the older plumber watched them. The apprentice slid his cock in and out of her mouth in a slow, steady rhythm. Looking up, she caught his eye. She fixed his gaze as his rigid tool probed her soft mouth again and again.

"Yeah," the older plumber grunted, stroking his cock. "Fuck her mouth! "

Suddenly, the apprentice switched to a hard, fast rhythm. He thrust his hard-on into her mouth with violent strokes in a frenzied tempo. Christy pulled away from him, but the older plumber grabbed the back of her neck, pushing her head forward. The apprentice fucked her mouth like a madman with his long, hard cock, making her gag. Finally, with a loud gasp, he pulled out of her.

The two naked men stood in front of her, showing off their huge erections. Gasping, Christy shook her head at them.

"You're crazy, both of you," she whispered.

The men just grinned at her.

"Sit back on the couch, honey," the older plumber said, "and we'll show you just how crazy. I said: Sit back!"

Christy obeyed.

"Take your clothes off," the plumber said, opening the toolbox.

Christy slipped out of her negligee and sat on the couch naked, except for her high-heeled shoes. The apprentice poured a glass of champagne, only to pour it over her naked breasts. She gasped as the ice-cold, bubbly liquid hit the skin of her breasts, and she felt her nipples stiffening.

The older plumber pulled a shiny steel vibrator from the toolbox and came towards Christy.

"Oh no," she protested.

The older plumber knelt down between her legs, and Christy felt the cold steel touching her labia.

"Spread your legs wide," the plumber commanded.

And she obeyed, placing her high-heeled feet wide apart in the soft carpet.

"Oh yesss," he whispered at the sight of her pussy.

Then he turned on the vibrator. With his free hand, the plumber parted her labia, exposing her tiny, pink clit. As the buzzing metal dildo hit her love button, Christy gasped out loud.

"Aaah," she cried.

Oh, she had tried to resist, she didn't want to give in to them. But this just felt too damn good.

"You bastards," she hissed.

But her excitement was showing, and the two naked men just laughed at her feeble protests. The apprentice stood above them, watching, stroking his long, hard cock.

The older plumber slowly slid the vibrator up and down her pussy lips. She quivered with pleasure as the cool, whirring metal brushed against her tender pink flesh, teasing it. The plumber rested the buzzing dildo against Christy's clit, making her gasp. She realized how wet she was, and spread her legs wide, letting the plumber explore her pussy.

He switched off the vibrator and slowly slid it into her pussy. The hard metal tool felt cold inside her hot slit, making her shiver. The plumber started moving the smooth vibrator in and out of her in a steady fucking rhythm.

"Mmm," Christy moaned, as the older plumber masturbated her.

Juices oozed from her pussy, covering the steel vibrator in hot, spicy liquid.

Suddenly the apprentice leaned over her and kissed her. His tongue explored her mouth, and she felt one of his hands grabbing her breast, squeezing it hard. She wrapped her arms around him and kissed him passionately. She smelt the excitement on his skin, their tongues caressing each other with wild playfulness.

The dildo slid in and out of her pussy, and suddenly the older plumber turned it back on. Christy's body jerked, as the metal tool started vibrating the tender insides of her flesh.

"Mmm!" she cried out, her scream muffled by the apprentice's kiss.

Then he let go of her mouth and she screamed again: "Aaah!"

"Yeah," the plumber grunted. "You love it, don't you, you nasty little slut?"

He held the whirring tool still inside her, thrust it back and forth a few times, then held it still again. He kept this up for several minutes, while Christy moaned and sobbed with unbearable pleasure. Finally he stopped, and threw the glistening wet vibrator back into the toolbox. Getting up on his knees between her legs, he stroked his thick, hard cock, showing it off to her.

"You want a man's cock now, honey?" he asked.

Christy didn't answer. She was so close to orgasm now, and somehow she didn't want to climax with the older plumber. If only the apprentice would fuck her instead...

But the older plumber grabbed her hips, pulling her forward, until her ass rested on the edge of the seat. The apprentice pulled on her arms from behind, stretching her body, exposing her to his colleague. The older plumber stared lustfully at her naked breasts, her nipples hard with excitement. A drop of clear liquid ran down the shaft of his cock, as he guided it towards the entrance of her pussy.

"No..." Christy whispered, but he pretended not to hear her.

"Yeah," he grunted, gently parting her pussy lips with two fingers to make way for his cock. "This is it! "

And with one powerful thrust, he forced the entire length of his cock into her wet slit.

"Ohhh!" she screamed, the apprentice holding onto her wildly struggling arms.

The older plumber grabbed her ass and started fucking her with hard, deep strokes. He was almost drooling with excitement.

"You fucking whore!" he yelled, driving his cock into her again and again. "You love it when I fuck your little pussy, don't you?"

Christy thought she was about to faint. The plumber's fat cock rammed into her, stretching her tender flesh, massaging the insides of her pussy with powerful strokes. As the apprentice held her arms, she threw herself about on the couch, squealing with pleasure.

As the apprentice bent down over her, she felt his teeth biting her nipples.

"Ah!" she cried out, as he bit down hard, his tongue flicking at the teat behind his teeth.

He let go of her nipple, sucking most of her soft breast into his wet mouth, his eyes fixed on her pussy. The apprentice watched intently, as the older plumber's cock thrust in and out of Christy's tight slit, glistening with the spicy wetness of her love juice.

"Yeees," she whimpered, her climax approaching.

She didn't want the older plumber to bring her to orgasm, and didn't want him to see her come. But she couldn't help it. The swollen cock plunged into her over and over, and as the apprentice's mouth started sucking hard at her other breast, the sensation brought her over the edge.

"Ahhh," she cried as she came. "Aaah!"

The sheer force of her orgasm took her by surprise. Both men grunted with approval, the older plumber still fucking her mercilessly.

"Yeah," he murmured. "Suck her fucking tits!"

Christy was still breathing hard as he pulled out, his stiff cock dripping wet from her juices. He turned around and pushed the coffee table aside. Then he grabbed her arm, pulling her up from the couch.

"Come here," he ordered. "On your knees. "

The older plumber forced her down on all fours on the soft carpet.

"Yeah," he grinned. "Now you fuck her! "

Still dizzy from her powerful orgasm, Christy gasped, knowing he meant the apprentice. The naked, older plumber grabbed the bottle of champagne. Then he sat down on her sofa, showing off his huge erection, and chugging champagne straight from the bottle.

Christy felt the apprentice's hands on her ass-cheeks and bit her lips in anticipation. The tip of his cock poked at the mouth of her tender pussy. God, it was hard. The apprentice grabbed her breasts and slowly let the entire length of his long, stiff cock slide into her.

"Ohhh," she gasped.

The apprentice slowly pulled his cock all the way out of her juicy slit – and slowly back in. He kept moving slowly back and forth, back and forth, making Christy feel every inch of his hard, excited shaft.

The older plumber bent down and put his face next to hers.

"You like that?" he whispered hoarsely. "You love it when we fuck you hard, don't you, honey?"

"Oh yeah," she moaned.

Holding on to her breasts, the apprentice increased his speed, poking her moist flesh with deep, steady strokes. Christy dug her nails into the carpet and arched her back, pushing her firm, rounded ass towards her lover.

Still holding the champagne bottle, the older plumber got up from the couch. As the apprentice kept fucking Christy, the older plumber began pouring champagne over her ass. She gasped from the cold, as the bubbling liquid flowed over her ass-cheeks, trickling over her pussy-lips and down her thighs. She heard the apprentice gasping, too, as the cold champagne hit his hot, pounding cock.

"That's a cute little ass you've got there, honey," the older plumber said, as he pulled the metal vibrator from the toolbox again.

Christy heard the apprentice laughing wickedly.

"No," she gasped. "Please don't. No..."

But immediately she felt the cold tip of the vibrator against her rectum. The apprentice grabbed her hair with both hands and drove his cock into her pussy harder and harder, turned on by the sight. Turning it slowly around, the older plumber screwed the dildo into her tight ass. Christy sobbed helplessly, her flushed face touching the soft carpet.

The older plumber had forced the vibrator several inches into her ass.

"Okay," he whispered. "Get ready for this, baby."

And he turned it on.

"Oooh," Christy whimpered, as the motor started buzzing, stimulating the tender inside of her ass.

The apprentice grunted with excitement, hammering his stiff cock into her pussy over and over.

"Please," she gasped, out of breath. "Please stop. Please..."

"No fucking way," the older plumber barked. "Take it."

And as he let go, the apprentice held onto the vibrator with one hand and Christy's hair with the other, still pounding away at her juicy cunt. The older plumber knelt down in front of her face and guided his thick cock into her mouth.

Christy felt the pleasure washing over her, as both her ass and pussy were stimulated at the same time. Greedily, she parted her lips, letting the older plumber's cock enter her wet mouth. As she started sucking hard, making wet, smacking sounds, he groaned with lust.

"Oh yeah," he moaned. "I'm coming, baby. Keep your mouth closed."

As Christy felt the hard cock bulging, ready to ejaculate, she wanted to let go, but the older plumber grabbed her chin, pushing his cock into her mouth.

"Closed, I said," he commanded. "And you swallow every fucking drop, baby!"

As the apprentice's long cock pounded her aching slit, the vibrator buzzing in her ass, she came again.

"Mmmm," she yelled, her voice muffled by the older plumber's cock.

And at the same moment he suddenly froze, his cock swelling incredibly in her mouth.

"Unnnh," he yelled, as he started ejaculating.

Obediently, Christy held her mouth closed, as hard, salty jets of spunk shot into her mouth. Jerking madly, the older plumber's cock squirted its creamy load down her throat, as Christy swallowed mouthful after mouthful of his hot, spicy semen.

"Unnnh, unnnh," he grunted, as Christy sucked every last drop of sperm from his fat, twitching cock.

And behind her the apprentice gave a loud cry as he, too, surrendered to orgasm:

"Aaah!"

Thrusting the entire length of his hard tool into her flesh, he started ejaculating deep inside her tender cunt. She felt the stiff shaft swelling and contracting, as the first hot spurt of semen exploded into her. With incredible force, his cock shot jet after jet of creamy spunk into her helpless pussy.

As his orgasm subsided, he turned off the vibrator and held his cock still inside her, letting her feel every last twitch. As he finally pulled out, he pulled the dildo out of her ass, too, placing it back in the toolbox.

Exhausted, Christy collapsed on the floor. She faintly heard the men dressing, finishing off the champagne. She heard footsteps and the sound of her door closing.

She sighed. They were gone. She had wanted sex with the apprentice, and now they'd both fucked her and left. Shit!

As she got up off the floor, she saw that the apprentice was still there – sitting naked on the couch, holding the toolbox. He pulled out a pair of handcuffs, dangling them in front of Christy's face.

She smiled.

The Churchyard

As Anne opened the gate to the churchyard, the hinges creaked. They creaked again when she closed it behind her.

Why did churchyard gates always creak? It was such a cliché – and it almost felt like a deliberate attempt to make the churchyard experience even spookier. Fortunately, Anne wasn't easily spooked – especially not on a sunny summer day like this.

Clutching the bouquet in her hand, she walked briskly towards Scott's grave. The big, black granite headstone lay flat in the ground. Scott's name stood carved in gold letters with his dates underneath – and space enough below it to carve Anne's when that day came.

She stood for a few seconds, contemplating the gravestone. She was dressed in black, as she always was when visiting the churchyard. In fact, Anne secretly enjoyed dressing up in the classic widow's outfit – because she looked so damn good in it: A black dress and gloves, black stockings and high heels, her favourite little black handbag – even the traditional black hat with the black veil.

She put the bouquet on the ground and knelt down in front of the grave.

No, there was no doubt in her mind: Their marriage had been a mistake from the start.

They'd met at a party, where she'd gotten a bit drunk – and brought him home for some amazing sex. The next day they had more amazing sex, and the next, and the next... Three months later, they were married. And the sex was still great. But gradually, Anne discovered that Scott was a complete bore.

He had a nice job in a bank, with no ambition to be promoted. He dressed in dull grey suits – at least Anne tried to buy him more colourful shirts, the least colourful of which he sometimes wore. And every summer they went on vacation to the same, little sleepy village in the country. Sure, the nature was beautiful, but it was dull, dull, dull...

But still the sex was amazing. Anne and Scott went at it like rabbits whenever possible, his long, thick cock hammering into her

moist pussy until she lost count of her violent orgasms. And then, after a little rest, they went at it again, sweaty, out of breath, climax after climax until they were utterly exhausted.

For two years, Anne considered the pros and cons of their marriage. Scott's dullness would drive her up the wall sometimes. But the next act of furious lovemaking would make her so delirious with pleasure, it made her think that maybe she loved him after all.

And so it went on, until the day she got a phone call saying that Scott had been found dead of a heart attack. In a hotel room. With a prostitute.

Of course she cried. For days and days. And she was shocked – Scott had only been in his early thirties like herself. But most of all she was angry.

Not so much that he'd been to see a prostitute – although it did surprise her that his libido had been so strong that even their intense sex life hadn't been enough to satisfy it. No, it was the deceit – the meaningless deceit: He must have known that Anne was open to anything. If he'd wanted to be with a prostitute, he could have just brought her home. And what man ever said no to a threesome? But no, for whatever reason, he had chosen to deceive her.

And what remained now – six months later – wasn't so much a feeling of sorrow or even loss. All through her marriage, she'd imagined life without Scott time and time again. No. Most of all she was horny.

Sex was very important to Anne, always had been. That was what made her put up with her husband's otherwise terminal dullness for two years.

She could still remember the sight and sensation of his cock – always hard, always ready. It never took much to get him excited: She'd show him her breasts, whisper some dirty words in his ear, or just give him a long wet kiss – and instantly she'd feel his long, thick cock swelling to full erection. What she wouldn't give right now to feel that hard piece of meat plunging into her slippery pussy...

Shivers ran down Anne's spine as she looked down at the gravestone. What if the dead could still see the living? What if Scott was looking up at her from six feet under? She looked around – the churchyard was empty. It usually was at this time of day.

Anne put down her handbag and lay on all fours over the headstone, her legs spread slightly.

"Can you see me?" she whispered at Scott's name.

She grabbed her breast with her gloved hand. The sensation made her shiver just a little.

"See my tits?" she whispered. "Do you wish you could grab them and give them a good, hard squeeze?"

She let her other gloved hand slip inside her panties and touch her pussy. God, she was wet!

"And what about my hot little cunt?" she whispered to the gravestone. "Doesn't that deserve a good hard fuck?"

She vividly remembered her late husband's long, swollen cock — what it had looked like, what it had felt like buried inside her sensitive flesh. Trembling with pleasure, Anne began masturbating, gasping excitedly on the shiny headstone.

"Oh Scott," she panted. "Oh, fuck me. Oh, yes."

I have an erection already. I feel my cock stretching inside my jeans, hot and stiff against my thigh. Hiding under the shade of the trees, I cautiously walk around the churchyard to see who's there.

"Oh... yes... ahhh..."

I turn my head at the sound. And I can't believe my eyes: This gorgeous babe in a black dress and hat is on all fours on top of a grave, masturbating like crazy.

If my cock wasn't hard before, it certainly is now: So hard, in fact, it's kind of painful. I zip down and pull it out. What a nice long, thick cock I have! That little slut in the black dress needs to see how hard I am. I grab my cock in my fist and step out of the shade. I walk towards her, stroking my shaft.

And when I'm only a few feet away, she looks up at me in surprise.

Anne just stared at the flasher. He seemed to have come from out of nowhere — and now he just stood there grinning, masturbating in front of her, dressed in jeans and t-shirt- He was about medium height, thin, sort of gangly, with a dark mop of hair and stubble that looked scratchy. And she just froze.

They say that when your life passes before your eyes, it's not because you're at death's door. Your brain is trying to figure out a way to survive. And to do that it just fast-forwards through every experience you ever had, trying to find a match. And lying there on all fours on her husband's headstone, one hand on her breast and one on her pussy, a grinning flasher jerking off in front of her, Anne felt her brain doing exactly that. Fast-forwarding. But nothing came up.

"Yeah, keep going," the flasher gasped. "Play with your cunt, you slut."

His words made her snap out of it. Well, sort of. At least she became acutely aware of the erect cock a few feet away from her face – and noticed that it wasn't at all unlike Scott's: Long and thick with a bulging reddish head.

Of course she knew it wasn't Scott's cock that had come back from the dead – but her mind couldn't quite tell them apart. She saw the clear liquid oozing from the tip of the flasher's cock like it had always done from Scott's. And now she felt the urge to taste it.

"Come here," she whispered. "Let me lick it."

She was surprised at the sound of her own voice – deep and husky, like a parody of a corny porn actress. But oh, she was so incredibly horny now. Her gloved hand resumed the circular motions around her clit, and she felt pleasure rippling through her body.

"Yeah?!" the flasher said. "You like that? Okay – stick out your nasty little tongue."

He stepped closer, bringing his cock just within range of Anne's outstretched, pink tongue. She eagerly licked the head of his cock, tasting the clear liquid. Which didn't really taste like much. But what it did taste of was all sex.

She let her wet tongue tickle the underside of the head of his cock. It swelled and grew, and she heard his breathing become fast and hoarse.

"Yesss..." he whispered.

Suddenly, he pulled away. He stood there looking at her, clenching his throbbing, erect cock in his fist.

"Take your clothes off," he ordered.

With a sigh, Anne stood up, reached around the back of her dress, and slowly zipped it down. She let it fall to the ground and stepped out.

The flasher looked at her lasciviously: Anne stood there in black lingerie and stockings, heels, gloves and the black hat with the veil.

"That's it!" he gasped. "Keep the rest on..."

Anne smiled. Yeah, she knew: She looked pretty damn hot in that outfit.

The flasher stroked his cock, his eyes gleaming with lust.

"Yeah," he said. "Lie down. On your back."

And slowly, carefully, Anne lay down on the gravestone – her late husband's gravestone. The sensation of cold granite against her naked back made her shiver. The flasher stepped closer, still masturbating, showing off his erect cock to her.

"Spread your legs," he ordered.

And as Anne spread her thighs apart, he knelt down between them. With one hand, he pulled her panties to the side, with the other he guided his fat, throbbing cock towards her wet labia. Anne felt the swollen head against her flesh. He pushed forwards, forcing his cock into her, until she felt her pussy lips yielding, opening to his hard, prodding shaft. He held on to her ass cheeks with both hands and slowly let his hard cock sink deep into her slippery cunt.

"Oh, God," she gasped.

The flasher let go of her ass and instead grabbed her shoulders, pinning her down on the granite stone. She felt her sensitive cunt stretching around his cock, as he pulled out – and then began thrusting rhythmically into her.

"Yes," he whispered in time with his strokes. "Yes. Yes. Yes."

Her juices oozed abundantly around his cock, as it entered her again and again. She felt the wetness squirting from her cunt, dripping on to the black gravestone. Again, she imagined the spirit of Scott being somehow down there, his ghostly tongue reaching up to taste her juices one more time.

Gasping for air on the cold, hard gravestone, Anne looked up at the blue sky, at the trees, gently shaken by a mild breeze. With each thrust of the flasher's stiff cock, Anne's excitement grew. She grabbed her breasts hard, kneading them, massaging herself to even higher levels of intense sensual pleasure. She purred lasciviously.

The flasher thrust into her with all his strength, his face a grimace of determination. Almost utterly out of breath, he kept plunging into her sensitive cunt, burying his cock to the hilt with each stroke.

He was sweating now, drops of perspiration dripping on to Anne's veil. She pushed it aside and caught a few drops of his sweat on her tongue. Savouring the salty taste, she wondered whether his semen tasted anything like that. The thought made her gasp. She spread her legs wider, inviting him to thrust even deeper into her cunt, bringing her closer, ever closer to orgasm.

"Oh yes... " she whispered, "oh yes..."

"Ahhh!" the flasher yelled, his cock bulging and throbbing inside Anne's cunt. "I'm coming! I'm coming hard!"

"Yes!" Anne cried. "Go ahead! Come all over me!"

She couldn't believe the sound of her own voice – it was the voice of a madwoman, delirious with primal lust. The flasher thrust hard into her. And again. And again. And then Anne felt the orgasm surging through her body like a jolt of electricity, making her shiver and thrash about on the gravestone, hardly sensing that the flasher's cock kept plunging into her with even greater force, until finally...

"Aaah!" he yelled. "Aaah!"

He pulled out of her trembling cunt and grabbed his cock in his hand as he began to ejaculate. Long, powerful jets of white semen shot from his jerking cock, spattering Anne's black lingerie. She felt the white-hot spurts burning her skin, as she writhed in orgasmic pleasure on the black granite gravestone. The flasher masturbated, making his cock squirt again and again, forcing every drop of sticky spunk from his pumping shaft.

But eventually, it was over. Breathing heavily, he squeezed the last, thick drops from his cock and saw them drip onto Anne's quivering thighs.

"Yeah..." he whispered. "Like that..."

He kept tugging at his cock, as if disappointed that his ejaculation didn't last.

I made the bitch come. I covered her in my cum. She was asking for it, the filthy slut. But I'm not done with her yet.

I pull the brown leather belt from my pants. I can see he's too exhausted to move. I bend down over her and quickly tie the belt around her wrists. She whimpers slightly as I pull it tight. But I know she loves it, the nasty little whore.

I step back to look at her. She's writhing on the gravestone, my sticky cum glistening all over her slutty lingerie.

There's a bouquet lying next to the stone. I pick it up and unwrap it. It's roses. Their stems are full of thorns, and as I hold them in my hand, one of the thorns prick my finger, drawing blood. Yeah, there's an idea.

I pick one flower from the bouquet and bend down next to the dirty little slut.

"Look at me," I say.

She looks at me nervously, biting her lip. I pull off her bra and throw it aside. What a nice pair of tits she has.

I lay the stem of the rose down across her skin, right above her breasts and press down. She shivers as she feels the thorns pricking.

"No..." she whispers, her bound hands tugging at the leather belt. "Please..."

"Shut up," I said. "You know you like it."

Pressing down on the stem, I roll it slowly down over her skin, up over her heaving tits. The thorns prick all over her skin — and my hands — leaving tiny little scars. She whimpers helplessly.

I roll the stem all the way down over her belly, then up again toward her tits. I'm pressing down harder this time, making the thorns pierce her skin, leaving little cuts, drawing a little blood.

"Aaah..." she cries.

Anne squirmed on the granite slab, as the flasher rolled the thorny stems up and down her naked torso. The thorns stung her like a thousand tiny needles, making her skin tingle. No one had ever done anything like this to her body. And no sensation had ever so exquisitely mixed pleasure and pain.

The flasher grinned.

"Yeah," he said. "You like that, don't you?"

Anne was about to say yes — but stopped herself with a gasp. No, she couldn't be enjoying this — it was too sick, too perverted. But then the flasher rolled the thorny stem up and down her skin again. And the tingling pain made her gasp out loud with pleasure.

"Oh yeees..." she sighed. "I love it. Don't stop."

And at that exact moment — he stopped. Frustrated, Anne squirmed on the gravestone, her bound hands struggling against the leather belt.

The flasher held the flower in his hands, plucking off one of the thorns. The he bent down next to her. He held her stiffened nipple with the thumb and forefinger of one hand and with the other he forced the thorn into her sensitive flesh from below.

"Aaah!" she screamed.

The thorn pierced her nipple. The pain was violent, stinging — and amazing. Anne's head was spinning, her pussy wet with excitement.

"Oh yes," she whispered huskily. "Please — do the other one."

Chuckling fiendishly, the flasher broke another thorn from the stem and pulled on her other nipple. And again Anne felt the biting pain of the thorn piercing her tender skin.

"Aaah!"

The flasher was breathing heavily now.

"Yeah," he gasped, breaking another thorn off the stem. "Like that. You filthy little cunt. Stick out your tongue."

"No," Anne whispered. "Please..."

Why was she suddenly afraid of that? She didn't know. Maybe because she had absolutely no idea what it would feel like.

"Do as I say," the flasher ordered, raising his voice. "Stick it out!"

And obediently, Anne opened her mouth and stuck out her tongue.

Gently, the flasher pulled out her tongue with one hand and stuck the thorn into it with the other. The hard thorn pierced her soft, wet flesh completely, and she could taste her own blood. It was the same kind of stinging pain, but somehow completely different.

"Nggg!" Anne protested.

"Yeah," he gasped. "You love that, don't you, you kinky little slut."

With a brisk motion, he pulled her panties off, exposing her neatly trimmed pussy. The sight made him grunt and swallow with lust. He broke another thorn off the stem.

I push her legs aside and kneel down between them, taking a good look at her cunt. That's a nice little pussy she's got. I wonder how many cocks have fucked that dirty little hole and pumped her full of burning hot cum? Hundreds of them, no doubt — maybe even thousands. What a filthy little whore.

I grab the folds of skin with the thumb and forefinger of my right hand. The tiny little pink clit peeks out from underneath its hood, hard and shiny. I bring my left hand closer — the hand holding the thorn.

She starts kicking and moaning:

"Nooo! Please!"

But she really wants it. They all do. Every dirty little slut I've ever tortured has loved every second, and I've always made them cum. That's just the way they are. Whores — all of them.

I press the thorn into the hood of her clit, piercing the skin.

"Aaah!" she cries. "Aaah!"

I push it in, drawing blood, leaving it there. Her pussy lips quiver and tremble.

The pain made Anne gasp. Again it was stinging and powerful – and again it was completely different. The juices flowed from her cunt, forming a tiny pool on the shiny black surface of the gravestone.

Soon she felt the skin around her clit swelling up, clenching and squeezing her hardened love button, making her flesh tingle with lust. Anne tugged at the leather belt, writhing and moaning on the gravestone.

The flasher stood up, pulled off his t-shirt and jeans, and stood naked in front of her. His cock had once again grown to a full, twitching erection.

He picked a thorn from the stem. Then, looking deep into Anne's eyes, he put out his tongue and stuck the thorn into it.

"Aaah!" he cried, wincing.

Anne stared at him in amazement. When he'd stuck the thorns into her flesh, it had turned her on. But watching him torture himself almost made her crazy with lust. She kicked her heels impatiently – she couldn't wait for that big pervert to get excited enough to fuck her again.

He pulled off another thorn and pierced the left side of his scrotum.

Again, he cried out with pain, and again he pulled off another thorn. This time piercing his scrotum on the right side.

"Aaah!" he cried. "Yeah!"

His cock twitched uncontrollably, the reddish head swelling and throbbing.

"Please..." Anne gasped, besides herself with lust. "Fuck me again..."

The naked man stroked his hard cock a few times, then assumed the position between her legs.

"Oh, I'm gonna fuck you all right..." he grunted.

He guided the head of his cock towards her pussy lips, then applied pressure, sinking the erect shaft into her soft, wet flesh. It felt even larger than before – obviously torturing her and himself with the thorns had turned him on in a big way.

Anne swallowed, spreading her legs as wide as she could to accommodate him. Finally, he buried the entire length of his cock inside her again. And immediately he began thrusting in a hard, demanding rhythm.

"Aaah!" she cried. "Aaah, yes! Fuck me!"

Almost out of breath, the flasher plunged his swollen tool into her pussy again and again. Anne felt her cunt overflowing with juices, lubricating his rigid shaft as it thrust into her relentlessly.

The flasher opened his mouth to kiss her. Surprised, Anne parted her lips and felt the wet tip of his tongue gently touching hers. As he let his tongue play around hers, she felt the thorn in his flicking against the thorn in hers. Every poke shifted the thorn around, triggering a new sting of pain, adding to the tingling sensation in her tongue.

"Nnng!" she moaned, licking at his tongue eagerly.

She couldn't get enough: The play of their excited tongues – the taste of the flasher's saliva – the sensation of his breathless gasps into her mouth – the sweet tingling pain every time their thorns scraped against each other. All this drove her into a sensual frenzy, bringing her closer, ever closer to another orgasm.

"Don't stop!" she gasped. "Please don't stop!"

Grunting like an animal, the flasher thrust harder and deeper into her. Anne felt her ass being pushed back and forth over the cold, hard gravestone, sliding in her own spicy juices. If Scott was watching from inside the grave, he would be shooting his load by now. In a flash, she imagined the familiar spurts of Scott's thick white semen spattering the inside of his coffin.

And then she came. Even harder than before, a violent orgasm surged through her entire body, making her thrash about on the gravestone. She shook so hard, the flasher had to grab both her arms to hold her down – while still vigorously plunging his cock deep into her tender cunt.

"Aaah!" she cried. "Aaah!"

"Yeah!" the flasher gasped. "That's it! You're gonna make me come. Aaah..."

He pulled out. Through the haze of her orgasm, Anne watched as the flasher picked up the rose once more. He broke one final thorn of the stem.

He hesitated slightly, his cock twitching, ready to come. Anne stared at him, her eyes now open wide.

"No..." she whispered quietly to herself.

But yes, he did. With a swift motion he stuck the pointy thorn deep into the swollen, red head of his cock.

"Aaah!" he yelled, quivering from the pain. "Aaah!"

And as a tiny drop of blood oozed from his tender flesh, he started ejaculating. Jerking wildly, his cock released a long, white jet of hot semen, shooting several feet across Anne's body, spattering her thighs, her belly, her breasts.

Immediately, his cock fired again, the thorn wriggling with every contraction. Jet after jet of piping hot sperm squirted from the pumping shaft, as the flasher cried out loud in ecstasy. He grabbed his cock in his fist, masturbating, emptying his tool of every last drop of creamy semen.

"Huhhh," he grunted, clutching his cock as his ejaculation finally subsided.

He closed his eyes, trying to catch his breath. And finally he reached over and untied the leather belt, freeing Anne's hands. She rubbed her aching wrist and just stared up at the sky. Lying there. she felt the final electric tingling of her last orgasm – and the heat of the flasher's semen on her skin.

Fluffy, white clouds blew across the sky. Birds flew from branch to branch, chirping and trilling. Anne couldn't imagine she was ever going to get up again.

Did she pass out – or fall asleep – for just a few seconds? She didn't think so – but the next time she looked up, the flasher was gone.

Breathing deeply, Anne sat up. She carefully removed the thorns from her clit, her breasts, her tongue. It felt slightly numb where the pain had been. Then she found some tissues in her handbag to wipe the flasher's semen off her skin. And slowly, she got dressed.

Before she left, she placed the remainder of the roses in the little vase by the grave. Then she once again lay down on all fours and kissed the stone.

"Did you watch that?" she whispered huskily. "I hope you did. You'd have loved it."

And calmly, Anne stood up and walked away.

To any random observer, she would have been just another beautiful young widow – closing the creaking churchyard gate behind her as she left.

Outdoor Service

Part 1

Rachel sat at a table in the sidewalk café, sipping her latte and savouring the heat of the summer sun on her face and her naked arms.

She was reading her book – which actually turned her on a bit. Sure, it was an ordinary crime story. But she'd just gotten to the part where the vicious serial killer had kidnapped the female detective. And even though the book didn't say so, Rachel couldn't help imagining that the serial killer would force himself on the detective. Reading, she saw juicy sex scenes in her mind's eye. The rough male hands of the serial killer, ripping off the heroine's clothes...

Rachel felt herself getting slightly horny. It felt a bit strange and wrong – so she put her book down and looked around the café. In front of the tables the waiter stood smoking a cigarette. He was tall and dark, with chiselled features and day-old stubble. Quite sexy, really. There were only a few guests at the other tables: An older, distinguished gentleman with greying temples in a formal, dark suit. A pretty young girl with big sunglasses. And a rather unattractive man – big and chubby, with a reddish face and crew cut red hair.

She read on. In fact, there was no sex at all in the book – it was all in her mind. It must be the heat. But she really wished that serial killer had just jumped on the heroine and ravaged her violently. That would have been so hot.

Rachel's imagination ran wild: The heroine completely naked – the killer unzipping, pulling out his cock. She could just see it: Long and stiff, its head bluish and swelling.

The thought made her all wet. No, that wouldn't do. Getting all aroused here in the café – in the middle of the street for everyone to see. She slammed the book shut and focused on her latte. And that's when she noticed.

The waiter still stood there smoking. But now he'd pulled his black apron to one side, unzipped his pants and pulled out his stiff cock. He was calmly caressing it with one hand.

Rachel gasped. This was madness! She wanted to look away – but couldn't take her eyes off the waiter's cock. Long, smooth and hard, it looked exactly like the cock she'd just been fantasizing about. The waiter held it, masturbating leisurely. The elongated bluish head swelled, all shiny in the summer sun.

Rachel looked around. None of the other guests even seemed to notice the waiter exposing himself to them. They were so indifferent, she wondered whether she'd been hallucinating. But when she looked back at him, he was still masturbating. And now he caught her gaze.

Without letting go of his cock, he smiled at her.

Rachel gasped again. That guy was fucking insane! Shamelessly exposing himself to the female guests. What the hell was he thinking?

But she still couldn't take her eyes off him – and certainly not off his cock.

The waiter put out his cigarette. And slowly he walked towards Rachel's table. She stared in fascination at his rigid cock, bouncing up and down with each step. He stood behind her chair.

She knew that now was the time to get up and leave – just get away from here. But for some reason she stayed seated.

Rachel felt the waiter's hands on her shoulders; then they slowly slid down over her breasts. He grabbed them with both hands, took her nipples between thumb and index fingers and squeezed them hard, making her moan. She sat there petrified, letting him do as he pleased.

The waiter bent over Rachel, slipping his hands down over her belly. He unbuttoned her jeans – and she felt his hand slipping under the edge of her panties. His fingers slid in between her pussy lips, then slowly out again. She gasped, as he grazed her clit and let his middle finger circle her love button.

She grew more and more wet, and felt her clit swelling and poking out.

Rachel had an unusually large clitoris – and now it stretched pink and glistening from its fold of skin, as the waiter rubbed and massaged its surroundings, making her sigh with pleasure. Again he

forced his fingers up into her cunt and began to thrust in and out, massaging her long clit with his thumb.

"Oh yes," she whispered, shivering with delight.

He kept going endlessly. His finger twisted and turned deep inside her succulent pussy. And suddenly she felt she was already about to come.

Trembling, Rachel grabbed the seat of the chair hard with both hands. She could hardly believe it – never before had she climaxed so quickly. Could she really be this excited? It was too embarrassing. There were people sitting next to her at the other tables. She bit her lip, trying her best not to scream.

The waiter's fingers thrust a few more times up into her cunt – then everything went black, as the orgasm surged through her body.

"Ohhh!" she screamed, writhing in ecstasy on the chair. "Ohhh!"

Her pussy muscles clenched the waiter's fingers hard. Juices gushed over his hand. Her entire body thrashed about spasmodically.

Slowly the orgasm subsided – only a deep, warm feeling of pleasure remained. Rachel sighed deeply and savoured the sensation, as the sun beat down on her face.

The waiter pulled his fingers from her cunt and stood in front of her. He put his dripping wet fingers in his mouth, letting her watch as he slowly licked up her juices. Rachel looked at his cock, still just as long and hard.

"Show me your tits," he said.

She looked up at him with glazed eyes, still dizzy after her surprise orgasm. Then she slowly began unbuttoning her thin white blouse. She wasn't wearing a bra today, and opening her blouse exposed her round, voluptuous breasts. Her nipples stood out stiff in the sun.

"Yeah," the waiter whispered randily and began masturbating.

His big fist flew back and forth over the stiff shaft of his cock. The veins swelled and throbbed underneath the skin.

Rachel looked around the café. By now the other guests seemed to have finally noticed what was going on. The grey-haired man watched them with interest, the girl with the sunglasses had at least turned her head in their direction – and the fat man stared at them, his face even redder than before.

"Grab your tits," the waiter ordered.

Rachel looked up at him. He smiled viciously, his eyes twinkling with lust. Without letting go of his gaze, she grabbed her breasts and slowly began kneading them.

"Yeah," the waiter panted.

He tugged hard at his cock in an ever more vigorous pace. Rachel enjoyed the sensation of massaging her breasts – and showing them off turned her on even more. A tiny drop of clear liquid glistened on the tip of the waiter's cock and slowly ran down the shaft. He had to be extremely aroused by now.

"Stand up," he ordered.

On trembling legs, Rachel stood up. The waiter let go of his quivering cock and grabbed her shoulders. He turned her around, making her bend over the table, her ass in the air. Then he zipped her jeans all the way down and pulled them down to her heels. She kicked them off – and suddenly his hand slapped her on the buttock.

Slap!

Rachel gasped. The waiter hit her again.

Slap!

Her skin burned, but the waiter just kept on and on hitting her.

Slap! Slap! Slap!

Blows rained down on her ass-cheeks, making her sob quietly, holding on to the table. But she also felt her cunt growing wetter and wetter. She was getting spanked – and she loved it.

Slap! Slap! Slap!

"Yeah, like that!" the waiter said. "You like that?"

"Oh yes," Rachel whimpered. "I love it. Please don't stop."

Slap! Slap! Slap!

Rachel felt her juices running slowly down the inside of her thighs.

The fat man had gotten up from his chair and now stood staring at them, his face bright red.

Suddenly the blows stopped. Instead she felt the waiter pushing her panties aside – and then the head of his cock pushing against her labia. She gasped loudly.

The waiter grabbed her hips and slowly forced his stiff cock up into her cunt. She opened herself to him, letting the long hard shaft bury itself inside her.

"Ohhh," she moaned.

The waiter began thrusting, hard and relentlessly, making the cups clatter on the table. His stiff cock pumped like a piston inside Rachel's juicy cunt. She shivered with pleasure.

"Yes!" he gasped. "Yes, like that!"

His voice was hoarse with excitement – and the sound of it turned Rachel on even more. She spread her legs, allowing herself to be fucked right there in the café – in plain view of the other guests. It was just so insanely hot! She felt her juices oozing out over the waiter's rock-hard cock.

With a grunt he pulled out of her.

"Turn around," he ordered.

With a swift move of his hand he wiped Rachel's cup off the table. It landed on the pavement and shattered. He pointed to the tabletop.

"On your back," he said.

His cock twitched, wet and glistening from Rachel's juices.

She lay on her back on the little table; and he quickly pulled off her panties, throwing them on the ground. Her long clitoris poked slick and pink from its little fold. The waiter stood between Rachel's legs and guided his cock into her cunt once more.

"Ohhh yes," she whimpered, as he buried the rigid shaft inside her.

The waiter grabbed her thighs hard and began fucking – hard and deep, making her dripping wet cunt smack loudly with each thrust.

The other guests had got up from their chairs and stood around the table, watching the waiter fucking Rachel with hard, deep thrusts. The elderly gentleman smiled wickedly, the girl in the sunglasses slowly licked her lips. And the fat man's face was now bright red with excitement, as he rubbed his crotch through his pants. Rachel saw his cock bulging and growing beneath the fabric.

Again and again the waiter thrust deep into her juicy cunt. Helplessly, Rachel held onto the table, feeling her excitement growing and growing – driving her towards yet another inevitable climax.

"No," she gasped. "Wait. I can't... oh! Oh!"

But the waiter showed no mercy. With an evil grin he thrust his cock into her in a hard, relentless rhythm. Until Rachel felt her juices gushing and squirting around his pumping cock, as another orgasm completely took her breath away. A shimmering sensation

of pleasure surged through her entire body. Gasping for breath, she shivered in convulsions.

"Aaah!" she cried. "Aaah!"

"Fuck, I'm gonna blow," the waiter gasped. "I'm coming."

He held his throbbing cock still inside her cunt. Rachel felt it swelling and jerking – and with a grunt of lust the waiter ejaculated inside her. She felt the first squirt of spunk shooting deep inside her pussy. And then another.

But then the waiter pulled out, grabbing his pumping cock in his hand, letting her watch as he kept coming. The next long jet of white-hot sperm flew in an arch over her, spattering her belly and her breasts. Again and again he spurted, masturbating intently – as if to empty himself completely of semen.

Finally he finished ejaculating. Sighing deeply with satisfaction, he let his cock drip off on the pavement. Then he zipped up and adjusted his black apron.

Rachel looked around, dazed. The elderly gentlemen produced a briefcase and opened it. It was full of a neatly wound rope.

"Well," he said with a vicious smile. "Yes, she's a naughty little number. But now, let us just get this situation under control."

The waiter, the girl, and the fat man held her down, as the elderly gentleman skilfully began tying her to the table with the heavy ropes.

Part 2

Rachel was too exhausted to protest. The elderly gentleman tied the rope around her wrists; then he pulled her arms above her head, and fastened the rope to the small table's solitary leg. He tied a loop around each of her thighs and pulled them apart, making her lie spread-eagled on the table. All ropes were fastened and tightened around the table leg.

When he was finished, the bound Rachel couldn't lift her arms, and couldn't pull her legs together. The ropes burned her skin, and the waiter's semen and her own juices slowly oozed from her cunt onto the blank steel of the table top.

She turned her head and saw that the fat man had began to undress. His skin was pale; he had a big belly and chubby legs. And Rachel almost burst out laughing at the sight of his cock. It was now hard and stiff – but was almost the spitting image of its owner: A bit shorter than the waiter's, but rather thick and very pale. Its head was almost spherical and as bright red as the head of the fat man himself.

He stood between Rachel's legs.

"No!" she cried.

No – she didn't want to – she just didn't want to be fucked by that horny, flabby man. She struggled desperately to free herself. But the taut, scratching ropes just dug deeper into her wrists and thighs, pinning her down on the table in the same position: Arms over her head, legs spread, her moist pussy wide open for all to see.

The fat man's cock stood straight up. He grabbed it with his fist, pointing it down towards Rachel's cunt. Then he thrust forwards, burying the entire length of the wide cock inside her.

"Oh!" she gasped.

The fat man grabbed the two ropes holding Rachel's thighs, as if they were the reins of a horse – and began to fuck her in hard, fast strokes. She screamed. His face was bright red with excitement and his belly and flab bounced in time with his thrusts.

Rachel couldn't bear the sight of the horny fatty. She closed her eyes. That spared her the sight – but somehow enhanced the sensation: The feeling of how deep he entered her – how his fat cock stretched the flesh of her cunt – how hard and vigorously he thrust into her again and again.

She whimpered with lust there on the table top – while the fat man held on to the ropes around her thighs, ruthlessly plunging his hard, fat cock into Rachel's wet, slippery cunt.

She climaxed again. This time she was too exhausted to even scream. She just sobbed helplessly, throwing her head from side to side as another powerful orgasm surged through her body. This couldn't be happening: The disgusting fatty had made her come.

The fat man's cock swelled and jerked inside Rachel's cunt. He grunted loudly and pulled out. As he grabbed his fat, glistening member in his fist, it immediately began squirting. The shaft contracted violently with each spurt – but it didn't shoot as far as the waiter's had. The fat man's cock spat out its thick white semen onto Rachel's trembling belly in burning hot globs.

The fat man masturbated, uttering deep, grunting sounds. When he was finished he stepped away and stood next to the table. Rachel noticed that his pale cock was still just as erect.

The girl in sunglasses came over and knelt down between Rachel's legs. She placed her open mouth over Rachel's tender cunt and began sucking up the semen of the two men. Rachel sighed. The girl forced her thighs apart, slurping vigorously at Rachel's pussy. She licked up the spunk of the waiter and the fat man, swallowing repeatedly.

Then she took Rachel's long, erect clitoris in her mouth and began sucking it like a cock. Rachel cried out with surprise – and felt an incredible lustful sensation streaming from her clit into every fibre of her shivering body. The girl in sunglasses sucked at her stiff love button in an intense rhythm. Rachel's juices flowed abundantly from her cunt, and the girl sucked them up, moving her head up and down over the long, quivering clit.

Rachel came again.

"Ohhh!" she cried, writhing helplessly in the taut ropes. "Ohhh!"

The climax coursed through her as the girl's mouth sucked in her twitching, swollen clitoris. It just went on and on – Rachel thought she'd never stop coming. But slowly the mad, animal orgasm subsided, leaving a calm, lusty tingling throughout her bound body.

The girl in sunglasses gave Rachel's cunt a final wet kiss, then stood up next to the table. The waiter walked over to her and asked:

"You have a dildo?"

"Of course," she said.

"I mean," he went, "Have you brought one with you?"

"Always," she replied smiling.

And from her purse she produced a bright red latex dildo the size of a standard cock. The waiter took it with a crooked smile.

Rachel was too tired to struggle.

"Oh no," she whispered helplessly. "Now what?"

Now the waiter stood between her legs, placed the vibrator against her long, protruding clit – and turned it on. A deep, electric buzzing ran through Rachel's cunt, spreading through her entire body.

"Aaah!" she cried.

The waiter ran the vibrating toy in circles around and around her clit – then slowly down between her labia and into her cunt. Rachel's juices flowed around the dildo, soaking the waiter's fingers. He turned off the vibrator and thrust the latex member into her pussy a couple of times. Then he pulled it out, instead placing its tip against her anus.

"No. No!" she protested.

Grinning maliciously, the waiter slowly forced the dildo up into Rachel's ass. And she couldn't help it: She enjoyed the sensation. It felt so incredibly filthy, the hard rubber cock entering her smallest and tightest hole. Rachel writhed lustfully on the table top. And then the waiter switched on the vibrator.

"Ah!" she cried. "Ah!"

She jerked violently from surprise and lust, making the little table rock back and forth. The waiter held her still, forcing the buzzing dildo further up her ass.

The elderly gentleman, the girl in sunglasses and the naked fatty stood around the table, watching them. The fatty's pale, thick cock was still completely erect. From time to time, it gave a little twitch, spitting out a spurt of semen that spattered onto the pavement.

Rachel trembled, as the dildo whirred inside her tender ass. Her long, erect clitoris stuck out, pink and glistening, twitching with lust. The waiter gripped it, gently masturbating it like a cock. Rachel cried out with pleasure:

"Aaah!"

The waiter turned off the vibrator and pulled it out of her ass. Then he pushed his apron to one side and unzipped his pants. His long cock was hard and stiff again. He thrust two fingers up into

Rachel's sopping wet cunt. Then he pulled them out and put them in her mouth.

"Taste yourself," he panted.

Eagerly Rachel licked up her own juices. She savoured the spicy taste of pussy juice – but thought she could taste the semen of the waiter and the fat man – and perhaps the saliva of the girl in sunglasses? The aroma excited her – the waiter's fingers had the taste of lust and shameless sex in the sun in the outdoor café.

Again the waiter drove his cock into her and began thrusting. Rachel looked up at him. Oh, it was that lovely long cock again. And a man she really fancied. So handsome with his dark, chiselled features, his day-old stubble – and the muscles in his arms and chest, flexing vigorously beneath his shirt as he fucked her.

Throwing her head back, Rachel savoured the sensation of the long, rigid cock, pumping away at her sensitive cunt. She noticed the fat man; he had grabbed his cock and stood there masturbating.

What was going on? How long would they keep going? Why was everyone so deliriously horny? Was it something about her that excited them on so much? She'd noticed men gazed longingly at her when she walked down the street. But was she really sexy enough to turn an entire café on to a wild open air gangbang?

The girl in sunglasses knelt down in front of the naked fatty and stuck out her tongue. He masturbated himself to yet another ejaculation – thick, white spurts shot from his pale, fat cock. The girl caught every glob on her tongue, swallowing it. As one more little droplet ran down his swelling shaft, the girl in sunglasses carefully licked it up. Afterwards, his cock remained as stiff and hard as before.

Rachel whimpered. The waiter's hard brutal thrusts into her cunt drove her towards yet another orgasm. She no longer remembered how many times she'd come. She couldn't... she...

"Ohhh!" she cried as she climaxed again. "Ohhh!"

Her orgasm was so violent it was almost painful. Rachel's pussy contracted in spasms – she felt as if it would squeeze the life out of the waiter's cock. But he seemed to enjoy the sensation of her cunt muscles gripping his hard shaft. He grunted with pleasure, thrusting deeper and deeper into her, her juices gushing and squirting around his pumping cock.

"Oh yeah..." she whimpered huskily. "Oh yeah..."

Suddenly the waiter pulled his cock from her cunt, grabbed it with both hands, and pointed it up over her bound body. He was so close to coming, he didn't have to move his hands. His hard cock jerked violently, its head swelling madly. And then he climaxed.

"Yeeeah!" he cried, shaking with pleasure. "Ohhh!"

He first, hot spurt of the waiter's semen flew through the air, hitting Rachel's left breast. The next hit her belly. And the cock just kept spurting and spurting. She felt semen hitting her chin, her cheek, her left breasts – and landing in long, white lines across her skin.

Panting, the waiter let go of his cock, one final thick drop of spunk oozing from its head.

"Oh yes," he whispered. "Like that."

The elderly gentleman had zipped down and pulled out his erect member. It was long and slender, curving slightly upwards. The veins were clearly visible beneath the taut skin of the shaft. He stood next to Rachel's face.

"Open your mouth," he ordered.

Obediently, Rachel parted her red lips – and the elderly gentleman guided his erect cock into her wet mouth.

"You filthy whore!" he said harshly. "Suck my cock. Suck it, until I come!"

Rachel was surprised to hear the distinguished, elderly man talk so dirty to her. He must be very excited. She began sucking rhythmically at the hard cock – and felt how he slowly let it slip in and out of her mouth.

Now a hard cock pressed against her labia. It was the fat man again. Snorting with lust, he forced his fat tool all the way into her cunt. Again he grabbed the ropes around her thighs and began thrusting away – hard and deep, making the table rock and dance on the pavement. With loud slurping noises, Rachel vigorously sucked the elderly gentleman's cock.

On edge of the next table, the girl in sunglasses sat watching them. Now she lifted up her skirt. She wasn't wearing panties, and her pubes were neatly trimmed, exposing her moist, pink slit.

Her fingers found her clit.

"Oh yes," she whispered hoarsely. "Fuck her."

And the girl in sunglasses began masturbating – slowly and intensely. She looked from the elderly gentleman's cock in Rachel's mouth to the fat man's furious pumping into her cunt, and once in a

while to her own lap, each time prompting a deep sigh. She clearly enjoyed watching herself masturbate.

Rachel writhed and squirmed on the metal table, the rough ropes scratching the skin of her arms and thighs.

The fat man was sweating with excitement, his face a deep red. His sweat dripped onto her face, her breasts, her belly – ran down between her thighs, mixing with her juices, and pouring over his thrusting cock. Rachel stuck out her tongue, catching a few drops of his sweat. It had a salty, spicy taste that for some reason made her even more randy.

Grunting like a beast, the fat man fucked Rachel with savage energy, driving her ever closer to yet another orgasm. The elderly gentleman fucked her mouth, making her swallow several times. And leaning on the neighbouring table the girl in sunglasses massaged her smooth pussy, juice trickling down the insides of her though.

"Keep going!" the girl gasped. "Fuck her fucking brains out!"

She plunged her fingers up into her own cunt – sobbing loudly with pleasure. Snorting and grunting, the fat man thrust his thick cock into Rachel again and again.

"Ohhh!" the girl in sunglasses cried, her fingers buried deep inside her own juicy cunt. "I'm coming!"

She gripped the edge of the table, and a powerful jet of juice shot from her cunt, as orgasmic spasms shook her entire body.

The fat man thrust a few more times up into Rachel's pussy – and she came again.

"Mmm!" she cried, her mouth full of the elderly gentleman's cock. "Mmm!"

The fatty pulled out of her, grabbed his fat cock with both hands, and masturbated like mad. He roared like an animal, as his pale, fat cock began ejaculating again. He pumped his sticky semen all over Rachel's belly and thighs.

And then she felt the first hot spurt in her mouth.

"Yeahhh!" the elderly gentleman cried. "There's a good little whore! Swallow it all!"

His long cock jerked fiercely inside Rachel's mouth, spurting jet after jet of spicy, hot spunk down her throat. Gulping, she swallowed one mouthful after another, as he emptied himself into her mouth, gasping with pleasure.

Then silence fell on the sidewalk café.

The girl in sunglasses adjusted her clothes and hair. A puddle of her juices glistened on the pavement. The elderly gentleman's orgasm subsided, and he pulled out of Rachel's mouth and zipped up his trousers. The waiter stood a few steps away, smiling lustfully. And the fat man? He still walked around, stark naked, still sporting a full erection. Rachel saw him swiftly masturbating again, making globs of thick semen spurt from his cock, spattering the pavement.

Carefully the elderly gentleman untied her ropes, letting Rachel crawl off the tables and get dressed. She sat on her chair, trying to recover. The elderly gentleman shook her hand.

"Thank you, miss," he said politely. "It was a pleasure."

Rachel stared at him. Seconds ago he had hurled obscenities at her. And now...

The girl in sunglasses came over and sat next to her. The waiter walked into the café and brought them two glasses of cold white wine.

Clinking their glasses, they drank in silence.

But soon the girl leaned over, kissing Rachel passionately. Surprised, Rachel pulled away. But then she opened her mouth, meeting the girl's lips again. Their tongues flicked playfully at each other. The girl grabbed Rachel's breasts, kneading it hard.

Rachel squirmed with pleasure. This day in the café had kindled something inside her. And she wasn't done yet...

The sun was going down, as Rachel and the girl in sunglasses got up from the café table. And together they walked back to Rachel's flat.

Part 3

"By the way," the girl in sunglasses said. "My name's Kitty."

The stopped on the sidewalk, looking each other over. The air was still warm, and in the last reddish rays of sunlight Rachel found Kitty incredibly beautiful.

"Kitty," she replied. "I like that name. Sounds slutty."

She pulled her close and kissed her long and deep, their wet tongues eagerly playing with each other. Rachel grabbed Kitty's soft breast, then let go, instead slipping her hand up under her skirt. Kitty was dripping wet, and Rachel slid her finger in between her labia.

Kitty pulled away, startled.

"Not in the middle of the street," she whispered.

Hand in hand the two women walked back to Rachel's flat.

Inside the flat, Kitty took off her sunglasses. She had lovely, green eyes.

"Would you like a glass of wine?" Rachel asked, taking a bottle of white wine from the fridge.

"Oh, yes, please," Kitty said.

Rachel poured two glasses. Kitty looked around Rachel's kitchen timidly. She took the glass and quickly gulped down a couple of mouthfuls.

"Take off your clothes," Rachel said.

Kitty stared at her. Then she began undressing. She tossed away her blouse, showing off her pretty, round breasts. Her short skirt fell to the floor, once again revealing that she wore no panties. Rachel sipped her wine, savouring the sight of the naked girl's body.

"Now put your sunglasses back on," she said.

Kitty obeyed, making Rachel smile with satisfaction. An attractive nude girl with big designer sunglasses was somehow just so hot. She put down her glass and took Kitty's hand.

"Come here", she said, pulling her into her bedroom.

Kitty followed willingly. Rachel's bed was covered by a soft, black blanket.

"Lie down," Rachel said.

And Kitty lay down on her back, looking around her curiously. Rachel crawled on top of her, kissing her softly on the mouth. Then she reached down behind the headboard.

Rachel and various boyfriends had often enjoyed tying each other up – and eventually Rachel had bought a pair of black leather bracelets, attached to metal chains. Now she pulled them out, swiftly chaining Kitty to the bed.

"What?" Kitty gasped. "No..."

"Don't worry," Rachel whispered soothingly. "It's okay."

She moved down between Kitty's legs, letting her tongue caress her pussy lips. Her taste was sweet and spicy.

"Oh yes," Kitty sighed, squirming.

Rachel sucked Kitty's tiny clit into her mouth. She sucked it vigorously, making it harden and quiver with lust between her lips. Kitty gasped with pleasure, as Rachel slurped and drooled around her stiffened clitoris.

Rachel's fingers slipped into her own panties. She was sopping wet with excitement. Still sucking at Kitty's sensitive clit, she began masturbating in a furious rhythm.

Rachel let the stiff button slip out between her lips. Wet and swollen it stood there, twitching in its little fold of skin. Now Rachel forced her wet, meaty tongue up into Kitty's cunt and began thrusting her head back and forth, her tongue rhythmically poking her pussy like a cock. Kitty whimpered with lust.

"Ohmigod, I'm coming," she sobbed. "I'm coming..."

"Not yet," Rachel replied. "Wait."

She had been too excited to think about undressing. Now she jumped out of bed, quickly tearing off blouse, jeans and panties. Her long clitoris stood out hard and swollen, pointing at the chained Kitty on her bed. Kitty stared at it, fascinated.

"It's so beautiful," she whispered admiringly.

Rachel caressed her clit with two fingers.

"You think?" she asked.

Then she crawled back into bed to Kitty.

"Spread your legs," she ordered.

And Kitty spread her thighs, her moist pussy opening like a wet, pink flower. Rachel gently lay on top of her, guiding her long, hard clit up into Kitty's cunt.

"Ohhh!" the two girls cried out in unison.

The sensation was beyond description. Wild with excitement Rachel began thrusting her pelvis, slipping her clit in and out of Kitty's wide open cunt. Sobbing, Kitty tugged at her bracelets, making the chains jingle. Rachel kept thrusting away in a hard, demanding rhythm – like a brutal and very horny man. Kitty's juices oozed from her pussy, drenching Rachel's long, stiff clit, making it glisten.

Kitty threw herself about on the bed, senseless with excitement.

"I can't take anymore!" she sobbed. "I'm coming."

"Ohhh..." Rachel gasped, sensing that orgasm was coming, too. And this time with that special kind of excitement that meant she was going to squirt.

She thrust once more into Kitty's cunt. And twice. And thrice. Then she couldn't hold back any longer.

"Aaah!" she screamed, pulling out.

Juices gushed from her cunt, a violent orgasm surging through her body.

Kitty, too, climaxed. Letting out a bestial howl of pure lust, her body shuddered spasmodically, her chains jingling. And a long jet of love juice squirted from her cunt, spraying Rachel's breasts and belly.

Whimpering with pleasure the two girls bathed each other in the clear fluids of their lust, emptying themselves in long, warm spurts. Still quivering from her orgasm Rachel collapsed over Kitty's soaking wet body, kissing her passionately.

They lay there for a while, kissing and caressing.

"That was so good," Kitty whispered.

Rachel kissed her again.

"And I can taste my cunt on your tongue," Kitty whispered huskily. "That's just so hot."

Getting out of bed, Rachel stood watching the chained, naked girl, her skin glistening with sweat and love juices. And she still looked so hot in those big sunglasses.

"Can I have some more wine?" Kitty asked timidly.

"Of course," Rachel said nodding.

She was on her way to the kitchen as the doorbell rang.

"Oh my," she said smiling. "I think we have a visitor."

Again Kitty pulled at her chains, making them jingle.

"But," she protested. "What about me?"

Rachel went to answer the door – still stark naked. She looked back at Kitty, smiling sarcastically.

"What about you?" she echoed. "Well – we'll just have to see about that, won't we?"

Rachel opened the door. Outside was the fat man from the outdoor café. Naked, flabby and red in the face – and still sporting a huge erection. His fat, pale cock stuck straight out, twitching.

"Come on in," Rachel said cheerily.

The fatty followed her into the bedroom.

Before leaving the outdoor café Rachel had slipped him her address. But how did he get here? Had he walked all the way stark naked? And knowing the fat man, he'd probably been masturbating on the way – his fat, erect cock always had some globs of semen to spit out.

"Look," Rachel said to Kitty. "I have a present for you!"

The fat man grunted lustfully at the sight of the chained girl, his pale, fat cock twitching with excitement.

"Nooo!" Kitty screamed. "No, not him!"

Her protests seem to turn him on even more. He grabbed his cock with both hands, masturbating until a little load of thick spunk oozed from his cock, dripping onto Rachel's shiny wooden floor. As usual his cock remained hard and stiff.

"There you go," Rachel told the fatty, indicating Kitty, her voice dropping to a husky whisper: "Here's a naked, horny bitch for you. She just needs a proper pounding with that big, fat cock of yours until she can't take it anymore. Okay?"

Snorting, the fatty crawled onto the mattress to Kitty. Springs and bedstead creaked under his weight.

"No," Kitty sobbed. "Don't!"

The fatty assumed the position between her thighs, grabbed his fat cock with both hands and guided it up into Kitty's cunt. He buried the entire length of the huge member inside in one single stroke.

"Aaah!" Kitty screamed.

The fatty began thrusting in hard and relentless strokes – out and in, out and in, the chained Kitty moaning in protest.

Rachel stared at them, fascinated. What an incredible cock the fat man had. Thick and wide, it forced Kitty's smooth pussy lips apart, forcing her cunt open, pumping vigorously in and out of her dripping wet crevice.

"Yeah," Rachel whispered excitedly. "Keep going. That's the way she likes it."

She sat on the bed next to them. The mattress rocked and creaked with each of the fatty's powerful thrusts. Rachel spread her legs, her fingers touching her long, hard clit. Slowly she began masturbating, savouring the sight of the fatty's pale, swollen cock thrusting rhythmically into Kitty's slurping cunt. Rachel shivered with pleasure.

Kitty could no longer conceal her excitement. She whimpered with joy each time the fatty buried his thick cock inside her – all the way in with every thrust. Rachel watched him, wild with lust, entering deeper and deeper into Kitty's juicy cunt. Yes, Rachel almost wished she was the one lying there, chained to the bed, mercilessly fucked by the sweaty, flabby man. Turned on by the sight, she masturbated like mad.

Then Kitty could take no more. She let out a loud scream as another orgasm washed over her.

"Aaah!" she cried. "Aaah!"

The fatty's face was bright red from the strain. Grabbing his cock in his fist he pulled out of Kitty's pussy. And once again Rachel watched in fascination as a jet of love juice spurted from her quivering cunt.

This was too much for the fat man as well. Roaring, he clenched his cock in both hands, as it spat out long globs of his thick sperm over Kitty's thighs and belly. His sweaty flab shivered in ecstasy, as he eagerly masturbated, forcing out the very last drops.

Rachel sat, her mouth wide open, watching the lascivious scene.

"Fuck..." she whispered.

The fatty stumbled out of bed and walked restlessly around the room, stroking his indefatigable hard-on. Kitty lay on the bed as if sedated – still trembling slightly from her orgasm

Rachel bent over her.

"It's okay," she said. "I'm letting you go now."

"Mmm," Kitty replied.

It was hard to tell whether she understood. Rachel unlocked the bracelets, freeing Kitty's arms.

"Was it very bad?" Rachel asked.

But before Kitty had time to answer, Rachel felt a strong fist grabbing her arm, brutally pulling her out of bed.

"No!" she protested. "What...?"

The fatty dragged her into the kitchen. Rachel tried to struggle away, but he was incredibly strong – even after God only knows how many ejaculations that day.

Gripping her arm firmly he looked around the kitchen. He ran his eyes over knives, vegetables, wine bottles, spice racks. Rachel tried to pull her arm away, but he held on so firmly it hurt to even try.

With a satisfied grunt the fatty reached for a bottle of olive oil. Unscrewing the cap, he poured the thick, yellowish fluid over his cock. Then he took some on his fingers and forced them into Rachel's ass.

"Ow!" she cried. "No!"

Wild with excitement the fatty poured more olive oil over Rachel's buttocks, using his fingers to squeeze even more oil into her anus. He placed her – bottom up – over her little kitchen table and guided his fat cock in between her shapely buttocks.

"Oh no!" she protested. "Please don't."

Rachel had tried anal sex previously. Sometimes it hurt, but she'd grown accustomed to it and taught herself to relax. And when her lovers knew what they were doing, fucking her ass could trigger utterly amazing orgasms. But not today! Not with him! Rachel simply wouldn't risk coming with the fatty's cock buried in her ass – that would just be too humiliating.

Snorting with excitement, the fatty forced his thick member up into Rachel's anus. She felt herself opening for him in an indescribable mixture of pain and pleasure. He grabbed her hips hard and pulled her towards him, impaling her ass on the entire length of his meaty shaft.

Then he began fucking. Rachel let out a scream of pain and surprise. The oily prick pumped in and out of her ass, but not as furiously as usual. He still thrust deep and hard, but somewhat calmer this time – as if to savour the sensation of Rachel's tight, little hole.

Rachel's fingers found her pussy, and again she began masturbating. Her other hand grabbed and kneaded her shapely breast as the fatty forced his pale, fat cock in and out of her ass. He let his cock slip out almost completely with each thrust, letting her feel the swollen edge of its head slipping in and out of her anus again and again.

"Damnit," she gasped. "You bastard!"

He thrust Rachel hard up against the kitchen table repeatedly, his oily cock impaling her tight, stretching hole. An intense mix of pain and pleasure surged through Rachel's naked, quivering body. She masturbated in a vigorous rhythm, feeling her pussy juices flowing over her fingers.

"Ohhh..." she moaned. "Ohhh..."

She felt his giant cock bulging inside her ass. With a loud roar the fatty thrust all the way into her one last time. Then he just stood there, as Rachel felt his fat cock jerking with excitement deep inside her ass.

She cried out with surprise, feeling the first spurt of piping hot sperm inside her. The fatty grabbed her hips hard, grunting loudly with lust, his cock ejaculating again and again. Sobbing, Rachel kept masturbating – she was almost there. Yes – now she was coming. She was coming...

"Ohhh!" she cried. "Ohhh!"

Juices spurted wildly from Rachel's cunt, splashing over the kitchen floor. The orgasm shook her thoroughly, her eyes glazing over. The fatty's thick cock kept twitching inside her ass, spitting out a few more globs of semen inside her.

Slowly he let his slippery cock slide out of Rachel's tight hole. She felt wide open. Gasping, she lay over the kitchen table, still shivering from the strength of her orgasm. The fatty's slimy semen oozed from her anus, running down the insides of her thighs.

Rachel sighed. He'd had his way with her, she thought. It was all over now.

But grunting he grabbed her upper arm and brutally dragged her from the kitchen, clutching the bottle of olive oil in his other hand. Rachel tried struggling – but what strength he had! (There had to be some muscles under all that flab, after all) Stumbling, she followed him back into the bedroom.

"No!" she protested. "No more!"

The fatty threw her on the bed, face down. Next to her Kitty sat stark naked, still wearing her sunglasses. Her bright red vibrator lay next to her.

The fatty's hands forced Rachel's thighs apart, and she felt him pouring more olive oil into her ass. Then she heard the slurping sound of him spreading the oil over his cock. He snorted lustfully, and again she felt the huge head of his cock pressing against her anus.

"Oh!" she cried as he thrust forward.

Kitty watched them, her mouth wide open. Her fingers found her cunt, and she slowly began rubbing her clitoris. The she grabbed the dildo, turning it on. Slowly she let the buzzing vibrator circle her clit. She moaned with pleasure.

The fatty's cock penetrated the depth of Rachel's ass. It was as if he went even deeper this time. His flabby fingers grabbed her hips hard, and again he began brutally fucking her ass. Grunting with pleasure he buried his thick member inside her again and again. Rachel shivered. She was so horny now she didn't even have to masturbate. Every thrust of the fat cock inside her anus drove her closer and closer to another orgasm.

Watching them, Kitty let the dildo slip into her cunt.

"Oh!" she gasped.

She kept it whirring, sliding it in and out of her succulent pussy. She fucked herself with the vibrator, enjoying the sight of the fatty thrusting his cock into Rachel's ass.

Rachel lay with her cheek against the blanket, her eyes fixed on Kitty's cunt – and just let it happen. Again and again the thick, rock hard cock thrust into her ass, as she whimpered helplessly, feeling the climax approaching.

Kitty thrust her vibrator all the way up into her cunt, crying out loud as she came. The juices squirted from her pussy over her fingers and the blanket. A couple of drops hit Rachel's face, and she licked them up, savouring the taste of the young girl's cunt.

The fatty's cock thrust harder and harder into Rachel's pussy – and now she felt it bulging, ready to spurt. She knew that when the fatty ejaculated into her ass again that would make her come, too. And now he let out a loud roar, holding his cock still inside her. The huge member contracted – and she felt it firing its first load of thick, hot semen deep into her ass.

Then Rachel felt her body going limp. And everything went black...

When Rachel opened her eyes again, it took some time for her to realize where she was. But eventually she recognized her own bedroom and her own bed.

She was alone. Both Kitty and the fatty had gone. Outside her windows it was now completely dark. How long had she been unconscious?

Naked, she lay on the bed, thinking back on everything that had happened that day. From seeing the naughty waiter masturbating in the café – to being brutally fucked in the ass by the fatty.

She sighed, turning over on her back. Then she let her fingers slide towards her cunt.

Rachel closed her eyes, slowly beginning to masturbate.

Volume 5

Little Thief

Nervously, Rachel let her eyes wander over the shelves of the sex shop. It had been a difficult decision to enter here - and it still felt awkward. Very awkward. But she'd decided that now was the time: She was going to buy a vibrator.

One shelf was just porn films, another was magazines: All covers showing large-breasted females in various states of undress - being fucked in bizarre positions by virile and well-endowed men.

Rachel turned around. Here - next to latex masks and handcuffs - the vibrators were lined up in transparent plastic boxes. Big, small, thick, thin - skin-coloured, steel, pink and purple. Her heart beat a little faster. The thought of using one turned her on - and she couldn't wait to get home and try it.

The young, male shopkeeper sat behind the counter, unshaven, wearing a white t-shirt and jeans. He glanced over at Rachel - but discretely looked away again.

Rachel picked up a box. The vibrator was in pink plastic, not too big - almost like an average cock - and had three speeds. That would do. Now all she had to do was pay and get the hell out of the shop.

She walked towards the counter. The shopkeeper had his eyes on his computer screen, but as she approached, he looked at her quizzically.

She stopped. No - she couldn't do it. It just felt too weird putting a sex toy on the counter in front of a guy her own age. She was certain he'd immediately picture her naked, vibrator between her legs, approaching an orgasm. How couldn't he? And wouldn't that turn him on?

Damnit!

Rachel looked around. The shopkeeper focused on his computer screen again. Oh, sure - she could have bought the thing online, as well. But right now she just wanted to get home and play with her new toy.

Discretely, she stepped behind a shelf and dropped the vibrator in her purse. Done. Taking a deep breath, she headed for the exit.

Looking up, the shopkeeper nodded as she passed. She pushed the door open and walked out...

... and the alarm went off.

A piercing siren cut into Rachel's eardrums. Panicking, she froze, her heart pound. The shopkeeper jumped up and grabbed her arm.

"What the fuck are you doing?"

Confused, Rachel gasped, unable to answer.

The shopkeeper pulled her back to the counter and pressed a button underneath it, turning off the alarm. The siren had been deafening, but the sudden silence was an almost greater shock.

The shopkeeper opened her purse and produced the vibrator. He sighed and shook his head.

"I-I'm sorry," Rachel whispered. "I was going to..."

The door opened and a policeman entered. He was tall, with broad shoulders, wearing a uniform, cap and black leather gloves.

"What's going on?" he asked.

"This lady tried to steal a vibrator," the shopkeeper said, placing the box on the table.

"I-I didn't mean to," Rachel stuttered. "It's all a mistake."

The policeman opened the box and took out the vibrator. He tried to switch it on, but nothing happened.

"It needs batteries," the shopkeeper said, opening a drawer beneath the counter.

He took out three large batteries, put them in the vibrator and screwed the lid back on. Then he passed it to the policeman. He switched it on and it made a buzzing noise.

"Hmmm," the policeman said curiously.

He stood right next to Rachel.

"So we have a little thief here," he said amiably.

Rachel felt the shopkeeper grabbing her upper arms, holding her with her back against the counter.

"What...?" she gasped.

The policeman lifted up her skirt and pushed the humming toy down into her panties.

"No..." she protested.

The policeman let the vibrator buzz against her clitoris, moving it around in little circles. Rachel's legs jerked spasmodically. Next, the policeman slid the dildo over her labia. Gently, he pushed the tip of the vibrating toy into her cunt. She felt herself starting to get wet.

"Oh!" she gasped.

She writhed in the shopkeeper's grip, but his strong hands held her in place. Helplessly she rubbed her behind against the counter, the vibrator buzzing inside her pussy.

The policeman pulled out the dildo, turned it off and placed it on the counter. Then he slipped two leather-clad fingers into her panties, forcing them up into her wet crevice.

"Ah!"

He thrust the rough leather fingers in and out, in and out of her succulent cunt. She heard rhythmic slurping noises between her thighs and squirmed lasciviously in the shopkeeper's grip.

As the policeman finger-fucked her with one hand, he grabbed her throat with the other, letting her feel the rough leather against her skin. He bit her lower lip hard, making her whimper.

"Yeah," he whispered. "You little thief, you..."

Letting go of her, he unzipped his uniform pants. His cock was as hard as stone, long and thick. Rachel felt his leather gloves against the inside of her thighs, as he forced her legs apart. Then he grabbed his cock, pulled her panties to one side and placed the swelling head of his cock against her labia.

The policeman thrust his hips forwards, and she felt her pussy yielding. Slowly he pushed his fat cock up into her wet, slippery hole. His gloved hands grabbed her hips, and looking deep into her eyes, he began fucking her. Rachel felt her love juices flow lustfully around the policeman's swollen cock, as he thrust up into her, hard and deep, over and over.

"Ohhh," she moaned.

She shivered with lust. Every thrust of the policeman's cock drove her closer to orgasm, and finally there was no turning back.

"Aaah!" she screamed. "I'm coming!"

Rachel wriggled in ecstasy as the two men held onto her. A violent orgasm surged through her entire body.

With a satisfied smile the policeman pulled his cock from Rachel's cunt. Her juices dripped from the hard tool.

"Turn around," he ordered.

The shopkeeper let go of Rachel's arm. Her legs trembling, she turned her back to the policeman. Obediently, she bent down over the counter, sticking her ass in the air. The policeman swiftly pulled her panties down to her heels, and she willingly kicked them away.

Spreading her legs, Rachel felt her pussy opening like a hungry mouth, ready to swallow the policeman's horny cock.

But instead he slapped her buttock hard.

Slap!

And now the other one.

Slap!

Over and over he hit her soft buttocks hard with his leather-gloved hands.

Slap! Slap! Slap!

Rachel bit her lips. She loved a good spanking. She wriggled her ass lasciviously - getting wetter and wetter with every slap.

Finally, his gloved hands grabbed her hips hard. And she shivered with pleasure, as his cock entered her from behind.

"Yes..." she gasped. "Fuck me."

The policeman started fucking Rachel in a slow, teasing rhythm. With every thrust he pulled nearly all the way out of her cunt - then buried the entire length inside her. And pulled and. And all the way in. Again and again and again.

With trembling hands Rachel grabbed the vibrator and switched it on. Then she guided the buzzing toy towards her cunt. Slowly she let the dildo circle her tiny, hard clit as the policeman pumped his cock into her juicy pussy.

The shopkeeper sat on his chair, his pants undone. His cock was completely erect - long, thin and curving slightly.

Oh my god, Rachel thought - now he wants me to suck him off.

But he didn't. Calmly, he just sat there masturbating at the sight of Rachel getting fucked hard over his counter.

The policeman pulled off his gloves and threw them on the floor. Then he unbuttoned her blouse and grabbed Rachel's firm, round breasts. He pinched both stiff nipples hard. She squirmed.

"Ow!" she cried.

But that, too, only increased her sensations of pleasure. Faster and faster the hard, wide cock thrust into her dripping wet cunt. And she felt another orgasm coming on.

The shopkeeper looked at her coldly, stroking his cock. The clear fluid seeped from its tip and flowed over his hand.

"Is it good?" he asked.

"Yeah..." Rachel whispered, beside herself with excitement.

"Yeah," the shopkeeper murmured, stroking his cock like a madman. "A little thief like that. What a dirty, little whore. Needs to be fucked with a giant cock. Yeah..."

He let go of his cock, leaving it pointing straight out, ready to squirt. Rachel stared at it, fascinated. His balls contracted, becoming little, hairy globes - and his cock jerked and twitched like in a cramp. And finally the first long spray of semen erupted from it.

"Ah!" the shopkeeper yelled. "Ah!"

He grabbed his chair with both hands as spurt after spurt shot from his stiff, dancing cock. Long globs of white sperm landed on the shop floor.

Whether the sight of that did it - or the policeman's pumping cock inside her cunt - or the buzzing vibrator on her clit - Rachel couldn't fight it any longer.

"Ohmigod..." she gasped. "Ohmigod..."

Her second orgasm was even more powerful than the first on. She held on to the counter, as her screams of pleasure filled the sex shop.

"Aaah! Aaah!"

Rachel's juices flowed around the policeman's cock. Her pussy trembled spasmodically. She felt him thrust deep and hard into her a few more times. Then he held still, his cock swelling madly inside her.

"Yeah," he grunted. "A little thief like that..."

Roaring like mad, the policeman ejaculated inside Rachel's cunt. His massive cock jerked violently - and she felt his boiling hot semen spurting with incredible force deep into her sensitive insides. His orgasm just kept going, releasing what felt like a torrent of sperm.

The shopkeeper looked at her derisively, his long cock still half erect.

The policeman's ejaculation subsided. He kept his cock deep inside Rachel's pussy, letting her feel it twitch - the last, powerful jerks. Finally he pulled out - and she felt his thick semen flowing from her cunt and down the inside of her thighs. She sighed with contentment.

Quickly, the policeman zipped up his pants.

"Alright," he said. "That settled it, then. Have a nice evening."

And just like that, he exited the shop.

Confused, Rachel stood up, buttoning her blouse. She wiped off the juices with her panties and stuffed them into her purse.

"Yeah, yeah," the shopkeeper said, pointing to the vibrator. "You can have it. As a token of my appreciation."

Hesitantly, Rachel took the dildo and put it into her purse next to the soaked panties.

"Anything else I can help you with?" the shopkeeper asked.

Rachel stared at him. He still hadn't zipped up his pants, and his cock was still half erect.

"I thought so," he said sarcastically. "Anyway, I'm rather busy."

With a few clicks of the mouse he brought up the shop's surveillance cameras on his computer screen: Four different angles, two of them with a perfect view of the counter. Rachel froze.

The shopkeeper rewound to where the policeman entered the shop.

"Yeah, like that..." the shopkeeper gasped and started masturbating again.

Rachel ran out the door.

It was dark outside. Through the windows of the sex shop she could just make out the silhouette of the shopkeeper. Who was now masturbating to a video with her in it?

Rachel shook her head. What a night. Men were just plain crazy, that was for sure...

She headed straight home to bed. With her new toy.

The Babysitter

"So," Rebecca said, as I pulled the car into the driveway. "How do you like the new babysitter?"

"She seems nice," I said.

"'Nice'," Rebecca sniffed. "Oh, sure. But do you think she's hot?"

I stopped the car.

"Yeah, she's kinda cute," I said.

"Would you like to fuck her?" Rebecca asked.

I laughed. Emily, our new babysitter was a cute, young thing – about nineteen years old, with big blue eyes and shoulder length blonde hair. She was neither too tall, nor too skinny and always wore jeans, tightly fitted around her cute little ass. And even in those big sweaters she liked to wear, you could tell her breasts were remarkably well developed. So – good question: Would I like to fuck her?

"I haven't," I said. "If that's what you mean."

"Oh no," Rebecca said. "But maybe you should."

She opened the door and got out of the car. I followed her.

"What do you mean?" I asked.

"Oh, you know," she said. "It's healthy for a man your age to have a bit of young pussy."

"You're crazy," I laughed.

We walked into the house. In the hallway, Rebecca stopped me.

I looked at her. She was really sexy in her long, black, strapless dress - her long, black hair flowing down over her bare shoulders. She'd been the focus of all males at the dinner party, and I could see why.

"You wait here," she said.

"Why?" I asked. "Oh. Oh, no, you wouldn't..."

"Don't' worry," she said, smiling. "I'll be gentle. You just stay here and... well, I suppose you might as well get undressed. See ya."

And she walked into the living room, closing the door behind her. I laughed and shook my head. What can I say? I have a kinky wife. And I love her very much.

"Good evening," I heard Emily the babysitter's voice from the living room. "She's asleep now. She's been very good."

"Oh sure." This was Rebecca's voice. "Never mind that. I hear you've been sleeping with my husband."

I heard Emily gasp. Smiling, I took off my jacket and shirt. Call me a vain bastard, but I couldn't help admiring my muscular torso in the mirror. I believe I'm in great shape for a man in his late thirties.

"No," Emily protested in the next room. "I never... You can ask him yourself."

"Right," Rebecca said. "But now I'm asking you. And I don't believe you."

I heard scuffling sounds, and Emily shrieked. I was pretty sure Rebecca had grabbed her. I kicked off my shoes and socks.

"Take your clothes off," Rebecca said.

"No, please," Emily sobbed. "Please, madam...."

I unbuckled my belt and pulled off pants and underwear. Naked in the hall, I saw my long cock quivering. I took it in my hand, stroking it gently.

"Shut up," Rebecca said. "Take your clothes off, you little slut."

I looked at my cock in the mirror as I stroked it. Long and veiny, it began to harden and rise in my fist. It felt good.

I heard a metallic jingle from the living room. Emily was still whimpering.

I looked at myself in the mirror – flexing my muscles I savored the sight of my erection. I could hardly wait to see what Rebecca was up to.

They were quiet now. Naked and excited, I walked slowly through the door to the living room.

Emily sat on our big white leather couch, naked, her arms behind its back. Her pretty blue eyes were already wide open, and as she saw me entering, she gave a loud gasp.

Emily was even prettier in the nude: She was well proportioned, with full hips and shapely breasts, young and firm. And between her legs, Rebecca was kneeling, still wearing her evening dress.

I walked closer. Rebecca's fingers were gently pulling at Emily's labia, her tongue slowly licking her young pussy. It was a lovely

sight: My wife's long, thirsty tongue tasting the flesh of our babysitter. Emily sobbed helplessly.

I watched them, masturbating. Rebecca intensified her licking, slurping away at Emily's tiny pink clit. I saw Emily getting wet, and knew that Rebecca now tasted the girl's excitement. Emily squirmed on the couch, moaning.

Looking over the back, I saw the handcuffs. While I was undressing, Rebecca had cuffed Emily's hand behind the couch. My cock twitched. This was good. This was really good.

Rebecca was slurping loudly between Emily's thighs.

"Ah!" Emily cried, her slender legs kicking into the air.

My cock was thick and erect, dripping clear liquid onto the carpet, as I kept stroking it.

Rebecca looked up at me, her face wet with Emily's juices. She was smiling.

"I think she's ready," she said and got up.

Emily looked up at me. The size of my cock seemed to frighten her.

"No!" she cried. "Please!"

"Ungrateful bitch!" Rebecca said. "Most young girls would love to be fucked by a stud like my husband."

I knelt between Emily's legs.

"No..." she whispered.

Her pussy was wet from Rebecca's licking. Slowly, I slipped a finger into her soft, pink slit. I moved it back and forth a few times, making her moan. She was not a virgin. Not that I had expected her to, but I couldn't help wondering what lucky young punk had had the pleasure of deflowering our little babysitter.

Fascinated, I put my face next to Emily's cunt, inhaling the smell of the young girl's flesh.

"You like that?" Rebecca asked. "Young pussy. That makes you hot, doesn't it?"

I didn't answer. Keeping my finger inside her slit, I buried my face between Emily's legs, sniffing the sweet scent of her delicious, young flesh. Tenderly, I kissed her cunt, then began sucking. She gasped. I pushed my tongue forwards, forcing it in between her labia. Greedily, I licked the insides of her pussy, my tongue lapping up and down. The taste of her juice was sweet and spicy, and as she got wetter, I sucked it up and drank it down.

Emily was kicking and squirming on the couch. But with her hands tied behind the back, she was helpless. I grabbed her ass as I kept sucking her pussy. Her nipples stood out, erect and excited.

Next to us, Rebecca had zipped down her dress. Now she stepped out of it and stood naked, except for her high-heeled shoes. I glanced over at her. She's gorgeous: A tall, thin woman with voluptuous breasts – and a fine pussy crowned by a tiny bush of jet-black hair. And, watching us, she let her fingers gently part her labia. Her tiny pink clit peeked out, glistening with juice. Then she began to stroke her own flesh in a slow, sensuous rhythm.

I kept licking Emily's cunt, while looking at my wife. I love to watch Rebecca masturbate. She really gets into it, teasing herself to incredible heights of pleasure. And a beautiful woman having a powerful orgasm is always a lovely sight.

Emily was watching Rebecca, too, utterly amazed. She'd never imagined that the nice lady who hired her would do anything so filthy: Standing naked in front of her, masturbating shamelessly. And the nice lady's husband on his knees, licking her cunt. Again, Emily pulled at the handcuffs behind her back. They jingled loudly, but it was no use: Her hands were tied. She moaned.

I gave Emily's pussy one last, wet kiss. Then I straightened up, still kneeling and grabbed my cock. Licking her cunt had turned me on so much I now had an incredible hard-on.

"Look at it!" I said, slowly stroking my cock.

Emily looked at my erection and gasped. You never know how experienced these young girls are, but obviously, Emily had never been with a man who was hung like me. Not that my cock is monstrously huge, but around nine inches seems to be enough to please most women.

Rebecca was still touching herself, excited at the thought of what was going to happen next.

"Yes," she whispered. "He's going to fuck you now, Emily. Better open wide, 'cause he's going to fuck you with that big, fat cock of his."

"Please…" Emily whimpered, squirming on the couch.

I couldn't tell if she was being serious, or if she was just acting. For all I knew, our babysitter was as turned on as we were. Slowly, I guided my cock towards her wet slit. She bit her lip, as the swollen helmet made contact with the mouth of her cunt.

Breathing deeply, I pushed forwards. Emily's pussy opened, letting my hard cock enter. Deeper and deeper, I slid into her, savoring the sensation of her hot flesh wrapped around my shaft.

"Ahhh…" I groaned.

I'd buried the entire length of my cock inside her. Rebecca masturbated at the sight, gasping with pleasure. Emily sat motionless on the couch, trembling, obviously waiting for me to start fucking her.

So I did. I pulled back, then thrust deep into her tight, wet slit. She gave a loud cry. Again and again, I poked her, feeling her soft flesh stretching around my cock. I fucked her in a steady rhythm, entering deep and hard with every stroke. Emily was moaning now – moaning with pleasure.

"Yeah," I gasped. "You love it, don't you? You nasty little bitch."

"Yes!" Emily shrieked. "Oh, please… Aaah!"

Panting with lust, Rebecca drove two fingers into her own cunt and began thrusting them in and out, in and out – fucking herself.

"Give it to her!" she gasped. "Fuck her real good!"

Grunting like an animal, I thrust even deeper into Emily, making her scream. Over and over, my swelling meat entered her tender pussy.

Then suddenly, Rebecca leaned over and kissed me. Opening our mouths, we kissed passionately. It was an incredibly kinky sensation: Kissing my wife, while I was fucking the babysitter – and my wife masturbating like mad. Our tongues played sensuously with one another, until I heard Emily's cries growing louder – and I knew she was about to come.

Rebecca pulled back, watching intently.

"Are you coming?" I asked, giving Emily a few more powerful thrusts.

And then it happened.

"Aaah!" Emily cried, my glistening cock pumping in and out of her cunt. "Aaah!"

Her young body trembled uncontrollably, overcome with pleasure. She threw her head back, lost in the sensual rush of a violent orgasm.

Rebecca lay on her back on the carpet.

"Oh, God," she gasped. "Come here, both of you!"

I pulled out of Emily, my cock dripping with her lovely juice. Then I grabbed hold of her, pulling her up from the couch. She was nearly unconscious, delirious with pleasure.

I pushed her down on her knees. Her hands were still cuffed behind her back. Rebecca spread her legs, and I placed Emily's face just above Rebecca's pussy. Then I assumed the position behind Emily, my reddened cock pointing straight up. I grabbed Emily by the hair, pushing her face into my wife's cunt.

"Now lick it," I said. "Lick it good."

Expectantly, Rebecca reached down and parted her pussy-lips with two fingers, exposing the wet, pink insides of her excited cunt. Emily hesitated for a second, but as I kept pushing her face down, she opened her mouth, her lips gently kissing my wife's pussy.

"Oh, fuck!" Rebecca gasped.

Slowly, Emily began sucking at her clit, rhythmically munching at her soft flesh.

"Mmm," Emily said.

I knew she was tasting my wife's spicy juices, and the thought made me mad with lust. I guided my rigid cock towards Emily's wet opening and pushed forwards. She was so wet, that my thick cock easily penetrated her. With a little slippery sound, I entered her to the root.

Rebecca lay squirming on the floor, while Emily sucked her pussy. Our babysitter obviously did an excellent job – Rebecca was beside herself with pleasure.

"Yes!" she cried. "Now fuck her! Fuck her hard!"

I grabbed Emily's hips and thrust into her savagely. I heard her muffled moans, as I drove my cock into her again and again. Rebecca was gasping for air, and I knew her orgasm was approaching.

"Good girl, Emily," I whispered. "Make her come!"

I saw Emily's little wet tongue lapping away at my wife's cunt, making slurping sounds. And then it happened.

"Aaah!" Rebecca screamed. "Yeahhh!"

She arched her back, trembling violently as she climaxed. A powerful orgasm washed through her body, making her thrash about on the carpet.

I grabbed Emily's hair, pulling her head away from Rebecca's pussy. Then, still fucking her savagely, I kissed her on the mouth. I pushed my tongue in between her soft lips, tasting my wife's

delicious juices in her mouth. Excited, I thrust into Emily's cunt over and over.

"Mmm!" she screamed, trying to pull away from me. "Mmm!"

She had come again. The young girl was shivering, overcome with sensations of ecstasy she hadn't known before. She was limp in my hands, letting us use her body as a toy for our kinky pleasures.

At the height of my excitement, I pulled out of her slit and stood up. Still holding onto her hair, I stood in front of the trembling girl, pointing my swelling cock at her mouth. Obediently, she parted her lips and let me enter. She sucked me vigorously, while I thrust rhythmically into her mouth.

Rebecca sat up on the carpet, watching us.

"Yes," she said. "Come in her mouth."

I could hardly hold out any longer. My cock was throbbing, and I felt the pressure of my semen boiling up through the shaft.

"Yeah!" I cried. "Here I go!"

I almost passed out with pleasure, as the first long burst of sperm shot into Emily's mouth. I ejaculated so hard, it was almost painful. With each violent contraction, my cock shot another load of semen down our babysitter's throat.

"Swallow!" Rebecca ordered. "Swallow every last drop! You bitch!"

Grunting and yelling, I emptied myself in rhythmic spurts. Obediently, Emily just sat her, hands cuffed behind her back, gulping down my spunk. As my orgasm subsided, I grabbed my cock and masturbated into her mouth, squeezing out a few more drops. Finally, my cock went soft and I let it slip from her mouth.

"Yeah," I whispered. "Hell yeah..."

Rebecca got up and untied Emily's handcuffs.

"You've been a good girl," she said. "Now put your clothes on and go home. We don't want your parents to worry about you."

"Yes, ma'am," Emily said.

She stumbled over to the pile of clothes on the floor and hurriedly began dressing. Rebecca looked at me, smiling.

I sat down on the couch, exhausted. I didn't even bother to get dressed. Rebecca put her dress back on.

"By the way," she said. "Emily, can you come over on Thursday?"

Emily thought for a second.

"Sure," she said. "Are you going out?"

Rebecca laughed.

"Not on your life!" she said. "We'll be right here. Waiting for you."

Emily's big blue eyes opened wide.

She giggled.

The Phone Call

The phone rings in the dark.

Startled, Cindy opens her eyes and checks the glowing numbers on the alarm clock next to her bed.

02:14. It's late at night. Who would possibly call her at this hour on a Tuesday night? Everyone knows she'll be in bed by now.

The phone rings again.

Cindy sits up. She is naked. She never wears a nightdress in the summer months.

Who could it be? She's worried that there might be something terribly wrong. On the other hand, if it is an emergency, she absolutely should pick up the phone.

And after the third ring, she does.

"Hello?" she asks.

A deep voice – a voice she does not recognize – answers.

"Cindy?" Is this you?"

"Y-yes," Cindy says. "Who is this?"

There is no answer.

"What's happened?" she asks nervously. "Is there something wrong?"

"Oh no," the deep voice replies. "Everything is fine, Cindy. Just fine."

"So..." she asks. "What do you want?"

"I want you to do something for me," the voice says. "Are you in bed?"

"Y-yes," Cindy says.

"Are you naked?" the voice asks.

Cindy hesitates.

"Yes," she says. "But why...?"

"I want you to touch yourself," the voice says calmly.

Cindy gasps quietly. Who is this?

"Where?" she asks.

"You know where," the voice says. "I want you to touch your cunt."

"N-no," Cindy says. "I... I can't..."

"It's okay," the voice says. "You're safe in bed. I can't hurt you over the phone, can I?"

"N-no..." Cindy says.

"All I want is to listen to you, as you touch yourself," the voice says calmly. "Will you do that for me?"

He's right, Cindy thinks. He couldn't possibly hurt her. And it's late at night – and she's naked – and the unknown voice has planted a thought inside her head. A thought that turns her on - just a little bit.

Cindy lies back on the bed, holding the wireless phone to her ear with one hand. The other slowly slides towards her pussy. As she touches her labia, she sighs under her breath.

"Are you doing it now?" the voice asks. "Are you touching yourself?"

"Yes," Cindy whispers.

"Do it like you do when you masturbate," the voice says.

And Cindy begins stroking herself, slowly massaging the base of her clit. She moans deeply at her own touch. She is very skilled at masturbating. In fact, she can bring herself off in a few minutes - if she wants to.

"Tell me what you're doing," the voice says.

"I'm touching myself," Cindy gasps. "Near the clit. I'm masturbating..."

"Is it good?" the voice asks.

"Oh yes," Cindy says. "I love it. Aaah..."

"Yes," the voice says, "let me hear you moan. Louder."

Cindy masturbates, slowly, sensuously. She's writhing on the bed now, pleasure rippling through her naked body. She hears the man on the phone breathing. Is he masturbating, too? She wants him to keep talking. His voice is turning her on.

"Are you wet?" he asks.

"Yes," she gasps. "My pussy's getting wet. Do you like to hear that? Want me to tell you about my pussy?"

"Yes," the voice says. "I want you to tell me how you do it."

"Ahhh," Cindy moans, masturbating vigorously. "Are you hard? Are you masturbating?"

"Of course," the voice says calmly. "I have my cock in my hand. It is very hard. I'm stroking it as we speak."

"Mmm!" Cindy cries.

Her pussy is very wet now. She feels the moisture all over her fingers as she keeps massaging her tender slit.

"Now," the voice says. "Put your finger inside your cunt."

Excited, Cindy obeys. Slowly, she slides her middle finger in between her moist labia. The walls of her pussy feels slick around it. She pushes deeper, burying her finger inside her soft crevice.

"Aaah," she moans loudly into the phone. "Yesss..."

"Is it in?" the voice asks.

"Oh yes!" Cindy gasps.

"Now fuck yourself," the voice commands.

Cindy sits up in bed again, throwing the sheets away. She wants to see this.

And in the pale moonlight, Cindy looks down at her pussy, sees her own finger slipping out slowly, wet and glistening. Eagerly, she slides it in again, then out, then in, over and over. She clenches her pussy muscles around it, making the sensations even more intense: Her finger feels the wetness of her pussy, her pussy feels the finger moving back and forth, stimulating her tender flesh.

"Yes," she whispers into the phone. "I'm fucking myself. With my finger. In and out."

"Keep going," the voice says. "Faster."

Cindy obeys, sliding her finger in and out of her sensitive cunt, increasing the rhythm.

"Oh... oh... oh..." she moans in time. "Are you... masturbating, too?"

"Yes," the voice says. "I have my cock in my hand. It's big and hard. And I'm stroking it now."

For one second, it is as if Cindy feels the stranger's cock inside her pussy. She almost feels it stretching her flesh, pumping into her, thick and erect.

"Aaah!" she cries. "Ohmigod!"

"Now," the voice says, still completely calm, "take your finger from your cunt and taste it!"

Slowly, Cindy slips her wet finger out of her pussy and puts it to her lips. She licks it, hesitantly.

"Taste good?" the voice asks.

"Mmm," Cindy says. "Spicy. Sweet and spicy."

"Lick all the juice off," the voice says.

Cindy puts the finger in her mouth, sucking off her own love juice. It's a strange sensation, tasting female juices – almost like having sex with another woman.

"Mmm," she purrs.

"Again," the voice commands. "Stick your finger inside, then lick it off."

Cindy dips two fingers into her succulent slit, then sucks them off. She does it again and again, savoring the taste of her own excited flesh.

"Mmm," she says, slurping loudly, making sure the stranger can hear. "Mmm..."

"Yes," the voice says. "Nothing like the taste of pussy. Now - I want you to masturbate again."

"O-okay," Cindy whispers, out of breath.

She looks down at her cunt and begins stroking herself again. Her labia open slightly, wet and pink, as she rubs the base of her clit.

"Ah yeah," she gasps. "Ohhh..."

"Keep going," the voice says. "I want you to come for me."

"Ohhh," Cindy gasps, masturbating vigorously. "Are you coming, too? Ah! Please! Stroke that big cock and come with me. Ahhh..."

Cindy is doubled over, her legs spread wide, as she massages herself rhythmically, harder and harder, driving herself towards an orgasm.

"I'm ready when you are, Cindy," the voice says.

Gasping loudly, Cindy increases her pace. Now there is no turning back.

"Now!" she cries. "I'm coming now!"

Whimpering helplessly, Cindy feels the climax coursing through her body.

"Yes," the man says coolly. "I'm coming, too."

Cindy shakes all over as the orgasm hits her, all her senses taken over by the violent sensation of pleasure. In her excited state, she imagines the stranger's cock ejaculating, spurting long jets of semen into her. Squirming on the bed, she cries out again and again, cries of pure lust and satisfaction.

Finally, Cindy falls back on the bed, still clenching the phone in her hand. She thinks she heard the man breathing slightly harder.

But apart from that, there is no way of knowing whether he has actually come.

"Ohhh..." she moans.

"That was good, wasn't it?" the deep voice says into her ear. "You came hard, Cindy. And so did I."

"Did you?" she gasps. "Oh, God..."

Again, she just hears him breathing.

"Thank you," she says.

The voice laughs. A deep, friendly laugh.

"Oh no," it says. "We're not finished yet."

Cindy swallows.

"What...?" she asks.

"Get up," the voice says.

Cindy fumbles for the switch on the lamp next to the bed. She switches it on, illuminating the bedroom in soft, yellowish light. Still trembling, she gets out of bed.

"Go to the door," the voice says. "And open it."

"But..." Cindy protests. "I'm naked."

"Just do it," the voice insists.

And naked, Cindy walks through the bedroom into the hall. She stands in front of the door, the phone pressed to her ear. She's shaking, hesitating, not knowing what to expect.

"Open the door," the voice says calmly.

And she does.

Light flows into the apartment, as the door swings open. Outside is a dark figure holding a cell phone. And Cindy realizes that the man has been outside her door all the time. He's dressed in black and wears a ski mask, concealing his face. As Cindy hesitates, he pushes her into the apartment and closes the door behind him. He drags her into the kitchen, pressing her up against the wall, his breath hot and excited from inside the ski mask.

"Wait..." she gasps.

The man gently places his hand around her neck, pinning her to the kitchen wall. Swiftly, he pulls a black latex dildo from his pocket and guides it towards her pussy. Looking down at his hands, she sees the dark brown color of his skin. Somehow she never expected the stranger to be a black man.

"Spread your legs," he says.

Whimpering, Cindy stands with her legs spread wide, and the tip of the plastic tool enters her cunt. It's big, and she feels her labia stretching, as the smooth surface slips into her wet flesh.

"Oooh..." she moans.

She hears the man breathing heavily, excited, as he rhythmically moves the dildo back and forth, in and out of her slick pussy. Her head is spinning. The whole situation is like a kinky fantasy: Standing there naked in the dark, as the strange black man fucks her vigorously with the dildo. And soon she can't help herself any longer.

"Ohmigod" she cries, losing control.

And pinned to her kitchen wall, Cindy comes again. Comes even harder than before.

"Aaah!" she screams. "Aaah!"

Grunting with satisfaction, the man steadies her. Otherwise, she would have collapsed on the floor, trembling in her powerful climax. Cindy feels her juices trickling down the insides of her thigh, as the man pulls the dildo back out.

Next, he brutally forces her down, making her lie on her back on the kitchen floor. Kneeling between her legs, he fumbles feverishly with his belt and zipper. Eventually, he pulls out his erect cock. Cindy stares at it. It's chocolate brown and even bigger than the dildo. The veins stand out, swelling under the dark skin of the shaft, as the man masturbates before her eyes.

"N-no..." she whispers.

But it's no use. Too excited to wait now, the man swiftly positions himself between her legs. She feels the head of his rigid cock pressing against the mouth of her pussy. Cindy screams, as he penetrates the depths of her juicy cunt. And immediately, he begins thrusting into her, a hard, relentless rhythm.

She whimpers quietly, as he fucks her with savage determination. The hard cock slips in and out of her slippery pussy, in and out, making wet noises. Cindy feels his breath through the woolen mask, panting hot against her neck.

He grabs her wrists hard, holding her down as he thrusts into her again and again. The floor is hard and uncomfortable, but Cindy hardly notices that. Her body feels only the lustful stimulation, as the stranger's giant cock fucks her with amazing force. He keeps pumping, deep and hard, taking her to new levels of unbearable pleasure.

"Oh God," she hears herself saying. "Fuck me! Fuck me hard!"

I can't believe I'm saying this, she thinks. Usually, she's a nice, quiet girl. But here, on the floor of her own kitchen, the man has freed something inside her. Cindy's mind is taken over by animal lust. She's in heat now – completely fixated on the swollen cock fucking her, driving her to yet another climax.

Whimpering with pleasure, she touches her cunt. As she man thrusts into her, she begins masturbating, massaging the flesh around her hardened clit. Already in ecstasy, somehow she wants more, wants to know just how much pleasure a girl can experience. She feels as if she's about to faint – but she keeps going.

"Yeahhh!" she cries. "Give it to me! Harder! Yes!"

The man is grunting loudly, his cock flying in and out of Cindy's pussy in a frenzied rhythm. He's sweating and gasping for breath. He's trying not to come, wants to keep fucking her, every muscle in his body so tense he's almost shaking.

Masturbating, Cindy squirms on the kitchen floor. She throws her head back, as the pumping cock inside her drives her towards another climax.

"Aaah!" she screams. "Aaah!"

"Yes!" the man shouts. "Come for me!"

Sobbing loudly, Cindy keeps rubbing her clit impatiently. The man increases his tempo, driving his cock into her, ready to come.

"You too!" Cindy gasps. "Squirt all over me! Aaah!"

She comes again. She thrashes about on the floor, as the man keeps fucking her in deep, powerful thrusts.

"Unh!" he grunts in time with his strokes. "Unh! Unh! Yes! Here I come, baby! Take it all!"

Cindy is still stroking her clit, as he pulls out. Kneeling between her legs, he grabs his long, dark cock and holds it, as it immediately begins to ejaculate.

"Aaaah!" he yells.

The first squirt of semen shoots several feet across Cindy's naked body, hitting her on the cheek. The jerking cock keeps pumping, the next jet spattering her left breast. Then another - and another - and another. White-hot spurts of creamy spunk sprays from his twitching cock. He masturbates, grunting, squeezing every last drop from his swollen tool.

"Yeah…" he says, satisfied, as one last, thick drop spills onto Cindy's thigh.

Cindy lies completely still, as he gets up. In a daze, she senses her fingers are wet from her own juices. She puts them to her mouth, tasting her own sex again. Then she wipes a glob of semen from her breast, tasting that, too. Soon, she has wiped and licked off all of the man's sperm.

The man zips up, getting ready to leave.

"Thank you," she says again.

The man opens the door.

"I'll call you," he says, his calm voice trembling slightly from his orgasm.

"Tomorrow night?" Cindy asks.

"Sure," he says, closing the door behind him.

And for some reason, Cindy knows he will call again. She just knows.

Sighing, she relaxes on the kitchen floor.

Insomnia

It was three o'clock at night, and I'd just woken up with a massive erection. I'd dreamt about her again.

The same beautiful woman had appeared in my dreams night after night. She was pure imagination – I'd never seen anyone like her in real life. But in my dreams she was incredibly lifelike: Every time the same long, billowing, dark hair – the lovely, slender figure – always dressed in a long, blue silk dress wrapped around her elegant curves.

There were dreams where I only saw her at a distance. I could be at a party, suddenly noticing her across the room. In other dreams I visited her home – a large, dark apartment that seemed strangely uninhabited. Sometimes I pulled off her dress and saw her perfect body – her soft, round breasts, her long, shapely legs – and the tiny triangle of dark pubes around the pink slit of her pussy. Sometimes we lay together in her bed – my cock hard as a rock with arousal – but I'd never dreamt of us having sex.

Not tonight, either. I just lay there staring up into the darkness, my erect member stretching, forming a tall bulge in my blanket. What should I do? Usually, once I'd dreamt of her I couldn't go back to sleep. My thoughts would keep returning to her, replaying every situation I'd seen her in. And I'd fantasize about what fucking her would feel like – her wet cunt wrapped around my eager cock – how I'd vigorously thrust and thrust into her, making her scream out loud in ecstasy …

Sometimes I'd get up to masturbate. But although releasing the pressure of lust always felt good, it was also somewhat disappointing. Having just dreamt about the most beautiful woman in the world, letting my cock spit hot semen into a paper towel just felt too sad.

I pulled off the blanket and got up. My stiff member bounced as I walked. I closed my eyes and banished the dream woman from my thoughts – and slowly I felt my erection subsiding. Then I got dressed and went out.

It was a warm summer night – the time of year when the blue of twilight lasts almost until dawn – and I could feel the morning approaching already. I walked the old streets of central Berlin – I don't remember the exact location. The neighborhood was deserted and quiet. But as I turned the corner of a cobbled street near Alexanderplatz I suddenly saw her. The woman from my dreams.

I stopped in my tracks and stared at her. There was no doubt about it: I recognized her long, dark hair, the blue silk dress, the perfect curves of her body. But I also knew it was impossible – because she did not exist!

Then she turned her head to look at me. Her expression was quizzical – she didn't smile, wasn't flirtatious – and yet … She turned her back and began to walk. Her high heels clicked against the cobblestones, her hips swaying slightly as she walked. I hesitated for a second, then followed her.

She turned a corner down an even narrower street I didn't know. I kept my distance discretely. As I looked around the corner, I saw her disappear between two buildings. I chose the opposite sidewalk and slowly walked closer.

Standing across from where she'd disappeared I noticed a narrow passage – about three feet wide – between two old buildings. She stood leaning against the wall on the left. I heard muffled music coming from the other building – it sounded like old disco. The woman turned her eyes and looked at me – looked straight into my eyes, smiling faintly.

The music increased in volume as a door opened in the house. I smelled cigarette smoke – a sleazy red light lit the woman on the other side. A tall, bald man stepped out into the narrow alley, thin and athletically built, wearing a dark suit. The music faded as he closed the door behind him.

The man reached behind the woman's back – and I heard the sound of a zipper being swiftly pulled down. Seconds later he pulled the entire dress off over her head, giving me a perfect view of her naked body. She was not wearing a bra, but her shapely breasts stood out proudly. A black garter belt held up a pair of black silk stockings, but she was not wearing panties, either. Like in my dream her dark pubes were neatly trimmed around the pink slit.

The man dropped to his knees in front of her, his face on a level with her cunt. With a swift, vulgar motion she stood with her legs wide apart in front of him. My cock jumped at the sight. The

man let his tongue run up and down her pussy lips as if to taste her. She closed her eyes. Then he moved the tip of his tongue in circles around her clit. She moaned quietly with lust.

Hypnotized, I stood across the street just staring at them. The man's bald head moved eagerly up and down as he licked the cunt of my dream woman. Her arms quivered. Feverishly, her hands scrambled across the rough brick wall. She found a crack to hold on to, her entire body trembling with pleasure. I believe I heard the little, wet noises of the bald man's tongue against her pussy lips – and imagined him swallowing her love juice. What did she taste like? Spicy, yet sweet – like every beautiful woman in the world.

"Oh!"

She let out a loud gasp. I watched as the man grabbed her round buttocks, forcing his tongue all the way up into her juicy cunt. Again he began to move his head up and down – more vigorously this time – his tongue thrusting like a small cock into her tight crevice. She squirmed in helpless lust. Blood throbbed in my swelling cock.

Suddenly she threw back her head, her dark hair flying around her face. Every fiber in her body tensed up as she cried out her orgasm, mouth open wide:

"Aaah! Aaah!"

The bald man slurped and smacked all over her cunt, juices dribbling down his chin. I felt my cock slowly stretching to its full length inside my pants.

The man stood up. For a few seconds he savored the sight of the nude female body, still quivering in orgasm. Slowly he zipped down his pants and pulled out his cock – long and hard, impatiently twitching. The woman whimpered quietly at the sight. He'd just licked her to orgasm and now he wanted to fuck. And I'd be allowed to watch – my throat went dry at the thought.

The man grabbed his cock by the root, masturbating as he stared deep into the eyes of the naked woman. With the other hand he grabbed her thigh, lifting up her leg. The alley was so narrow she could press her high-heeled shoe against the opposite wall. He clenched his cock in his fist, slowly but deliberately guiding it up into her slippery cunt. She gasped and gasped again. He buried his member inside her and froze for a moment. Nervously, the women bit her lower lip.

And now he began to thrust.

"Ohhh!" she cried.

He fucked her at a slow pace – withdrawing the entire length of his shaft and drove it all the way in with every thrust. Again and again and again. Her gorgeous breasts bounced in time, and she moaned with pleasure.

My rock hard cock felt ready to burst through the fabric of my trousers. I quickly looked up and down the street – then I zipped down and pulled it out. The shaft throbbed hotly against my palm. I don't remember ever having a more impressive erection: My cock was long and unusually fat – its bluish head swollen with lust. A tiny, clear drop of liquid oozed from its tip, dripping onto the sidewalk. Slowly I began to masturbate.

The bald man increased his pace. Mercilessly he drove his cock up and up into the naked woman's cunt, slamming her up against the wall with every thrust. She clutched his muscular buttocks, hoarsely screaming in ecstasy as he fucked her. I gripped my cock hard, massaging the shaft, making it swell and lengthen. It was so hard it was almost painful.

The woman's nails scratched into the wall – and again I heard her screaming in orgasm:

"Ohhh! Ohhh!"

The man grit his teeth. He grabbed her breasts hard and fucked her with even greater force.

"Nng! Nng!" he grunted.

His entire body shook with lust. And suddenly he buried the entire length of his shaft deep inside her cunt with one single powerful thrust. And froze.

"Ohhh!" he roared. "Yesss!"

The woman put her arms around him, holding him tight. They stood like that for a while, the orgasm surging through her naked body. I assumed he was ejaculating – imagined his long, hard cock spitting jets of white-hot sperm up into her quivering cunt. The clear fluid oozed from my cock as I masturbated at the sight.

Finally the man pulled out. His bald head was bright read and sweaty from the strain. He staggered a bit, fumbling to get his semi-erect cock back into his pants and zip up. Sighing contentedly, he leaned back against the wall across from the woman, pulled out a pack of cigarettes, and lit one. He took a deep drag, put his head back, and exhaled the smoke between the walls.

The woman turned her head, looking directly at me. I stopped masturbating, but still held on to my cock. She looked me deep in the eyes – and I looked straight back at her. She didn't even blink.

Slowly I crossed the street and approached her. The bald man opened the door in the wall, and again the sound of music and the odor of cigarettes filled the alley. He disappeared into the house, closing the door behind him. I stood in the alley, facing the woman. Her cheeks were flushed with excitement – the sweet and spicy scent of sex hung around her. I also detected the faint smell of the bald man's semen.

I swiftly pulled down my pants and stood there in the alley displaying my erection to her. Her eyes widened at the sight of my cock – it was rather larger than that of the bald man. I didn't speak, but stepped right up to her, feeling the warmth of her naked, sweaty skin.

The door opened behind us and I turned my head to look. A stocky, elderly man stepped out into the alley accompanied by a young redhead with heavy makeup wearing a sequined dress. She clung to him with a seductive look and I took her for a prostitute. The odd couple stood right next to us as the door slammed shut again. The man took a drag of a cigar, his eyes darting up and down the naked woman's body. The hooker whispered into his ear and he nodded slowly.

I looked at the woman of my dreams again – in the nude and incredibly beautiful. My cock twitched impatiently. I had to have her – have her right now. And if the old man and his whore wanted to watch, I was too horny to care.

My dream woman gasped with anticipation as I gripped my shaft and guided it toward her cunt. I shivered as I felt her succulent flesh against the head of my cock. Slowly I forced the head up into her – it swelled and throbbed, the cock jerking. Although in my mid-thirties, I almost felt like a teenager again: So horny I was just about unable to think clearly – with a cock that constantly felt about to ejaculate.

I took a deep breath and entered her all the way.

"Mmm!" she whimpered.

The sound of her lust almost made me black out. Wild with excitement I began thrusting savagely up into her cunt.

"Aaah!" she screamed.

"Yes!" I grunted. "Like that! Can you feel it? Can you feel my fat cock inside your cunt? Can you? Is that what you want? Yes! And like that! And like that!"

Drooling with lust I fucked the gorgeous woman up against the raw brick wall. Her juices flowed abundantly around my swollen shaft, dripping onto the ground. I grabbed her stockinged thigh, lifting it up – as the bald man had done – her high-heeled shoe pressing against the wall behind me. She whimpered. Mad with lust I lifted up her other leg, placing it similarly on the other side of me. There she hung - suspended in air, her back pressed against one wall, her heels against the other – at the mercy of my cock brutally thrusting into her soft cunt. I held her soft, round buttocks, fucking her as hard as I could. My cock jerked and twitched.

The redhead prostitute had her hand inside the elderly man's pants, apparently jerking him off as he watched us fuck. His face was blank – he just nodded in approval, calmly smoking his cigar.

I gasped with excitement, repeated thrusting my rigid cock up into the cunt of the woman of my dreams. And suddenly I felt her strong fingers grabbing my hair. She stared at me, her mouth gaping, her eyes wide open. I fucked her like a madman – feeling her soft pussy flesh quivering wet and slippery around my hard shaft. And then she came again.

"Aaah!" she screamed. "Aaah!"

How beautiful she was as she climaxed! Her face transfigured in sensual ecstasy. I felt her entire body shivering in orgasm. My cock jerked harder and harder – until I could no longer hold back.

"Ohhh!" I roared. "Yeahhh!"

Her pussy muscles clamped hard around my cock as I began to ejaculate. I never felt anything like it. It was as if my semen began to boil inside my balls. And from the depth of my bulging scrotum I felt the sperm bursting up through the bone-hard shaft until the first jet of spunk spurted way up into her velvet cunt. And again. And again. Piping hot sperm pumped from my spasmodically jerking cock, my entire body shaking in orgasm.

As I finally stopped squirting she sighed deeply, resting her warm head against my shoulder.

"Oh yes," I gratefully whispered into her ear.

She put her arms around me. Her legs quivered, but she was still suspended in air, her high heels propped against the wall behind me and my hands supporting her buttocks. I felt my thick semen

slowly running down my shaft and dripping from her cunt – felt her strong pussy muscles squeezing my cock. We stood like that for a while. And then I noticed: My cock was still hard.

My ejaculation had been so violent I expected to be completely spent. But whether it was because I was unusually aroused – or due to her amazing pussy's firm grip on my member – my erection was not subsiding. My cock stood proud, hard and ready for action, stretching her slippery cunt. I took a deep breath and whispered into her ear:

"I'm not done with you yet!"

And again I began to thrust. She gave a little scream, which only made my cock straighten even further. Grunting with lust I fucked her – even more vigorously than before. Her cunt slurped and smacked with semen and juices as I drove my hard shaft up into her again and again.

"Ohhh ..." she whimpered.

She was helpless in my grip. Never – neither before nor since – have I fucked a woman so relentlessly.

The prostitute had zipped down the elderly man's trousers and taken out his cock. It was of rather ordinary length, but thicker than even mine. She began massaging it – her fingers could hardly reach around it – and a droplet of spunk oozed from its tip. He still regarded us blankly, but the hooker's eyes glistened, and she licked her painted lips lasciviously.

The woman of my dreams screamed again. I grabbed her soft buttocks hard, feeling my cock jerking wildly. We came together. She screamed her orgasm into my ear just as I began to spurt again.

"Ohhh!" I yelled.

The ejaculation felt even more violent this time. I'd almost emptied myself of spunk before, but my painfully swollen cock kept pumping and pumping inside her cunt – forcing the very last thick drops out of its bulging head.

"Ah!"

The elderly man gave a brief gasp. Held by the redhead hooker's hand, his member had begun to ejaculate. I watched as long, white jets of semen spurted from it, landing on the ground in the small alley.

My body felt drained of all energy. Carefully I put the woman of my dreams back on the ground. She just looked at me, drawing breath in fast, deep gasps.

Every moment I expected to wake up and find it had all been a dream. But I never did. Exhausted, I leaned against the wall, pulling up my pants. I wanted to say something – but what?

The prostitute opened the door and led the elderly gentleman inside. Then it closed behind them, leaving us alone in the alley.

The woman of my dreams smiled quizzically at me, brushing her dark, wavy hair from her sweaty face. She picked up her blue silk dress and pulled it over her head. She turned her back to me, and I zipped it up. Leaving the alley she turned her head to look at me one last time. Her gaze was steady and calm. What was she trying to tell me?

Then she left. I followed the sight of her wiggling hips until she turned a corner and disappeared, leaving me alone in the small alley.

I haven't dreamed about her since then. But every night I walk the same neighborhood in central Berlin. I can't tell whether I'm walking the right streets – and I haven't been able to locate the small alley. I haven't met the woman since that night. But I know it's bound to happen. The thought alone excites me. And the memory of her cunt turns me on, making my cock swell inside my trousers – ready to fuck her again.

The woman of my dreams.

The Tattoo Shop

Part 1

The electric needle buzzes against Megan's thigh, repeatedly puncturing her skin, and spraying black ink into the microscopic holes. The tattoo artist with the black beard and glasses follows the lines of the sketch, and dot by dot the tattoo takes shape. Little and petite, Megan lies on her back on the table in her pink t-shirt. Her pale blue jeans are around her knees, exposing her little white panties. It is a hot summer's day and little beads of sweat glisten on her skin.

The tattoo artist lays the needle on the small metal cabinet by the table. He replaces the black ink cartridge with a red one and changes to a thicker needle. Using a paper towel he wipes the blood and excess ink off her skin. He studies the result – the black lines form the outline of a flower.

"Well," he says. "We just need to fill it in. We'll be done soon."

Megan wriggles about to get comfortable on the table.

"Is it bad?" the tattoo artist asks.

She shakes her head, her cheeks blushing. The tattoo artist smiles, puts the needle to her skin, and starts the machine again. It pricks and buzzes against Megan's skin, and she closes her eyes.

When he's finished he switches off the needle and wipes her skin again. He pulls off his thin latex gloves and wipes the sweat off his forehead.

"Try and have a look," he says.

Megan glances at the finished tattoo and smiles. An elaborate rose, its fiery red petals boldly outlined in black.

"It's so pretty," she whispers, her voice trembling.

"It is, isn't it?" the tattoo artist says proudly, getting up from his chair. "I'll get some lotion for you."

He disappears into the back room and Megan closes her eyes again. Her entire body is quivering. Slowly she slides her little hand down into her panties, and slowly she begins to masturbate. She's

already sopping wet, the soft flesh of her pussy slippery with her juices. Her tiny clit stands erect with excitement, and she runs her fingers in little circles around it, making herself gasp for air.

Even as she hears the door opening, she continues. As she opens her eyes, the tattoo artist stands there, a little jar of lotion in his hand, calmly watching her, a friendly gaze in his grey-blue eyes.

"Keep going," he says calmly. "It's okay."

Megan whimpers with pleasure. The tattoo artist puts the jar down on the little metal cabinet. Then he stands right in front of her, watching her attentively as she masturbates. Gradually she accelerates the rhythm, moaning louder and louder.

The tattoo artist pulls her jeans all the way off. Then he grabs her panties, sliding them down over her legs and all the way off, exposing her pink cunt to his gaze. Megan's fingers energetically work her clit. The tattoo artist gently pushes her thighs apart – spreading her legs. Her wet, pink labia gape hungrily towards him.

"You have such a beautiful cunt," he says calmly.

Inside his pants, his cock begins to grow. Long and hard it pokes against the fabric of his black jeans.

"Oh!" Megan gasps. "Oh!"

She arches her little body as she orgasm surges through her. The tattoo artist stares at her – his eyes shiny with lust behind the glasses.

"Was it good?" he whispers hoarsely.

Megan whimpers with pleasure.

"Yes," she replies.

The tattoo artist nods, his gaze running lasciviously up and down her quivering body. Then he picks up a new stencil and shows it to her.

"Would you like a bonus tattoo?" he asks. "You can have it for free."

Megan squints at the little drawing.

"An orchid?" she says. "That's nice. Yes, please. Where?"

The tattoo artist places the stencil on the inside of her left thigh – barely an inch away from her warm pussy.

"Here," he says.

With two fingers he rubs the plastic, copying the drawing onto Megan's thigh. He pulls on a fresh pair of latex gloves and changes the ink cartridge back to black.

"Um," Megan asks hesitantly. "Isn't the skin rather sensitive right there?"

"Yeah," the tattoo artist replies, putting the needle against the skin. "It might hurt a bit."

He immediately switches on the machine, and Megan cries out: "Ow!"

The tattoo artist turns off the needle.

"Too much?" he asks.

Megan brushes a lock of blond hair from her sweaty forehead and gasps.

"No," she replies. "I love it. Keep going."

Smiling, the tattoo artist grabs his crotch.

"Just a second," he says. "My cock is so fucking hard."

He zips down his pants and releases his long, hard member. Megan gasps at the sight, her mouth wide open. His fingers reach inside his pants, pulling his round, bulging balls out of the fly as well. The cock stands straight up, jerking with lust.

"Yeah, like that," he gasps.

Again he applies the needle to the inside of Megan's thigh and switches it on. It buzzes loudly as he begins tracing the new outlines. Megan writhes on the table, her wet, pink slit quivering with excitement.

"Ow!" she whimpers. "You're torturing me. You evil bastard – I love the way you torture me!"

Breathing hard, the tattoo artist finishes the outline – then wipes it off with a paper towel. He stands up slowly, gazing lustfully at Megan. His long, hard cock throbs and jumps. Clear fluid oozes from its tip. His latex-gloved hand grabs the shaft firmly, guiding it towards her cunt.

"Are you ready?" he gasps. "Are you ready for my cock?"

The head of his cock pushes hard against the soft mouth of her pussy. Megan nods, her cheeks flushed.

"Yes!" she whimpers. "Oh, yes!"

The tattoo artist thrusts his hips forwards, burying the entire length of his shaft inside Megan's soft cunt. She cries out loud:

"Aaah!"

Immediately he starts fucking – out and in, in deep hard thrust, making Megan's sensitive flesh slurp around his bone-hard cock. He's still wearing pants and t-shirt – the jeans fabric rhythmically scratches against her fresh, tender tattoo.

"Oh!" she cries loudly. "Oh! Oh! Oh!"

Her shapely breasts bounce beneath her t-shirt in time to the tattoo artists thrusting – her nipples stiff and hard under the thin fabric. She spreads her legs, allowing him to enter her completely – grips his powerful, jeans-clad ass, pulling him towards her. Her hands feel the muscles flexing in his buttocks, as his hard shaft impales her cunt again and again. Gasping loudly, she feels her orgasm approaching.

"Oh yeah," he grunts. "That's good fucking pussy!"

He grips her t-shirt and starts pulling it off her. His cock is still relentlessly pumping inside her juicy slit. Megan lifts up her arms, letting him pull of the shirt and throw in on the floor, leaving her stark naked on the table beneath him. His strong, gloved hands grab her full breasts and squeeze them so hard she screams:

"Aaah!"

The tattoo artist thrusts harder and harder up into her slobbering cunt, his cock hard as a rock with lust. Megan grips the edges of the table, holding on tight as a powerful climax hits her.

"Ohhh!" she yells. "Ohhh!"

The tattoo artist's cock jerks inside her pussy.

"Yeah!" he roars. "Like that! Yes!"

Suddenly he pulls out of her trembling, wet cunt. He grips his cock with his big, gloved fist, pointing it at the fresh tattoo as he begins to ejaculate. The first, white spurt of semen hits the tender drawing with incredible force.

"Ow!" Megan cries, still shaking from her orgasm. "It stings!"

"Mmm!" the tattoo artist grunts,

His cock fires again and again – jet after jet – covering the little tattoo with creamy, white spunk.

"I love it ..." Megan sighs. "Spurt your fat spunk all over me ...!"

The tattoo artist keeps masturbating, completely emptying himself of sperm. His swollen balls jump. When he can't come anymore he begins to rub his semen into the tattoo with his latex-gloved fingers. Megan's eyelids flutter deliriously.

"Oh, yes," she whimpers lasciviously. "Into my skin. Mmm. You ought to jerk off into one of those cartridges – then you could give me a cum tattoo ..."

The tattoo artist shakes his head.

"You kinky, little slut," he grins.

He swiftly pulls t-shirt and pants off, standing naked in front of Megan – his wet, glistening cock still fat, but slowly growing soft. He pulls out a drawer in the metal cabinet, producing two pairs of handcuffs.

"No!" she gasps. "What ...?"

Skillfully he cuffs her left wrist to the table with one pair – the right with the other. Megan pulls at the cuffs. They jingle, but her hands are hopelessly stuck. The tattoo artist reaches for the machine, switches to the thick needle again, and selects a cartridge of pink ink.

"Well," he says. "Should we get it finished?"

He puts the needle against the fresh tattoo on Megan's thigh and turns on the machine, making it buzz and sting.

"Owww!" Megan cries. "It hurts! Keep going! Yes!"

Juices flow from her cunt, her stiff clit jumps with excitement – and her lusty moans almost drown out the buzzing of the needle. She throws her head back, her hands pull at the cuffs – and then it happens:

"Ohhh!" she cries. "Ohhh!"

A long jet of love juice spurts from her trembling pussy, hitting the tattoo artist's cheek. Megan's cunt squirts again and again, a violet orgasm shaking her young body.

"Oh, you dirty slut!" the tattoo artist hisses.

Megan collapses on the table – her entire body shaken by convulsions of pleasure. The tattoo artist fills in the outline and wipes off the tattoo. He stands up, peeling off his latex gloves.

"I want to fuck you again," he gasps.

He grabs his semi-erect cock and begins massaging its head. Megan shakes her head.

"No," she whispers. "You can't. No so soon after ..."

"Shut up!" the tattoo artist snarls. "Shut the fuck up and look at me! Look at my cock!"

Megan opens her eyes wide, staring at his cock. He masturbates vigorously.

"I want your delicious cunt so bad!" he gasps. "Yeah! Like that!"

As he squeezes its head hard, his member slowly grows to almost a full erection. Sweating with excitement he steers his cock towards Megan's dripping wet cunt, forcing it in between her soft pussy lips. It twitches and soon becomes as bone-hard as before.

"Ohhh!" Megan shouts, pulling at the cuffs and making them jingle. "Fuck me!"

"Yeah!" the tattoo artists grunts – and immediately begins thrusting rhythmically into the pussy of the bound girl.

If you walk past the tattoo shop now you have a direct view of the table. Here you can see Megan naked and handcuffed – see the tattoo artist naked on top of her, see his muscular buttocks flexing with every stroke as he thrusts his hard shaft up into her trembling cunt. And you can hear the sounds: Megan screaming with pleasure, the tattoo artist grunting with lust – and perhaps even the little, wet sounds of the long, rigid member rhythmically thrusting into her succulent pussy. Perhaps you'll stop for a while – I know I would – to enjoy the arousing sight of the two horny, sweaty people fucking like animals.

"Aaah!" Megan screams into the shop. "Fuck me! I'm coming."

"Oh, yes!" the tattoo artist roars, impaling her over and over. "Come on. Come on!"

Megan thrashes about on the table, squealing with pleasure as yet another orgasm overpowers her. The tattoo artist's cock jerks wildly inside her cunt as it starts squirting its hot sperm deep into her. He grabs her, hugging her hot body tightly.

"Ohhh!" he roars.

"No!" Megan protests. "I want to watch you come! Spray me!"

The tattoo artist manages to pull his pumping cock from her cunt, directing the spray over her naked body. The first, long jet hits her right breast. She opens her mouth, catching the next spurt with her tongue. Grunting, he once again drives his cock up into her juicy pussy. It twitches again and again as he empties his balls of hot, sticky semen.

They lie like that for a while. Megan whimpers with pleasure. The tattoo artist's cock throbs rhythmically until it finally goes soft. As he pulls out, his semen slowly seeps from Megan's cunt onto the table below her.

Still naked, the tattoo artist picks up the jar of lotion and begins gently spreading it over the two new tattoos. The lotion feels cool against her hot skin and she writhes lasciviously. He wipes them with paper towels and applies bandages.

"Thanks," Megan whispers.

The tattoo artist remains seated in his chair, watching her with a quizzical expression behind his glasses. She pulls at the handcuffs.

"Hey!" she says. "Aren't you going to … untie me?"

The tattoo artist smiles viciously as he opens a drawer in the metal cabinet. As the sunlight hits a long, metallic vibrator, it gleams. Megan gasps at the sight.

"Take a wild guess," he says hoarsely.

Sighing, Megan gets comfortable on the table. She closes her eyes. Now he is in charge – and she is just his chained toy. Not until the tattoo artist is done with her will she finally be allowed to leave his shop.

And that won't be any time soon.

Part 2

Megan hears the buzzing noise as the tattoo artist turns on the vibrator. She watches as he slowly brings it closer and closer to her cunt – so slowly it almost hurts. Her handcuffs jingle as she writhes impatiently on the table. And then she gasps loudly as the tip of the whirring toy grazes her clit.

"Oh!"

Staring up at the ceiling she feels the hard steel dildo vibrating against her sensitive nub. The tattoo artist moves it in tiny, slow circles around her clit. Juices flow from her cunt and over the table. He doesn't say a word, but Megan can't keep herself from moaning loudly.

The tattoo artist slips the vibrator in between her labia, pressing the tip up into her succulent crevice.

"Ah!" she cries.

With small, careful motions he begins fucking her with the toy. Turning her head, she sees him sitting naked – completely focused on stimulating her with the steel cock. His eyes gleam behind the glasses, and his soft cock starts to swell.

He thrusts the dildo deeper and deeper up into her wet cunt. Helpless, Megan kicks her trembling legs. If he keeps going much longer, he's going to make her come. Ever more out of breath, she gasps, sensations of pleasure rolling through her entire sweaty body.

Now she hears the sound of the tattoo artist's electronic doorbell. Heavy footsteps approach. And suddenly a big, dark-skinned man appears in the doorway. Widening his eyes, he looks from Megan to the tattoo artist and back.

"What the hell?" he says, grinning. "You're having fun, aren't you?"

If Megan could move her hands, she'd push away the tattoo artist. She'd jump from the table, run away, and hide. But she's chained – and nothing can hide her naked body from the eyes of the stranger. His gaze seems lustful – fascinated, he looks down at her lap, where the tattoo artist drives the buzzing dildo in and out of her slit. It's embarrassing. But it's also arousing – and suddenly Megan feels she can no longer fight it. She cries out loud as a violent orgasm hits her.

"Ohhh! Ohhh!"

She thrashes about on the table, beside herself with excitement as she just comes and comes. The stranger grins sardonically.

"Cool," he says.

The tattoo artist turns off the vibrator and lets it slide out of Megan's cunt. Droplets of juice make it glisten. He wipes the sweat off his forehead and looks at the stranger.

"Yeah," he replies. "She's one horny slut. But I'm determined to give her what she needs."

The stranger nods thoughtfully.

"Can I have a go?"

Megan wriggles on the table, still out of breath from her recent orgasm.

"What?" she gasps. "No!"

"Of course," the tattoo artist replies calmly. "Knock yourself out."

The stranger unbuttons his jeans and pulls them down a bit. His cock jumps out, almost completely erect. Megan widens her eyes. It's slightly more than average length – but quite unusually wide. She can't help thinking how it would stretch her cunt – if she were to get it inside her.

The stranger takes his thick member in his fist and strokes it a bit. Soon it is hard as a pole – pointing straight at Megan's slit.

"Thank you," he said. "I've been craving pussy all fucking day. How about you, honey? Ready for some real cock?"

Megan shakes her head, pulling helplessly at the handcuffs. But the stranger guides his wide member in between her slick labia, forcing it all the way in.

"Aaah," he sighs.

Megan spreads her legs, feeling her tight pussy opening to his fat shaft. And now the stranger begins to fuck. The cock slides in and out of her stretching cunt. His member is so huge, it's almost painful – but his rhythmic thrust teases her sensitive flesh, making her shiver with pleasure.

She looks up at him. Muscles flex under his black t-shirt. His facial expression is one of deep concentration – his eyes blank from excitement as his cock plunges up into Megan's tight slit again and again. The tattoo artist stands up and bends over her, pressing his mouth against hers. He kisses her greedily as the stranger fucks and fucks. She feels the tattoo artist's hands on her breasts. He kneads them, pinching her nipples hard, until she whimpers into his open

mouth. The stranger's thrusts get deeper and deeper – and now Megan can hold back no longer.

"Aaah!" she screams. "Aaah!"

Her juices flow around the stranger's pumping cock. She throws her head back. Her orgasm is so powerful, she almost passes out. The stranger ceases his fucking motions. She feels his wide member throbbing – buried to the hilt inside her juicy cunt.

"Ali," the tattoo artist says calmly. "What about that tattoo you wanted?"

Ali wipes the sweat from his forehead, nodding.

"Oh yeah," he says. "How about we make it right here and now?"

The tattoo artist shrugs. Megan looks from one man to the other – still gasping for breath. The tattoo artist picks up a stencil showing a small five-pointed star – a pentagram. Ali pulls just a few inches of his member out of her, and the tattoo artist places the stencil on his wide cock.

"Here?" he asks.

Ali nods, and the tattoo artist carefully rubs the stencil, until the image appears clearly defined on the skin of the shaft. Ali admires the result.

"Cool!" he says. "That'll be great. You go right ahead."

The tattoo artist puts a black cartridge on the needle, placing the point on Ali's cock. Immediately the needle begins buzzing as he starts tattooing. Ali grits his teeth, and Megan feels his swelling cock jerking inside her.

The buzzing of the needle spreads through the stiff shaft, letting Megan feel it, too. The tattoo artist holds Ali's fat cock with one hand, the other carefully tracing the drawing with the needle. Dot by dot Ali gets the pentagram tattooed on his member. He closes his eyes. Megan feels his cock jump.

"Are you okay?" the tattoo artist asks.

"Hm," Ali replies out of breath. "Yeah, I ... I'm good. Keep going."

It buzzes inside Megan's pussy. It's wrapped tightly around Ali's member, letting her feel it swell – feel every contraction. The tattoo artist has finished three out of five lines and starts on the fourth.

"Ohhh!" Ali moans.

His cock feels even thicker than before.

"Hold on!" the tattoo artist says.

"I'm about to ..." Ali gasps. "Ah!"

Wide-eyed, he stares down at his fat shaft, following the tattoo artist working on the final line. Megan feels his cock jumping violently inside her cunt.

"I'm almost ..." the tattoo artist murmurs. "I'm completely done ... now!"

"Ohhh!" Ali roars. "Ohhh!"

Megan gasps loudly as she feels the semen spurting from Ali's pumping cock, far up into her sensitive flesh. A violent ejaculation, making Ali tremble with excitement as his swelling member jerks wildly. He comes and comes. Megan feels his sperm oozing out of her, onto the tattoo artist's table. As his orgasm finally subsides, he grunts with satisfaction.

"Yeah," he sighs. "Like that."

He slowly pulls his cock from Megan's cunt. The tattoo artist wipes blood and excess ink off the skin of his cock, and Megan notices he still has an erection.

"Was it good?" she asks.

"Fuck, yeah," Ali replies. "That was fucking great."

Megan looks at the tattoo artist.

"Can I have one right next to my clit?" she asks.

"Of course," he replies. "What do you want?"

"Make it a little arrow," Ali says. "A little arrow pointing straight down at her cunt."

"Good idea," the tattoo artists says. "That sends the right message. She wants every cock in the world to go there."

Megan giggles quietly. Ali stands with his still erect member in his hand, stroking it softly. The tattoo artist leafs through a binder until he finds a stencil with a small arrow. He places it on Megan's belly, right above her pussy.

"Further down," she whispers.

The tattoo artist's eyes widen behind his glasses.

"Okay," he says, moving the stencil slightly downwards. "But here it's almost touching your clit."

"Yes," she whispers. "That's where I want it."

The tattoo artist rubs the stencil, replicating the little arrow on Megan's skin. Meanwhile, Ali is getting undressed. He pulls off his t-shirt, revealing his muscular torso. Then he drops his pants, standing naked in the shop. His cock juts straight out, hard and

wide, wagging slightly up and down. The tattoo artist brings the needle close to the skin above Megan's pussy.

"I'm so excited," she gasps.

"Wait a minute," Ali says.

He stands betweens Megan's legs and slowly guides his fat cock up into her cunt.

"Oh!" she gasps.

He buries it to the root. Then he nods to the tattoo artist.

"You go right ahead," he says.

The tattoo artist looks severely at Megan who writhes on the table, the massive member inside her.

"It's important that you lie completely still," he says sternly.

Megan nods at him. She's breathing in little, short gasps. She jumps as he turns on the needle and it begins to buzz. He places it on her skin, drawing the first line.

"Ohhh!" she cries. "I feel it all the way into my pussy. Aaah!"

"Don't move!" the tattoo artist commands.

Ali's cock is throbbing. Her pussy quivers around the wide shaft as she feels the prickling pain from the needle – and the whirring sensation of the motor, spreading through her clit and into her entire abdomen. It's almost impossible for her not to squirm with lust. She tries tensing up all muscles – but that only intensifies the feeling. Juices seep from her trembling cunt.

"Oh!" she gasps. "Oh! Oh! Oh!"

"Yeah," Ali says. "Squeeze my cock."

Megan tightens her cunt muscles around the fat member, feeling it bulge, growing fatter still. Lustful sensations spread all through her hot body. She forces herself not to come – because she knows her orgasm will be so powerful, it will make her jump. The needle buzzes, pricking her skin. She sighs deeply.

"Lie still, damnit!" the tattoo artist cries.

"I ... I'm trying," she sobs.

"What a horny little slut," Ali says. "Are you ready to come?"

Megan nods helplessly. Ali's cock jumps inside her cunt as the tattoo artist finishes drawing the arrow.

"I'm almost done," he says. "It's done ... now!"

It's as if he applies extra pressure with the needle – right above Megan's clit.

"Ohhh!" she cries as the orgasm hits her. "Ohhh!"

The tattoo artist switches off the needle, and Ali starts thrusting his cock in and out of her trembling pussy.

"Mmm," he grunts. "Now all it needs is a bit of sperm."

With a low groan he pulls out of her and immediately begins ejaculating.

"Yes!" he gasps. "Ah! Ah!"

Fat spurts pump from his dancing cock. The fresh tattoo is like an open wound, and when Ali's semen hits it, it stings, making her scream.

"Aaah!"

"More!" the tattoo artist says. "She likes it. Dirty slut."

Ali masturbates the last sperm from his cock, letting it drip onto Megan's tattoo. The tattoo artist gets up from his chair. He has a powerful erection. Ali steps aside, and he assumes the position. With one brutal thrust the tattoo artist forces his long, hard shaft up into Megan's tender cunt.

"Oh!" she moans.

"Shut up!" he growls. "Shut up and feel my cock. You little whore!"

He grabs her hips hard – he's still wearing latex gloves – and begins fucking in a hard, furious rhythm – harder than ever before. The table squeaks and wobbles – the tattoo artist's thrust pushes it across the floor inch by inch as Megan squeals with pleasure. Ali stands behind the table. As he pushes against it with his entire bulk, it only rocks a bit back and forth.

"Ah!" Megan cries. "Ah! Ah!"

The tattoo artist's eyes gleam with excitement behind the glasses. As he fucks Megan, his mouth is open wide – almost drooling with lust. Megan's cunt smacks loudly in time with his thrusts – again and again his long, hard cock penetrates her to the root. Ali watches with a cheeky grin – one hand stroking his still erect cock.

The tattoo artist thrusts deeper and harder. It is as if he's gone completely mad with lust: He grunts and roars like a savage beast, impaling Megan's cunt with incredible stamina. Ali climbs onto the table and guides his fat member into Megan's mouth.

"Mmm!" she protests.

But he insists. He forces his cock in between her lips and starts thrusting back and forth. Megan opens wide to accommodate the fat member. She drools around the pumping shaft, gagging a bit

each time the head of his cock hits the back of her throat. The tattoo artist fucks her savagely, and she feels she's about to come again. This orgasm will be the most violent yet.

"Mmm! Mmm!" she cries, her mouth full of Ali's cock.

"Yeah!" the tattoo artist yells in response. "Like that! Take it! You fucking whore!"

Ali grabs her hair and freezes in mid-thrust. His fat cock swells inside her mouth, and he lets out a loud roar:

"Ohhh!"

Megan feels Ali's member jumping as it fires the first spurt of semen – deep down into her throat. It keeps on pumping and pumping. She whimpers with excitement as the tattoo artist's deep thrusts make her lose control – and a violent orgasm surges through her body, making her shake with convulsions. Juices spurt across his vigorously fucking cock. And finally he can't hold back his ejaculation either.

"Ohh!" he yells. "Fuck it!"

He holds his member still inside her, and she feels it swelling and jerking in her cunt. The tattoo artist roars with pleasure as the first violent spurt pumps from his cock – far up into Megan's cunt. She writhes in the throes of orgasm, making the handcuffs jingle, as the two aroused men ejaculate into her mouth and pussy – emptying themselves of all their thick, hot sperm.

"Mmm," Ali grunts as his orgasm subsides.

He slips his fat cock out of Megan's mouth, climbs off the table and kisses her greedily. The taste of his own spunk doesn't seem to bother him – perhaps he actually likes it? Megan feels dizzy from her latest orgasm. The tattoo artist's cock is still inside her cunt. It's finished spurting, but she feels it contracting a few more times. Eventually it grows soft and slides out of her.

The two men stand around for a while, just looking at her – naked and sweating, their members half-erect. Then they start getting dressed. Finally the tattoo artist finds the keys and unlocks Megan's handcuffs. She sits up on the table, rubbing her sore wrists. She's sweating, too. The tattoo artist sinks to the floor, seemingly completely exhausted. Ali sits on a chair, smiling contentedly. Megan looks around for her clothes, pick them up, and put them on.

"Well ..." she says.

Her voice is hoarse and slightly out of breath.

"Yeah," the tattoo artist says almost inaudibly. "You may go now."

Ali laughs.

"Come on," he says. "Don't be rude to her. She's been a really good girl today."

"But ..." the tattoo artist says. "I'm done for today."

"That's fine," Megan replies. "I have to get home, anyway."

She walks towards the door. Ali grabs her arm.

"But – we'll see you again?" he asks.

Megan's eyes widen. Then she smiles happily.

"Sure," she replies. "Why not?"

"Here's what we do," Ali says quietly. "We'll just meet here in the shop again tomorrow."

He points to the tattoo artist.

"Then he'll be ready to go again. And if not ... we'll just handle it ourselves."

Megan shakes her head, grinning slightly.

"You're fucking nuts," she replies. "Both of you."

"Yeah," Ali says. "And you like that, don't you?"

Megan is exiting the shop. In the doorway she turns to Ali and replies:

"Yeah. You bet I do!"

As the door slides shut behind her she hears Ali laughing and the tattoo artist sighing deeply. Her legs tremble slightly as she starts walking down the sidewalk.

She's already looking forward to tomorrow.

Live Sex Show

Part 1

"Damn – that looks good!" Kaj said.

Gitte placed the dish of meatballs on the table and smiled at him cheekily.

"I hope you like it," she said.

"You make the best meatballs in the world," Kaj replied.

He took a swig of beer from the bottle. Gitte sat across the table from him.

"Well, help yourself then!" she said.

She popped open a beer for herself and tipped the glass as she poured. Kaj helped himself to potatoes, meatballs, gherkins and sauce. Gitte sipped her beer and asked:

"How were things in the shop today?"

"Couldn't be better," Kaj replied. "They love it. The shop is full of Germans and Japanese. They can't believe their eyes."

Cheerfully, he began cutting up his food and wolfing it down.

"And now it's even legal," Gitte added.

Kaj and his friend Jørgen had opened the small sex shop in Copenhagen's red light district in 1967 – and the police had paid them a few unpleasant visits the first couple of years. But as time went on, the cops had stopped bothering, and last year – 1969 – it had finally happened: Denmark had been the first country in the world to fully legalize pornography – and Kaj and Jørgen had found themselves with a completely legal business on their hands. Feeling at ease, they'd started placing ads in the papers. And customers were pouring in – not least the male tourists, who'd never seen anything like it in their home countries.

Both Kaj and Jørgen made a good living off the shop – and Gitte, too, enjoyed the money coming in. Kaj was a generous man who loved to surprise her with expensive presents. Gitte rarely visited the shop, but wasn't shocked by it when she did – she

enjoyed walking among the shelves stocked with glossy magazines of nude women and men – naked breasts and long, stiff cocks. Sometimes Kaj would bring a few magazines home for them to look at together. And they always ended up fucking afterwards.

Kaj took another swig of beer.

"By the way," he said. "Jørgen had an idea. And I just need to discuss it with you."

Gitte nodded, chewing her meatball.

"You know, we have this little backroom for showing movies," Kaj went on. "And we were thinking: Maybe we should do what the other shops do – start having live sex shows."

"Live sex shows?" Gitte asked.

"Yeah, you know." Kaj gesticulated, fork in hand. "Real sex. A couple fucking in front of an audience."

Gitte's eyes widened.

"Oh my!" she said. "Well, I bet there'd be good money in that." Kaj nodded.

"But who will you get to perform?" she asked.

Kaj took another sip of beer and cleared his throat.

"Well," he said. "There's this big guy from the brewery. Bjarne. You know him, don't you?"

"Sure," Gitte said, nodding. "But why him, exactly?"

"I've heard rumors," Kaj said. "He's supposed to have one hell of a giant cock."

Gitte laughed,

"Well, I see," she said. But ... does he know how to use it?"

"Apparently: More than enough. The girls are crazy about him."

Gitte squirmed on her chair.

"Ooh, that sounds hot," she said. "I never thought about Bjarne in that way. He's rather big and brutish. But yeah – now that I think about it ..."

Kaj nodded slowly.

"Anyway," Gitte went on. "I suppose you'll also need some hot babe for him to fuck. Who's that going to be?"

Kaj hesitated before answering.

"Well ... We wondered whether you'd be interested."

Gitte gasped.

"Me?" she exclaimed. "But ..."

"Well, first of all, you are absolutely gorgeous," Kaj went on quickly. "You have nice tits, you're great in bed – and we already discussed that you're turned on by people watching ..."

Gitte poured the rest of her beer into the glass and shook her head.

"But still," she said. "And ... and with Bjarne ..."

"Lots of girls are dying to do it with Bjarne," Kaj said. "And you'll even be getting paid."

Gitte giggled.

"Really?" she said. "Is that the kind of thing you and Jørgen get up to down in the shop? Your wife getting fucked for money?"

Kaj sighed.

"Yeah, it's sort of crazy," he said. "I know that. But what if ... What if you gave it a try just once? And if you don't enjoy it, you never have to do it again."

Gitte stood up, took Kaj's plate and placed it on top of her own.

"I believe I need to think about that," she said.

She turned around, carried the plates to the kitchen, and put them in the sink. Kaj emptied his beer in one swig and followed her.

"I don't know," he said. "It seems to be turning you on a bit."

Gitte stood with his back to him, rinsing the plates in running water.

"Well, what do you expect?" she finally whispered. "Sitting there talking about monster cocks over dinner."

Grinning cheekily, Kaj stood right behind her.

"So you liked that?" he asked. "Getting all hot and bothered, are you?"

She didn't reply. Kaj lifted up her skirt and put his hand between her thighs. Gitte sighed. She wasn't wearing panties – she usually wasn't. He let his fingers slide slowly across her labia. They already felt wet.

"You naughty little girl," he whispered in her ear. "You're going up on that stage for a taste of that monster cock. Aren't you, now?"

Gitte turned to face him, her plump breasts swelling inside her blouse.

"Alright," she said huskily. "I'll think about it. On one condition."

Kaj nodded.

"And that is?" he asked.

"You have to take me," she replied. "Right here. Right now."

Kaj grunted with lust. He zipped down his pants and took out his cock. It was already half erect, and as he began stroking it, it grew long and hard. Looking at it lustfully, Gitte licked her lips.

"Mmm, yes," she whispered. "That's a real man's cock."

She looked him in the eyes and asked earnestly:

"Kaj – you really think, Bjarne's cock is bigger than yours?"

"I have no idea," Kaj gasped.

He lifted up her apron and skirt to get a look at her hairy cunt. As she spread her legs, the pink slit opened, wet and glistening.

"But what if I can't take it?" she asked. "If it's far too big for me?"

Kaj grabbed his hard cock in his fist, pressing it against the mouth of her pussy.

"I think it's huge," he panted. "I don't think you ever tried anything like it."

Then he thrust forward. Pressing Gitte against the edge of the kitchen table he buried his rigid member inside her slick cunt.

"Aaah!" she cried. "Yes!"

Kaj stood like that for a while, his cock jumping and twitching inside her. Ever so slowly he pulled out, the thick shaft shiny with juices. He grabbed Gitte's buttocks hard and began thrusting – a hard, deliberate rhythm, making her whimper with joy.

"Fucking great pussy," he hissed. "Bjarne's got something to look forward to."

Gitte's hands flailed backwards. Glass and plates clinked until she got a firm grip on the edge of the kitchen table. Her breasts bounced in time with Kaj's eager thrusts. Juices flowed over his long, hard cock, dripping on to the vinyl floor.

"Oh yes," she gasped. "Oh yes. I'm coming. Oh. I'm coming."

Kaj grit his teeth, his stiff member pumping in and out of Gitte's quivering pussy. Orgasm shook her entire body like cramps, droplets of juice squirting from her cunt with every thrust.

"Yeah?" Kay gasped. "You like that? That's what a horny little bitch wants? Turn around!"

He suddenly pulled out of her succulent pussy. When she hesitated, he grabbed her and turned her around, bending her over the kitchen sink, her ass turned toward him. Again he thrust his stiff cock into her, making her cry out loud with pleasure. And again he

started fucking – even faster and deeper than before. He slapped her on one buttock with his open hand.

Smack!

"Ah!" she cried.

He hit her again. Smack! Smack! Smack! Her buttocks glowed red, burning hot from the spanking. Kaj ripped her blouse open and grabbed her full, round breasts with his huge hands. He kneaded them roughly, his cock thrusting and thrusting all the way up into her sopping wet cunt.

"Ohhh!" he roared. "Fuck, that's good!"

"Yes," Gitte sobbed. "Don't stop! I'm ... I'm going to come again!"

Kaj clenched his jaw and shut his eyes tight, his face a grimace of wild, lustful concentration. He increased his rhythm, making Gitte cry out loud. Her hands held on to the tap as Kaj's cock kept hammering away inside her trembling cunt. The fat member swelled and jerked in her juicy crevice.

"Come on!" Kaj gasped desperately. "Come on!"

Gitte let her hand slide in between her thighs and began feverishly massaging her little, hard clit.

"Oooh," she whimpered. "Yeahhh!"

She thrust her ass up in the air. Her entire body froze as she came again. Shaking and quivering, she sobbed helplessly as Kaj thrust up into her once again. And again.

"Ohhh!" he roared. "Ohhh yes!"

He grabbed her hips hard, pulling her towards him and burying his cock inside her to the root as it began to twitch and squirt. From his swollen balls semen shot up through the shaft and deep into Gitte's sensitive cunt. Spurt after spurt after spurt, as both of them trembled and gasped in an explosion of incredible pleasure.

Then all was quiet in the kitchen.

"Damn it," Gitte whispered. "I thought I was going to faint."

Kaj held his half erect cock inside her. He bent over to lick the sweat from the back of her neck.

"Mmm," he said. "Maybe next time."

Gitte shook her head and laughed.

"And with Bjarne," she sighed. "What a ride that's going to be!"

Kaj kissed her passionately.

"I hope so," he growled. "I sure as hell hope so."

Part 2

Cigarette smoke hung heavily in the room, filling it with a spicy scent. It loomed like soft clouds in front of the two deep red spotlights illuminating the small stage. Entering, Kaj looked around. There were about fifty seats, and the house was nearly full. Unsurprisingly, the audience was almost entirely male. Only a single red-headed woman sat locked in embrace with a man. Kaj took them to be a prostitute and her client.

On stage was a writing desk with a typewriter and an old office chair. When Jørgen noticed Kaj he crossed the room to shake hands. He wore the rust red corduroy suit he always wore at such occasions and held an open beer bottle in each hand.

"So," he said cheerfully. "This is it. Want one?"

Kaj took the beer, nodding.

"Yeah, thanks," he said. "How's Gitte?"

Jørgen winked at him.

"Excited," he said. "A little nervous, perhaps – but most of all excited. She's back in the dressing room getting ready."

The "dressing room" was a small storage room they'd equipped for the day with folding chairs and tables, mirrors and a small fridge with beer and mineral water. Kaj took a swig of his beer.

"Okay," he said.

Jørgen looked at his watch.

"Hey – it's time, buddy," he said. "I'll handle it. Just sit down and enjoy the show."

Jørgen walked up to the desk next to the stage where the record player was. He put on a record – some slow, groovy funk music – the horniest music they could find. Jørgen turned to put out the house lights. Only the small stage remained lit by the soft, deep red light, reminiscent of a brothel. A few audience members applauded enthusiastically. Kaj found an empty chair in the middle of the room. Jørgen took a seat right in front of the stage.

Seconds later, Gitte nonchalantly strolled on to the stage floor. She was dressed up as a decent, yet slightly saucy secretary: Her hair in a tall hairdo, big horn-rimmed glasses, a low-cut silk blouse, miniskirt, black nylons and heels. She sat at the desk, put a sheet of paper in the typewriter and began to type. The clacking noise of the machine cut through the music. Once in a while she paused to

caress herself – let her hand slip under her blouse or up under her skirt. Then she resumed typing.

The stage floor creaked as Bjarne entered. He was a tall, muscular man, dressed in worn overalls. He stood at the edge of the stage, ogling Gitte with a filthy leer. She looked up at him.

"Yes?" she asked. "Can I help you?"

"Did you call the janitor?" Bjarne asked in his deep, rough voice.

Kaj and Jørgen had discussed whether to have dialogue at all – knowing that their native Danish would be incomprehensible to most of the audience. But they had agreed on just a few lines in English for the benefit of the tourists. Lines that Bjarne – with his limited grasp of language – had learned more or less phonetically. Kaj sipped his beer.

"No!" Gitte exclaimed. "I really didn't call anyone."

"Have I come here to no avail?" Bjarne asked.

"Yes, I'm truly sorry. But you have to go now."

"I believe I can be of some assistance," Bjarne growled, stepping right up to the desk.

Gitte got up from her chair, brushing a loose lock of hair from her face.

"What do you mean?" she asked.

"Just a little service check, miss. Of your cunt."

"Well, I never!" Gitte exclaimed. "Such a coarse and lecherous type!"

Bjarne walked around the desk and kicked away the chair away. His huge fist swept across the desk, knocking the typewriter to the floor with a crash. Papers flew. Gitte gasped loudly. Bjarne grabbed her wrist, forcing her onto the table on her back.

"Shut up!" he said. "I can tell when a little fucking whore like you needs a real man's cock!"

He lifted up her mini-skirt. She wasn't wearing panties, and the sight of her hairy cunt made the crowd gasp. Grunting, Bjarne knelt down between her thighs and began to lick. Grabbing her ankles, he spread her legs, giving the audience full view of his fat tongue dancing across her labia. Gitte's pubes glistened with his saliva.

"Ohh!" she moaned loudly. "Ohh!"

Kaj looked around the room. All faces were turned to the stage, engulfed in the show. Only Jørgen turned his head towards him, grinning and winking. Kaj took a swig of beer and focused on the

stage. Slurping loudly, Bjarne lapped up Gitte's juices. Muscles quivered in her slender thighs. Kaj felt his cock jerking – stiffening and stretching inside his pants.

Bjarne's powerful thumbs spread Gitte's labia apart. The pink inside of her pussy glistened in the red stage lighting. He made his tongue hard, thrusting it up into her cunt like a small cock. Jerking his head back and forth, he fucked Gitte with his tongue.

"Ohhh!" she cried. "Yes! Yes!"

Her hands trembled as she tore open her blouse. Buttons flew off, rattling across the stage floor. She began to knead her full breasts, lasciviously thrashing about on the desk. Quiet sighs and moans were heard from the audience. Several guests squirmed on their chairs. And suddenly Gitte's cries of ecstasy cut through the funky music:

"I'm coming!" she squealed. "Ohhh! Mmm!"

Pressing his face against her pussy, Bjarne buried his tongue deep inside her. She writhed and shivered. Kaj felt his cock stretching and pushing against the fabric of his pants. Discretely he slid his hand over the bulge, feeling how hard it was. Bjarne stood up, savoring the sight of Gitte, lying half naked and quivering in front of him.

"Play with your cunt, miss," he ordered.

Gitte slowly spread her legs. As her fingers found her clit she sobbed quietly. She began to masturbate, as Bjarne stared deep into her eyes.

"Yeah, like that," he growled in appreciation. "You'd better get ready ..."

He zipped down the fly in his overalls.

"... for the cock."

The entire room gasped as Bjarne produced his huge, semi-erect cock. Gitte breathed deeply, her eyes open wide. It was both long and thick. The dark blue head must have been the size of a pool ball – and beneath the wide shaft bluish veins throbbed, giving it a bumpy and brutal look. Bjarne grabbed it with his huge fist, stroking it until it was hard as a rock.

"No ..." Gitte whispered.

She massaged her clit vigorously, her warm juices running down her thighs and over the desk. Bjarne stood between her legs. Gitte was not a tall woman, and Bjarne's enormous cock made her look even smaller. His huge fist grabbed it at the root, forced it

downwards, and steered it towards Gitte's cunt. She spread her legs. Several spectators stood up halfway to catch the sight of the wide head of Bjarne's cock squeezing in between her pussy lips. She panted. Slowly, slowly, he drove his huge member up into her.

Kaj's cock twitched. He looked around the room – then he placed his beer on the floor, quietly zipped down his pants, and released his stiff member. He sighed. The red-haired hooker, too, had let out her client's long, hard cock and now sat massaging it. Her long nails were painted bright red. Her customer panted, mouth wide open, staring at the stage.

Inch by inch Bjarne's cock penetrated Gitte's cunt. She threw her head from side to side, whimpering helplessly. Bjarne grunted loudly with the strain:

"Ng! Ng!"

Grabbing her ankles, he forced her legs even wider apart. Her slick labia stretched around his giant cock – about the size of a grown man's forearm. Finally he impaled her to the root, throwing his head back as he held still inside her.

"Aaah ..." he sighed.

Gitte swallowed a couple of times and put her trembling hand against Bjarne's belly as if asking him to wait.

"Well, miss," he said. "Are you ready for a good, hard fuck?"

Gitte gasped.

"I ..." she panted. "... mmm ..."

Bjarne laughed harshly.

"Well, here's some cock for you, then!" he said.

He pulled his glistening member all the way out of Gitte's cunt and buried the entire length of it in one thrust. She screamed. He thrust again. And again. The giant cock drove up and up into Gitte's cunt in deep, fast thrusts. Her arms flailed in the air, pushed against Bjarne's powerful torso, and gripped the edge of the desk. Howling, she squirmed about on the table top, his cock brutally fucking her with loud smacking sounds.

The spectators writhed on their chairs. A number of men had zipped down and sat openly masturbating as they watched. Kaj looked down at his cock. Hard and stiff, it pointed vertically upwards. A tiny droplet of fluid seeped from its tip and ran down the shaft. Gripping it firmly, he slowly began to masturbate.

"Ah! Ah!" Gitte cried. "I'm coming! Aaah!"

Bjarne increased his rhythm, thrusting and thrusting up into her dripping wet cunt. Juices squirted around the fat shaft. Quivering, Gitte screamed her orgasm into the room. But Bjarne did not stop. He buried his swelling cock inside her cunt over and over, drooling with lust.

"Yes!" he suddenly yelled. "Here I come!"

He pulled the huge member all the way out of Gitte. It glistened and dripped with her juices. He put his hands on the hips of his overalls and watched his fat cock. It twitched uncontrollably, and now it released the first, long spurt of semen. The jet shot across Gitte's sweaty skin, landing on her left breast. And another spurt. And another. Swelling and jerking, Bjarne's cock pumped white-hot sperm across Gitte, who squirmed lustfully on the desk.

"Aaah!" Bjarne cried. "Aaah!"

"Mmm," Gitte purred.

Bjarne grabbed the root of his cock and began to masturbate.

"Yeah?" he gasped. "You liked that?"

Gitte's eyes opened wide as she stared at the huge member. A thick drop of semen dripped from the tip and onto the stage floor, but the cock did not go soft. Massaging it skillfully, Bjarne kept it as hard and stiff as before. Gitte sat up unsteadily.

"No ..." she whispered.

Bjarne laughed mockingly.

"Surely, miss – you didn't think I was done with you, did you?" he said. "Turn around!"

He grabbed her and placed her on the desk, face down. He lifted up her shapely bottom and guided his swollen member up underneath her. Gitte screamed as his cock penetrated her cunt from behind.

"Aaah!"

"Yeah!" Bjarne yelled randily. "Like that! Damnit, that's good pussy!"

He began pumping violently back and forth. The desk squeaked and moved across the stage in time with his powerful thrusts.

In the house, Kaj stood up. Clear fluid oozed from his stiff cock as he slowly masturbated. His gaze fixed on his wife, he walked towards the stage.

"Oh!" Gitte cried. "Oh! Oh!"

Grabbing her soft buttocks, Bjarne thrust up into her with all his might. Her entire body quivered with pleasure.

The stage floor creaked as Kaj stepped up to stand in front of Gitte, his stiff cock jumping before him.

"Well?" Bjarne said. "You like that, huh? Watching your life getting fucked like a proper little whore?"

"Yes," Kaj whispered. "That's the way she likes it. Suck my cock!"

Gitte blinked. She slowly parted her bright red lips. Grunting, Kaj steered the head of his cock into her mouth. She closed her lips around the shaft, and he began thrusting back and forth. Gitte slurped around his meat, her saliva making it glisten in the red stage lights. Kaj looked across the room. By now about half of the men had their members out, shamelessly masturbating. The red-haired hooker's client sat gasping, his mouth wide open, as she vigorously jerked him off.

"Oh!"

The first ejaculation in the house. A man in the back row bent forwards, his cock spitting semen in long, hard spurts.

"Oh!" "Ah!"

Spectator after spectator succumbed to orgasm. Kaj thrust in and out of his wife's slurping mouth, while Bjarne fucked her relentlessly from behind.

Smack!

Bjarne slapped Gitte's buttocks hard.

Smack! Smack! Smack!

He kept hitting her shapely bottom, thrusting up into her cunt again and again. Kaj's cock jumped.

"Yeah," he whispered hoarsely. "Spank her! Spank her good!"

He grabbed Gitte by the throat, pumping his cock in and out of her drooling mouth. She choked. Bjarne's face was bright red. His huge member swelled, stretching Gitte's cunt with every thrust.

"Ah!" he suddenly cried. "Yes!"

He pulled out and grabbed his jerking cock in his huge fist. A long, white spurt shot out of it, landing as a sticky stripe across Gitte's back. The cock fired again – and again. The bulbous head of his cock swelled, his hairy balls contracted. Bjarne masturbated slowly and thoroughly – emptied himself of spunk.

"Ohhh!" Kaj gasped.

His entire body tensed up as in a cramp as he began to ejaculate into Gitte's mouth. He spurted – harder and more violent than ever

– deep into his wife's throat. She greedily swallowed his semen, as Kaj shook with lust.

"Damn, that felt good!" Bjarne's rough voice announced.

He shook off the last drops of semen on the stage floor. His half-erect member still hanging out of his overalls, he walked to the edge of the stage and bowed deeply several times. The audience hesitated for a second, then a round of applause erupted. The sound echoed in the small room. Kaj swiftly pulled out of Gitte's mouth and managed to tuck his cock back into his pants.

"You too," he whispered to her. "You're the star."

Hair and clothes in disarray, Gitte slid off the desk and stumbled to the edge of the stage. Squinting into the lights, she slowly licked her lips. The applause rose in volume – many piercing whistles were heard. Gitte giggled shyly and looked around the stage, where both Bjarne and Kaj nodded appreciatively. She curtseyed coyly. Then she turned around, showing first her breasts, then her pussy to the audience.

"Bravo!" someone shouted from the house.

Kaj held her shoulders and led her from the stage to the small dressing room. Bjarne followed. Immediately after, Jørgen came through the door, clapping enthusiastically.

"Goddamn!" he exclaimed. "Goddamn, that was great!"

Kaj nodded, his face still red with excitement.

"A man could do with a brew," Bjarne said.

"But of course," Jørgen replied. "There's beer in that fridge."

Bjarne opened the fridge, passed bottles of beer around for the other, then took one for himself and popped it open.

"Well," Jørgen said. "I'll leave you to it. But it was fucking awesome. It really was."

He turned and left the room. Bjarne followed him, drinking from his beer.

"I think I'll go meet my audience," he said cheerfully. "Perhaps someone wants an autograph."

He closed the door behind him. Gitte and Kaj sat on two folding chairs.

"How do you feel?" Kaj asked quietly.

Gitte wiped the sweat from her forehead and sipped her beer.

"I'm all excited," she said. "That was fucking crazy."

"Crazy?"

"Yeah. That's one hell of a cock that guy has. I can feel it inside me still ..."

"So ... you liked it?"

"Fuck, yeah – couldn't you tell?"

She smiled wickedly.

"And so did you, right?" she asked.

Kaj took a swig of his beer and nodded.

"Yeah," he said. "Watching you get fucked like that. Made me damn horny ..."

Gitte laughed.

"Mmm," she said seductively. "Two nice, big cocks at once. I liked that."

"So you're willing to give it another go?" Kaj asked.

Gitte nodded.

"Sure," she replied. "But ... do we have to wait that long?"

Kaj looked at her, confused.

"What do you mean?"

"Perhaps you could ask Bjarne," she whispered, "if he ... if he wants to come home with us afterwards?"

"Home with us?"

Gitte giggled shyly.

"We could continue where we left off ..." she said quietly.

Smiling, Kaj took a swig of his beer.

"If that's what you want," he said, "it's fine with me."

Beneath the fabric of his pants, his cock was already growing hard again.

What It's Like With A Girl

Part 1

What a waste, Jennifer thought.

She stretched out on her beach towel and looked up at the clear blue afternoon sky. What a waste.

They could probably see her now, she realized. Their house wasn't far from the beach, and if they looked out of those big, expensive windows they could definitely see her.

Their names were Adam and Jake, and as the sun warmed Jennifer's bare skin, she couldn't stop thinking about them. They were both so hot - and such really nice guys. But gay. And a couple. They had each other and were really happy that way, so she didn't stand a chance with either of them. What a waste.

Jennifer grabbed a handful of warm, dry sand, letting it slowly run through her fingers. Was she just jealous? A bit, of course. Adam and Jake were obviously so happy together. And she knew she had no right to be disappointed that they weren't attracted to her. There were lots of straight guys in town, after all - so why did her thoughts keep returning to the only two friends unavailable to her? But damn - they were hot.

Which one was her favorite? That was kind of a tough question. They were quite alike in many ways - same height, same athletic body type. But Jake was a bit more serious and aggressive, while Adam was slightly more quiet and sensitive. Which one did she like the best? Ah, she wasn't really sure. And what did it matter anyway?

Jennifer sighed. Oh, well. She could always fantasize about them. She'd done it before and would surely do it again. No harm in that. They'd never know - and although it wasn't as good as having sex with one of the guys, she'd managed to masturbate herself to orgasm several times by thinking about Adam or Jake. Or both, if she'd been in an especially kinky mood.

She looked around. The beach was almost empty. Far away to the left here was a couple splashing about in the water. They wouldn't be able to see what she was doing. Jennifer adjusted her sunglasses and exhaled. Then she closed her eyes and thought of ... Adam.

The quiet one. But what is they said about quiet guys? Maybe he was really... She bit her lip. In her fantasy he was wearing a t-shirt and tight jeans, showing an impressive bulge. What if she reached out and stroked it? And kept stroking it, making his cock grow long and hard ...

Jennifer slipped her fingers into her bikini panties, finding her clit and gently caressing it. Mmm ... what if? Once she'd gotten Adam excited what would he do? If she kept going for long enough, would he turn mad with lust? Wouldn't he?

"Mmm ..."

Would he grab at her clothes, his cock jerking inside his jeans? Rip her top off, exposing her breasts? Yes, he would. He would zip down, letting his stiff cock out. And she'd fall on her knees in front of him and take it in her mouth. She'd suck it eagerly, grabbing her naked breasts.

Jennifer masturbated at the thought, her body shivering on the beach towel.

"Oh. Oh."

God, she was so wet! The thought of Adam's cock bulging and twitching on her tongue made her increase the rhythm. She felt the juices flowing from her cunt. And when he was completely erect, he would grab her, pull her to her feet and ...

"Hi."

A male voice. As Jennifer opened her eyes, she didn't see anyone, and for a moment thought she'd been imagining it. But as she looked around, she saw a young man walking towards her, wearing only a pair of swimming trunks. It took her a few seconds to realize it was Adam. And she couldn't help noticing the curve of his shapely cock clearly visible beneath the fabric of his trunks.

"Hi, Jennifer," Adam said, sitting down in the sand next to her.

She swiftly, but casually, slipped her fingers out from her bikini panties and lay her hand in the warm sand beside her.

"Oh, hi Adam," she said cheerily. "I just had to scratch myself. All that sand ... It's ..."

Stupid, she immediately thought. Stupid, stupid, stupid. Adam hadn't mentioned where her hand had been - maybe he hadn't even noticed. And now she'd gone and drawn attention to the fact that she'd been masturbating. Scratch myself, indeed. She sat up, wrapping her arms around her ankles and turned her head to face Adam.

"So, how are you?" she asked, her voice almost breaking with excitement. "And Jake? Everything okay?"

"Oh, yes," Adam said, smiling. "I'm fine. We're both fine. It's all good."

Jennifer shook her head, smiling, too.

"You guys," she said. "You're really happy together, aren't you?"

Adam looked out over the calm blue sea.

"Absolutely," he said. "Couldn't be better."

Jennifer felt the sand sticking to her wet fingers. She took a deep breath.

"I have to admit that I'm ..." she began. "Well ... that I'm a bit jealous."

Adam looked at her curiously.

"Jealous?" he said slowly. "But - why?"

"Oh, I don't know," she said. "It's really silly. But I'm single, you know - and you seem so happy. And ... I can't help thinking of all the sex ..."

Adam smiled.

"The sex?" he said.

Jennifer blushed, immediately regretting her words.

"No, no," she said. "I didn't mean ..."

"It's okay," Adam said quietly. "I understand. You're alone, and you know we're having sex?"

Jennifer looked away and nodded, then looked back at Adam. What beautiful blue eyes he had.

"Yes, and I can't ..." she said. "I can't help thinking about it ..."

Adam shook his head.

"Wait. You can't help thinking about Jake and me having sex?"

"I keep picturing you naked. Touching each other. Sucking each other off. Fucking ..."

Jennifer felt herself blushing. She hardly knew what she was saying anymore. Adam reached out and stroked her arm gently.

"You poor thing," he said, smiling. "And does that turn you on?"

"Oh," Jennifer gasped, louder than she'd planned. "It ... it makes me so horny I have to masturbate."

"Really?" Adam said. "Well ... I didn't know. I suppose we should be flattered."

Jennifer swallowed twice, her throat dry with excitement.

"In fact," she went on. "In fact I'm quite horny right now. Really horny, in fact. So ... do you mind if I masturbate? Just a bit? You can watch if you like ..."

Adam smiled.

"Go right ahead," he said. "In fact, as you may have guessed, I've never seen a woman masturbating before."

Jennifer felt herself trembling, as she slowly pulled off her bikini panties. What was she thinking? This was madness. But an overpowering urge had flooded her brain, and she didn't really know what she was doing any more. She undid the bra as well, and lay naked on the towel as Adam looked her over.

"You have a beautiful body," he said earnestly.

"Thank you," she whispered.

Her fingers found her clit, and she let out a deep sigh of pleasure.

"Oh, fuck ..." she gasped.

Closing her eyes, she began moving her fingers in small circles around her love button. Slowly at first, then faster and more vigorously, feeling the wetness oozing from her cunt.

"Oh ..." she moaned. "Oh ... oh ..."

It felt so good. And it felt even better - turning her on even more - knowing that Adam was watching her. How would he react?

When Jennifer opened her eyes, she saw that he had moved closer. He sat right next to her, his gaze fixed on her cunt, fascinated. Whimpering, she kept masturbating, looking at his face, judging his reactions. He had soft, gentle features that would almost have been feminine if not for the dark stubble on his chin and upper lip. God, she wanted him so badly.

She closed her eyes and resumed her fantasy. Imagining that she'd finished giving Adam a blowjob - that his cock was now long and hard - that he would pull her up. Oh God, he'd probably press her up against the wall. She would see his cock jumping with excitement. He would grab her wrists, pin her up against the wall.

She would be so horny by then, she'd spread her legs wide and wait for him to guide his cock towards the mouth of her cunt. Oh, and when he did ... The sensation of the bulging head against her labia. Pushing against her. Oh, fuck. Forcing her pussy lips apart. Entering her ...

She masturbated like crazy, juices flowing abundantly from her quivering cunt onto the towel.

"Ah. Ah. Ah."

"You're so wet."

She opened her eyes. Adam stared intently at her cunt.

"So ... so wet," he said. "Can I ... can I taste it?"

"Hm," Jennifer whimpered. "Yeah ... go ahead ..."

Gently, Adam ran a finger along her wet, pink flesh. He put it to his lips and sucked her juices off, savoring her taste.

"Mmm," he said. "Not bad. Not bad at all."

Jennifer's eyes widened.

"You ... you like the taste of my pussy?" she whispered.

Adam nodded slowly.

"Keep going," he said. "I want to watch you come."

She took a deep breath and spread her legs wide, opening her crevice to his curious gaze. If wanted he watch, she wanted to show him everything. Everything. Her fingers resumed the circular motion around her clit - even more vigorously than before.

"Like what you see?" she gasped.

Adam stood up, the sun behind him. Jennifer squinted at the silhouette of his athletic body towering above her. Still masturbating, her eyes zoomed in on his crotch. She thought she could just make out the contours of his bulging cock - but she couldn't be sure.

She let out a gasp of surprise as she felt her climax approaching.

"Oh, fuck," she whispered. "I think I'm gonna come ..."

"Yeah," Adam said. "Come for me. Let me watch."

He calmly pulled off his swimming trunks and kicked them aside. Jennifer whimpered loudly. She watched him take his cock in his hand and slowly stroke it.

"Ah!" she cried.

With Adam masturbating above her she brought herself to orgasm. She came hard, almost painfully, her body tensing up as pleasure surged through her. Whimpering, she threw herself about on the towel, little spurts of juice gushing from her flesh.

"Oh! Oh! Oh!"

Jennifer felt Adam's big, warm hands against the insides of her thighs. He had knelt down between her legs and was now pushing them further apart. His cock was fully erect, stretching long and hard in front of him. He smiled.

"You have such a pretty little cunt," he said. "I want to feel what it's like."

Jennifer whimpered, still shivering from her orgasm as he assumed the position. She couldn't believe what was happening. Adam was gay. Had been for as long as she'd known him. And he and Jake were so happy together. All her fantasies about having sex with either of them had just been silly nonsense. Nothing to be taken seriously - completely unrealistic.

Yet here he was, grabbing his cock in his fist to force it down towards the entrance to her cunt. As she felt the swollen head against her wet flesh, she couldn't help thinking that he'd never felt a pussy before. What would it be like for him? He pushed forwards, the bulging head of his cock just entering her cunt.

"So wet," he gasped. "It's so wet."

Slowly, carefully, he pushed deeper. Jennifer felt the entire length of his hard shaft entering her and couldn't stop herself from moaning out loud:

"Ohhh ..."

Adam took a deep breath, and began thrusting rhythmically into her. She felt ... no, it couldn't be ... she couldn't believe it. She felt Adam's cock, long and swollen, hammering into her cunt with great force. Adam's cock. Adam who was gay - who wasn't turned on by women at all. Yet here he was: His cock fully erect with excitement. Turned on. By her? What was going on?

Adam was moving faster now, his entire naked body slamming against hers, driving his hardened tool into her flesh again and again. The sensations overwhelmed her. Her head was spinning, and she heard herself whimpering with pleasure:

"Oh, Adam ... Fuck me. Fuck me, Adam."

The sound of her voice seemed to excite him even more. His thrusts got harder, deeper, faster. Jennifer squealed with pleasure, squirming with lust on the towel, her entire body shaking. Adam was sweating now, his handsome face a grimace of intense concentration.

"Yeah," he gasped. "Like that. Such a wet little cunt."

"Does my pussy feel good?" she whispered. "Does it feel good around your cock?"

"Yes," Adam said. "Ah. It's so good. I'm gonna ... I'm gonna come ..."

Jennifer's fingers found her clit again, and she began masturbating. Even if Adam was coming soon, she knew she'd be able to bring herself off again. Oh, God ... the thought of coming with Adam's cock inside her. She was so aroused she could almost faint.

"Aaah!" she cried. "Fuck me, Adam! I'm coming!"

Adam grunted with strain, thrusting again and again into Jennifer's trembling pussy. She lifted her abdomen from the towel, pressing it against his cock as she came.

"Aaah! Aaah!"

Juices gushed from her cunt as the climax shot through her like electricity. Adam's big hands grabbed her buttocks as he thrust into her again, again, again. And then ...

"Hunhhh!"

He pulled his cock from her flesh and grabbed it in his fist as he began to ejaculate. Jennifer stretched out on the towel, shivering in the throes of orgasm. The first spurt of piping hot semen hit her naked breast. Another shot all the way to her chin. Again and again Adam fired, masturbating like mad, his cock pumping and jerking.

"Ah! Ah! Ah!" he gasped, still masturbating long after his ejaculations had ceased.

Adam was on his knees between her legs, breathing hard.

"That was amazing!" Jennifer said.

She realized it might refer to his ejaculation, to her own orgasm, or the sex in general. But really, it referred to the fact that she had been fucked by a man she still believed to be 100% gay. Except, he couldn't be. Or ...?

Adam looked away, his eyes confused.

"Yeah, um ..." he said, holding his softening cock in his hand. "I ..."

"Was it ...?" Jennifer began.

She wanted to ask "was it good for you, too?" But she somehow felt it would be wrong. If it had been good, would that be questioning his sexuality? She's rather have him speak for himself, unasked.

Adam picked up his shorts, stood up, and pulled them on. He wasn't looking at her anymore.

"It was nice meeting you," he said quietly. "But I think I ... I'd better get going."

"Um ... okay," Jennifer said.

"Bye," Adam said quietly, immediately turning and walking away.

Jennifer lay back on her towel. She sighed. The sun was slowly sinking, a deeper shade of yellow. Had it been wrong? It wasn't as if she had planned it - and neither had he - it had just happened. Should she have fought it? But he'd been as excited as she was - so wasn't he to blame, as well? Had she embarrassed him now? Oh, fuck. Why did everything have to be so complicated?

Part 2

The keys jingled in the lock. Jake turned from the large windows with their view of the beach. That would be Adam. Seconds later he heard the sound of plastic sandal footsteps in their hallway.

"Is that you?" he asked.

There was a slight pause before Adam's voice came back. "Yeah."

"So what was it like?" Jake asked cheerfully. "Was it good?"

Adam came through the door, dressed only in swimming trunks, a worried expression on his face.

"What?" he said. "Was what good?"

Jake couldn't help laughing.

"The beach," he said. "Was it nice down on the beach?"

"Oh," Adam replied, smiling back. "Yes, it's a beautiful day."

Jake sat down on the couch.

"And, oh," Adam went on. "I met Jennifer there. Remember her?"

"Jennifer," Jake replied cheerily. "Yes, sure. Nice girl - rather pretty, isn't she?"

"She's ..." Adam began. "Yes."

Jake shook his head curiously.

"Anything wrong?" he asked.

"Mmm, no," Adam replied, turning towards the kitchen. "I could do with a beer. Do you want one?"

"Sure," Jake replied. "There's plenty in the fridge."

He leaned back in the couch as Adam flip-flopped into the kitchen. He heard beer bottles clinking inside the fridge, then two bottle tops popping. What was the matter with Adam today, he thought. He seemed confused - troubled. Had anything happened?

Adam came back with two open bottles, dewdrops clinging to the cold glass.

"There you go," Adam said, offering one to Jake.

"Thanks."

Jake expected him to sit down - either next to him or in the armchair across from him. But Adam just stood there, staring into space and sipping his beer with the same curious expression. Jake took a sip of his, too.

"Is anything the matter?" he asked.

"Why?" Adam snapped.

Jake almost smiled. Adam had to be the most hopeless liar in the world. If he really wanted to pretend there was nothing wrong, he could at least start by answering "no", instead of going all defensive. Now Jake knew there was something.

"It's just that ..." he said slowly, "... well, you seem a bit edgy. Or am I wrong?"

Adam drank from his beer and shook his head.

"I'm sorry," he said. "Yeah, I guess. I've been under a lot of stress lately. Work, you know ..."

Jake didn't know. He'd never mentioned it before. As far as Jake knew, Adam liked his job at the small architecture firm, he got on well with his co-workers, and there were no stressful deadlines approaching. But of course, he could be wrong.

"That sucks," Jake said. "Just let me know if there's anything I can do."

Adam stared back at him. For a few seconds his hazy, confused gaze was suddenly replaced by an intense glare. It was almost frightening. Jake laughed lightly.

"Not that I know how I could help," he said.

Adam placed his hand in front of his swimming trunks, grabbing his cock.

"Maybe you could," he said, taking another swig of the bottle.

"Take the stress off, you mean?" Jake said smiling. "Sounds like a good idea."

Adam slipped his hands inside his trunks, slowly stroking and kneading his cock.

"Get up," he said.

His voice was slightly slurred. He'd only had half a beer - so it wasn't that. Jake stood up.

"Take your clothes off," Adam said.

This wasn't like Adam at all, Jake thought. He was usually quite timid, and Jake usually had to initiate any sexual activity. Adam must be really horny. Good for him. This could get interesting. Jake pulled of his t-shirt, jeans and underwear and stood naked in front of Adam, his cock already stirring in anticipation. He took a quick sip of his beer.

"Okay," he said. "I'm ready."

Adam pulled off his swimming trunks. His cock jumped up, almost completely erect. Jake looked at it, smiling. He loved the sight of that cock - the thick, hard shaft, the swollen, rounded head.

What a lucky guy he was, having a boyfriend with a cock like that. Not speaking a word, he walked over to Adam, knelt in front of him, and took his cock in his mouth.

"Yes!" Adam gasped.

Jake immediately began sucking it, sucking it hard. He took it as far into his mouth as he could, until the head poked the back of his throat. He slipped his tongue up and down the shaft, his mouth applying suction in a steady rhythm. Adam groaned. Jake grabbed his hairy balls, feeling them jumping and contracting in his grip.

Adam began thrusting in and out of Jake's mouth. Saliva splashed around his shaft, running down Jake's bearded chin. Harder and harder he thrust, gripping the back of Jake's neck to enter deeper into his throat. Jake slurped and gagged.

Adam was never this aggressive - not unless he was unusually aroused. He'd been like this a few times when they'd just met - and every now and then if they'd been watching porn together, and a particular scene had turned him on. Some weeks ago they'd watched a police-themed porn flick, and they'd fucked for hours afterwards, Adam besides himself with lust. That had been a night to remember, Jake thought, his own cock rising and hardening as Adam eagerly fucked his mouth.

"Hunh!" Adam yelled, his pelvis pumping back and forth. "Yeah! Like that!"

Jake reached for his own cock and began stroking it, feeling it swell and stiffen. Oh, that was good. His cock was slightly longer than Adam's and could become hard as a rock. But it didn't have the same girth that Adam's had.

With a popping sound, Adam let his cock slip out of Jake's mouth. Saliva dripped from the shaft onto the wooden floor.

"Get up!" Adam ordered.

Jake got to his feet, and Adam pointed to the dining table.

"Bend over," he said.

Jake bent over the table, spreading his legs wide. The lacquered tabletop felt cool against his hard nipples. With a look of intense concentration, Adam spat on his cock again and again, covering it in saliva as he masturbated.

"Hm, yeah," he grunted. "Get ready for my cock, Jake."

No - this wasn't like Adam at all. What had gotten into him? Jake gasped as he felt Adam grabbing his buttocks hard, pulling them apart. And then the sensation of Adam's hard, dripping wet

cock pressing against his anus. Jake relaxed, yielding to the pressure, and the head of Adam's member entered his ass.

"Aaah!" he cried. "Fuck!"

Adam let out an animal grunt as he drove his cock forwards, forcing it deeper into Jake's ass. Inch by inch Jake felt the big, hard shaft entering. His own cock jumped with excitement. There was a slight sensation of pain, but that was completely overpowered by that of intense sexual pleasure. Damn, that cock felt good in his ass. Adam grabbed his hips hard.

"Oh yeah," he said, his voice hoarse with excitement. "I'm gonna fuck you so hard ..."

He pulled back and thrust into Jake's ass with incredible force. Then back, and forward again, and back, and forward. Jake groaned. Adam increased the rhythm, thrusting into Jake's stretching anus with incredible vigor.

"Ah!" Jake gasped. "Ah!"

"Yeah," Adam roared. "Like that! Unh! Unh!"

He grunted loudly with each brutal thrust, his cock hammering into Jake's stretching ass. Mad with lust, he wasn't trying to please anyone but himself. But his savage fucking turned Jake on as well, making his cock twitch and jerk under the table. Jake held on to the table top with his left hand and found his erect shaft with the other, stroking it, feeling it hot and throbbing in his fist as Adam fucked him ferociously.

Adam was like a man possessed. The sturdy table creaked and rocked with every brutal thrust. Jake was gasping for air, his mouth open wide, as Adam relentlessly penetrated his anus again and again.

"Aaah!" Jake gasped, his cock twitching in his hand. "Aaah! I'm gonna come!"

Incredibly, Adam was able to increase his rhythm. Jake had never felt anyone fucking him faster than now. He grit his teeth and grabbed his cock hard as he began ejaculating.

"Hnnnh!" he cried.

He felt a long, powerful spurt of semen shooting from his cock. And another, and another, spattering the wooden floor with loud, wet, splats. He let go of his ejaculating cock to grab the table top hard with both hands, letting his shaft fire again and again as the orgasm shook him.

Adam froze, his cock swelling inside Jake's tender ass.

"Ah, fuck!" he cried. "Yeah!"

He grunted like a beast as his cock began ejaculating. Jake felt hot jets of spunk shooting into his ass, filling him up. Adam ground his pelvis against Jake's ass, as thick semen dribbled down his thighs.

"Huh!" Adam gasped, squeezing the last drops from his still jerking, but already softening cock.

Jake exhaled, eyes closed, resting his body on the table, exhausted.

Minutes later they had cleaned up, and Jake had wiped his semen off the floor. Adam didn't say a word. His eyes seemed to dart around the room in confusion. Jake got dressed, while Adam still stood there on the floor in the nude, shaking from his orgasm.

"So," Jake asked curiously. "What got into you?"

"Hm?" Adam said. "What do you mean?"

Jake let himself fall into the couch and picked up his beer, happy to see that more than half was left.

"You were like a wild animal," he said. "Not that I'm complaining. In fact, I rather liked it. But ... why?"

"I dunno," Adam mumbled.

"C'mon," Jake insisted. "Talk to me. You came home all confused and stressed out. Then suddenly you jump me and fuck the living hell out of me. Don't tell me it's nothing special."

Adam smiled vaguely.

"I want to put some clothes on," he said and left the room.

Seconds later, he was back, wearing a pair of blue jeans and pulling on a black t-shirt as he entered the room.

"Okay," he said, sitting down on the armchair across from Jake. "Something happened today. But I'm not really sure what it means."

"So tell me," Jake said.

"Promise me you won't get mad," Adam said quickly.

He's fucked someone, Jake immediately thought. He's met some guy and fucked him. They had an open relationship, so Jake was okay with that. But it wouldn't surprise him if Adam felt guilty about it, anyway. Jake shook his head.

"Sure," he said. "I promise."

Adam took his beer and took a swig.

"Like I said," he began. "I met Jennifer on the beach. I told you. And she's ... well, she's really pretty, and really ... sexy."

Jake blinked.

"I think she was feeling a bit horny," Adam went on. "She was masturbating, and she let me watch."

"Really?" Jake said with a surprised laugh. "She did?"

Adam nodded silently.

"And I watched her do it," he said. "It was pretty sexy. Then she let me taste her pussy. And I ... I somehow got turned on, too. And I ... well, I fucked her."

Jake's mouth fell open. He didn't speak for a few second.

"You ..." he finally said. "Jennifer?"

Adam nodded again and took a big swig from his beer bottle.

"Was it good?" Jake asked.

Adam squirmed in his seat.

"I guess," he said. "But now I'm really worried. I mean - am I turning straight? And ... what about us? What if I start fucking girls instead? I can't ..."

"Woah, woah, woah!" Jake interrupted. "Calm down. Do you know how many straight guys have a gay encounter every now and then? Not to mention straight women. Look, Adam. Look at me. It's just sex. Don't worry about it. You just added to your repertoire. That doesn't mean you don't still prefer boys, does it?"

Adam stared at the beer bottle in his hand, as if it would eventually be the source of revelation.

"I dunno," he said. "I guess not."

Jake learned forward.

"Listen," he said. "Trust me. We're still lovers. You're still gay. You just had an experience with a woman. She's really hot, isn't she?"

Adam smiled.

"Oh yeah," he said shyly.

"And sex is sex," Jake said. "If a person is hot enough, you want to fuck them, no matter what your persuasion."

He emptied his beer.

"Want another?" he asked. "I'm gonna get one,"

Adam nodded. Jake fetched two cold beers in the fridge, popped them open and returned. He handed one to Adam and immediately took a sip of his own, as he sat down.

"So..." he said, "that Jennifer girl. She's damn hot, is she?"

Adam laughed coyly.

"I ..." he said. "Yeah. She must be. Never been attracted to a girl before."

"And ... fucking her?" Jake asked. "What was that like?"

Adam emptied the first beer bottle, then sat turning it in his hand.

"Kinda weird," he said. "But nice. Very soft. Very wet."

Jake took a large swig of his beer.

"Sounds interesting," he said. "I'd like to try it one day. What do you say ..."

He put the bottle down. A new idea had formed in his head, and he could hardly believe it.

"What do you say," he went on. "We meet her on the beach tomorrow?"

"Both of us?"

Jake laughed.

"Yeah, why not?" he said. "Both of us. Should be a nice little surprise for her."

Adam's eyes widened.

"Well," he said. "I believe she goes to the beach whenever she can. And tomorrow's Sunday."

"Right," Jake said, sipping his beer. "So there's a good chance she'll be there. Let's just go and see, right?"

Adam smiled sneakily.

"Really?" he said. "It's not ... too much?"

Jake shook his head.

"No, no," he said. "It's not a fucking ambush or anything. We're not gonna jump her, you know. We'll just be there and say hi. We won't even touch her unless she wants us to. Right?"

"Right."

Adam nodded. Jake took another sip of his beer and looked through the big windows facing the beach. The sun was going down now. The sky and the sea were both slowly turning red.

"No big thing," he said, leaning back in the couch. "Just, you know ... a nice surprise."

Part 3

Adam kept falling behind slightly. Jake had a nervous energy in his gait, climbed up every dune with determination, and let himself run downhill on the other side every time. Meanwhile Adam walked at a leisurely tempo and climbed up and down the dunes without exerting himself.

They'd reached the beach just after 10 am, but the hot sun was already high in the clear blue sky. Today would be even hotter than yesterday. Only a few locals were out in the water, even fewer were sunbathing. Jennifer would be easy to spot.

"Are you coming?" Jake called out.

Adam stood on the top of a dune, looking out over the ocean. Jake was several feet below him, wearing his checkered swimming trunks and clear plastic sandals. He was slightly out of breath after clearing the last three dunes in an impressive pace. Adam smiled.

"It was just around here," he said, cautiously walking downhill, his feet sinking into the warm sand. "But of course, I can't guarantee she's here today."

Jake shrugged.

"Of course not," he said. "But it would really be a shame if she's not."

They both laughed and walked side by side along a flat stretch of the beach. Adam noticed how quickly Jake caught his breath again. Apparently, the thought of meeting Jennifer really excited him. Adam was more reluctant - still somewhat ashamed about what had happened.

He had fucked her. Imagine that.

When they'd gone to bed last night, Jake had asked him for more details. What had it felt like? What did Jennifer look like when she came? Was she a screamer? How hard had Adam come? Eventually, it had really turned Jake on, and they'd had sex again. Jake had ejaculated into Adam's mouth with amazing force, yelling like an animal.

Almost immediately afterwards, Jake had fallen asleep. But Adam had lain awake for a few hours more. After all, this had been the day he'd fucked a girl for the first time ever.

Anyway, Jennifer was truly beautiful. Even though Adam had always felt 100% gay, he could still appreciate female beauty. They had bisexual friends who snickered and joked about the whole idea

of sexual "orientation". We're all human beings, they'd say, and if you're attracted to someone, why not have sex with them? Why does the whole gender thing even have to be an issue?

They might have a point, Adam thought. In fact, he'd just been fucking someone really beautiful - and this time it just happened to be a girl. Wouldn't that be one way to look at it?

"What are you thinking?" Jake asked.

"Oh, I ..." Adam replied. "Nothing, really. I ... I think it was around here somewhere."

"Who's that over there?" Jake asked, pointing. "Can you tell?"

In the distance, a woman in a black bikini was lying on a red blanket. They walked closer.

"Looks like Jennifer," Jake said.

He seemed aroused, Adam thought. Did Jennifer remind him of Adam's story? Did it make him picture the scene when Adam was fucking her? Or had the story triggered some hidden urges? Was Jake developing a sexual attraction to Jennifer? Was Adam? Or was he just imagining?

By the way, what was the difference? Can sexual attraction even be imaginary? If you're aroused, you're aroused. If the thought of Jennifer made his cock hard, didn't that qualify as attraction?

They walked closer.

"Yeah," Adam said. "It is her. Hi, Jennifer!"

Raising her head, Jennifer looked around. As she recognized Adam and Jake, she waved.

"Hi!" she said cheerily.

The men stood right next to her.

"You're both on the beach today?" she asked.

"Yeah," Adam said. "Just out walking. Perhaps go for a swim."

"Did Adam tell you I met him yesterday?" Jennifer asked Jake.

Jake smiled fiendishly.

"Oh, he did," he said. "He sure did."

Adam winced. This could really get embarrassing. What was Jake thinking?

"Why ...?" Jennifer asked. "Why are you looking at me like that?"

Jake laughed.

"Why do you think?" he said. "He told me everything."

Jennifer's flinch was barely noticeable. She froze for a second, then her eyes turned to Adam, her brow furrowed. But she didn't speak.

"Yes," Jake went on, visibly savoring the awkward mood. "Everything. I understand the two of you had a really good time."

"Jake," Jennifer said. "I'm sorry. I ..."

Jake smiled.

"Sorry?" he said. "But why? You shouldn't be. It's perfectly okay."

Adam nodded, hoping it would calm her.

"But," Jake went on, "I think you owe me."

Jennifer looked up at him, confused.

"Owe you?" she said. "How? What do you mean?"

"Look," Jake said. "I don't mind you fucking my boyfriend. But you could at least let me watch."

"But ..." she replied. "I don't see ... how ...?"

Jake laughed again.

"What's done is done," he said. "Can't be helped. But you can let me watch - now."

"What?" Jennifer gasped.

"Yes," Jake said. "Take that bikini off. Now."

Jennifer looked at Adam, shaking her head. Adam shrugged. He knew there was nothing he could do. Once Jake got an idea like that, he'd never let it go.

"Now!" Jake repeated, breathing hard. "I want to see you naked. I want to look at your tits and your cunt."

Jennifer undid the bikini bra and slid it off, exposing her beautiful, round breasts. Then she pulled of the bikini panties and sat naked on the towel.

"That's better," Jake said smiling. "Now lie back and touch your cunt."

With a sigh, Jennifer lay down on the towel. Her hand slowly moved towards her pussy. Two fingers found the fleshy mound above her clit. Closing her eyes, she began to masturbate.

"Yeah," Jake said. "That's a good little slut. Play with your cunt while you think about my boyfriend's cock. Did you like having his meat inside you? Did you?"

"Mmm," Jennifer whimpered.

"I bet you did," Jake said. "I bet you just loved feeling his big, fat cock inside your cunt. Did he fuck you good? Did he?"

Adam noticed Jake's cock stirring inside his trunks. It would soon be completely hard.

"Yes," Jennifer sobbed, masturbating. "He fucked me. It felt so good ..."

"Serves you right," Jake said. "Like the whore you are. That's all you're good for. You should have strong men with big cocks fucking you all the time. Think about that."

Jennifer gasped. Her fingers trembled as they rhythmically stroked her clit. Her labia glistened as wetness slowly leaked from her cunt.

"Yeah?" Jake said. "You'd like that, wouldn't you? Big, strong men fucking your tight little hole with their long, hard cocks. Hammering into your cunt for hours, making you come again and again. You think you could handle that? Could you, you little slut."

Jake slipped off his swimming trunks and his cock jumped out, fully erect. Jennifer opened her eyes and gasped at the sight. Adam wondered whether she'd ever seen a cock quite as long as that. Jake immediately grabbed it with his fist and began masturbating.

"Yeah," he gasped. "Go on, touch yourself."

Jennifer kept looking at his cock as she masturbated. Adam looked at them both, fascinated. The beautiful, naked girl, forced to expose herself by his gay boyfriend - who was already turned on by the sight of her tits and her cunt. And Adam couldn't blame him - there was something about Jennifer's beauty that transcended gender and sexuality. He bet straight girls were turned on by her, too. How many happily married women lay in bed at night, secretly masturbating at the thought of

Jennifer? Adam was getting an erection, too.

Still stroking his cock, Jake looked at Adam.

"Come over here," he said.

Adam stood in front of him.

"On your knees," Jake said.

Adam knelt down, and Jake let go of his cock. It bounced rigidly in front of Adam's face, a droplet of clear fluid seeping from its tip.

"Suck it!" Jake ordered.

Obediently, Adam opened his mouth and wrapped his lips around the warm, erect shaft. He heard Jennifer gasping behind his back.

"Oh my God!" she sighed.

"Yeah?" Jake said, as Adam began sucking his cock. "You like to watch that? You like to see Adam sucking my cock?"

Jennifer whimpered and sobbed.

"Oh, oh yes," she said. "I love it. Suck that cock, Adam. Suck it good."

Adam moved his head back and forth, Jake's hard cock slipping in and out between his lips, covered in saliva.

"Aaah!" Jake gasped. "Yeah. Like that."

Adam heard Jennifer moaning louder and louder, apparently turned on by the sight of him sucking Jake's cock.

"Ohmigod, keep going!" she cried. "Keep going. I'm gonna come..."

Jake slipped his cock from Adam's mouth with a loud pop. Adam turned to look at Jennifer. She sat up on the towel, masturbating at a furious pace, juice gushing from her pink cunt.

"Oooh!" she cried. "Oooh!"

She fell back on the towel, her entire body shaken by convulsions. Moaning loudly, she forced two fingers into her cunt. She lay there shivering, as the orgasm surged through her.

"I need some of that," Jake said softly

He walked over to Jennifer and lay on his knees on the edge of the towel. His big hands grabbed her ankles and forced her legs apart. Jennifer looked up at him, her face flushed. Adam stood up, adjusting his position to get a better look.

"Jake ..." she whispered.

Jake's long, erect cock jerked with excitement.

"I want to feel your pussy around my cock," he said.

He grabbed the shaft in his hand and assumed the position, the head of his cock pressing against her labia. She whimpered.

"Yeah," Jake gasped, pushing forwards.

Her pussy lips yielded to his hard cock. Inch by inch his stiff shaft entered her cunt. Adam watched as his boyfriend buried the entire length of his cock inside Jennifer's soft, wet flesh.

"Ohhh!" she cried.

Adam had an erection, too - quite strong in fact, almost painful. He swiftly slid off his swimming trunks and kicked them away.

Jake held still inside Jennifer's cunt, catching his breath in deep gasps.

"Are you ready?" he said. "Are you ready for my cock? I'm gonna fuck the hell out of you, you filthy little slut."

Jennifer threw her head from side to side, sobbing with pleasure as she felt Jake's cock inside her. Jake pulled back, slipping nearly all the way out of her cunt. The shaft glistened with her juices in the bright sunlight.

"No answer?" he said, teasingly. "Well, I'm ready - and that's all that really matters. Here I go, baby!"

And immediately he began thrusting into Jennifer's cunt in hard, fast strokes. She screamed. Which only seemed to turn him on even more. With powerful thrusts he hammered his erect cock into her pussy again and again.

Adam stared at them, his cock twitching with excitement. Jake fucking Jennifer. It had to be one of the sexiest scenes he'd ever seen. He couldn't keep his hand off his cock. He just had to masturbate.

"Ah! Ah! Ah!" Jennifer cried.

Grunting with pleasure, Jake kept thrusting into her. Adam could hear the wet sounds of her succulent cunt, slurping around Jake's shaft every time he entered her. His muscular ass moved up and down between Jennifer's wide open thighs. Adam kneeled down behind them. He put two fingers in his mouth, covering them with saliva, then thrust them into Jake's anus.

"Aaah!" Jake cried.

He didn't miss a beat - just kept thrusting relentlessly into Jennifer's pussy. Adam turned the fingers around and around inside his ass. He pulled the fingers out and spat on his cock several times, spreading the saliva all over the shaft. With both hands he grabbed Jake's rhythmically pumping buttocks, forcing them apart to reveal his anus. He placed the tip of his cock against it. And as Jake pulled back from his next powerful thrust, Adam held still, letting Jake's ass impale itself on his erect cock.

"Fuuuck!" Jake yelled.

Still, he kept fucking. Adam merely had to hold still. Jake's ass moved back and forth, letting his cock penetrate his tight anus, then slip out, then in ... Damn, that felt good! Adam looked down at Jennifer, her eyes and mouth wide open, as Jake relentlessly fucked her.

"Oh, God ..." she cried. "I'm coming ..."

"Yeah," Jake gasped, increasing his rhythm. "Come on. Come for me."

"Aaah!" Jennifer cried.

She tried to wriggle about, as another orgasm hit her. But Jake grabbed her shoulders, pinning her to the towel. She cried and cried. Jake kept thrusting into her cunt, impaling his ass on Adam's cock with every backstroke. Adam whispered into Jake's ear:

"She looks great when she comes, doesn't she?"

"She sure does," Jake gasped.

"Make her come again," Adam replied.

"Huuunh!" Jake roared, relentlessly hammering his erect cock into her slippery slit.

They were all sweating now. Drops of perspiration dripped from Adams face, ran down Jake's back and dripped all over Jennifer's naked body.

"Play with your cunt!" Adam ordered.

Jennifer gasped, out of breath.

"I ..." she said. "I ..."

"Do it!" Jake commanded. "Make yourself come again!"

Trembling, Jennifer began stroking her clit. She whimpered loudly at her own touch.

"I have my cock up Jake's ass," Adam said. "I'm fucking him."

"Ohmigod!" Jennifer gasped, masturbating like mad. "That's so hot."

"Yeah," Adam went on. "His ass feels so tight around my cock."

Describing it made his cock jump excitedly inside Jake's rectum. He felt Jake's buttocks bouncing rhythmically against him, whenever his cock slipped out of Jennifer's cunt. Jake groaned with pleasure.

"Aaah!" Jennifer cried. "Aaah!"

With a loud gasp, she opened her eyes wide as another orgasm hit her. Her body trembled uncontrollably, held in place by Jake's muscular arms.

"Ohmigod!" she whispered. "Ohmigod!"

Jake increased the pace of his thrust, hammering into her cunt with brute force. Adam felt his body tensing up, trembling.

"Oh, shit!" Jake gasped. "Oh fuck, I'm gonna come!"

Adam pulled his cock from Jake's ass and stood up.

"Yeah!" he cried. "Come in her mouth!"

"Hunh!" Jake grunted, pulling his twitching member from her cunt.

He stood above Jennifer's head, forcing his shaft down, pointing it at her face. The head of his cock swelled madly in his fist.

"Open your mouth!" he ordered.

Jennifer promptly obeyed. Jake was so excited, he didn't even need to stroke his cock. It immediately began contracting, firing a long spurt of semen into Jennifer's mouth.

"Aaah!" he cried. "Yeah!"

Adam stood on the other side of Jennifer's face, watching Jake ejaculating, his cock pumping jet after jet of semen. Jennifer caught his spunk in her mouth, swallowing repeatedly. With trembling hands, she grabbed her shapely breasts, kneading them vigorously. Adam grabbed his cock, masturbating at the sight of his lover shooting his sperm into the mouth of the beautiful girl they both desired.

"Hunh!" he groaned.

He felt the contractions of orgasm throughout his cock, so strong they were almost painful. Everything went black, and he thought he was about to faint. A long white jet of hot spunk shot from his jerking shaft, spattering Jennifer's breasts. Jake's ejaculations had almost subsided, and as she swallowed the last mouthfuls of his spunk, Adam took over, pointing the pumping cock at her mouth, firing his semen in between her lovely red lips. He masturbated like mad.

"Huh!" he gasped. "Yes! Aaah!"

Jake just stood there, looking at him, as he emptied himself of his spunk. Adam grabbed his cock hard, squeezing a last, thick glob of semen from its tip, breathing hard. Jake fell to his knees, bent over Jennifer and kissed her on the mouth. Adam saw his tongue playing with hers, licking her lips, tasting the spunk of both men. Excited, he too lay down next to Jennifer and pressed his mouth against both hers and Jake's lips. He felt both of their tongues, savored the strong taste of semen, not knowing which was his and which was Jake's.

Eventually, out of breath, they let go of each other's mouths and just lay there, sighing, stroking each other's hot, sandy skin. Tears of joy welled up in Jennifer's eyes.

"Oh, guys," she sighed, "that was wonderful. Just wonderful."

"You're wonderful," Adam replied.

"Yes," Jake said calmly. "You're a lovely girl."

He stood up and put his short back on. Adam gave Jennifer one last, gentle kiss.

"Thank you," he said. "Thank you for a lovely morning."

"Are you coming?" Jake asked.

Adam, too, stood up and got dressed.

"Sure," he said. "Bye, Jennifer."

With glazed eyes, Jennifer waved at the men as they walked.

"Bye, guys," she said, her voice breaking. "See you around."

Sighing, she stretched out on her towel. She was still naked, it wasn't a nude beach, but she didn't care. She just didn't care. It had happened. Everything she'd fantasized about had just happened. Adam and Jake had been all over her and it had been just amazing. Her head was still spinning from her powerful orgasms.

Jennifer sighed again. She just wanted to lie here for a bit, relax, get her strength back. Then a dip in the ocean, and then – what?

She thought of her friend Karen. She realized she was just dying to tell her. Maybe they could meet for a glass of wine later, and Jennifer could tell her all about her morning of passion in the arms of Adam and Jake. How would she react? Shocked? Jealous? Hopefully excited.

Yes, she wanted to get Karen aroused. Because if she was, maybe she could seduce her later. Karen was a beautiful girl, and Jennifer had often fantasized about having sex with her

Jennifer closed her eyes. Mmm, Karen. She wondered what Karen's pussy tasted like.

Her fingers found her clit. She sighed as she began to masturbate.

# # #

More Frank Noir online

Keep in touch with Frank Noir – his stories, his books, his dark desires.

Official website

https://franknoir.com/

Social Networks

Frank Noir on Twitter: https://twitter.com/talesoflustxxx

Frank Noir on Facebook:

https://www.facebook.com/FrankNoirAuthor

Frank Noir on Tumblr: http://talesoflustxxx.tumblr.com/

Stories

Frank Noir on Literotica:

https://www.literotica.com/stories/memberpage.php?uid=213440

Frank Noir on Stories Online

https://storiesonline.net/a/Frank_Noir

Printed in Great Britain
by Amazon

36670070R00223